THE U

Andrew Sanger was born in London in 1948. A professional travel journalist who has lived in several countries, he has contributed to a wide range of UK national press and international print and online media. He worked as a consultant editor and project manager for leading UK and US travel publishers, and for ten years was editor of French Railways' English-language customer magazine *Top Rail* (later *Rail Europe Magazine*). He is the author of more than forty guidebooks, mainly on France and the French regions.

The Unknown Mrs Rosen is Andrew Sanger's fourth novel. His first work of fiction, *The J-Word,* was published in 2009 and in the same year featured at Jewish Book Week and Hampstead & Highgate Literary Festival, and was made into a Talking Book by the charity Jewish Care. His other novels include *The Slave* (2013) and *Love* (2015). He now lives in the New Forest, on England's south coast. Website: www.andrewsanger.com. Twitter: @andrewsanger.

THE
UNKNOWN
MRS ROSEN

ANDREW SANGER

FOCUS BOOKS

London, England

www.focus-books.co.uk

FOR GERRY AND JOSH

. . .

In loving memory of my parents
Hilda and Joe Sanger

THANK YOU

Alison Abrams and Tom Cunliffe, for advice on sailing & boats;
Antje Khalil, for correcting my German;
Magda Sikora-Nowak for insights into the work of a carer;
and above all, thank you Gerry, for your
endless patience and help
every step of the way.

'**D**arling?' Marjorie set the crossword aside and gazed at her husband. She meant, didn't he agree that it was bedtime. From a mahogany cabinet in the corner of the room he looked back, the face impassive, a man forever in his fifties. She studied the tight-lipped smile, the dark scrutiny of the eyes, the pointed, disputatious arc of thick brows. Drawn across the bald dome, a few threads of hair. A sports jacket with wide lapels. Tie not quite in place.

The framed photograph was black and white, everything without colour, the nostalgic grisaille of yesteryear; eyes, hair, the light falling on his right side, the tweed jacket, the shirt and tie, all in shades of grey. Yet Marjorie saw hazel eyes sparkling, the green tie she bought at Arding and Hobbs, a blue cotton shirt she ironed many times. It was at the height of Harry's career, this picture, half a lifetime ago, or another life altogether. She still felt the touch of tweed under her hand, the bristle of his cheek against hers.

The room was quiet. Marjorie listened attentively; all was well. Small sounds from the other flats, young voices passing in the street, a television faintly. Bracing herself, she leaned forward, pushed on the arms of her chair and rose to her feet. Tomorrow was another day, and the day after, yet another. May she live to see them. Constant frustration, endless irritation, yet Marjorie had become used to pain and weakness, accustomed to it, the struggle for breath, the hazy vision, the awkwardness of simple movements. Step by step she crossed a living room Harry had never known.

She knew she was going too quickly. About half way on the long journey from the armchair to the door, a nauseous dizziness enveloped her, then a savage determination to remain upright, then an indifferent abandon to the great tide of darkness as the sitting room carpet came rapidly towards her.

* * *

'Miss, not so fast! No running!' Nanny calls, 'Don't run, don't run, Miss Marjorie, ne cours pas, you'll fall.' Mother's voice behind: 'Fräulein, nicht Laufen!' No running! But then Father's voice: 'Pust' ona bezhit, dyevushka.' Let her run, the lass.

Father, Mother, Me. Three pieces in a perfect little puzzle.

Up, down, across.

Ex, why, zed.

Three, two, one.

Zero.

These are Our Days, the good days, when Mother must force herself to be nice to me, pretend to love me because Father is with us and everything fits together as it should. The puzzle is solved. I skip home from school, gymslip like a sail.

Nanny is not wearing her coat. She has been allowed out in her indoor uniform. Nanny's name is Millie. Really it's Mélisande. Running is not allowed. Skipping – 'carefully, Miss!' – is allowed. Skipping is nearly as fast as running, fast as a breeze, and myself like a skiff skimming the stream.

'How long can you stay?' I ask Father. He laughs and raises me in his big hands, lifts me high, to his mighty red whiskers and bristles on the back of his neck rough as a maid's scrubbing brush. 'Don't worry about that, moya malen'kiya milyy!' My little darling! I love his big, puffy white shirtsleeves, the silvery armbands so manly, and the silky back of his waistcoat.

For my eleventh birthday, Father gives me a bicycle. It's a Hopper, from Barton, just across the river. I think he has had it specially made for me. We race to the river on our bikes, Father and I, and stand together in a long silence, looking across the estuary's swelling waters, oil-stained and brown. Edged with piers and towers, masts and warehouses, timber, steel and brick, the river is a huge open-air workplace under shifting clouds, a workshop of ships moored or moving. The funnel of the Humber ferry belches smoke as it paddles slowly to New Holland, faint in mist on the other side.

'Reckon you could swim across, Marjorie?' asks Father mischievously.

'No!' I shriek, clenching fists in a shiver of fear at the thought. 'It's too far! Anyway, it's too rough, and too dirty.'

'Bet you could, though. One day.'

His impossible challenges are a joke between us. It's Father's way of saying he's fond of me. We lean the bikes together and step down to my own little sailboat tied to the bank. A lapping tide drags through the mud and gravel on the foreshore, sounding quietly in and out, in and out, sh-sh, sh-sh, the water like breath, like breath.

Without a word, we climb into the boat. I rig it as Father watches. I take an oar and push against the bank. The shore releases us at once, and we are away, heading for the estuary and the open sea.

* * *

Marjorie did not press her panic button on the way to the floor, since she was not wearing it. No one was alerted to her fall until the next day. Getting no answer at Marjorie's door, the morning carer rang the Rezniks on the other side of the road. If the panic button had been pressed, it was in any case to the Rezniks that the message would have gone. Mr Reznik would have let himself into Marjorie's flat and found her. That's what he did now, with Shelley, the carer, at his side.

Marjorie lay wide awake, had a crippling headache, terrible bruises where she'd fallen and couldn't lift her own weight. She had trouble moving her arms and hands. The phone was out of reach and she could not even make herself crawl to it. When Marjorie saw Joe Reznik walk into the room she began to cry – just a little, more like a whimper. It was something he had never seen before. Marjorie was not the crying type. She was the dauntless, hard-as-nails, resolutely good-humoured type. The few tears were blinked away at once. With as much cheerfulness as she could muster, she said, 'Hello, Joe. Hello, Sharon.' She was breathless, the voice barely audible.

At once they lowered themselves to the floor, the lean elderly man on one side of her, the plump young woman on the other. 'It's Shelley, Mrs Rosen. I'll phone for an ambulance.'

'No, I'm fine,' Marjorie whispered. 'Really I am. No ambulance. Absolutely not. I caught my leg and fell. Thank goodness you came in straight after. No broken bones, nothing serious. Get me back on my feet, would you?' The thudding headache beat against her like a thing visible and audible, shrouds of sailcloth slapping rhythmically between herself and her words.

Shelley and Joe moved Marjorie with difficulty, each placing a hand under the moist, soft flesh of her upper arms. She was not a small woman. The sturdy, once muscular frame had years ago taken on a layer of fat. Her body was as uncooperative as a hundredweight sack of wheat. Carefully they heaved her from the floor to a chair.

'No ambulance,' she gasped, 'but you can call my doctor. Ooph! First of all, I'd like to go to bed.'

'The surgery won't be open, Mrs Rosen,' the carer pointed out.

'What time is it?'

'About seven o'clock. I came early.'

'Seven in the morning?'

'Yes, Mrs Rosen. I'm Shelley. I come in the morning.'

'Leave a message. They'll call back later. Tell them I tripped.'

'How long have you been lying there like that?' Joe demanded.

'Stop asking silly questions, Joe. Make me a cup of coffee.'

'Did you have another blackout?'

'No, of course not.' She worked to articulate every word. 'This leg of mine won't do as it's told. Blasted foot caught on the chair and I lost my balance. That's all.'

'Really?' Joe's glance flicked towards the chair. 'When was this?'

'For goodness' sake, Joe! Ten minutes ago. Help me back to bed, Sharon, via the bathroom.'

It might have been clear that the bed had not been used this night, nor the bathroom. If asked, Marjorie would say she had made the bed herself. But in the step-by-step struggle, Shelley did not notice.

'Mrs Rosen, my name's not Sharon, it's Shelley,' said Shelley with cheerful patience, 'shall I get you some breakfast?'

'No thank you, Shelley dear, I've had something. Just bring the coffee. And a flask for later, and a glass of water and my pills. I'm so terribly thirsty. And tired. I need a little nap.'

Shelley placed the medication in an eggcup. 'What about your family?' She guided Marjorie into place. 'Shall I call someone?'

On the bedside cabinet, a tiny silver frame held an even more treasured photograph of Harry, young, slim, with no smile, hair jet black, staring directly at the camera. Marjorie turned to meet his inscrutable gaze, looked longingly at him for support, before leaning back into the soft pillows.

Shelley gently repeated, 'Should I call one of your children?'

'No, why trouble them? They've got their own lives to lead.'

Joe Reznik, the neighbour who had for years been such a good friend of Harry's, sat in Marjorie's kitchen. After leaving a message for the doctor, he dialled the number of her eldest son.

'Phil?' Joe's rich voice was sombre. 'I have a horrible feeling your mum might have spent the whole night lying on the floor. She says it was just a few minutes. She doesn't look well. She's not herself. Can you come down?'

'Not really, Joe. I'm very busy. Is she OK now?'

'Phil – your mum's *not* OK. She can't cope. Come down.'

'Not today.' He did not believe his mother couldn't cope. It was unthinkable.

'As soon as you can.'

Marjorie's children knew, as well as Marjorie herself, that Joe and Eva Reznik kept a close eye on her. Trapped by Joe's old loyalty to Harry, it seemed there was nothing they would not do for her.

'Let me talk to Mum,' Phil said. 'Can you give her the phone?'

'The carer's putting her to bed. You know, Phil,' Joe lowered his voice even further, 'she needs proper care, seven days a week.'

'Mum's fine whenever I see her. She told me she hates being looked after.'

'*We* are looking after her,' Joe insisted. 'Did you know, Eva does your mum's shopping?'

'I thought she had home delivery. She does online shopping.'

'That is a little fantasy of hers. Your mother can't possibly make an online order. The keyboard is tricky and she has trouble reading the screen. Did she mention that Eva often cooks for her? It's a pleasure. A pleasure. And helps her dress and undress? You didn't know? No, well how could you? Yes, and gets her ready for bed.'

'Really?'

'But there's more, Phil. I don't want to say it, but – Eva sometimes takes your mum to the bathroom and washes her.'

'Oh!'

'And even helps her on the lavatory.'

'My God!' At last Joe had found Philip's horrified conscience. 'That's not right! I'll do something. Yes, I will. Straight away. Thank you both for all your help, Joe. I'm so sorry.'

'Look, drop what you're doing, ask her doctor to organise home care. That's how it's done. Your mum won't discuss it. She thinks everything must be kept private.'

'That's what she's like. Very private.'

At that moment, Shelley came into the kitchen to write her care log in a big notebook. 'Be all right now, won't she?' She gestured in the general direction of the bedroom. 'She's having a lie-down. You staying here, Mr Reznik?' Joe understood he or Eva would have to wait until a doctor arrived later in the day.

Shelley picked up her bag and made her way out. Passing Marjorie's bedroom door, she called, 'Bye, Mrs Rosen.'

Marjorie, falling through fathomless dreams, made no reply.

* * *

even o'clock, he said. It's not even six. So worried about being late, I'm at Kensington Gardens more than an hour early. My heart is fluttering like an idiot. A low wall runs alongside the fruitful patchwork of allotments bursting with foliage which give the royal park an almost bucolic air. In the most inelegant way imaginable, I lift myself onto it. Feet not touching the ground, I perch upright as a post, handbag on my lap, knees together, keeping my precious stockings away from the brickwork.

I peer at the platform of every number 9. Is he standing there? Making his way along the aisle? Coming down the stairs? No, it's far too early. I'm swinging my legs like a child. I try to calm myself. I check my seams and smooth my skirt, straighten my hat, cast a quick eye at the looking-glass of my compact, dab on some powder.

Yet suddenly he *is* there, ahead of time and not on the platform of a bus. He's walking hatless in the street, strands of jet black hair breezily unbrushed across that tanned, beautifully domed head. His sports jacket flaps open in horrible combination with suit trousers. Someone should take the man in hand. Over one arm a mac hangs untidily, while the other clutches a bundle of magazines and books and loose sheets of paper in danger of slipping free. Surely he didn't come all the way from Cadby Hall like that?

To some, he could be a comic spectacle. That, no doubt, is how Mother and my wretched brothers would see it. Yet for some reason, in me he arouses – I really don't want to scrutinise the feeling – an unaccountable excitement and – my heart beats harder. Something in me trembles at the thought of getting to know this man.

Since catching sight of Harry in a staff restaurant at Cadby Hall, I've been painfully conscious of him. We've hardly spoken, other than a few workaday greetings en passant in the corridors of the Administration Block, Building X.

Which is peculiar and inexplicable, because the only other place I've seen Harry, months ago, was at Bletchley Park, even before the mission to Germany.

He didn't notice me, though, in those days. I watched him flirt with other girls at BP hops, while I was overlooked! Beautiful dancer, light on his feet to the point of daintiness. No taller than me, not suave, not sophisticated, never a hint of brilliantine to smarten himself, tie always askew, but he brims with alertness and vitality. Light-hearted, full of humour and the joy of living, there's such tremendous physical energy as well as abundant mental horsepower. Even in that place, he was among the brightest.

When I was sent back to Cadby Hall after the mission, how impossible and mystifying it was to find Harry there as well. I did ask him what on earth he was doing in Joe Lyons' head office. He said he's in Systems Research. What does that mean? 'Hard to say, exactly. Maths, statistics and margins of error.' Of course, what I really wanted to know was, *Why the heck are you here instead of at BP?* That's not something one can ask. For that matter, he might want to ask me the same thing. I merely inquired politely, 'So is that about payroll? Or stock control, or what?' He rolled his eyes in hilarious indecision. 'It is – and it isn't.'

That smile! His face is illumined by it. He's delighted to see me. Or, no, perhaps amused. I too might look comical, balanced on the wall. I jump down and try to be more ladylike.

He surely doesn't consider me pretty. I'm clunky, big boned, too tall, too strong. My forehead's too high, too shiny and too commanding and too much everything, and the colouring horribly pale, ultra-blonde perm and washed-blue eyes as pale as midwinter. I've done my best with dabs of powder on the eyebrows and cheeks. There's no hair dye around for love or money, no foundation cream, hardly any make-up.

Nor am I glamorously dressed. Today's costume is as good as it gets, a neat grey Utility suit with a functional pleated skirt. The high-necked white blouse might strike him as prim and schoolmarmy, or decent and demure, or, with luck, girlishly charming. I'm not svelte, but nor am I – well, I hope it all adds up to something that appeals to the respectable male mind.

Or, absent-minded, head-in-the-clouds type that he is, perhaps Harry Rosen hardly notices such things. A girl's hair and figure probably never enter his mind. Mathematical theorems are his world. Except… he positively basked in female admiration at the hops.

'Hello, Harry,' I call out casually, as if I already know him. There's a thrilling intimacy in saying his name.

He attempts a ridiculous wave from under the draped mackintosh. His first words to me: 'Have you read this article by Professor Joad, about chess and mathematics?' He attempts to hold up a copy of *John O'London's Weekly*.

'Give me those,' I answer, seizing pages from under his arm. 'Joad, is he that chap on the Brains Trust? I don't know anything about maths and can't play chess, so I don't think I'll read his piece.'

'Can't play chess!' he laughs, incredulous. 'I thought everyone at BP could play chess.'

It's horrifying that he would refer to BP. 'I can do other things,' adding (before his mind races too far in the wrong direction), 'I'm a good cook.'

Harry's smile is quick and eyes alert. We both realise that cooking is not to be likened to chess. 'I know what you're good at,

Miss. I noticed you in Hut 3 and Hut 9C. I know about the work in there. And it's not cooking.'

I'm thrilled beyond words that he noticed me, bewildered that he knows about Hut 9C and, most of all, alarmed that he's so indiscreet. My voice is not even a whisper: 'Don't talk about it here, Harry. Or anywhere. It's not on. I never discuss it with anyone. Not anyone.'

I make a mental note that he's not to be trusted with a secret. I was already concerned that I might have to ward off questions about where I've been since leaving BP. Yet he doesn't ask. Maybe he assumes I've been at Lyons all the time.

His tone is jocular again. 'Well now, what would be the nicest way to spend our evening?'

'I thought we were just going to have a walk in the park.'

'Dancing it is, then! Shall we have a bite to eat first?'

'D'you want to share my sandwich? It's only Spam.'

'Half a left-over Spam sandwich,' he beams. 'Lovely! Then over to the WVS for a nice cup of tea.' Instead he proposes a five-bob meal in one of the smart hotels across the park.

'No!' I reply firmly. 'I truly *don't* want a slap-up dinner. I'd honestly prefer a sandwich or something at a milk bar or at a Lyons. Really I would. Especially with the staff discount.'

'Oh, come on!'

'No, really, my idea of a luxurious meal is bangers and mash. That's the truth.'

'Oh, me too,' he replies with gay flippancy. 'What do we want with that lah-di-dah nosh? Custard and chips, good enough for us.' We giggle idiotically, but presumably Harry is grateful. He'll be able to feed both of us for less than half a crown in a Corner House.

He doesn't hold my hand or put his arm round me, or any of that nonsense. We talk easily. He's interesting. As we stand watching the ducks and coots on the Serpentine, I'm quite sure there isn't another man in the world with whom I have ever talked so comfortably and intelligently. Harry Rosen has an opinion on every single thing, philosophy, politics, literature. Best of all, he listens attentively to everything I say, too. There's not a trace of that patronising smile men reserve for women they wish to indulge. Or be indulged by.

The thing I'm worried about is the dancing. I'm hopeless, and I know he's terribly good. 'Can I dance, though, dressed like this?'

'Course you can. Leave your jacket in the cloakroom.'

'No, I mean, are you talking about a tea dance? That would be all right, I s'pose.'

Harry grins. 'Not unless you know a tea house where we can jitterbug all night.'

I feel quite panicky at the thought. 'In this skirt?' There's no question of me jitterbugging, I've absolutely decided upon that. Let alone all night. 'No, Harry, I don't think so!'

'Well, why not? You can at the Royal Opera House.'

'What?'

'Have tea and dance the jitterbug. Or jive – that's more sedate.'

'No.' I shake my head with certainty. 'No, not even at the Royal Opera House. Anyway, I don't know how to,' I admit at last, 'you know, jitterbug and all that.'

'Nothing to it, honestly! Easy as one-two-three! Like chess – you just have to know the moves!' Harry grabs my elbow and suddenly we're dancing shaky, crazy jitterbug steps on the grass. I laugh out loud, and realise that I'm doing it, I'm actually jitterbugging, in this skirt, in the park, we're laughing our heads off, and no matter what happens, it'll be all right with Harry. Even if I look a fool, he'll still like me.

B

A phone call, an email, and your troubles begin. Or a text. Max read and re-read the screen. For once he gave not a glance into the open doorways of the poky little garment workshops, one after another along rue du Chemin Vert, that he normally found so fascinating.

Mum had another fall. She's OK. Joe thinks Mum needs a lot more care. It's unbelievable how much he & Eva are doing for Mum. Maybe we are taking them for granted? I can't afford to pay any more. Can we share the cost in future? Maybe the 3 of us cd meet up to discuss? XXX Phil.

Only then did Max notice that the text had also been sent to Nic. Instantly Phil's message took on the feel of a little family crisis. Philip would not contact Nicola for anything less.

As he waited at a pedestrian light, Max sent *Glad Mum is OK. Can't Social Services deal with this? XX, M.*

No way – the ungenerous thought sprang up immediately – could he and Jelka contribute towards the cost of Mum's care. The thought was followed at once by remorse, as he pondered whether they might, after all, be able to chip in, say, €20 a week. They couldn't easily spare it. Besides, €20 would not buy any care.

He had no objection to meeting Philip and Nicola. He even felt rather pleased to receive news that would throw them together. For all the differences between them – a vast gulf of mutual disapproval – he wanted to see them again. For they were the only family he had, other than Jelka and Olivier. And Jelka too was without kinship.

The last time he'd seen his brother and sister was three years before, on Marjorie's eightieth birthday. She hadn't been well then, and walked with a stick. Max found an uneasy satisfaction in these rare nursery reunions. The same emotion would always stir. Max was perplexed by it, by the sense – the sensation – of an intangible bond.

It wasn't *love*, surely, this feeling? For certainly he did not love his brother and sister.

There had been occasional messages since that last meeting, nearly always about Mum. *Mum had a fall.* And another, and another. *She hurt herself falling.* Then came the mini-strokes. *A mini-stroke is not the same as a stroke.* Philip texted that Mum had been taken to hospital in an ambulance, kept awake all night in Acute Admissions and brought back home by Joe the next day. It didn't affect Max. After all, he was in Paris. He would phone afterwards to ask if she was all right. She said she was *very* well, and he believed her.

As Max reached avenue Parmentier, his phone sounded again. *Mum doesn't want the SS prying into her affairs.*

He typed, *What affairs?* Their mother had no affairs of any kind. She was a modest elderly widow with modest savings living on a modest pension. Her mania for privacy was ridiculous.

He arrived at his door on rue Rochebrune, passed the stack of mailboxes in the echoing hallway, dashed up the wide stairway. Jelka and Olivier were not due home for over an hour. Inside the apartment, he tapped out his mother's number on his phone.

In a comfortable flat by the sea in a resort town on England's Channel coast, Eva sat in an armchair at Marjorie's bedside, waiting for a doctor to ring the doorbell. Apparently more unconscious than asleep, Marjorie lay half propped up, duvet pulled high, her pale eyelids ceaselessly flickering. Eva, delicate as a wren, skeletally thin, almost as old as Marjorie herself, did not pick up the ringing phone.

I can't take your call at the moment, said the answering machine in Marjorie's quavering voice. *You may leave a message.* She gave no name, no number, no sorry, no please, no thank you.

Max adored the look and sound of Paris before it wakes, the black-and-white darkness, the depravities of night being washed away. Hard-pressed refuse men passed quickly along the wide street, sweeping and emptying. Occasional shattered revellers still wandered abroad. A faint aroma from locked boulangeries, unseen basements and back rooms revealed that bakers were already at work, rolling out croissants, taking loaves from ovens, preparing for a new Parisian morning of pleasure. The first number 46 bus of the day rattled along empty avenues and boulevards to the Gare du Nord, where Max stood in Eurostar's comfortless waiting area until ushered to a train.

Philip left his home early too, quietly shutting the back door. He paused on the terrace to listen and watch as the pure note of a single owl disturbed the stillness. It moved through a black lace of branches and settled in silhouette atop the stables.

On empty Cotswolds backroads with no speed cameras he passed through sleeping villages and waking countryside. Driving in darkness, the windows blackly opaque, always the car seemed eerily animate, low radio voices intimate, Prayer for the Day murmuring its soothing platitudes and promises, Farming Today its earthy mysteries of stock and market, the sweeping oracular span of the shipping forecast, rhythmic and relentless as the ocean waves, a saga of the old seafaring kingdom. The first news bulletin and the Today programme awakened the new day in earnest. Clouded sunrise streamed across the rooftops of High Wycombe. Philip passed beneath the M25, reaching the North Circular before the rush. That was the idea: miss the worst of the rush hour, park in Hampstead (he knew all the streets where one could park), and walk across the Heath to catch a number 24 bus to Nicky's.

Nicola struggled to open her eyes. She turned towards poster-covered windows to gain some impression of the sky they obscured. As soon as the girls were fed, dressed and out, she rushed the vacuum cleaner around the ground floor, wiped the dining table and checked there were three clean mugs and plates. It was time for them to arrive. Philip would be early, she supposed, Max late.

The posters on the windows cried out Nicola's impassioned certainties: a blood-spattered "NO" (Stop the War Coalition), "Vote Against Climate Change!" (the Green Party), "No GMO" (Friends of the Earth), "No War!" (CND). The largest blazed with a single non-word, "BLIAR".

Topics to avoid, Philip warned himself. It was long established about Nicola, in the Rosen family, that her main preoccupation was war, about which she knew as little as anyone – beyond the usual, that innocents were hurt. Nicola held that this alone justified her stand. Violence solved nothing, she declared.

Philip had no such opinion. Why should violence not solve a problem sometimes? As for Marjorie, she argued that 'all history is the history of war' and 'war is the greatest driver of progress'. Nowadays, Marjorie avoided discussion with her daughter. She needed to keep her children on side. Philip admired Max's approach. Like the Queen, Max expressed no opinion on anything.

'I brought you some apples,' Philip announced genially. 'They're organic.' His fifty-year-old little sister smiled in welcome. She pecked his cheek and peered into the bag. 'Oh! Thank you, Phil! I'll make a crumble. I see you got rid of the ponytail! I never liked it.'

'Really, you didn't like it?' Without the ponytail, what was left of his hair fell in silvery waves over his ears, and his grey beard was clipped short. He smiled as if brimming with good humour. 'What's happened to *your* hair, Nic? The Françoise Hardy look suited you.'

'Françoise Hardy has it like this now. It's grey, and she's sixty. Sorry.'

Max joined them earlier than expected. The impression *he* gave was of remaining uncannily the same as years passed. He still had his head of unruly black curls. There was something youthful in his manner, the quick movements, taut nerves. He remained fey, mercurial, hard to observe. He had not brought a gift, and began at once, irritatingly, to take photographs of Nicola as she arranged Philip's apples in a bowl.

She said. 'Let's talk about Mum.'

* * *

The train door swings open. Brisk women, buttoned-up in khaki greatcoats, stride on the dark platform, marshalling us with shouts of "R.O.F. Elstow", like someone's name. We step down and are commanded into silence. There is no word of welcome. Torch beams dart about. I make out that we are all girls, hundreds of girls, no fellers. A sharp wind stings my ears.

Perhaps I was expecting a bus, or maybe a walk. Our wardresses urge us straight into the backs of army trucks. We're pushed shoulder to shoulder, and driven at reckless speed through the blackness to a horrid collection of dingy huts – they tell us it's called Chimney

Corner Hostel. Along the way we learn that R.O.F. means Royal Ordnance Factory.

We're to share the Chimney Corner dormitories with a mob of jocose, hoydenish northern lasses who arrived a fortnight ago. Straight away they have fun telling us about the "powder girls" who've already lost an eye or two, a finger or two, a hand or two, or a leg or two, or simply been blown to smithereens. What's a powder girl? I ask. You are, is the cheerful response.

'Oh, and the powder ruins your skin and hair. Lots of powder girls will get a bald patch on top sooner or later. A man won't look at you afterwards.' Some girls guffaw at that. Some smile uncertainly, puzzled, a little frightened. Others withdraw, stepping out of the dormitory for a panicky cigarette – or a cry.

The 'shop' is a vast hangar full of waist-high wooden workbenches lined with girls. A scrawny chap in an oversized brown warehouse coat explains how to do the job. Everyone is bewildered, eyes darting around and struggling to take in what the little fellow is saying.

To stop the "powder" yellowing our skin and hair, we're to put a protective cream on our faces every day before work. 'Never forget – you're working with TNT. Yes, ladies, "powder" is a mix of TNT and worse. Much worse. Dangerous stuff. Or,' he corrects himself, but the warning has been duly given, '*potentially* dangerous. No room for slip-ups. A slip-up could be fatal. Follow *every* rule in the Rule Book. That's an order. Bear in mind, it's not just yourself you endanger, but your workmates, or everyone in the whole shop.'

If there's one thing particularly unusual about the job, it's the glass of milk at the start and end of every shift. This is to combat the effect of the powder on our bodies. We *must* drink it, he says, because TNT leeches the body's chemicals and minerals. It's true, then, about the hair. Which is a nuisance, as my hair is too thin already.

We're not to wear anything made of metal, either. Not so much as a clip or a button, not even on any part of – 'sorry, ladies' – our 'undergarments'. That's in the Rule Book, too. A wedding ring is allowed, though it must be covered with special tape, but as all women called up under the new law must be unmarried, that doesn't apply to any of us. And something else: don't knock anything or drop anything. 'One tiny jolt or jog could cause a great big explosion.' Some girls who were smirking have stopped smirking and look frightened.

There's a faint air of disbelief and fear. Surely they wouldn't really put innocent young women in such peril? Yes, they would. There really have been accidents. Everyone grips her copy of the red cloth-covered Rule Book. I open the book. On the inside cover, my name and number have already been filled in. Miss Marjorie Louisa Behrens. Facing it, the sobering words, *Rules of the Danger Area – Elstow Ordnance Factory*. Beneath that, *J. Lyons & Company Ltd., Managing Agents*.

There's a surprise! Instead of being run by the Ministry of Supply or the Ministry of War, R.O.F. Elstow is run by good old Joe Lyons & Co. I smile at the thought. A business whose name is synonymous with tea and cake also makes bombs!

'What if there's a raid?' I hear a girl ask.

'What if there's a raid, Miss?' Warehouse Coat repeats ominously. 'Good question. Right, ladies, listen very carefully. When the *first* bell sounds, be alert, be ready, but carry on with your work. If a *second* bell sounds, stop what you're doing and go straight to the shelter. Wait for the second bell! The first bell only means Jerry is heading this way. We don't stop just because Jerry is coming, because he usually flies right past. The second bell means Jerry is dropping bombs, so that's when we run for cover. Except, don't run. In this place, we need great calmness during a raid. No running. No clumsiness. Great calmness, ladies. Don't dally, but make your way to the shelter in an orderly fashion.'

The Chimney Corner girls have promised me a drink tonight, in honour of my twenty-first. There's no question of any time off, let alone a home visit. I wonder if, apart from them, anyone in this world or the next is thinking of me, sending me many happy returns. As I handle the shell casings on this day, my fingers on the cold metal, I think continually and furiously of Father. A shred torn from something exactly like this, a scrap of metal made in Germany, lay deep inside Father's body all the time I knew him.

I never asked if it hurt, or if it affected him in any way. I never thought about it at all. When he was at home we never spoke seriously. I'm sorry now that I threw away the chance to talk with Father properly. Until they are dead, it's hard to understand that one's parents are as real as oneself.

I feel bitter about Father. It took him twenty years to die, but they murdered him. Of all people in my life, the only one who had any real fondness for me, the only one I was happy with, was the one they killed. In the looking-glass, I see Father's face, his expression, his blond hair and blue eyes. My face is Father's face – as a woman.

When it was announced that unmarried women were to be called up, Father was outraged. Not the thing for women, he said, the Forces. He said he never wanted to see me in uniform. By the time my papers came, he was dead. Even so, for his sake I couldn't join the WVS or ATS or WRNS. He might not have minded had I become a Land Girl, though they do wear a uniform. I felt his eyes watching from some hidden vantage point. Besides, I was glad to go into a factory. There's something appealing about a production line.

The workbench process is unnecessarily laborious, treating us as serfs whose energies can be thrown away on trifles. Instead I place everything on the bench in sequence, everything the correct distance apart to fit with the swing of my arm, cases, filler, pellets. Like this, the powder is easier to press into the casing. The girls to either side can't keep up. Nor do they want to. 'Blimey, you're quick,' comments one, with acid looks. I show them what I'm doing. They are bemused. One cautions, 'you'll get no thanks for it.'

She's right – I don't. Our foreman – the Overlooker, he's called – reprimands me. 'Follow your instructions, young lady.' Soon I refine the technique further, with components aligned to do two things in a single movement, first as the arm moves towards the casing, then as it moves away again. My neighbours eye me even more suspiciously.

'You're not doing it right, pet,' the girl next to me explains kindly. 'Look – like this.'

'This is much quicker,' I tell her.

'More 'aste, less speed,' she warns. 'Might not be safe. It's TNT, remember! You'll cop it. Anyway, it's not piecework.' And our shabby Overlooker again barks 'Don't try to cut corners.'

'I'm not cutting corners – this is faster,' I tell him, 'see?'

Other girls look up astonished, some smirking at my cheek, some shocked by it. Quiet falls around the benches. Girls whisper and look in my direction. There is agreement that Behrens has got above herself. It's one thing to have a bit of spirit but answering back is going too far. Worse, they think I'm putting them in danger.

Our foreman orders me to stop work, and bustles indignantly back, accompanied by two well-spoken chaps in spotless white shop coats over dark suits. On their brogues they have tied canvas overshoes.

'All right,' says one of the suits, 'what's the trouble?'

'No trouble, sir,' I reply crisply.

'Not working as per instructions?'

'This way, the girl doesn't move about so much. It's easier and breaks down the process.'

Our brown-coated foreman winces as if struck by a twinge of toothache. Heeding the advice of a factory girl probably seems as foolish to all of them as listening to the comments of a mewling cat or a songbird in a cage.

'Easier!' The men are outraged. One replies with icy politeness, 'That's enough, Miss Behrens. While you want it easy, you do realise that *other* people are being called upon to give their *lives*?'

It's boyish bluster. I suppose being a supervisor in an ordnance factory is a reserved occupation – although a woman could do it, which would free these three to do proper men's work. I bet these jobs are divvied out to chaps with contacts. Sons of local bigwigs.

'People don't give their lives,' I say. 'Their lives are taken away.'

It sounds a little anti-War, which I hadn't intended. With stony faces the interview ends abruptly. 'Work as instructed, Miss Behrens. A Reprimand Notice will be sent up. Thank you.'

Even before changing into my overalls in the morning, I find Icily Polite waiting for me. With a suitably chilly expression, he asks me to come to the Administration Block, which is, he tells me, 'outside the Danger Area.' In fact it's so far away that we travel there by car.

He drives in silence, staring ahead. He appears to be furious.

'Trouble?' I ask. Meaning, for myself. – 'Can't say.'

'Who'm I seeing?' – 'Mr Dickson.'

Dickson's a suave fellow in his thirties, with neat brown hair and gentle brown eyes behind tortoiseshell glasses. He half rises from his desk as if unsure whether this is a friendly encounter or a disciplinary one. A chivalrous impulse wins the day and he holds out his hand. 'Miss Behrens! Ray Dickson. Morning.' He has a soft, educated Yorkshire accent. I expect he hears a trace of the same in me.

'Morning, sir.'

'Well now, Miss Behrens. Reprimand Notice! Refused to follow the instructions. Bad start.'

'Yes, sir. Sorry, sir.'

'Very well, let's hear your side of it.'

'I came up a few little techniques to get the work done faster. Your chaps ran a time check. It was literally three to one. I was told to go back to doing it slowly. Happy to comply, sir.'

I brace myself for a lecture, and here it comes.

'Your conceit does you no favours, Miss Behrens. Nor does your cheek. On the other hand,' Dickson concedes condescendingly, 'your zeal does you credit. But Elstow Management Committee devised and *thoroughly tested* the production procedures as required by the Ministry of Supply. You must realise, Miss Behrens, the material you're working with is high explosive.'

He fixes me with a stare that demands my full attention, as if he thinks I hadn't understood that bombs contain high explosive. 'Something called tetryl goes into the pellets. It's extremely volatile and handling it is extremely harmful to health, damaging to skin, hair, eyes and lungs. It creates a dangerous dust which has to be got rid of safely. Even a speck can ignite. The amount of powder inside the shop has to be kept at an absolute minimum. Yet there are –'

'I'm aware, sir. We were told –'

A raised hand stops my interruption. I must let him finish. 'Yet there are pressing targets to meet. We need staff, but staff need wages and facilities, which mean risk and expense, and if they have to travel too far, there is a problem of absenteeism. Our problem is balancing safety, efficiency and cost. Within all these constraints, I'd say we've achieved the maximum output possible.'

'Really, sir, would you?

He thinks I am being impudent. 'What are you getting at?'

'It's to do with the little techniques I mentioned. If I may, sir, I'd like to show you in the shop. You'd need a stop-watch.'

As they see us walk into the workshop together, the girls at the benches instantly view me as an outsider. Just by talking to Dickson, I am altered. Like a chrysalis emerged, their workmate has become a new creature and flown out of their ambit. Dickson makes notes and says nothing as I explain. Heading back to the car, he comments drily, 'I'll get Supply to come in and have a look. I suspect they'll say your ideas are impractical. Staff would need to be retrained.'

'Yes, sir. And I believe you'd get more productivity with girls who've had secondary education. And with a three shift system.'

'That would require many more workers!'

'With one and half times as many workers, I think you'd get twice the output. Am I right that married women are to be conscripted?'

He nods. 'That's not definite.'

'One or two other things, sir. Hundredweight sacks are too heavy for women, so you're using men for the heavy lifting. Use half-hundredweight sacks and put the men onto work that women can't do. Don't waste men's strength on labour that women could do.'

To this he says nothing at all. I fear I have gone too far. After a few minutes, we are waved out of the Danger Area once more.

'Miss Behrens, where are you billeted?'

'At Chimney Corner.'

He pulls a face. 'We can find somewhere better for you.'

As I'm pondering this, he speaks again. 'By the way, Miss Behrens, you doing anything after work? Free to pop out somewhere? The tea room at the Red Lion, or something like that?'

Now, surely, *he* is being impudent. Whatever a man's private thoughts, it's not appropriate to ask that while at work. Put out by his forwardness, I reply sharply that I'm not sure.

'No, no, I mean,' he adds hastily, 'to discuss a work matter. I want to put something to you about your role at Elstow. Connected with the war effort.'

C

'Let's talk about Mum.' They liked talking about their parents in those days. Now, they never meet and would have nothing to say to each other. It was all they had in common. As she sliced the fruit, Nicola told the tale of arriving to visit Marjorie and finding her up a ladder, clearing the gutters. 'I kid you not. Her walking stick was leaning on the bottom step! I called up, "Mummy, that looks extremely dangerous." She just laughed and said, "No, darling, not extremely." It was mad, but admirable.'

'"Mad but admirable" – yes, that sounds like Mum.'

Max's strangest memory was of the time she vanished on a family holiday. 'You'd left home by then,' he said to the others, 'but do you remember Erika, her friend in Vienna? They met up with friends in some French wine village. Then Mum drove off without telling anyone for twenty-four hours.'

'Wow.'

'And the next day, Erika and her husband were found dead in a mysterious car accident.'

'Oh my God – weird.'

Philip would never forget, he said, driving their mother to the airport for a final trip to Israel. He took her into the terminal, he recalled. Among the hectic crowd and queues, excited groups, uncouth men, tetchy families, he worried that Marjorie was too vulnerable for such a place, an elderly disabled woman on her own. At Security he kissed her goodbye. When he turned to make sure all was well, it struck him – all *was* well.

'You should have seen her standing there. Plain headscarf, ordinary cardigan, flat shoes, a skirt with pockets. So unostentatious.'

'Mum's never showy,' said Nicola. 'All good quality, though. The headscarf is Hermès. Jaeger, the skirt.'

'Is it? Well, it's not just the clothes, Nic. Mum had no luggage, just a little shoulder bag. She radiated that she can manage, and needs no one. Well, the point is, that's not true any more.'

Max looked at him. 'She always needed Daddy, didn't she?'

'Daddy needed her,' said Nicola. 'She didn't need him. I think she finds it easier to relate to Daddy now he's dead.'

'What a terrible thing to say!' Max smiled.

'No, but it was like she carried no baggage of *any* kind.'

'She's a great one for travelling light,' Nicola agreed.

'No, Nic, I don't mean that. Everyone else,' Philip insisted, 'was bogged down with companions and luggage and print-outs. Mum seemed alone, calm and quiet, with her walking stick and shoulder bag.' He was proud of her, he told them, 'I don't even know why.'

Yet Marjorie had returned home ill, and looking much older. Joe Reznik revealed to them that she had passed out in a Jerusalem street.

'Fainted, you mean?'

'Well, yes, collapsed unconscious. A young couple took her to a clinic. It turned out your mum has a serious heart condition.'

'Really?'

'Injured her bad knee, too, when she fell. After coming home, of course she had those appointments at the cardiac department, didn't she?' He had taken her and collected her himself after her angiogram. 'None of you knew?' Joe's tone implied it was their own fault.

Philip challenged her on his next visit to Sandcliffe. 'Why didn't you tell us, Mummy?'

'Because it was nothing, just the heat. I was covered in bruises,' Marjorie grimaced good-humouredly, 'from landing so hard on the pavement. The young couple were marvellous.'

'But you're not well. You have heart problems, Joe says. And you had an *angiogram* without *telling* us!'

'Honestly, Phil, what do you want from me? An angiogram is no big deal. Joe worries too much. I'm perfectly well.'

But Marjorie abruptly gave up driving and from then on hardly even left the flat. She concentrated on creating a beautiful balcony garden of luxuriant pots and tubs overlooking the quiet street. She spent a lot of time out there, working on the plants, eyeing passers-by as if waiting for someone to turn up.

The three children could not get to the bottom of it. What exactly was wrong with their robust, tireless mother? Nicola demanded to know the name of the clinic where she had been taken by the young couple, what she had been treated for, what it had cost and who paid. Marjorie laughed that she remembered nothing of such details.

There was no hiding it, though, when the cardiac specialist instructed Marjorie always to wear compression stockings to manage her low blood pressure. Her damaged fingers made it a struggle to put the stockings on or take them off. She could not do it by herself and decided not to bother. Philip said he would pay a hundred pounds a week for a woman to come in and give her a hand with them every morning and evening. That was how it started, the care.

'I have a feeling Mum's heart problem dates from that break-in at the pâtisserie,' Philip guessed. 'She was never the same afterwards, was she? That's why she moved to Sandcliffe.'

They knew their mother had endured a moment of fame as a local hero for getting the better of three intruders at her shop in Saltington. Her left hand had been injured in the struggle. About her heart, it was just speculation.

'No, it was Joe and Eva, they encouraged Mummy to move,' argued Nicola.

'But that was *your* idea, wasn't it Phil?' said Max. 'You offered to buy a flat for her.'

'No-o-o,' Philip reminded him, 'after the break-in Mum sold up, bought the flat and moved just like that. Afterwards I bought it from her only so she'd have cash in the bank for her retirement.'

Marjorie didn't keep the money to enjoy in her old age. She divided it into four; one quarter for herself, the rest for her children. In that way, she said, they could spend their inheritance now instead of waiting for her to die and paying inheritance tax.

Nicola used her share to do up her little house. Max, to move from Athens to Paris and equip himself with new cameras. As for Philip, at least he now had a seafront flat in Sandcliffe to add to his portfolio of property investment. Marjorie's own share was spent on a knee operation and trips abroad. She visited old friends in Jerusalem, in Washington DC, in Paris, in Berlin, people she had 'not seen in years.' The children had no recollection of them ever being mentioned before. They were people who shared her interest in gardens and gardening, she said.

Philip gave the other two a resumé of his phone conversation with Joe Reznik. 'If you each gave fifty pounds a month, that would cover another hour a day. That's not much.'

It galled Max that this sum would be so hard for him to find, and so easy for Philip. 'What about if she needs more care in the future?'

Nicola said, 'We can ask Social Services for help.'

'Why "we" can ask?' said Max. 'You mean she can ask.'

'Mum would never ask.'

As it happened, Nicola knew more than the others what Marjorie's choices were. 'The council contribute if your assets are under, I think about £23,000 or so. Otherwise, you have to pay for your own care.'

'Are you sure?' Philip quizzed. Nicola admitted she was not sure.

'What assets *does* Mum have?' Max wondered. Philip surmised, 'Over £23,000, I suppose. At least she doesn't own the flat.'

'The council work it out,' Nicola revealed. 'You ask Social Services for a Care Needs Assessment, it's called, to find out what they'll give you.'

'Mum won't do that,' said Max. 'She won't ask the council.'

'Well, for a start, she should claim Attendance Allowance,' Nicola said. 'That's a weekly payment. She might qualify for Disability Living Allowance as well.'

'What else is there – anything?'

'Yeah, masses of stuff. Meals on Wheels, that sort of thing.'

Max grimaced. 'Shouldn't we just ask Mum what help she wants? She's compos mentis. She can decide.'

'Not really,' Philip pointed out. 'She can't decide how much *we're* willing to spend on her.'

'We're talking like she's *wrong* to need help at the end of her life.'

'End of her life?' Nicola said. 'It's not the end of her life!

That strange sensation Max felt sometimes, that was not love, was almost choking him now. 'Are you scared for Mum? Is she dreading the future? Is she afraid of becoming old? Afraid to die?'

This woolly philosophising, thought Philip, is so typical of Max.

He said tartly, 'Let's not try to work out what Mum feels. Let's just get the extra help she needs.'

Nicola rolled the words around, trying to get the sense out of them. 'Scared? Afraid? No! If there's a problem, she'll solve it, or we will.'

Max looked at her. 'No, Nic. *Nobody* knows how to solve this one. Mum can't get out of the flat by herself, can't wash, can't dress herself, can't walk properly, and can't cook her own dinner.'

'All right,' she said, 'I'll call Social Services.'

'If she agrees.'

* * *

Otto has stopped whatever he was doing. He's observing me thoughtfully. 'What?' I protest. 'I'm on my lunch break – that's all right, isn't it?'

'Of course, Marjorie. That's fine. I was thinking.'

'Oh, I wouldn't do that! Don't you know there's a war on?'

Poor Otto struggles to make sense of such mindless ripostes. Although he can't be much above forty, Otto's the very pattern of dull respectability, a solid citizen, unflappable and measured. His voice, accented with something not especially Germanic, is quiet.

'I've been impressed by your work. Your memory for detail is astonishing. I would almost describe it as a cognitive abnormality.'

'Goodness. Thank you, Otto.'

'As a matter of interest, what sort of thing do you tend to forget?'

'What I forget is… actually I forget what it is I forget.'

'Ah, yes, I see.' It passes him by that I am joking. He does not even smile. 'And I notice you do that Times crossword puzzle every day without fail. While eating a sandwich.'

'Well, yes. Any objection?'

'You always do the hard one, don't you? The cryptic one?'

'Otto, are you serious? What do you take me for?'

'Do you always finish it?'

I gaze back incredulous. What a patronising, question! I suppose he doesn't mean any offence. 'What, my sandwich, or the crossword?' I ask sweetly. At last Otto smiles as I inform him that I manage to finish both, unless I leave some of the sandwich.

'Well, d'you remember that crossword puzzle in the Telegraph, back in January?' he asks, '"Can you complete this crossword in twelve minutes or less?" Did you try it?'

'In *January*? No. I didn't see it.'

'You ought to have a go,' he persists. 'It was especially tough. There was some kind of prize.'

'What, books to the value of thirty shillings? A pack of playing cards? Otto, I don't want a prize.'

'I know, but it would be interesting.'

'No, it wouldn't. A crossword puzzle is just a crossword puzzle. Anyway, no one would know whether you'd done it in less than twelve minutes. So how could there be a prize?'

'I'll bring it in for you.'

'What – you mean you've kept it since January? Why?'

'I didn't keep it but I can get a copy. Do have a go, Marjorie.'

'*Get* a copy? Why?' It's impossible to refuse, as Otto's my boss.

Otto and I are still getting the measure of each other, but from the start there's a curious rapport. As soon as Ray Dickson and I had implemented the changes at ROF Elstow, I was sent here. Officially, Dickson had to recommend the transfer, although I had the distinct feeling he wanted to keep me. A professional relationship, obviously. Yet here I am again alone in an office with a man. I keep everything reserved, correct and modest, but one ought not to be too distant.

'Did you know, you're the youngest person, and the first woman, ever to work in Lyons' head office as a manager?' It's clear Otto regards this as some sort of achievement, although it's none of my doing. I was given the job without even applying for it.

'When my call-up papers arrived, I volunteered for factory work. Instead I'm doing a desk job for a chain of tea shops.'

We're in the company's Labour Planning Office, which is all about Work Study. Otto Weigert's little section doesn't occupy itself with tea and cakes, though. We deal solely with the company's Government contracts – war work. It's not only ordnance. As well as making both biscuits and bombs, Joe Lyons also makes the army rations and does the army's laundry.

Otto straight away sends me on a course in time study, to be instructed in how best to squeeze the maximum production out of workers. It's interesting to learn the number of minutes normal healthy human beings need to rest every hour, and how many times a man has to visit the lavatory, as compared with a woman, and how long it takes each to spend a penny.

Our job is to come up with faster, cheaper, more efficient ways of working. Otto sends me to warehouses and workshops and factories to look at the personnel, and study the equipment they are using, their clothing, desks and work benches, everything. I'm scrutinising managers as well as workers. What must they make of this chit of a blonde with her clipboard and stop-watch? I write up my report and give it to Otto, and Otto passes it on to the powers that be.

Seems odd that war work would be entrusted to a German, but it turns out – Otto tells me – he isn't a Lyons' employee either; like me, he was ordered here by the War Office.

At first, Otto called me Miss Behrens and I called him Mr Weigert. It was easy to relax with him. So easy, that one day at lunchtime I said that we had probably been put in a room together, far from the others, because we both have German names. He didn't find this amusing. 'Can you speak German, Miss Behrens?' he asked.

I replied in German: 'We might just as well talk German to each other. Perhaps it would be more correct to call you Herr Weigert?'

'Goodness, you speak it like a native!' In true German fashion, he explained (in English) with deadpan concern that because of the war, it would be better to say "Mister" – as if I might really call him "Herr"! I said drily that I had not been serious.

Continuing the humourless vein, he then vouchsafed, in a thoroughly un-British way, that he had been naturalised and was now truly British. 'I left Germany in 1934. I saw how things were going.'

With dreadful lack of tact, I burst out, 'So you really *are* German!' and straight away began to apologise effusively.

He halted the apology with a graceful wave. 'No, as I say, I am naturalised British,' he repeated. 'If you like, please drop "Mister" and call me Otto.'

'And please do call me Marjorie. Thank you, Otto. Please forgive me for saying that. But I mean, presumably you can't be allowed to… I mean, after all, we're at war with the Germans.'

'No,' he replied patiently, 'Britain is at war with Germany, which is not at all the same thing.'

'It's not the same thing, but I wouldn't say it's not *at all* the same.'

'Well, plenty of people of German origin are serving in the British armed forces. Germans are also working in British intelligence.'

This seems a rather wild remark. Neither of us can possibly know whether it is true. 'What about your family? Did they come with you? Or they didn't want to?'

'No, no. It's not that they didn't want to. My parents are in Berlin. I urged them to get out. They said they were too old, but the truth is, they were too optimistic. They believed they could accept life under the Hitler regime. My sister stayed because she would not abandon them. They needed her help.'

I try to imagine what possible circumstances could cause me to do what Otto has done; to renounce England and become the citizen of another country, and fight against my own brothers. Then I realise, my own family *did* do as Otto has done. Father fled here to fight for England against his Jew-hating native land.

Otto has moved me across the river for three days a week to Hayes Laundry, where Lyons does the army's washing (there's a joke in there somewhere: privates, linen). It's a long way from my digs, bus to Victoria, tram to Camberwell, but I love the journey. The awful truth is that after a raid I like it even more. The landscape changes, roads are closed, buses suddenly on detour, the way ahead blocked with scattered masonry and girders, and curtained with floating dust.

Steamy with our breath and wet coats, overloaded with standing passengers, the bus lurches sharply, diverted along narrow backstreets of broken terraced dwellings. Here and there a house is absent, or a roof half missing. Women in rags crowd around glowing braziers on the pavement, using as fuel their own once-precious furniture, now ruined and splintered. I wipe condensation from the window with the side of my hand and stare into the privacy of a bathroom ripped apart. A washstand hangs off the shattered wall, yet a toothbrush still stands in an unbroken glass upon a shelf.

The bus runs over some toys lying in the road, turning slightly as if to avoid them. The driver works his way forward, each passenger quiet. The bus fills with cigarette smoke. There is some coughing from the upper deck. 'Bastards. Bloody boche,' mutters a lone Cockney voice behind me. There is no reply other than the resounding sense that she speaks for everyone.

Again wiping the misted glass, I see queues, inexplicable, patient, waiting eternally. Ordinary, undistinguished-looking volunteers in tin hats and armbands hand out blankets. With rather theatrical posturing and shouts, others keep order, the order which is everything we own, everything we are, marshalling the bereaved and broken-hearted.

'Sorry folks, everybody orf!' cries the conductor, as the double decker judders to halt at a policeman's command. The passengers alight in the midst of nowhere. Scarves and mufflers are tightened, collars raised against the cold, mouths and noses shielded with handkerchiefs to keep out the dust as we continue on foot, hoping to get to work somehow. Following one another in single file, we step gingerly through broken glass, seeing into people's homes torn open, their pitiful quotidian struggle exposed to view, intimate family treasures lying where we tread.

Life will go on. Of course life does go on, one way or another.

In the last resort, I could simply walk the whole distance to work. Why not? There is no God-given right to travel by bus or tram. All the orderly, daily world can be blown clean away. The more it is, the more the mystery of the city is revealed, its bone and sinew, and a life that cannot be vanquished. Beneath the relentless good cheer lies relentless doggedness. The ironic bonhomie of the English conceals a cynical resolve peculiar to England. Everyone is stoical. I admire them, these Britons, these tight-lipped Londoners, their coolness. Among shards and rubble, women in cheap housecoats sit in silent, dignified despair. People whose world has been destroyed are comforted with a mug of tea.

Hayes Laundry is a huge place and a huge operation, with huge clanking lorries moving in and out all day and all night. The number of efficiency improvements to be made is overwhelming. When I first arrived I discovered the linen was moved in tall bins on castors, designed to be shifted by a man, or two men. With men all gone to the Forces, women were brought in. Yet sometimes even three women working together can't manoeuvre these bins.

I've had smaller, lighter baskets made, half the height and weight, easy for a girl to handle on her own. Men need never be used for this work again. Women's wages are much less – so small baskets make the job cheaper as well as quicker. As a rule, men should only be used for work that women can't do. Management could be left entirely to women unless a man has some special aptitude for it.

The other two days a week, I'm back in Cadby Hall with Otto. When he drops the crossword into my in-tray, I leave the thing lying there and carry on with my work. After all, it's not yet our lunch break. And it's only a crossword.

I can't ignore it, though. I'm almost nervous at the thought of failing to complete it in time. At the start of the break, without any haste, I take out my Thermos, unscrew the cap and pour out some tea. Slowly and carefully I unwrap my sandwich and bite into the Spam as if the crossword has been altogether forgotten. I studiously avoid Otto's glances. Eventually the moment comes. 'All right, this puzzle of yours.'

Otto raises his eyebrows as if he too has become quite indifferent to it, and we each look at our watches. 'Go on, then,' he says.

7 Down (6 letters), a boat which is also a tailor. Not tricky, this one. I quickly pencil in "cutter". 4 Across (5, 3) is along similar lines, combining a "direct route" with "Roundheads", of course to do with their famous hairstyle, and as the third-from-last letter is the C of "cutter", the words "short cut" are hurriedly pencilled-in.

I wonder if all the clues will be to do with cutting, but as I keep going the common theme seems to be witty puns. 13 Across (5, 4) – "much that could be got from a timber merchant" – I smile at the answer, "great deal." It's funny, fits with 7 Down, and opens up possibilities for 5 and 6 Down as well.

The clues aren't what I'd call cryptic. Some are just simple anagrams, or mere definitions, some nothing but general knowledge. The only worry is the time limit. 29 Down (5), "Famous sculptor", I leave until last, thinking it's an obscure word play until the penny drops: it's literally nothing more or less than the name of a famous sculptor. The only one that fits is "Rodin".

I put down the pencil and look up. 'All done.' I check the time. If there's a prize, I'm eligible.

Otto frowns and smiles at the same time. 'Truly?' His eyes turn to his wrist-watch and rise again to peer with undisguised wonder, as if he's just learned that I am an oil billionaire or the author of a best-selling novel, or a rare insect. 'Let me see it.'

'How long?'

'Nine and half minutes,' he says. 'A second under.'

'Yes, that's what I make it, too.'

I fear I may have a self-satisfied glow, which doesn't suit my complexion. Any kind of flush makes my pale skin look awful.

'May I see?' he says again. He holds out a hand.

I step across the room and stand at his desk as he reads some of the clues and answers. Otto clears his throat. 'I have a colleague,' he says most mysteriously, 'in Signals. He tells me they would like to meet anyone who cracked this in twelve minutes. I'll show it to him. You'll hear from him.'

'So, what's the prize?' I ask.

'You are.'

Marjorie put on her reading glasses, surprised by the sight of a real letter. It was headed Sandcliffe Borough Council Social Services Directorate.

Dear Mrs Rosen, she read, *The Pensions Service and Sandcliffe Borough Council Social Services Directorate are working in partnership to provide a combined service for our customers.*

She would certainly delete 'combined.' Indeed, the whole first sentence after 'partnership' could go. Of course, she would never refer to residents of the town as the council's 'customers', but that was a battle lost long ago. It was not clear whether she was supposed to have heard of the Pensions Service or Sandcliffe Borough Council Social Services Directorate. She read on. *A Joint Team Officer will visit you on May 4th to assess your care needs.*

Privately, Marjorie had a horror of officialdom. Red tape was her bête noire. That every arm of the British state has a benign purpose, she did not doubt. Nonetheless she hoped to be spared contact with its functionaries, the myriad worthies with delegated powers who carry out the spadework of government. As for local government… local councils all over the land she viewed as nests of backscratching, inefficiency and profligacy. They were in place to serve the people, yet everywhere the people were in fear of their local authority, its power over their street, their house, their family, their daily lives. She found it distasteful to be 'assessed', and considered the words 'care needs' obtuse. Yet despite her horror of officialdom, Marjorie now flew with open eyes into its web.

Seasons arrive and depart one degree at a time; one leaf, one bud, one bird at a time. Spring adds a little more each week until long after the first signs of summer have appeared. Summer is still arriving when already the first signs of autumn are seen. Seasons are not absolute, nor the days of our lives, and the years progress, uncertain and incremental, youth and age overlapping. So it was that on this day Marjorie felt that she passed from one season to another.

The Joint Team Officer was an awkwardly pleasant, gawky man in his thirties, lanky as a thistle. He wore a well-worn business suit and battered casual shoes. With diffident smile and gentle handshake he introduced himself as Den, kindly explaining to Marjorie that he was her Care Manager but she should think of him as a friend, since he would be always on hand to make sure her care needs were met. 'Now, Marjorie, would you prefer to be known as Marjorie or as Mrs Rosen?'

'Oh, Marjorie is fine, Dennis, as we're to be friends.'

'Denzil,' he corrected her.

Until this day, Sandcliffe Social Services held no file on Mrs Marjorie Rosen. That she could hardly use a bathroom on her own, found it nearly impossible to dress herself, depended on friends to do her shopping and wasn't safe to lift a saucepan were facts unknown to them, and nor did she want them known. There was no record anywhere of how Marjorie moved slowly and carefully, making a small bowl of soup or half a cup of coffee, always taking advantage of any help or favours offered; that she revelled in the emptiness of her diary and the freedom to tend her balcony flower pots; or leaned back in her chair with poets and plays and histories, or a new novel, or an old one, and a sparkling glimpse of Sandcliffe Bay.

Then came May 4th. Denzil sat in one armchair with a pen in his hand and a clipboard on his lap. Marjorie faced him in the other armchair, her expression as frank and friendly as she could muster.

'Now, Marjorie, it's important to answer everything truthfully.' – 'Of course! What a thing to say, Den.'

Having established her full name and date of birth, he asked, 'So, what's your religion, Marjorie?' – 'You're asking if I have tried prayer?'

'No, no,' he responded politely, 'it's for our records. You know, cultural needs.' – '*Cultural* needs? Oh, in *that* sense. To be honest, I'd rather you didn't write anything for religion, Den, or culture.'

'Oh, it's quite confidential, Marje, under the Data Protection Act. And it's useful for us to know, if for example, someone passes away.' – 'Oh well, all right then. I suppose I have to say I'm Jewish.'

'Jewish! Ah! Go to Sandcliffe Synagogue, then, do you?' – 'Well, yes. I don't keep kosher, though. Or, I do, but not really.'

'And how do you get there, if mobility is such a problem?' – 'My friends over the road, they take me.'

'Ah-ha. And Marje, your ethnic origin?' – '*Ethnic* origin? You ask people that, Den? Can of worms, isn't it?'

'No, Marje, not at all. It's normal now. I mean, are you Asian, Black, Chinese or White? Or Irish? It's only for our records.' – 'The council is keeping a record of everyone's race?'

'We have to, Marje, to be sure cultural needs are met, you know. It's Ethnic Monitoring, Marje, for inclusivity. No problem if you don't want to answer. I can put "Refuses to say" or "White British".'

'Don't say I refused, Den, it looks bad. But White British surely isn't an ethnic origin, is it?' – 'Yes, yes, it is. I'll put White British. Anyway it's only a formality.'

Denzil quizzed Marjorie about her physical difficulties, nodding sympathetically as with a rueful grin she enumerated them. At last they rose to their feet. Walking ahead with her stick, Marjorie cheerfully showed him around her little home. He observed Marjorie's books, the volumes on their dark shelves from floor to ceiling, the colours of their covers pressed randomly together, the cascade of text on their spines, the unheard-of titles and authors.

'I see you are an educated lady,' he said. 'What a lot of books!'

'That's just a few of what my husband and I used to have in our old house. It's very painful getting rid of books.'

'Yes, people say that.' He glanced at the photographs of Harry, the souvenirs and knick-knacks, framed prints and paintings hanging in every room. He inspected the bedrooms, bathroom and kitchen, exclaimed that she had bookshelves everywhere. With a laugh she demonstrated why it was difficult to use the toilet. He laughed too, and made a note.

They returned to their armchairs in the sitting room. Denzil took up a separate bundle of papers. 'Obviously everyone must make the correct financial contribution for home care services,' said he. 'We call this the Financial Assessment.'

If Marjorie thought his earlier questions were impudent, she was even less prepared for the Financial Assessment. 'If your assets come to more than £23,250, the excess has to pay for your care. Under £23,250, we contribute on a sliding scale. You contribute and we contribute. That's fair, isn't it? So I need to see your recent bank statements. What's your monthly income? Your husband left you with a good pension, didn't he, Marje? How much did you get from selling your house in Saltington? From selling your pâtisserie business? Where are the proceeds?

Denzil spoke about profit from her pâtisserie as though it were a pot of gold that had appeared at the end of a rainbow. She thought ruefully of the days and nights of work she had put into it! *It would be better now if I'd sat with my feet up all those years.*

'And how much from selling this flat to your son? When did you sell it to him? You didn't sell the flat to avoid paying for care, did you – or did you? Why sell it, then? Where is that money now? Do you own other property, Marjorie? Anything abroad? Do you have any other shares, bonds, accounts, pension funds? What other property do you have, Marje, valuables, jewellery, things like that?'

Handing Denzil documents one after another for him to scrutinise, a savings certificate for £12,000, a building society passbook with a balance of £24,173, shuffling to fetch statements, she detected in Den a disapproval of her little nest egg.

Of course, they allow a certain amount for outgoings: would she fetch her utility bills, latest council tax demand? What about holidays? Gosh, she spent so much on holidays, Denzil remarked dryly. All her money went on holidays, she admitted. Was she being wasteful, he wondered, was she deliberately depriving herself of assets? 'Because that,' he warned gently, 'is not allowed.' They chuckled, and Marjorie assured him she had no such scheme in mind.

As alert to danger as she had been in years, Marjorie sweetly composed her replies. She felt as though she were pushing through trackless thickets of needle-sharp gorse, uncertain which way to turn.

The money in Israel, she could not mention, nor the money in Switzerland. Either would demand explanation – to Denzil, to the children, to nameless officials. Creating a paper trail for it at this stage would be impossible. In any case, both accounts together didn't add up to a fortune. Even if she had to spend all her other funds, she must not touch those accounts.

On the other hand, she did need someone to dress her. And help in the bathroom. And in the kitchen. Such things cost money. Someone had to pay. Who should it be? Ay, there's the rub.

The Israel money, she had always wanted to give back to Israel; the Switzerland funds, to share between her three undeserving children. She had put that hard-won money aside *especially* for them, and there it had lain, destined as a farewell gift to her little darlings. One thing she would certainly *not* do was spend it on herself, on her 'care'. That would be horrible, she felt, akin to a sort of narcissism. The sum total of your life should be carried forward into the future, not back to yourself.

Denzil thanked Marjorie for the coffee. He apologised that he had taken so much time, and hoped to see her again soon. As soon as the door closed behind him, Marjorie dropped exhausted into her chair. Her mind began to pick at this puzzle: whose responsibility was it, she asked herself, that she be decently washed, dressed and fed? The community's, the family's or her own?

In enigmatic reply, Sharon opened the door. Or rather, 'Not Sharon, Mrs Rosen – I'm Sherry.' Marjorie laughed at her mistake. Sherry warmed some soup, and made a flask of Ovaltine, led Marjorie to the bedroom, removed the compression stockings from the soft flesh, rinsed them with her own hands in the bathroom, and hung them in the airing cupboard to dry. She helped the old woman undress, guided her pale buttocks onto the toilet, wiped between her legs, pulled the nightdress over her head, watched as she took her medication, arranged the pillows, patted the duvet, made her snug. Marjorie thanked her like a child, and lay in bed, and pondered and remembered and half-slept, alert always for the first notes of dawn, its first pale glimmer on the curtains. At last it was there, and in came Shelly or Shannon, opening the bedroom door, drawing the curtains. 'Morning, Mrs Rosen. How are you today?'

Now Marjorie received letters nearly every day. Envelopes large and small arrived from the Joint Financial Assessment and Benefits Team and the Social Services Directorate. She put on her reading glasses.

She should read and check her copy of the Eligibility Criteria Checklist, partly typed, partly handwritten, partly printed. Marjorie had a sensation like seasickness as she rowed through its turgid text. In a single paragraph she found herself in the third, second and first person: *MRS ROSEN HAS RECenTLY HAS TO STOP DRiviNG BUT HAS Still THE DESiRR TO GO Out; You are unable to manage some aspects of your involvement in work/learning/education indicating some risk to your independence either now or in the foreseeable future; I confirm that I agree.*

Then her Care Plan, setting out Denzil's decision that she needed care three times daily. *The service user*, in Denzil's assessment, *can make the maximum weekly contribution*. Where previously Philip had sent cheques, Marjorie must now send them. For Philip to make the payment was not allowed. It would constitute an undeclared addition to her assets.

Marjorie turned to the mahogany cabinet in the corner and protested sharply to the photograph of Harry. Contributions to the cost of care, she exclaimed, ought to come from income, not assets. Harry glared back. Plainly that was what he thought, too.

Sign and return, she read. *I confirm that I was involved in this care plan and agree with what is documented.* In an unsteady hand she signed, M. L. Rosen.

* * *

A naval officer, spruce in peaked cap, crisp shirt and tie, and jacket brightly buttoned, pushes over a sheet of paper. 'Give this a read-through.' It's headed *Official Secrets Acts and Confidentiality Declaration*. 'When you've fully understood it, kindly append your signature to the dotted line.'

I am fully aware of my obligations under the Official Secrets Acts. I understand that it applies to me at all times during and after completion of Crown service.

I borrow a pen and sign, M. L. Behrens.

Without explanation the officer says we're off to Hut 3. I can only imagine that's some sort of code name. 'I hope you can keep a secret,' she says, 'because if you can't, you could end up in clink, or worse.' I'm not sure what could be worse! Is she threatening me with being shot at dawn?

She leads and I follow in the grounds of a stately red-brick mansion, a Victorian Gothic pile. The air is damp and cold, and dusk falling. Above our heads, autumn leaves race in a blustery wind, like birds. On our left stands the house itself, and to the right, a pretty lake and a lawn. Soon I make out groups of huts ahead, glorified cabins and large sheds clustered together with alleys between.

It has the look of a factory yard or a shanty town. Yet people are strolling in the twilight, some in uniform, some not, some in bizarre hybrid outfits. Many seem quite odd. A man cycles past us wearing his gas mask. Another, in a tweed suit with plus-fours, is doing gymnastics on the lawn. And I do believe that is a couple embracing with impunity on the chilly ground under some trees. It's hard to work out what is going on here, if anything. This is no shanty town, nor a factory. It could almost be a hospital. Mental asylum, perhaps.

My letter and travel warrant came from the Foreign Office. What has the FO to do with me? And what has this place to do with the FO? I didn't apply for a position at the Foreign Office. Have I somehow been transferred from Lyons? Surely one can't be conscripted into the Foreign Office – can one? Or am I still working for Lyons? Or for whoever sent me to Lyons in the first place?

'Officially,' says my Wren officer, 'this is the Navy, and I'm on a ship.' Yes, it's definitely a mental asylum. She and I are both deluded inmates. 'Always remember, you've signed the Act.' The way she says it, it sounds like a line from Kafka. She means, the Confidentiality Declaration.

'Never,' she counsels, 'never say your work is secret. It gets people a-wondering. That's a danger.'

'But what work *am* I here to do? No one will tell me.'

'No idea.' She shakes her head briskly. More Kafkaesque. 'If people ask, tell 'em Foreign Office staff have been evacuated here. Tell 'em you're a clerk. Say you're a telephone operator. Or a writer. No one knows what a writer does, so that should shut them up.'

'Yes, all that was impressed upon me.'

'It's quite a lot of fun here sometimes,' she confides. 'Better than being shot at. We have ENSA and all that, shows, the latest films, lots of dances. The civvy staff are very strong on that, put on their own revues, plays, serious stuff you know, a bit highbrow, first class though, professionals some of them. Food's not much cop, though. Where you billeted?' I tell her I'm with a family in Bedford. 'That's no good!' she exclaims. 'Ask your section head to get you nearer.'

'What section am I in?'

'It'll all be explained to you. I don't know anything. Hut 3 isn't Navy. It's Army and Air Force. Though, of course, they have naval officers in there. Obviously.'

Oh, obviously. This is more Lewis Carroll than Franz Kafka. Myself in the role of Alice. 'It'll be explained to you,' she adds.

Curiouser and curiouser. In keeping with the mad logic of the place, Hut 3 is not between Huts 2 and 4, but is round the back of Hut 6, and it's not one, but several linked timber sheds in an L-shape. Something sturdier than an ordinary hut, it even has a chimney.

Inside, it's as plain as a barn, with rough timbers, bare wooden walls and bare floorboards. A passageway runs between mysterious partitions which break the space into work areas. Some look cosy, with rugs and paraffin stoves. Yet so poor is the insulation the rest of the shed is freezing cold, despite noxious billowings from a coke fire at one end. A blue-grey fug of cigarette and pipe smoke swirls up from behind every partition.

My Wren officer walks me to the desk of – according to her, it is Wing Commander Eric Jones, 'Head of Hut'. Just beyond, WAAF girls are busy at clattering teleprinters and typewriters. Commander Jones flicks through a folder. 'Welcome, welcome, Miss Behrens! Welcome to Bletchley Park. Or Station X, rather.'

'Thank you, sir. What are my duties here, sir?' I ask.

He shrugs. Even Commander Jones can't tell me.

The job is easy in essence, maddening in practice, and required no instruction other than the good old "Next to Nellie" method: sitting alongside an officer in uniform who carried on with the task as though I were not there at all until I understood what I had to do.

Placed in a rickety chair, I puzzle over quarto sheets covered with screeds of unpunctuated German text arranged in blocks of five letters, the quintets rising on the page like a wall of bricks. These orderly, inhuman lines of pentalogies, stacked in neat columns and rows, look to me like square-jawed Teutonic grins – with dozens of gaps where letters are absent, as if the smiling Teutons have lost a few teeth in their punch-up with the civilised world.

This section of the Hut is called the Watch, and I'm one of the Watchkeepers. All my colleagues are men, some in uniform, others in the sloppiest open-neck shirts, cardigans, corduroys. Our shared desk is cleverly horseshoe-shaped, and we work together filling in those toothy gaps and correcting errors to reconstruct the military German, render it into functional English and make an assessment of its significance. This is interpretation or inspired guesswork rather than translation, and it is urgent. Often we are reading about imminent or ongoing enemy action. Completed papers are thrust into the hands of the Head of the Watch – "Number One", we call him.

Bundles of raw decodes from which no one has yet tried to make any sense constantly arrive down a cunning wooden chute linking us to Hut 6, or else they are brought in by rushed but cheery WRNS and WAAF girls. The Wrens and Waafs know nothing about what we are doing and must not be told. They, in their turn, have been ordered not to ask. They must have guessed, though. On one side of the paper the original coded message can be seen, while pasted in strips on the other side is the partially deciphered version from Hut 6.

Everyone on the team has a knack for grasping the sense of a message from a few fragments. Number One has decided I'm good at traffic analysis – spotting patterns and picking up details, names, dates and words that were used in previous intercepts, that a certain brigade was sent to a particular place on such and such a mission.

Number One has half a dozen phones, direct lines to commanders and officials, and one to the PM himself. Some decodes he rushes along the passageway to military intelligence – Army, Navy and Air Force. Instructions are hurried back to send the information immediately to this or that commander in the field of battle, and let Churchill know. Every message is rephrased to look as though it's from sources behind enemy lines, because even the top brass are not to know about our work.

There's a wonderfully anarchic egalitarianism on the good ship

Bletchley Park. Deference to class and rank has been forgotten. Forces people don't even bother to salute their officers. They just say, 'Oh, hello, sir.' All ages and backgrounds are thrown together. No one takes any notice of such things. Uniformed working-class girls predominate, good-humoured throngs of them mingling in saucy camaraderie with the second-largest group, young middle-class academics, mostly not in uniform, mostly in need of a haircut. Among the girls there's another type too, the cut-glass contingent, ladyships and honourables with pearls and connections, and blood as blue as His Majesty's. Whole gaggles and giggles of them do their irksome duty with uncomplaining good humour.

And then, unbeknownst to their fellows, an astonishing proportion of mathematicians, decrypters and analysts are Jewish. I haven't seen so many Jews in years, not since I last went to synagogue. There are five in Hut 3 alone, another five next door in Hut 6. It's just one more thing to keep quiet about. Naïve gentiles think a German name like mine shows that one is of German origin. They assume such people must have been thoroughly vetted. As I'm sure one has.

'*Marjorie Behrens!* Good heavens! It *is* you, Marje!' A Yorkshire accent. It's one of the Wrens with raw decodes from Hut 6.

'Peg?' In one second we have flung our arms around one another. I'm thinking, *Where does this leave our oath of secrecy?* Peggy is a great friend from when we lived and worked side by side as war volunteers in Melthorpe tank factory, but she likes to gossip and I wouldn't trust her with a secret. Now she knows where I work.

'You're not a Wren, Marje, or a Waaf or ATS. So *what* are you?'

My colleagues stare in disbelief at this indiscretion, but Peggy is not asking about my work. 'Well, I'm, you see… I'm a civilian.'

'Anyway, can't stop now,' says Peggy, to my relief.

I see her to the door and she pulls me out into the night air. I take a deep, refreshing breath. It's quiet outside. The lake looks calm and inviting. 'Peggy, you've signed the Act, haven't you?'

This reminder of the Official Secrets Act makes Peggy abruptly lower her voice to a whisper, as if secrets whispered are in some way not really divulged. 'Oh, that! Don't worry, I won't tell any German spies,' she giggles. 'But *we* don't have any secrets, do we?'

Before we signed the Act, that might have been true. In the tank factory, we went out like kids at the end of the shift. The war had hardly started. There were no raids and no rationing. We'd joke stupidly, take turns to bake a cake for tea and went shopping for cheap dresses.

'Secrets! Course we don't, Peg. Still, you remember this bit of the Act? *No mention whatsoever may be made either in conversation or correspondence regarding the nature of your work*. Don't know about you, Peg, but I don't fancy spending a few years in jail. Better not talk about our work. Walls have ears and all that. For all we know, spies may be working with us here.'

She laughs merrily. 'Well, if they're already here, it's a bit late to worry about them. How *did* you get the job, Marje? Most of the decode people are university types, toffs with double-barrelled names and that. Their fathers all knew each other at Eton and whatnot.'

'Well, I'm just a lass who never went to college and doesn't know anyone. A letter came in the post, telling me I must report for interview at the Admiralty. It didn't even say what it was for.'

'My goodness! What happened?'

'Well, I put on my coat and my best hat and went to the Admiralty.'

'Did they send a car?'

'Did they heck! No, Peg, I had to catch a bus.'

'Does it go all the way?'

'Yes, Peggy.' Peg's mind is impossibly scatty.

'Were you still living with your aunt in Fulham?'

'Yes. Auntie Frances.'

'And on that day you went to the Admiralty?'

'Well, yes, that's right, Peg.'

'How terribly grand! In your best hat! You must've been nervous.'

'I don't know that I was, really. I arrived, a chap came out to meet me, and we talked for a few minutes.'

'What, without going into his office?'

'Worse than that. He interviewed me in the street.'

'Well I never!'

'Yes, strange isn't it? I suppose because it's all so hush-hush.'

This further reminder of the Official Secrets Act makes Peggy lower her voice again. 'Golly! What did he ask you about?'

Now Peggy's venturing into territory that I can't discuss. 'Nothing much,' I say, before deciding to tell her just a little more, 'He asked what languages I can speak, so I told him.'

'Oh, you speak everything,' she laughs.

'Not quite everything, Peg. Three or four things.'

'Then what happened?'

'That was it. Took less than five minutes, on the pavement in Whitehall. Then he said, "You'll hear from us."'

'And did you?'

'Well, yes. As you see, here I am.'

I can't tell Peggy how the Admiralty chap and I strolled slowly along Whitehall. He asked how come I speak both Russian and German.

'It's complicated, sir.' In the end there was no choice, unless I'd told him to mind his own business. I tried to explain how the Leveens – or Levinskiys, rather – art dealers, connoisseurs, came from Odessa via Vienna and Frankfurt, and the Behrens family, wealthy from shipping, from a German-speaking part of Latvia which belonged to Russia. The menfolk of both families used German or Russian according to what sort of thing they wanted to say. Among the women, though, it depended on who they were talking to. 'Father left Russia alone when he was a teenager and made his way here. He enlisted in the British Army and won a medal, and after the Great War, started a fisheries business. At home my parents spoke German and Russian. In public they'd speak English rather badly. Or spoke, rather; my father's dead.'

'Oh, I'm sorry,' he said politely. 'And when you say a German-speaking part of Latvia, do you mean Courland?'

'Yes, Kurland. The Russians expelled all the Jews during the last war, but a lot, including father's family, went back afterwards.'

'Ah yes, I see. Where did you get the French?'

'I had a French governess who ran a little schoolroom, and my nanny was French. My mother is practically fluent in French. *Her* parents spoke French routinely. It's quite usual in that circle. They consider that only the most uncouth people can't speak French.'

'So, to be clear, which is your first language, German or Russian?'

'Wouldn't put it that way, sir. Fluent in both, but I was born here and grew up as an English-speaker. My brothers and sisters, we only ever spoke English amongst ourselves. When we were allowed to talk, that is; Mother was very strict,' I laughed. 'She forbade us to speak without permission. Literally a case of "speak when you're spoken to."'

'Well, they do say children should be seen and not heard.'

'Yes, that's how it was. Father was a bit naughty, though. He encouraged us to defy Mother whenever he was at home. But he was hardly ever at home.'

He seemed genuinely interested. 'What an unusual family. And, ah, forgive me – Jewish, aren't you?'

He had arrived at the very topic I most wanted to avoid. 'I'd prefer people to think I'm an ordinary Yorkshire girl.'

He raised his eyebrows. 'That you're not.' We passed Horse Guards on the other side of the road. 'As a matter of interest,' he said, 'have you spent any time in Germany?'

'Not going to be interned, I hope? Yes, I've been many times. One of my uncles fled to Hamburg to escape the Russians. Married a local Jewish girl, namely, my aunt. Their children were our two German cousins. One in particular I used to be close to. Father and my uncle did business together, I don't know what, exactly – fisheries, shipping. Father went there in the firm's boats, across the North Sea. In the school holidays, he often took me with him. We would stay for a while. When I was thirteen Father said my uncle's business had been Aryanised and it wasn't safe to go there any more. No idea what's happened to them since. My parents wouldn't have told me.'

'He worked there, in Germany, on those trips? Your father?'

'I suppose. I don't understand what the arrangement was.'

We walked a few paces in silence as the chap digested this. Out of the blue, he threw me a question: 'I hear you like crosswords! Would it be possible to have a crossword with no clues at all, do you think?'

Who knows I like crosswords? Only Otto. No one else. So is this his friend in Signals?

'Of course, there would be many possible solutions. Wouldn't really be a crossword, though, under the meaning of the Act.'

'What Act?' The man had no irony in his soul.

'The Cross Words Act,' I answered, straight faced. He cast an eye at me sharply, not sure whether he was being ribbed.

We turned away from Whitehall, through a great square gateway and across a fine circular courtyard. I craned my neck this way and that, admiring majestic Baroque facades all around, very stirring and splendid. I asked where we were, and where he was taking me, but the chap answered only, 'Have you ever done a raven's matrices?'

'No, sir.' Embarrassment stopped me asking what he meant.

Briskly into a doorway, along a high corridor, our heels echoing on decorated stone tiles, we walked without another word. It began to feel as though I were being led to a place of execution. I wondered whether I dare request a final meal. At an alcove, furnished with a handsome polished desk and chair beside an enormous hearth, we came to a halt. 'Take a seat, Miss Behrens.' On the desk was a sheet of paper and a pencil.

The chap unlocked a cabinet behind the desk and took out a school exercise book with a brown cover. That, at least, is what I thought it was, until he handed it to me. Printed on the front were the words *Standard Progressive Matrices, Set A, B, C, D and E, Prepared by J. C. Raven.*

'Have a crack at these,' the chap said. 'Raven's Matrices. Write your answers on the sheet of paper. If you can't answer a question, don't worry. We just want to see how you get on.' He looked at his wrist-watch. 'Begin when you're ready.'

I flicked the book open and saw page upon page of those "What's the next in the series?" type of puzzles. No words, just patterns with pieces missing and a choice of pieces to fill the gaps. When I'd finished them, I closed the book and handed him the paper.

The chap was scrutinising me with a small, tight-lipped smile. He looked at my answer for E12, the last page in the book. *That's* when he said, 'You'll be hearing from us.'

Philip rang the doorbell and walked in. 'Good *morning,* Mum!' He carried bags of shopping, a bunch of flowers too. Marjorie was delighted, laughing with surprise. Philip occasionally dropped in like this, without warning. After weeks of yearning to see one of her children, Marjorie sometimes caught herself daydreaming that he might appear. And there he was.

'Take me into the Forest, darling. I'll cancel the midday carer. Let's pick blackberries! Bring some boxes.' Marjorie longed to get out of the flat, to go somewhere, anywhere.

'We'll stop for lunch. Let me treat you.' He knew all her favourite spots for lunch or tea.

He settled Marjorie in her wheelchair and off they went, out of the building and across the car park. Even that she found exhilarating. She struggled to raise her legs into the car. Lately, she said, they felt almost too heavy to take a step. Philip cupped her calves gently in his hands and swung them round, unused to such intimacy with his mother. The folded wheelchair he lifted into the boot of his car.

With the window half open, an exquisite breeze caught her face along the clifftop avenues. It reminded her of being young and maybe happy. Or was that someone in a film? Young, carefree, driving by the sea with Cary Grant – hopefully not with Hitchcock directing. The road gave wide, thrilling views across Sandcliffe's shining bay to distant headlands hazy along the coast. Glimpses down to the beach showed miles of sand covered with parasols, blankets, sunbathers, family groups. Thousands of people were in the sea. White sails were scattered out towards the horizon.

A pretty scene. She would never again, she supposed, hoist a sail. Oh, she would still be *able* to do it, she told herself, if someone took her out on the water. If only she could still stand, and move about.

'So, darling – how are things?'

He replied that everything was fine. She asked about Kim, his glamorous companion. She asked about Nina, the only one of the six children in Philip's home who was definitely her own grandchild. One of the others might be, he wasn't sure. Nina, smiled Philip, was a little sweetie. Marjorie dreaded to think how Nina would turn out. 'And the other children?' Yes, yes, he assured her, the kids were fine, everyone was fine. Marjorie did not know how to address, even how to think about, Philip's ménage à trois (or quatre). She asked about Adèle, another woman in the house, Nina's deplorable mother. Marjorie abhorred Philip's way of life. And the drugs, of course. It sickened her, but it was so. Even at his age, still taking drugs. He was no fool, though, and she preferred to think well of him if she could. It was actually quite touching that he loved the children equally whether they were his own or not.

'Everything going well with the carers?' he asked. It was the sole point of his visits, to see that she was being properly looked after.

She grimaced. 'In and out with hardly a word. Mindless tasks done in the quickest way possible.'

'That makes sense. I'd have thought you approve.'

'Oh, I do. Anyway, they can't talk because they can't speak English. Not that I want to chat, but some don't even notice one is a fellow human being. Maybe it doesn't matter. Still, compassion is the whole raison d'être of the thing, isn't it? If you couldn't care less, don't be a carer. One day they'll get robots to do it. Program them to show a little humanity. They'll be more compassionate than people.'

'Haha! Good idea.'

'Philip, serious question about the carers. I'm vulnerable. Quite a few are from Eastern Europe. One or two are German. I had a Ukrainian. They soon realise I'm Jewish. Is it safe?'

Philip nodded emphatically. 'Absolutely, Mum! No one cares about that any more. It's another world. Shall we stop here for something? And we could look at the plants.' They were approaching a garden centre with a decent cafeteria.

Marjorie preferred to keep driving. 'Some aren't properly trained. They're sloppy. They ring the bell and wait for me to open the door. They've been asked not to do that. That's what the keysafe is for.

And their timekeeping is atrocious. Sometimes the morning girl doesn't come until after ten. Then the midday girl will turn up at eleven! It's a comedy of errors. I never know what to expect.' She laughed, unamused.

Philip was astonished. He had hardly heard his mother complain about anything at all, ever. He scrutinised her more closely than for months. She sat quiet and calm as always. There was nothing visible; nothing in the face or the demeanour. Her features were completely at rest. Her back, always so upright, was becoming bent, he noticed. She wore sunglasses and a headscarf, a summer jacket and skirt, sturdy shoes with strap, and grasped a handbag. Smart, sensible and ordinary. No doubt, as Nic said, all good quality.

Then he observed again what he had described to his brother and sister – that curious aura of inconspicuousness, her *tarnkappe* of concealment. Until you had caught a glimpse of it, she was nobody, or at any rate, nobody of interest. Any respectable old woman. Any elderly widow. Anyone's grandmother.

He saw her, then he didn't. She was not anyone's anything. It seemed impossible, and irrelevant, that this person belonged to him and he to her, that she had cradled him in her arms, nourished him and suffered a mother's care for him. He knew his mother had a past of her own and private memories, for this everyone has; but there was something else there that he could not imagine.

'Ten o'clock!' She used always to get up at five. 'Mum, you don't wait till ten for breakfast?'

She replied that if the morning carer hadn't arrived by nine, 'I make my own damn breakfast. Dressing gown on. I *can* manage by myself. Cup of cold water and instant coffee in the microwave. Porridge too, an eggcup of oats in a mug with two eggcups of water, in the micro. Easy.' She did not mention the most recent attempt to make her own breakfast, when she scalded her fingers and knocked the coffee into the cutlery drawer.

'What about the stockings?'

'Yes. Dratted things! I do need help with those.' – 'And washing?' – 'I can manage my hands and face. I'm a bit slow.' – 'Dressing?' – 'I can manage an elastic-waisted skirt and a blouse with not too many buttons.' – 'You do this even though you're paying for carers?'

'Only when the carer is very late. I don't *have* to get dressed. I can manage all day in my dressing gown.' He didn't want to hear any more details of what she could 'manage'. They must phone the agency about this.

The main road was busy with traffic – it was the height of the holiday season. Philip turned to take a narrow lane winding between beech trees, rattling across a cattle grid. There was no one else in sight. They marvelled at great flats of water shining among the undergrowth. They exchanged bland comments: such a lot of rain lately; there had been downpours; it had come down.

Then she returned to her subject. 'Every day, new people. I have to explain the routine each time. It's extremely trying. More strangers, more names. It's not their fault. They're only girls doing a job, and I'm only a job that needs doing.'

There was something unusual in the voice. She was upset.

'On Tuesday,' she said, 'I had three different girls, morning, lunchtime, evening, all foreign, all hopeless, all new. What can one say about that? That I'd rather have clean, healthy, intelligent, capable women whose first language is English? I daresay it's a crime now to want such things.'

'Probably is, actually.'

'Oh, we know beggars can't be choosers. Perish the thought! But I've had a different person *every evening* for the last two weeks! I'm practically naked in my bathroom while someone I've never seen before is poking around in my living room. It's worrying.'

'What do you mean, poking around?'

She did not answer, for suddenly Marjorie wanted to stop the car. Just here, great leafy boughs made a marvellous green tunnel, light filtering through the shifting lacy intricacies of the leaves. To one side a stream had burst its banks, throwing out its waters to wander among the trees. The ground would be too rough and wet for the wheelchair. Philip helped her take a few steps with her stick. Water ran sparkling and glimmering between oak and holly, among banks of bramble, sweeping over a grassy clearing in front of them. '"In broad daylight, streams full of stars",' she mused. He did not ask what she was quoting.

At last she did reply, 'Yes, they poke around. Things are moved. Knick-knacks. Books. I notice biscuits have been snaffled. That's not important, is it? What can one say about a few biscuits? But tins have gone from the food cupboard. Who knows what else?'

Was she exaggerating, maybe? 'Difficult one. Unless you have real evidence, hard to see how you can do anything about it.'

'Oh, I know that. I'm at the mercy of the carers, the agency, Social Services. I have to be realistic. My options are limited. I'm trapped.'

'Mum, that's awful.'

'Truthfully, Philip, I don't want to carry on like this. This "poor life full of 'care'"', she jested tartly. 'I want to go back to coping on my own. Or not coping, if that's the way it has to be.'

'I thought we agreed you weren't "coping or not coping" *on your own*. Eva literally came in and looked after you.'

'That was her choice. I never asked. Oh, darling, look!' With another abrupt reversal of mood, she pointed eagerly at the tangled masses of brambles. 'Blackberries! Fetch our little boxes.'

Philip moved cautiously to avoid being scratched as he picked berries and dropped them into his box, trying not to squash them. Marjorie thrust herself among the thorny stems, picking twice as many with less effort, and eating them as well. She tottered forward, parted the plants with her walking stick, used the handle to hook down higher, fruit-laden branches. 'And you know,' she called out, 'the care agency don't take any notice of me. Just another batty old lady on the line. I phoned Denzil Parker, my so-called care manager at Social Services, but it made no difference. He was never there.'

'I'll phone him.'

'Would you, Philip? That's very helpful. Careful, though,' her voice from behind a bush, 'if I'm a complainer, they'll pay me back in other ways.' She emerged from the brambles.

'I'll ask Nicky to do it. She's better at that kind of thing.'

Suddenly Marjorie needed to rest. Ripe fruit filled her Tupperware box to overflowing. They returned to the car and she used her spray.

After several silent minutes, Marjorie looked at her middle-aged son brightly as if nothing had occurred. 'You know, a National Care Service is what's needed, part of the NHS. Paid for by National Insurance. Everything state run. Care homes attached to hospitals.

Qualified carers working for the state. No local agencies. No local input. No local officials. No local trusts. Nothing local. An efficient national care organisation run by the state.'

'That would become an absolute *nightmare* of bureaucracy. And a political minefield. And, the NHS is already bankrupt.'

'No, it isn't. Just mismanaged.'

'And people would want something better for their old Mum, if they had the means to pay. Like with private medicine.'

'Come up with your own ideas, then,' she challenged him.

'OK, you and your friends should pool your resources and live together, like a commune but with live-in carers. Run it as a trust. That's what I'll do. Seriously, I will.'

'Sounds like any ordinary care home. That's the last thing I want.'

'It's probably the last thing you'll get, as well.'

They laughed. 'No, I would *hate* to end up somewhere like the Ruth Cohen. I'd rather be dead. Don't *ever* let them send me there, whatever happens!' She meant, the Ruth Cohen Memorial Rest and Nursing Home for the Jewish Aged, in Sandcliffe.

'You're not going there, Mum, don't worry.'

'How would your commune scheme work for the millions of old people living alone in East End tower blocks?'

'I'm talking about what would work for us. Feeling better now?'

'Fine, absolutely fine.'

He started the engine. 'Think you could manage lunch?'

'Let's just go home, Philip, and eat our blackberries.'

* * *

My new billet is with a retired couple in a cottage out of town. It used to be their children's bedroom. Three narrow beds are pushed against the walls, but for the moment I have it to myself. Peggy's been moved too. They've corralled the Wrens into Woburn Abbey, several miles away. Its draughty staterooms and halls are crammed with bunk beds. As always with Wrens, the authorities make out it's a ship. I have to ask permission to 'come aboard'. They even refer to the BP bus as 'the ferry'! Peggy measures time by 'bells', and calls her off-duty hours 'shore leave'.

We both have young men now. Peggy's head over heels for a handsome, square-jawed airman, George Winslow, who danced into her life at a Wrens' hop, a down-to-earth chap with a streak of the daredevil. He's strong and manly, loves a laugh and a pint of stout, and has a heart of gold. He'll be ideal for her.

My feller is quite a different type. Bob Shaffer is taciturn, cultivated and shockingly clever. He's in the advance team of US Intelligence sent to prepare for work alongside BP in the "spirit of co-operation". Bob definitely wants to co-operate – with me. He's big-boned and tall. I've never seen a Jew so huge. One of his ancestors must have belonged to the Nephilim, lost race of angelic giants.

The four of us go dancing at the American base, driving there in George's Austin. Entertainment on the base is out of this world. While the band plays and the others dance, Bob and I smoke American cigarettes, gaze into each other's eyes, hold hands and discuss the most profound matters. Bob *adores* his country and what he calls its principles. Do countries have principles? Or merely interests? – discuss. Grandiloquently amidst the din he declares, 'From the War of Independence, to the Constitution, to the Civil War, to fighting the Nazis, freedom is the leitmotif of America.'

'Which is odd, for a nation built on slavery.' My voice is mocking. Bob pretends to be utterly shocked. 'You're not against freedom?'

'Who is against their *own* freedom, Bob? Everyone insists on it. Other people's freedom is more problematic. Anyway, in the contest between liberty and freedom, I'm on the side of liberty.'

'Freedom, liberty – no difference!'

Couples dance energetically directly in front of us, spinning past as drums rattle out the rhythm, clarinet and saxophone swing out *Sing Sing Sing* and *In The Mood*, fellers tossing their girls all over the place, skirts flying up.

I shout to be heard, 'Bob, the difference is law and order. Freedom is *curtailed* by law,' I yell, 'liberty *protected* by it. Freedom is a dream of children, liberty the aspiration of adults.' I'm embarrassed to have been so earnest, and resolve to shut up forthwith.

Bob leans forward to kiss my hand and speak into my ear. 'Well put, Miss Behrens! Did I ever tell you my hero is Thomas Jefferson?

He'd agree with everything say. He wrote on "rightful liberty".'

We listen to a piano solo, then the band plays *Begin the Beguine*, before we part company with a kiss. I feel elated by our discussion.

Two days later, a newly published volume on President Jefferson arrives. Tucked inside is a note. *To my dearest friend Marjorie, I have been transferred home. Sorry I have been ordered to leave so suddenly. I really enjoyed your company and sincerely hope we'll get together again someday. In the meantime, please do write me, care of the base. They'll forward all mail. Yours very fondly, Bob.*

I write to Bob three times, but there's no reply. There doesn't seem much point in pressing the case, unless he is likely to be sent back here. The Liaison office tell me that's not going to happen.

Disconsolately, I spend time with Peg. With no Bob, and George away as well, we've stopped going to the base. It's easier to get to the BP hops. British shindigs are comfortably disorganised compared to the slick American sessions. There's nothing funnier than our brilliant academics and eccentric geniuses and barmy boffins whirling around on a dance floor. I notice that Peg has become very cautious about her partners. No flirting or hanky-panky. She confides it's because she and George are to be married.

'It's serious, then? He proposed to you, and you said yes?' Peggy is the first of my friends to become engaged.

She nods, smiling bashfully. 'I said yes.' They'll tie the knot as soon as the war is over, she says.

'That's marvellous, Peg!' I give her a huge hug and a kiss.

'It's a secret. I shouldn't really have told even you, Marje.'

A short, stout young man in an unlikely three-piece tweed suit, embellished with fob-chain, silk cravat and pince-nez on a ribbon bustles uninvited into the Watch. My first thought is Billy Bunter.

'Could do with a German speaker, mother-tongue,' he announces.

'Can't spare anyone, Percy,' responds Number One.

Bunter explains that he needs native German speakers for a new hand-ciphers team, and has the authority – he adds with tremendous arrogance – to choose anyone he wants. He swivels his head rapidly towards me and demands 'Are you Miss Behrens?' He speaks in a pretentious, "refained" voice that could have been calculated to grate on one's nerves. He also throws an exaggerated guttural into the middle of my surname. None of this manages successfully to mask his own accent of an East Midlands city slum.

'Depends who's asking,' I reply.

He quizzes me with his annoying voice and impudent tone, his eyes appearing too small through thick lenses turned towards my bosom. 'Your file says you're a first-language German speaker.'

'Does it? That's quite wrong.'

'And you're familiar with boats. Ships, sailing terms, nautical matters, that type of thing. Marine vocabulary?'

'Well, you've read the file. You tell me.'

After some debate with Number One, he invites me to join him on a short walk, on the strict understanding that I 'still belong to Hut 3'. On the way, he pauses and introduces himself with ridiculously elaborate courtesy, taking my hand and bowing as if he might even kiss it. 'Parsifal Jarram at your service.'

With his affected drawl, it takes me a moment too long to realise there's an R in his surname. I tug my hand out of his and reply less graciously, 'Why have you taken me away from my work, Mr Jam?'

'I have done no such thing. Our work continues without cease. However, better use can be made of your skills.' He turns towards the mansion, and we arrive at Hut 9, near the tennis courts. Behind Hut 9 are two smaller buildings, unnamed and unnumbered, which Bunter calls A and C. I don't ask what happened to B. I am taken to a desk in 9C and, as far as I can tell, must begin my new duties at once.

Here most of the team are women, which makes a nice change even though Bunter waddles around staring at us indecently, criticising and praising with equal hyperbole and conceit.

We're working on Reservehandverfahren, or RHV, naval hand-cipher messages. These are encrypted not with machines but simply by using this month's codebook to change the letters. Codebooks can't always be changed everywhere on the same day because of delivery difficulties, so there's a precious transition when an urgent message may be sent in either the old or the new version, which – if we can quickly identify two different messages as having the same text – gives a crib, or a text to work from, to decrypt the new code.

Most decoded messages contain nothing of operational use. Their value lies in unravelling the latest naval Enigma settings, because the same messages have generally been sent using both hand-ciphers and machines. There's a sloppy thinking about this which one doesn't associate with Germans, but then of course, the whole of Germany's megalomaniac nationalism is an example of sloppy thinking.

We're also decrypting and emendating hand-ciphers of the Abwehr, the Nazis' intelligence service, mainly to provide cribs for Abwehr's Enigma. This is overwhelming stuff, as though we have been invited to peer through a keyhole into Hitler's bedchamber.

For both tasks, especially Abwehr decodes, we collaborate with a top secret unit of Polish mathematicians in London whom, Jarram says, 'our masters foolishly moved from machine ciphers to hand ciphers.' These men, Jarram tells us, are pioneer codebreakers who, 'overcoming great obstacles and peril, came voluntarily to assist Britain after their own country was seized by the Barbarian. On no account ever discuss, divulge, disclose, reveal or even hint to other BP personnel that we work with these foreign nationals, and nor is it to be placed on record, nor at any time referred to in writing.'

In Bunter's domain, intercepts are still brought to us by Wrens, but now there is nothing pasted on the back. Instead we must rack our brains, make guesses, be inspired, follow hunches, look for common themes, and one way or another find an opening and start to see sense in the endless five-letter columns. He can then use a machine on other messages to see if we have successfully cracked the code. If we have, we can start emendating messages almost soon as they're sent.

In addition to his supercilious courtesy and massive pomposity, Mr Percy Jarram takes any opportunity to turn on his phoney, effusive charm and chat. He informs me that he's a brilliant historian from Cambridge, a rising star in his field. His great passion, he says, is eighteenth-century America, on which subject, he has no doubt, he will one day be the world's leading authority.

Despite everything obnoxious about Jarram, somehow we hit it off. My interest is piqued when he makes a reference to Bob's hero, Thomas Jefferson. He likes discussing America and the Americans, and I like listening to him. At the end of today's shift he invites me to join a Christmas sherry party in his rooms. His digs are an easy walk from the Park. It's not a billet; he's renting a flat above a shop.

I step into a smoky room filled with clever-looking chaps and bluestocking-ish ladies. Among them are cryptanalysts from Hut 8 and Hut 6. I recognise the luminaries – Mr Welchman, prodding at his pipe; Mr Milner-Barry in conversation with Mr Alexander and Mr Hughes. Everyone is introduced to me by Percy with an embarrassing explanatory soubriquet, 'the great Egyptologist', 'the brilliant chess champion', 'the famous classicist'. One is 'the distinguished author, as I'm sure you know' and a dark-haired, dark-eyed woman, 'of the renowned banking family, of course.'

With genial handshakes and smiles they raise their eyebrows at Percy's florid remarks. As for me, his description is 'my invaluable new colleague' or, more cringe-making, 'a wonderful addition to my team.' I glimpse – hardly above shoulder height of those around him – the unmistakeable brainy forehead and unruly dark hair of Ernst Wardmann, the one person I know here, and make my way to him.

In such a crowd, Percy bustles about like a besuitted balloon, full of bluster, trumpetingly opinionated, playing the virtuoso of rhetoric, always eloquently acerbic, quick and incisive. No one says much about the war, and none of us is permitted to elaborate on our rôles, so in lively banter we debate the torrent of new ideas about society and class, the new politics, as well as the trivia du jour about West End shows. The only truly contentious issues are the price of a canteen lunch and whether anyone trusts Americans enough to share intelligence with them. I think of Bob, in an OSS bureau somewhere in America. Would I trust him with a secret? With my life.

The general view, though, is that Americans are indiscreet. 'They drink too much, are boastful and, worst of all, they think openness is a virtue,' declares Percy. I protest that not all are like that, 'Isn't it really only about vetting procedures?', but my two-penn'orth is ignored (was it foolishly obvious?). No one seems to have heard me, or even seen me. Percy – clasping a bottle of sherry – says, 'Well, I always say, thank God none of *us* is American! But remember, it was a *British* Prime Minister who threw away our intelligence advantage in 1927. Who's for a top-up?'

'What was that about a British Prime Minister?' I ask Percy.

'Before your time,' he murmurs. 'I was just a child myself. Stanley Baldwin read out a decoded Russian telegram in the House of Commons. The Russians that very day changed to a more secure cipher system which we haven't been able to break ever since. *And* he was one of the *Guilty Men*, as we call them, the appeasers.'

As the guests crowd towards the door and make cheery farewells, wishing Merry Christmas and Happy New Year, Percy indicates that I should stay. As soon as we're alone, he's transformed, subdued to the point of melancholy. He begins savagely to disparage his friends one by one, declaring that they had nannies, went to public school, and 'walked into' Oxford and Cambridge. 'They act as if they own the earth – which indeed they do.'

'I had a nanny, Mr Jarram.'

'I know. I've read the file. That's not what I mean.'

I'm wary of being alone with him. His lingering glances up and down my dress are distasteful and alarming. However, I sense that I'm here because he wants to discuss something serious. I always have a feeling about Percy that he's privy to a lot of things that others don't know. He seems to be on first-name terms with everyone of importance. They may not like him, but he knows them.

'Fancy a sherry?'

'Prefer a cup of tea, if you've got any.'

'Come into the kitchen.' I'm hoping he won't try anything.

We pass through a folding door into a kitchenette no bigger than a broom cupboard. Percy puts a kettle on a gas burner and brings out cups and saucers. 'Where were you during the War Cabinet Crisis?' he asks, apparently in idle conversation. He spoons tea into the pot.

'When was it?'

'May 1940. The War Cabinet wanted Britain to surrender to Hitler. Remember that? Make terms with the Nazis.'

'No. I was busy washing dishes in the Community Restaurant.'

'The PM's speech in Cabinet on 28th May 1940 is why we are fighting Nazism instead of living under it. He said, and I quote, "If this long island story of ours is to end at last, let it end only when each one of us lies choking in his own blood upon the ground." Colourful stuff, eh?'

'Yes, indeed.'

'Well now, are you prepared to lie choking in your own blood, Miss Behrens?'

'Rhetorical question, I hope, Mr Jarram. I'd rather the Germans and their partners-in-crime suffer that fate, if anyone must.'

'You've met a few of my friends. Most of them are cryptanalysts.' The kettle begins to rattle and steam. 'Codebreakers.'

'That's not something we need to discuss, is it?'

'The trouble with these chaps is they think the war is about mathematics. We historians have a better grasp of what a war is.'

Percy wearily fills the teapot. He asks if I'm aware that ciphers take many different forms. I say, yes, of course. 'So perhaps you know, then,' he says, 'that Germany's army, U-boats, tanks, government officials, police, fire-brigade, everything, each has its own set of codes, and some are devilish hard to break.'

Naturally I know this in principle. I am longing for him to stop talking about something that I assume is classified information.

'We're listening-in to over a hundred different systems of encryption. It's hard to decide which to bother with. Some don't help us at all. Even so, it may prove useful to decode them.'

'You know, Mr Jarram, frankly I'd prefer we didn't discuss it, unless this conversation has some operational use.'

'Don't worry. This conversation is covered by the Act. It's strictly between us and must go no further. Our work on RHV and Abwehr, for example. Two quite different ciphers. Yes?'

'Yes.'

'Captain Upman's group read intercepts of the Ordnungspolizei, the Order Police. Yet another cipher system. Is it really worth reading police reports? Turns out they contain almost nothing except the number of Jews they've shot today, where and when.'

He studies my face for some reaction. 'Yes, they reveal that police units sent to occupied areas in the East, working together with the Einsatzgruppen, kill thousands of non-combatants every day. Every single Jew. *All* of them. Searching for Jews house to house, street by street, whole families. According to the intercepts.'

This is implausible, and it feels unreal to hear such things in a little kitchenette, waiting for tea to brew. 'Are you making this up?'

'No, Miss, I am not.'

'What exactly are the Einsatzgruppen – also police?'

'No, a special force of SS whose job is to kill civilians, especially Jews.' At long last he pours the tea and stirs in a few drops of milk. He doesn't ask if I want sugar; there's no sugar just at present.

We carry our cups to the fireside and settle into armchairs. The fire casts a pleasant, cosy glow.

'What about Einsatzgruppen messages – being deciphered?'

'Their sensitive information goes by courier. That *is* unbreakable. But we find it out from the Ordnungspolizei intercepts.'

'Killing women as well? Children? Jews, rather than Jewish resistance fighters, say, or Jewish Communists?'

'Precisely. Though the intercepts do refer to Communists as well.'

My scalp and neck seem to have become several degrees colder. 'What d'you mean, "all" of them? In which areas?'

Percy makes a pained expression, which may be as near as he can get to human sympathy. 'Your file mentions family in Libau, in Latvia. Ships took some refugees out before the Soviet occupation. Libau was taken by Hitlerite forces last year.' He hesitates, possibly to spare my feelings, more likely for dramatic effect. 'We can't verify what happened to the Jews. A few may have escaped.'

'Mr Jarram, if I may ask… what about those inside Germany? We have relatives in Hamburg. Hopefully they escaped to Palestine or the Americas. I doubt if my mother would tell me even if she knew.'

'As for Hamburg, Miss Behrens, if your relatives haven't yet left, it's too late. Sorry. There's something worse than mass shootings. You know about the Nazi conference at Wannsee last January? It was agreed killing Jews by shooting is too costly and too slow. It endorsed a plan to exterminate Jews in a more systematic way, Die Endlösung der Judenfrage. Quite a word, Endlösung, isn't it? *Final Solution* of the Jewish Question. It's been implemented all this year.'

'Just what the world has been waiting for!' Exterminate! *That's* quite a word! It sounds exaggerated. You never know with Percy. I'm not sure how to respond. 'I haven't been in touch with anyone over there for ages. What point were you making?'

'That it's important to break ciphers even if they appear non-operational, or non-strategic. We read every report on the number of

Jews murdered. We pass everything to the PM. Most people would say, foreign gentiles killing foreign Jews, what's that to us?' He continues in German, as if reading: '*We went to this village or that town and executed two hundred and twenty six Jews; we joined with such and such a brigade and shot nineteen Jewish men, eleven Jewish women, six Jewish children, one thief, and three Bolsheviks.*' He looks up. 'Is it useful to intercept that kind of thing?'

I can't think what Percy expects from me. I know about the situation before the war, businesses being 'Aryanised' as happened to Uncle Josef, Jews being excluded from professions as happened to cousin Artur in the year he qualified as a doctor, people being refused exit papers, and Kristallnacht, and laws to stop Jews going to the library. I've heard *nothing* about "extermination."

'Why would they do that?' I ask. 'Waste time, men and bullets killing non-combatants?'

Percy shakes his head. 'We don't know yet what purpose it serves. Intercepts suggest they don't always use bullets, but gas vans. We believe they're constructing or have constructed, in Poland, special sites for the mass murder of undesirables, Slavs and Jews and so on.'

'Frankly that has the ring of those fantastical tales of the depraved and bestial enemy.'

'It's from Russian and German intercepts. The Americans have been receiving radio photographs from Poland since last year and sending them to the Photographic Division of the British Ministry of Information. Murder camps, atrocities against Polish civilians and so on. Even so, the Ministry remains sceptical, because it concerns Poles and Jews, both of whom FO officials consider unreliable witnesses. And they think the pictures may be fake, as indeed they may be. They suspect it's propaganda, intended to draw Allied efforts further east. They say, if these stories *are* true the best way to put a stop to it is to win the war. Well, we know that already.'

My guess is that he's told me for a reason. Yet in an instant he seems eager to change the subject. 'Friend of Wardmann's, aren't you? Nice chap. One of the cleverest. You in his Zionist Group?'

'No, but I agree with him about it.'

'You don't attend the Sabbath dinners either, do you?' A local family, said to be the only Jews in Bletchley, welcomes coreligionists at BP to join them on Friday evenings. 'Why – not religious?'

'That's not the way to look at it. I just don't feel the need.'

'Where was I? Ah, yes, which intercepts it's worthwhile to decipher. What wouldn't we do to lay our hands on some of their hand-cipher codebooks, eh?' He smiles at the thought. 'Splash more tea?' He touches the pot. 'Still fairly warm. Might be a bit stewed.' He lifts the lid and peers inside. 'I could make some more.'

I shake my head. 'Not for me, Mr Jarram. I'm fine.'

'Do call me Percy, Miss Behrens. I think we know one another well enough by now! May I call you Marjorie?'

Oh dear! I hope this is not leading to some attempt at even greater intimacy. 'Of course you can, Mr Jarram!'

'Thing is, Marjorie, they're looking for a woman for a special job,' Percy confides. 'Something exceptionally difficult. Something you'd be able to do. Can't go into detail.'

'Who's *they*?'

'Our masters. They need a type of person that's hard to find.'

'What type?'

'Ideally, a respectable, unobtrusive young woman, native German speaker, talented at code analysis, resourceful, with a memory like a bank vault. Someone who looks the part and keeps a cool head. Fit, strong and healthy type.' He's making it up as he goes along. 'The active sort!' He scans me with too savoury an eye. 'Charging about on your bicycle. Swimming in the lake in all weathers. A charming spectacle!' I raise a reproving brow.

'Looks the part, Percy? What part?'

Ignoring the question, he carries on, 'A woman who's one hundred percent discreet, dedicated to our national interest, and who has some personal reason to try harder than everyone else. Someone with no friends or family ties. A person who never talks.'

I feel quite abashed, and hurt. 'I have friends. I have a family. Five brothers living and two sisters, several aunts and thirty-three cousins. And a mother. As for not talking, we're talking now, aren't we?'

'You know exactly what I mean, Marjorie.'

Of course, he's right. I do know.

The voice on the line is strange. I don't recognise it at first. She gasps as if drowning, practically chokes as she tries to say my name.

It's so unusual for anyone to get in touch with me by telephone. We are urged to avoid using the instrument in case operators at the exchange listen in. She repeats in a frightened whisper, 'Marjorie…'

'Is that you, Peg? What on earth is up? You sound so peculiar.' Something inside me already knows. It's as though I am holding part of my mind in readiness.

'I can't talk.' She literally cannot. She struggles to utter the words, but sobs instead and hangs up.

It's past five when I find Peggy. She's standing in her uniform outside Hut 9, her face as lifeless as wax. She nods, as if she knew I'd arrive. I take her arm and we walk across the lawn towards the lake, just like that, arm in arm. I say nothing, almost as though she has told me everything without a word passing between us.

'George?'

'It was on a mission.'

'Is it definite?'

'Confirmed dead.'

I hold her, pressing my cheek against hers. Then we part and walk on, not arm in arm this time.

For a moment her voice is steadier. 'He was with three others. It seems the Resistance rescued them and did what they could. But George was too badly injured. They couldn't help him.'

'How did you hear?' I ask.

'His dad got the telegram. He asked them to let me know. The Super told me. Of course, it's much worse for his mum and dad and family. I'm nothing. I'll write to them.'

'Will you get any time off? Any leave?'

'Problem is, Marje, it's happening all the time. You're supposed to accept it. Just get on with it. "Carry on with your duties as normal." That's what she said, the Super.'

We walk among trees and shrubs. As soon as we're hidden from view, Peg drops to her knees, leans forward awkwardly onto her hands, then drops her head right down onto the damp soil. She begins to sob, pressing her whole face violently onto the soft earth.

I squat down beside her. 'Peggy, don't. Peg, you'll get so dirty.'

She pulls sharply away from the ground, tears flowing, and slaps her face with both hands in a curious, mad-looking gesture. She puts the side of her hand into her mouth and bites it, stifling a scream.

There are smudges of mud on her forehead and cheek and on her knees. I spit on my handkerchief and wipe them away. From her coat I pick off a leaf, a petal. 'Let's sit by the lake,' I suggest. But at the lake edge, the turf is too wet for us to sit.

We walk aimlessly through the woods, and along the paths behind the Park. There's no one about. 'I already thought of him as my husband. Mr and Mrs George Winslow. We spent hours and hours thinking how life would be. We lay on the ground and I'd, you know, pretend we were in bed together, me and him.'

I hadn't fully realised what she felt for George. As we return to the streets of Bletchley, the rain starts again. Peggy's eyes are bloodshot, but the tears have stopped. 'I'll never love anyone else,' she tells me in a flat, normal voice. 'In my mind I already gave myself to him. I am, I was, going to be his wife. This is how it will always be for me. George will be the only one.'

I steer her in the direction of Percy's flat. On the step, I introduce them. Mr Parsifal Jarram, Miss Margaret Olroyd. 'Percy, would you be willing to do me a great favour?'

Astonished, he replies unctuously that nothing on this earth would give him more pleasure, and would we like to come in out of the wet. We prefer to remain on the step, ice-cold rain dripping down our necks. I tell him what's happened to Peggy, or rather, to George. She adds her own few words. Her plain Yorkshire tones are nothing like his own stagey accents, but Percy's affectations and pretentiousness fall away as he sees well enough that Peggy and George, at least, did *not* have nannies. He is sorry for her. 'How can I help?'

I answer, 'Would you be able contact the WRNS Superintendent at Woburn and tell her that Wren Olroyd is engaged on urgent, important paperwork for your officers, details of which you are not at liberty to divulge, and that you would be grateful if she could remain on duty at HMS Pembroke V until it is complete?' HMS Pembroke V being the WRNS' nautical name for Station X.

He nods cautiously. 'And Percy – might I also mention? – Wren Olroyd is attached to Hut 6. Is there some way you could square it with Mr Welchman, or whoever is in charge there, that she's attached to our hut for a couple of days?'

'No one would object to that in any case. Look, you really can't just stand there. For goodness sake, do come in and get cleaned up. Get dry by the fire and have a cup of tea.'

We're persuaded, and glad of a chance to wash and tidy ourselves. He toasts some teacakes as well, and even says he'll telephone for a car. That offer we turn down. I don't want to be too much in Percy's debt. Besides, the rain is easing again.

My bike is at the gatehouse, and plenty of others have been abandoned there. After cycling to my billet, Peg is exhausted. It's lucky there are spare beds in my room. I offer the old couple ten shillings to let her stay and give her breakfast in the morning. When they hear about George, they're only too willing.

The next day, Peggy remains subdued. The rain has stopped. It's an ordinary winter's day, melancholy and quiet. She talks about George and says it's not worth going on without him.

'Here's my two-penn'orth, Peg, for what it's worth. You love George and you'll always love him. He was a good man and you'll never find a better. But George is dead and you're alive. Don't think about feelings, think about goals. If you want to be a mother and lead a happy life, you'll do it without George. You really will.'

I regret the words at once. It's too soon: Peggy throws her head down and begins to sob. Eventually she lets out a long, terrible breath. 'Marje, how good you've been to me. I'll never, ever forget.'

'Hi, Nic. I saw Mum. We went blackberrying. No, really. She picked more than me, actually.' Philip did call Nicola. 'But she has serious issues with the carers.' He explained it all. 'Could you phone them for her? You know how to talk to them. She's worried I'd put my foot in it.'

Nicola devoted most of the next day to three calls, spending forty minutes at a stretch on hold, hearing a hundred times the automated apologies and thanks for her patience, listening to music she hated, calling back, speaking to voicemail, redialling. Eventually she was put through to Denzil's supervisor at Social Services, to the manager of the care agency and to Marjorie's doctor. The next step was to call her mother and join the rush hour crowd at Waterloo Station.

At long last she was striding along the tranquil pine-shaded (and pine-scented) avenues of Sandcliffe listening to the evening trill of blackbirds. When she arrived at the flat, Marjorie was sitting contentedly on the balcony, listening to the same blackbirds. 'I cancelled the carer,' said Nicola. 'Shall we knock up a bit of dinner?'

Nicola made a quick, simple meal. They tried to chat, mother and daughter, avoiding contentious subjects. Every item on the Radio Four news – Lebanon, Iraq, Chechnya, PLO, Intifada – provoked friction between them without a word being said, an unspoken argument hanging in the air as they sat uncomfortably in their chairs.

Marjorie turned off the radio and asked for help with the crossword. They were on safer ground. Marjorie admitted it was becoming harder to do the crossword. 'If ever I can't do the Times crossword any more, I'll know I'm finished.' She said every mini-stroke 'tore pages' from her mind. 'I've lost scores of words. Poems and plays I knew by heart, they've gone.'

'That's called forgetting. You're finding out what life's like for the rest of us.'

It was ten o'clock. They did not watch the Ten O'Clock News. Marjorie pinned back the pages of a book with clothes pegs and read in silence with her magnifying glass. Nicola caught up with friends and groups on Facebook. She was tired and bored. She was angry with her situation, and, as she felt, the brothers who had placed her in it. She would have gone to bed, except that she had come especially to help her mother. At eleven-thirty she said, 'Shall I get you ready for bed, Mum?' Marjorie looked up in surprise.

Nicola made her a flask of Ovaltine. She learned that her mother took twelve kinds of medication daily, some twice or three times a day, before breakfast, with breakfast, with lunch, at teatime, with dinner and at bedtime. Several caused fatigue. It was amazing her Mum wasn't asleep the whole time. 'Yes,' Marjorie chuckled, 'alpha blockers, beta blockers, right through to omega blockers. I'm losing my sight, my marbles and my alphabet.'

Nicola undressed her: cardigan, shirt, stockings, unbuttoned the skirt and removed it. She found it unseemly and incredible to unclip the capacious bra, pull down the immense discoloured panties and put them in the laundry basket. It was unspeakably distasteful to rinse the stockings. She declined to rub cream onto Marjorie's thighs. Marjorie went to the lavatory on her own, but could not manage. She called out for a flannel and a towel.

Nicola had not realised how much help her mother needed now. 'Goodnight, Mum, sleep well. I'm here if you need me.' – 'Thank you, darling. Goodnight.' Nicola kissed her and went into the spare bedroom, where she covered her head with a pillow in a vain effort to still her exhausted, unhappy mind.

In the light of morning Nicola resumed the duties of a carer. 'This is hard for you, darling,' Marjorie acknowledged.

'Oh, I don't mind.'

Marjorie grinned, 'Philip thinks I should set up a commune with my friends and have live-in carers.'

'Doesn't sound like you.'

'Sounds like Philip, though, doesn't it?'

'Haha! Yes!'

'Do *you* have any thoughts about assistance for the elderly? Who should pay for it?'

'Big subject, Mum. Leave it for another time.'

'Tell me your ideas. We won't fall out.'

'Only this: it's the state's responsibility to provide care. That's it.'

'Well then, I don't disagree.'

'You don't?'

'No! How should it be paid for?'

'Well, by taxation, of course.'

'Not by making people sell their things and spend their savings?'

Nicola shrugged, 'Well, no, because the way I see it, all your assets should go to the state anyway when you die. No one should be able to pass on wealth. Inherited wealth is the root of privilege.'

'Goodness! I'll bear that in mind when I revise my will!

The phone rang. To the great relief of both of them, the care agency had found Marjorie a more suitable regular evening carer. So it was that Carol came into her life.

* * *

A single slate-grey cloud spreads across the land, and a mist of raindrops turning to sleet brushes the train windows. It's the sort of weather that makes one proud to be English. Bomb sites afford strange vistas in the wintry sunlight, sometimes almost a vision of what might have been had London never been built. Degraded and unrepaired, every neighbourhood gathers now around broken landmarks and splintered spires. The leafless trees too are torn and injured, branches ripped away and the wood cut open.

A puzzling letter instructed me without explanation to make this journey down to London from Bletchley today. I'm ordered to an address in Broadway, near St James Park.

The carriage fills with troops, smoking until the air is unbreathable. Thus wedged together, our mood is subdued. After a whole year with hardly a single raid, this year has started with attacks on primary schools in the Kent suburbs. Some of the youngest children brought back from evacuation are dead. Level-crossing gates slam shut across an anonymous street as we pass. Women wait at the barriers in shabby overcoats and hats or headscarves, shopping baskets on their arms.

I've a warm greatcoat and plenty of time, and like to walk. From the station I march briskly down Gower Street, past the British Museum, reaching the still-open theatres of hectic Charing Cross Road. I cross into the narrower streets of Soho, a notorious warren of temptations for menfolk, but not holding many terrors for a respectable woman before lunchtime. I'm still heading the right way for St James Park.

Suddenly there is a vast, deafening sound – literally deafening, as I seem instantly plunged into bewildering silence and inexplicably am sitting on my bottom in the very middle of the road. With one hand I am clasping my bag tightly, as if it were all that matters. The other hand rests on something with a curious texture. When I look, I find it is broken glass embedded into my palm, and the flesh is bleeding.

A series of thoughts struggle into my consciousness. The first is, *Why was there no siren?* My second, *German bastards – what gives them the right?* And then, *Have I lost a leg or anything?*

I look down at my legs, to discover my torn drawers, suspenders and stocking-tops are on show. One coat sleeve is unstitched and my irreplaceable nylons, a gift from Bob, ripped to tatters. I hastily pull my skirt into place as two men run to help me, but it has been torn open on one side. Now I see a length of thigh exposed, red with blood. I'm trying to understand if it's my own thigh, my own blood, and certainly it is, yet I feel nothing except a headache.

As my hearing returns there is a din of shouting far away. It's the two men asking if I am alright. I nod automatically. In front of me, a taxi lies on its side among smashed doors and furniture and blown-out masonry and a human debris of men and women lying in the road like rolls of red cloth soaking wet and running with liquid.

'Unexploded ordnance,' a man shouts directly at me. He's squatting, holding my hand, removing the glass, bandaging it. Behind him, some climbing plant, wisteria, ivy, I can't think what, torn from a wall, waves around, its limbs blowing in the wind like a cry for help. Unharmed in a doorway a wide-eyed cat watches us keenly, as though we are all mice. Has it too been deafened?

'Look after those people,' I say. My voice is strangely hoarse and weak, my throat bone dry. 'They're worse than I am.'

'Are you sure, Miss? How do you feel?' he asks. 'Cup of tea?'

'Fine, really.' As I say the words I begin to feel pain in several places, but not excruciating. No broken bones, I'd guess. Plenty of cuts and bruises though.

A woman in nursing uniform approaches. She's holding my hat. With a grim smile she hands it to me. 'Here you are, duck.' She too squats down, offers to get me a cup of tea, and tends to the cuts on my thigh, applying some staining, stinging liquid directly to them. What she is doing, I have no idea. I trust her only because she gave me my hat. At last she helps me stand, and only then notices that my shoes are missing. She looks around and picks them up from the pavement, feels inside with her hand, and carefully fits the shoes onto my feet as if I were Cinderella. I'm relieved to find my coat hides the rip in my skirt. Shards of glass snap under the heels as I take a few steps. Then comes my next thought: 'Oh dear! My appointment!'

As I'm shown into the room, it would be hard to say who is more astonished – them or me. Both men leap up with cries of dismay. 'Miss Behrens, what has happened? Are you all right?'

'Good Lord, it's you! Hello, Mr Hughes, hello, Ernst!'

'You're hurt! Sit down, sit down, sit by the fire!'

'UXB near Charing Cross Road. Quite a few hurt. But what on earth are you two doing here?' Since it was Alec Hughes and Ernst Wardmann who dropped me at Bletchley station, it seems almost a music hall comic turn to find them waiting for me in London.

'We must see to those cuts!' exclaims Hughes.

'Wouldn't mind a wash, if there's somewhere. I need a place to sit and mend my skirt. Have to borrow a needle and thread from someone. Couldn't find me a couple of aspirin and a glass of water?'

'Of course,' says Hughes at once. 'I'll call Nurse and a woman officer. The Army & Navy is a few minutes' walk. We have an account there. Get anything you need. Gosh, may I say,' he adds, 'I admire your sang-froid.'

'And I admire your dispatch, Mr Hughes, in being here before me. How was it done – were you already on your way here when you dropped me at Bletchley Station?'

He grimaces apologetically. 'We were, in truth.'

'Well, why not travel down together, then? In fact, why not just talk at BP? If I hadn't come to London I wouldn't have been almost blown to bits.'

'Because this isn't a BP meeting, Miss Behrens,' he replies. 'These premises belong to SIS, MI6. On the way here, Wardmann and I had confidential matters to discuss – about you, actually. This is an official SIS meeting.'

'Oh? So are you part of SIS? And you, Ernst? Is BP part of SIS?' Suddenly I feel terribly, unbluffably out of my depth.

'It's not quite like that. Look, Bletchley Park is only a place, after all; SIS were based there for a while. BP both is and isn't part of SIS,' says Hughes, 'but it's under the same chief. We, all of us there now, are GC&CS – cipher-breakers. While SIS – intelligence gatherers – are based here in Broadway. That's it and never the twain shall meet. Except in the person of the Head of Intelligence.'

'How madly complicated.'

'Precisely. SIS know we exist, but they don't know who we are, what we do or how we do it, or why. My account of this meeting won't even mention BP. To be clear: no one outside BP is ever to know about BP – not even SIS.' He offers no further explanation. 'Let's get you a cup of tea.'

Ernst concurs like an expert. 'One should always have a nice cup of tea after a shock.'

Washed, brushed, patched and decently dressed, and furnished with another strong cuppa, I sit down at last and wait to be put in the picture. Their manner is businesslike yet amiable. Mr Hughes insists I call him Alec. He says, 'An opportunity has come up that we don't want to throw away.'

This must be the 'special job' that Percy mentioned. Ernst and Alec, though, are not the 'our masters' that Percy referred to, surely? They are cryptanalysts in Hut 8 and Hut 6.

'Who's "we"?'

'SIS,' replies Ernst. 'We want to talk to you, Marjorie – this is classified – about a proposed joint operation of SIS and SOE to obtain something of great value to BP.'

'Oh dear! I'm not familiar with the SOE.'

He smiles slightly. 'Don't want to overburden you, Marjorie. One of our problems is precisely that neither SIS nor SOE may know what is to be obtained, nor why we want it.'

'No, really, I mean it – please explain, what is SOE?'

'If you're willing to help us, SOE will formally recruit you,' says Alec. 'At the start of the war, this mission –'

'What mission?'

'Coming to that. Before SOE was set up, this mission might have been carried out by SIS using their own people, Section D. A couple of years ago Section D was subsumed into SOE, the Special Operations Executive. That was the PM's idea. Churchill wanted something a bit more irregular, something more like a guerrilla group able to carry out, well, top-secret ops behind enemy lines – sabotage, subterfuge, covert action, that kind of thing, acts of derring-do outside the remit of regular forces.'

'Ignoring the rules of war?'

'Well, you know, hopefully not. Unless necessary.'

'I assume Percy Jarram put my name forward?'

'Not the right question, Marjorie. Never ask. In any case the answer is No, it wasn't.' Ernst taps a cigarette on the desk before lighting it. He blows out smoke. Perhaps it was Ernst himself who put my name forward. In obedience to his command, I don't ask.

Alec slowly fills in the detail. 'It's like this. The wife of a well-placed German official has made contact directly with SIS.'

'How did she do that?'

'You don't need to know. Better if you didn't.'

'Thou wilt not utter what thou dost not know.'

'Exactly,' Ernst agrees. 'Though perhaps you do need to know that it was through the Norwegians. SIS have no network in Germany. No harm in telling you this since the Germans already know – the Norwegians have a small network fighting the regime, people who can move freely in Germany, Norwegian officials, businesspeople.'

'If Norwegians can do that, why can't we?'

Alec quietly explains that there are many Norwegian volunteers in the German military. 'They're recruited in Norway, but can be sent to Germany. There are thousands in Organization Todt. Thousands even in the Waffen-SS. They are considered racially acceptable, Aryan.'

'Sometimes,' says Ernst, 'a lone individual in the Reich manages to get in touch with us offering to help the Allies, opponents of the regime who have not yet been rooted out. Invariably, we can't use them. This case is different. The lady and her husband are high-ranking Nazis, respected party members. The husband is a member of the government. Even so, the wife wants to help us.'

'Why, if she's a Nazi?'

'People had all sorts of reason to join the Party. Our guess is that she's a German nationalist of the old school, a supporter of DNVP rather than the National Socialists. Or someone nostalgic for Kaisers Zeiten, the Kaiser's time. We have a note from the Norwegians that she objects to the militias, the Stormtroopers and so on, and what she calls the moral decadence of Hitler's gang. She thinks Hitler is destroying Germany. Sounds topsy-turvy, but she's one of those who think the best outcome for Germany is to lose the war and restore the status quo ante. So far, we must assume the authorities, and her husband, are not aware of her views.'

I listen spellbound, reminded of Otto, another German patriotic traitor, or treacherous patriot. It's because of him that I'm here. Meanwhile I suppose he is still in the Labour Planning office at Lyons, working on Government war contracts. Perhaps Otto was referring to himself when he said there are Germans working in British intelligence.

'It's pretty hard to figure out what to make of this woman.' Alec purses his lips. 'She has nothing to gain from helping us. Everything to lose. So we think she's sincere.'

'Unless it's a ploy by German intelligence,' I venture. 'To root out traitors. Maybe *she's* the victim of a trap, not us. What's the husband's job? You say he's part of the Hitler regime?'

'Don't burden yourself with too much information, Marjorie,' says Ernst. 'Not knowing more than you need is one of your strengths, from our point of view. However, no, he isn't in the inner circle. He's a senior figure in Deutsche Reichsbahn, the German Railways.'

'Which as you know from your work with Jarram,' adds Alec, 'is a key part of the German military machine.'

'The man is inside the office of the Secretary of State at the Reich Transport Ministry,' Ernst reveals. 'We're talking about his wife.'

'And what do you want with me?'

'She has access to the Reichsbahn records and past, current and forthcoming codebooks.'

It takes a moment to grasp what Alec has said. I recall Percy asking – rhetorically, I presumed – what we wouldn't give to get hold of some of the enemy's codebooks. 'The physical books?'

'That's right.' Alec nods as if to confirm the incredible. 'The ciphers are in her husband's safe at their home. She has complete freedom to go in and out of the room, even when he is not there. Sounds daft, but it's not unusual. It's considered more secure. Officials are instructed not to trust their staff. Actually, it's the same in this country. He does trust his wife, though. A common mistake.'

'All the same, how could she remove any without him knowing? She'd be found out. Won't he have a record of how many are in the safe, how many have been distributed, and to whom, on what dates?'

'She says so, yes. She's satisfied she can deal with it. That is *her* problem, Marjorie, not ours.'

'*Our* problem is, how can we get them to BP?' says Ernst.

'What about via one of your Norwegian contacts, or through the diplomatic channels of a neutral country?' I suggest. 'Switzerland, for example. Or Sweden. Portugal, Ireland. Or maybe she can send something to our people in an occupied country, obviously France.'

'We've worked through all those and more. Tested them. It's not feasible. She can't travel alone, and there's no secure way to send anything within the Reich. The Norwegian groups are riddled with informers. And she's too close to the Nazi administration. We have to be mindful of her security. This lady may have other information. She might be able to help us again in the future. We've concluded the best way is to go in and collect them from her in person.'

'If you can find the right person.'

'Ultimately, the decision rests with SOE,' Alec points out.

It's extremely perilous, they warn straight away. 'Until now,' says Ernst, 'we haven't put anyone into Germany. It's too dangerous. Support for the regime is near unanimous. The whole population is on high alert, looking out for spies, traitors, foreigners, suspicious types, anyone who looks, sounds or acts even slightly unusual. Anyone may be reported, and the response is swift, brutal and merciless. Any agent captured would be tortured, emptied of all their secrets, and killed. So even if we did decide to put someone into enemy territory, it wouldn't be someone who knew anything significant. Least of all would it be wise to put a Jew into Germany.'

'Yet you still think I'm the best option in this case?'

'Because, one, a lady can only deal with another lady. A married woman speaking to a man attracts attention. And, two, a man moving about the country on his own is vulnerable. He has more explaining to do. Everywhere he goes, he is observed. So is a woman, but in another way. A young woman, if she is conventional and respectable, can even ask for help. A man may be challenged at every turn. A woman will not be. Then, number three, we must entrust this to someone who can identify what we need on sight and will know at once whether it is genuine and useful. And four, it must be someone who beyond question can pass as Aryan.'

'And, five,' I add to his list, 'if it goes pear-shaped, you need someone who has no secrets of her own and is totally dispensable.'

'Correct,' the unsentimental Ernst nods. 'You already know more than is good for you.' I admire his attitude. 'And let's be frank, being just a girl makes you appear insignificant.'

'Haven't you got a real German you could send? A refugee or someone?' As soon as the words are said, I see why that would not be a good idea. 'No, of course. Not a refugee.'

'We're working with the Americans to find German exiles to penetrate the Reich. We haven't identified any suitable people at all.'

There seems no choice but to accept the task. In any case I feel no reluctance. I am pleased, rather.

Alec looks at me with almost meditative calm. 'Well, it may not happen,' he muses. 'You'll be sent at once to SOE for assessment and training. Things will have to be expedited. If they think you're not up to the job, it won't go ahead. If you are up to the job, you'll be fast-tracked to Group A and straight on to Group B. We anticipate you'll carry out the mission within a month or two, if they're happy with you. At any rate it must be before the spring.'

'I don't understand what you're saying, Alec. What are Group A and Group B?'

'Group A is firearms training and so on. Group B is something quite different. It'll all become clear if you're selected,' he replies.

'Oh, and Marjorie,' says Ernst, 'just to repeat: SOE don't know what we do at BP. Not an inkling. Don't be drawn. Don't tell them anything. Nothing at all. Your BP record will be deleted to make sure there's no way to follow your tracks back to us.'

'What, do you suspect someone? Someone on our side?'

'No, it's just a precaution. Now, any questions?' Both men look at me in silence. At last I say, 'Any chance of another cup?'

'Frankly, you deserve a double whisky,' says Alec. Neither of them makes a move to have anything sent in. The meeting is over.

A rueful expression on his handsome face, Alec takes my hand and makes his simple farewell, 'Thank you and good luck, Marjorie.' Ernst seems more affected. He impulsively kisses me on both cheeks. 'No more of our little talks! I shall miss you.'

From which ominous remark I gather that he doesn't expect me to make it back to Bletchley. 'Oh,' I reply breezily, 'if the war ever ends and we come out of it alive, I expect we'll meet again one day.'

It's been a long sleepless journey among a crush of bodies, breathing the stench of male sweat and stale smoke. Travelling from Group A to Group B has taken me almost the length of the country, north to south, on trains puffing through the night. The warrant says Brockenhurst, which I've never heard of. Nor do I know anything of the New Forest where it is set. Seen from the train at first light, the Forest is an enormous military zone of camps and barracks, camouflaged ranges and makeshift airstrips, War Department signs, regimental insignia, barbed wire hung with glistening droplets and concrete barriers scattered across acres of mud and water and heath, everything sparkling under a curious sheen that could be hoarfrost. At this hour, veiled in thin mist, it has a heart-rending tranquillity. Between the martial installations, groups of ponies unkempt in winter coat stand quiet and motionless among rank bracken and gorse. Miniscule clouds, rose-tinted, drift low through a glorious sky, like pink confetti thrown into the blue.

Under this sweet daybreak I alight with crowds of men and women, civilians and military, even foreigners in unfamiliar uniforms. The melée of passengers disperses like steam, vanishing without trace into army trucks and buses. Their diesel roar fades away. I stand alone in the silence, uncertain what to expect.

The station has two exits, so I button my coat and wait on a bridge over the track, with a view of both. There was no mention of where I would be collected, or by whom.

A staff car pulls up slowly. A uniformed FANY officer at the wheel, in a rather fetching khaki beret, waves in greeting. She throws open the passenger door and I slip in. She's cheerful and bright, 'Hello! I'm Fiona,' shakes my hand vigorously, offers me a cigarette, laughs merrily and drives fast on a narrow lane. Her outfit looks really practical and comfortable, with jacket, trousers and boots that you could wear to run for a bus or climb a tree. We cross a wide plain cloaked in heather and fern, the sun beginning to cast a little warmth, the heath shedding its mist. The tiny clouds turn from pink to white, as if miraculously transformed from confetti into snowflakes.

Fiona brakes sharply, giving way to a group of the wandering ponies, untended on the road. She explains that the animals are free to roam at will. 'It's funny, they don't even know there's a war on,' she marvels. She turns into a driveway, where a gatehouse duty officer, with what appears to be a huge struggle of intellect, compares my letter with papers that she shows him. He stares at my face to confirm my identity, checking the colour of my eyes. Through barriers and gates we pass into a thickly forested estate. A tree-shrouded track rises to a mansion looking over a lake still as glass.

'Can we swim in the lake?' I ask.

'In this weather?' Fiona laughs mysteriously. 'All in good time. You're about to have a very odd interview, Group B selection. Don't be fazed. Stand your ground. And by the way, the lake is damn cold at this time of year.' She delivers me to a room where behind a long table sit four uniformed officers, two male and two female. They have a rather hard-bitten look about them that I like. One of the women greets me stiffly.

'Behrens? Take a seat.'

This feels impolite, even insulting. She could at least have said Miss and Good Morning and asked about my journey. There's something of the courtroom here, or the punishment block, which I am keen to dispel at once. I walk straight over to her with a smile and hand outstretched. 'Morning, ma'am! Sorry, I didn't catch the name.'

Displeased, she barks out a rank and surname, introducing the others in like manner. To them I turn with a courteous, 'How do you do?' They respond in kind, keen to get on.

The woman hands me a document. 'Read and sign, would you? It says you'll be committing a serious crime if you ever mention this place. Understand that it applies not just while you're here, but to the end of your days.' It's the old Confidentiality Document again.

I'm on the verge of saying I've already signed it, when it strikes me that even saying so would be a breach. As Ernst and Alec warned, they clearly don't understand where I'm from, who I am, or why my name has been put forward. 'You've been cleared by STS, you've done well in Group A and we know your background is in Signals,' says the woman officer. I'm wondering – goodness, what has she been told? 'What did you do in Signals? Where were you stationed?'

That's a tricky one, since I wasn't in Signals. I reply, 'Our work is confidential, ma'am.'

'But with the Foreign Office?' She's nodding as if it must be so. – 'My apologies, ma'am, not permitted to go into detail.'

'Or are you at the Admiralty?' – 'Sorry, I'm not to discuss it.'

'At Bletchley?' – 'Not at liberty to say.'

'Come on now, all on the same side here.' – 'Can't say anything at all, I'm afraid.'

'Very well. Are you a good swimmer?' – A surprising start, and a curious echo of Fiona's obscure comment! I answer honestly, 'Yes.'

'Can you drive?' asks one of the men, looking quite disagreeable. He's fiddling with a pencil in what could be nervousness. – 'No.'

'All right. What is your worst fault?' – 'Not being able to drive.'

'No, I mean…' – They have no sense of humour. 'Oh, you mean character flaw? No doubt my *worst* trait is that I never, ever waste time wondering about such things. Prefer to get on with the job.'

There's not a glimmer of response. 'What about knitting; can you knit?' – Even more surprising. 'Do our boys need cardigans?' I smile. They do not smile. I confirm that I can knit.

'Would you say you were courageous?' – 'Not the kind of thing one would say about oneself.'

'Quite so. *Are* you courageous?' – 'No idea, sir. I do what has to be done.'

'Would you be prepared to die for your country?' – 'Rather live to fight another day, sir.'

From the woman again, sceptically, 'We understand you speak German. Where did you study?' They probably know already that I had no further education.

'At my mother's knee.' There's nothing to lose by admitting I haven't studied it. I'm not applying for a job, after all.

'German, was she?' With raised eyebrows.

'Naturalised British. Spoke German at home.'

'Do you have any other languages?'

'English, French and Russian fluent.'

The other woman officer, who has until now said nothing, speaks in Russian, 'Where did you learn Russian?'

I answer in Russian that it too was at my mother's knee. 'Both parents were also Russian-speakers, bi-lingual.' There are raised eyebrows. Notes are made.

The second man takes up the questioning. 'Ever inflicted any serious violence or been the victim of any?'

'Apart from being half blown up, no. Although I have seen men brawling sometimes.'

'Does the prospect of inflicting violence give you any pleasure? Wouldn't it be satisfying to strike back against some Germans?'

'The only thing that gives me satisfaction is successfully completing my tasks.'

'Would you be willing to shoot someone?'

'Whom do you have in mind?' with what I hope is a slightly wry expression.

'What about using a knife, then?'

'That's something I'd avoid in my best frock.'

'These are serious questions, Behrens. Would you be able to use a gun or knife on a fellow human being, and possibly take their life.'

'Well, there is a war on.'

'Yes or no?' he insists. 'What we're getting at is, do you draw the line at killing someone?'

'Depends who it is. I do what has to be done.'

'Right,' very tetchily. 'And where do you stand politically?'

'Firm believer in the secret ballot.'

My interlocutors pass irritated glances from one to another. One of the ladies says sharply, 'Look, Miss Behrens, there are no such secrets here. When we ask a question, we shall have an answer.' She stares at me ferociously.

I retort matter-of-factly, 'You invited me here, ma'am, and here I am. With respect, if I'm not what you're looking for, send me away.' There's an outraged intake of breath. I can see their minds whirring as they run through their options.

Suddenly a question in German from the woman who earlier spoke to me in Russian. 'Which part of Germany am I from?'

'Sie sind überhaupt kein Deutscher. – You are not German at all. There's a trace of Sächsisch, but obviously you are not from Sachsen. Perhaps your teacher was from there?'

This seems to please all of them except the German-speaking woman. The first man has a brain-teaser for me. 'Could you tell me, Miss Behrens, what questions did we ask, and in what order?' As it happens I'm good at puzzles like that, and rattle off the list.

'Well, good. Let's see how you get on. You'll wear the uniform of an officer of the First Aid Nursing Yeomanry.'

This is surely a mistake. 'You do know I'm not in the Forces? I'm a civilian. I can't be seconded to FANY.'

'Seconded or not, female operatives wear FANY uniform while at Beaulieu. Bear in mind FANY are not part of the armed forces.'

There's no point in mentioning Father's wish that I should not wear military uniform. After all, he said only that he never wanted to see me in uniform. As he's dead, he won't see me. Yet I want to respect his wish and his memory.

'In that case,' I reply at last, 'I'm unsuitable for the task.'

'What task? Has anything been said to you?'

'The task, whatever it may be.' I already know I won't need a uniform to carry it out.

G

'**C**oo-ee, Mrs Rosen,' she hallooed, 'new carer here.' Carol put her head round the living room door. There Marjorie sat in silence, doing nothing. Neither the television nor the radio were on. The newspaper on her lap was folded open at the crossword. Apparently she was lost in thought.

Marjorie beheld a strongly-built woman in her forties, older than most of her carers. There was a touch of blowzy plumpness and slack affability. The wavy brown hair could do with a wash and a stiff brush. Marjorie knew the type: genial, good-hearted, hardworking, wouldn't say no to a drink. There was intelligence there: Marjorie could see that the woman's sweeping, smiling gaze comprehended all. They also recognised each other at once, from years ago.

Before going into the room, Carol had formed a clear idea of the person she was about to meet and the job she had to do. Some of the other girls nicknamed Mrs Rosen 'the Crossword Lady'. Arriving at Durbeyfield Lodge, Carol stayed a few moments in her little car reading the Care Plan. *Address the service user as Mrs Rosen. Allow her plenty of time to mobilise. Mrs Rosen likes everything done in a particular way and will instruct you. Put her book, pen, glasses, crossword and angina spray in easy reach – she will explain. She insists on everything in its place.*

Carol decided that Mrs Rosen sounded like a dragon. Or a battleaxe. Or a harridan. She softened her view as she read on. *Mrs Rosen is in constant pain, which she does not show. Dislikes sympathy. She is quiet and dislikes chatter. She is a very private lady.*

The page headed *Tasks* stayed open in Carol's hand as she took the key from the keysafe and let herself into the entrance hall of Durbeyfield Lodge. Carol had been into scores of such hallways: pale carpet, modern lift, pale walls hung with bland prints. Most clients of the care agency lived in places just like Durbeyfield Lodge.

'Hello, dear,' said the dragon, 'come in.'

'Hello, I'm Carol. Hey, I remember you – you're *the* Mrs Rosen, from Saltington, aren't you? The cake shop lady?'

Marjorie nodded slightly. 'You came to the shop four times, am I right? With an elderly, foreign gentleman. He liked Savoy cake.'

'Wow, you *remember* that? That's incredible! Yes, Grandad raved about your Savoy cake.'

'So, that was your grandfather, was it?'

'My mum's dad. He was Polish. He died a while back.'

'Ah, so he *was* Polish; I did wonder. He had the accent.'

'Really, you even remember his accent?'

'Because the Poles helped us in the war. People don't realise.'

'Actually, Grandad never talked about Poland, not once, nor the war either. How are you keeping after all this time?'

'*Very* well. The kitchen is through there.' Marjorie gestured with her head. 'Help yourself to a cup of something. I'll have a coffee. Very strong, dash of milk, no sugar. There are biscuits in the tin; have one. Sorry, there's no Savoy cake. I can't make cake any more.'

They reminisced about Saltington. 'Course, there's loads of Poles there now on the new estates. There's a Polish supermarket.' Carol pronounced the name like a local, 'Saltentun' (which happened to be the original Saxon name of the town); and sure enough, she said, she was born there, grew up there, went to school there and met her husband there.

'And what work does he do?' asked Marjorie.

Carol finished her drink, mindful of the minutes passing. 'Wayne? He's a plumber at the docks. Used to be a soldier.' She looked at her worksheet. *Take Mrs Rosen to bathroom. Toilet as necessary.* 'Enjoy your crossword, don't you? So I've been told.'

'I like solving problems.' She said she had done the Times crossword every day for over sixty years.

'What about on holiday, or in hospital? Did you do it then?'

Marjorie confessed, 'I was exaggerating. Tell you what, though, I'll never have another holiday. And never go inside a hospital again, either, if I can avoid it.'

'Why not?'

'I've had enough dreadful days and sleepless nights in hospital. Promise never to call an ambulance for me.'

Carol's playful promise was non-committal. 'Hopefully you won't need one. I used to be a hospital nurse myself once, worked in rehabilitation. Well, Mrs Rosen, we must get on! Feel like going to the toilet?' To emphasise the point, Carol put down her cup and put on a pair of surgical gloves.

In the bathroom, with Carol's help Marjorie cleaned herself laboriously. She looked at her face in the mirror. Her eyebrows had become mere naked ridges. The eyelids were as rippled as hanging drapery; the thin skin below the eyes, criss-crossed with hairlines and creases. The eyes themselves were glossed with watery film. The gaze alone remained constant and true, her own.

Arrange pillows on bed. Mrs R cannot lie flat. Apply aqueous lotion to body and legs. Rubbing cream into Marjorie's calves and thighs, Carol asked, 'What about your hair, Mrs Rosen? You don't leave it up like that, to sleep?' Marjorie's hair was in its usual bun, lacquered into position.

'Yes, I do. I'll deal with it.'

'I'll brush it for you.'

'Let me deal with it.'

'I can give it a quick wash for you. You'll be glad.'

Marjorie hardly knew how to respond. No other carer had stepped outside the allotted list of tasks. Carol was human and had noticed that others were human. She even reached out for one's humanity, wanted to feel it. Marjorie took a great step. Dealing with her hair had become impossibly difficult. 'Alright, if you put it up again afterwards. Thank you.'

As soon as it was unpinned, Carol saw the problem. 'Ah, quite bald on top, aren't you? That's why you keep it covered.'

'You're finding out more about me than even my husband knew.'

Carol laughed mischievously. 'There are no secrets when you have a carer.'

'Ah, is that so?'

'What is it, alopecia? Hair lacquer doesn't do it any good.'

'It started after I worked in a bomb factory. The chemicals were very bad for us.' (Carol was interjecting 'A bomb factory! Was it dangerous?' and so on, all of which Marjorie ignored.) 'It got worse when I was pregnant with Philip, my first baby; there was still rationing then. Anyway, I never had good hair.'

Carol ran warm water from the shower to shampoo and rinse the thin hair. It was the most sensuous thing that had happened to Marjorie since Harry was alive, and the most intimate. Carol wrapped a towel around her head. They call it care, Marjorie thought, the most false word in Newspeak, but Carol was the first carer to make her feel cared-for. 'Sit like that for a minute, Mrs Rosen, and I'll pin it for you.'

Make supper as Mrs R instructs. She can feed herself but has problems swallowing. Ensure medication taken (see list).

The two women continued their conversation in the kitchen-diner. Marjorie ate while Carol cleaned and tidied. 'I remember you had a little red-headed girl and a baby in a pushchair,' Marjorie remarked. 'Any others?'

'Two girls and a boy, now. Blimey, you *have* got a really *amazing* memory – you didn't even know me, but you remember that! Our boy's ten and a half now. Little tearaway. Damn nuisance.'

'A worry to you, is he?'

Carol snorted. She did not look up. 'You could say that.' She kept her eyes on the list of tasks.

'I know what that's like. Would it help him if you were at home in the evening instead of working?'

'Haha! I won't bore you, Mrs Rosen, but it's more complicated than that. I've just worked nineteen days without a break. Ten to twelve hours a day. Minimum wage. No pay while travelling between clients.'

'My God! This whole care business needs to be better managed.'

'*And* I asked for a couple more evening calls. You're one of 'em.'

'For the extra cash, I suppose?'

'Yup, we need the money. But it's not only that. To be perfectly honest with you, me and my husband argue all the time. It's best for Aidan if he doesn't see us. And I'd just as soon be out of the house.'

'What – he's not violent, is he, your husband?'

Carol turned her head away, embarrassed. 'Me and Wayne have

differences of opinion. It's Aidan. Wayne says I'm too soft with him. Aidan is a nightmare, always in trouble. He gets picked up by the police causing mischief in town'

'At that age!'

'Yup. Wayne gives him such a thrashing. It's horrible. Poor mite. I've stopped sleeping with my husband because of it. Oh! I haven't done your Ovaltine.'

Make small flask of Ovaltine using water only, no milk or sugar. Wash dishes etc, tidy, prepare rubbish to be taken out.

'Stopped sleeping with your husband! That's playing with fire, Carol.' The Ovaltine tin stood ready beside a small flask. 'Just water. No milk or sugar. Bring Aidan with you next time, if you can. I'd like to meet this troublesome child of yours.'

'Nah, you wouldn't.'

'No, really, I would. Don't boil the water, Carol. Make it nice and warm. Not boiled.'

Complete daily record sheet noting any concerns. Make sure flat is secure for the night. On leaving, take rubbish out to bins.

Marjorie considered that she had hit it off with the new carer. She could prove a useful ally, too. Meanwhile, Carol was thinking, A very private lady? They had been nattering for the whole half hour! On the other hand, she – Carol – had said far, far too much about *her*self, while Mrs Rosen had said hardly anything about *her*self.

Marjorie settled against the pillows. Raindrops pattered on the bedroom window, a soothing sound. She might sleep a little tonight, or she might not. She held a pen and wore her reading glasses. The emergency call button was strapped around her wrist. Her crossword and her book lay on the bedcover beside her. The angina spray and flask of Ovaltine were on the bedside table, next to the reading light, the alarm clock and the small photo of Harry.

'That woman,' she said to Harry, 'has a lot on her plate.'

As far as she could tell from his expression, Harry agreed. When she had finished the crossword, Marjorie let the newspaper slip to the floor, turned off the light and closed her eyes.

* * *

In this house we speak only German, all the time, even at leisure. Three of us are British nationals, two Czech, one Swiss, and the others Polish, but all are mother-tongue German-speakers. We're evenly split between men and women, each of us preparing to be placed alone into a Nazi-occupied country in the guise of a German civilian. In my view, some are not suitable. Too voluble. Too self-conscious. Too proud they were selected. Too optimistic. Egotistical. Pleased with themselves. Not enough grit. Not focused. Not good at planning ahead. Not unflappable. Others are perfect, a match for anything, cool, adept, fit. And so Aryan-looking it's scary.

For some exercises off-site I'm free to wear what I like. On every other occasion, I'm in FANY uniform; they've won on that point. Perhaps Father would forgive me, since at least I raised an objection. Besides, they are right that FANY is not part of the armed forces. And I get to wear a dashing khaki beret like Fiona's.

Indoor instruction and most outdoor exercises take place within the Beaulieu estate, which is huge, reaching across heath and woodland down to riverside water meadows and marshes on the shore of the Solent, and encompassing a dozen grand houses, each one a closed world devoted to preparing a group. I'm not clear who's in which house. The men murmur longingly that one of them is filled with gorgeous Frenchwomen.

Beaulieu River is packed with naval craft armed with Oerlikons. Around Beaulieu and across at Exbury village, and around Exbury House (HMS Mastodon, as Wrens and naval types call it), the country lanes have been widened and straightened for tanks and trucks. In meadows and paddocks temporary airstrips are laid out with wire mesh tracking. There's an anti-aircraft site on the Solent shore. Bofors guns are hidden among copses and hedges.

Despite our deadly purpose and the peril ahead, everything strikes me as highly enjoyable, wading in mud, crawling through effluent, climbing ten-foot walls, moving from tree to tree above ground level. Sometimes I have to swim (in my clothes) in our freezing lake. Some tasks are like party games: re-draw a map you saw yesterday, make a scale model from plasticine. All the time watched.

There are useful skills for dealing with life's little problems: how to slip a knife between ribs, break a neck or an arm, disarm a stronger opponent. How to resist interrogation, subdue a dog, jump from a moving vehicle. 'Now, girls,' says the instructor, 'are you willing to be raped, and if not, what are the alternatives?' How to follow, but avoid being followed; hide emotions, and detect them in others. How to skin, gut and cook a rabbit or a trout with nothing but a pair of nail scissors and a box of matches. Very handy for a girl to know.

One night I'm pulled from my bed without warning and ordered to cross the Solent, rowing alone in the dark without lights. On the other side I'm to run uphill to fetch a wireless and come back with it. On the way, I hear a puzzling, eerie sound in the distance – is it a threat, a trap, perhaps a real raid? No, that is geese. Geese, calling in the marshes. Even with all the military activity going on here, after dark there's a serenity to which I could fall victim. In rest periods I find myself drawn into daydreams of its heaths and moors and watersides.

Discussion topics for the group: when is it better to sacrifice one's own life rather than endanger others; when is it better to endanger others? Forming a mental strategy to deal with torture. We are shown footage of a muscular middle-aged man in his vest and underpants being tortured. He is chained to the centre of a concrete floor; a long baton repeatedly strikes him with terrible force across his shoulders, back and legs. He is in tears, tries to cover the places with broken hands, writhes to escape the blows. It is difficult to watch. One wonders about the people who are doing this. Where did the footage come from? We are told to expect something much worse if we are caught. We endure mock sessions, to give some small idea of what to expect. Pain. Horror. Cruelty. Drowning. Ways that leave no mark, solitude, confinement in a space too small to stand or sit or lie down, hunger, thirst. This is nothing, we are told, compared to what really does happen in a Gestapo cell. There will be blood, blades, body parts. You will be injected with drugs. Be prepared.

During the night we are rudely awoken, uniformed men shouting in our faces and shaking us violently, jabbing hard with truncheons. This is another exercise, in which instructors assess whether one remembers to speak German when in shock or in pain. There's no one to turn to for help. Succeed absolutely or fail absolutely.

The pilot shakes my hand in a friendly, manly way and says to call him Len. I already know that's not his name, but that's what I call him. He doesn't tell me his rank, and I don't ask. As instructed, I say 'Hello Len, I'm Traudi', but he simply calls me Miss. He's a foot taller than me, with no cap. I can't quite make out if his greatcoat is RAF uniform. My impression is of an upright, decent chap, hair neatly cut and moustache clipped.

A few threads of thin mist swirl like transparent voile, long slender wisps rising slowly from the Beaulieu river and the Solent. No time is wasted, lest the mist become thicker. The night skies in this unlit place are like the icy unfenced steppes, or boundless oceans, stretching far beyond what any man can imagine. Tonight in the New Forest, a third-quarter moon illuminates four engineers in overalls who crawl on the dewy turf around our little aeroplane.

My pilot mentions casually that the ride will be a long one, 'that's our maximum range.' After a moment he adds, 'well, it's beyond the maximum, but it should be all right.' After this troubling remark, we stand waiting side by side in the field and say nothing more.

In my huge handbag is everything the respectable young lady may need. Identity card, driving permit, hairbrush, clothes brush, permits for my rail journeys, a popular but serious novel (*Volk ohne Raum* by Hans Grimm, a stirring tale about how the German People shouldn't be afraid to take what they need), a needle and thread, a small photo of my husband, the very handy little German Army penknife with its saw and punchblade, a permitted torch for use during blackout, some cash, ration cards, ration stamps for use away from home, and some knitting, which the Führer strongly approves for us women.

SOE have created a lot of clever kit for agents, especially those who are sent to join resistance groups. That doesn't apply to me, and I don't have much of that sort. No map, no compass, no emergency rations, no binoculars, no transmitter. There mustn't be a single thing in my bag or about my person that might give me away. Still, the handbag handles quickly turn into straps to secure it to my body, and the knitting needles, tucked innocently into a ball of wool, are modified punch daggers, sharpened steel with points intended to kill.

A capsule (or rather, a tiny rubber-coated glass ampoule), called an L-pill, sewn into the waistband of my bloomers, is also intended to kill... me. The assumption is that if I am captured and have reached the point where I am down to my underwear, it's time to put the capsule in my mouth and bite on it, releasing the lethal dose of cyanide. In case the first L-pill becomes inaccessible, another is hidden inside the clip of my sanitary belt, which I am to wear at all time whether needed or not.

Every SOE agent has a personal cipher in case of an opportunity and urgent need to get in touch. In that way the cipher itself verifies one's identity. Mine is a line from the *Shema*, because I know it by heart and because it can't be decoded without having the Hebrew text beside you, which I trust most Nazi codebreakers not to have. Carried only in my mind is a string of passwords, true and false. What I can't have, and wouldn't risk, and in any case don't need, is a code card to remind me of them. As long as I live, my call sign if a mission is underway and still incomplete is to be Hilde. If the mission has failed or I am under duress, it is Hollybush. If the mission has been successfully accomplished, my call sign is Halcyon.

My papers are perfectly in order. Mein Name ist Frau Waltraud Weißmüller . My poor husband Unteroffizier Christian Weißmüller was killed in action in January last year on the Eastern Front. I am still waiting to find out exactly where or how he died. Then in March our beautiful home in Lübeck was destroyed by enemy firebombing.

This is plausible because it is true. I have taken the identity of a real dead woman, with a real dead husband and a real destroyed home. She was the same age as me, twenty-two years old. She had been married only two years when Officer Weißmüller was blasted to pieces by Soviet troops. She herself was burnt beyond recognition in the firebombing, one of many who could not be identified.

I don't suppose anything survives of Waltraud's wardrobe. My clumpy shoes and handbag, and my husband's monogrammed attaché case ("C.W."), and all my clothes from hat and coat down to vest and pants, everything well-worn but cared-for, are in popular pre-War styles sold by the (now Aryanized) Wertheim Department Store. Or copies of them, complete with labels. I like the look. Modest, dignified and womanly. Not at all showy. Sehr attraktiv.

As it happens, Waltraud and Christian Weißmüller were members of the Party. Among my papers is a red-covered NSDAP membership card. I wear a natty little black and red enamel swastika brooch in my lapel, just as – so I've been told – lots of women do who belong to the Party but are unable to show their support in any other way. After my terrible year I have nothing left except my devotion to our great Führer and the Party and the certain triumph of our great Reich.

Freed from its camouflage cover and pushed into place, the trim Lysander could almost be a boy's balsawood model. The pilot even calls it, boyishly, his Lizzie. The airstrip is nothing more than a band of steel mesh unrolled onto the earth and pinned into position. After we've gone, it will be rolled up again and taken away.

Len and I climb aboard and drive off without ceremony, for all the world as if we were riding an open-top car into the stars. That is how it looks and sounds. How astonishing the view! This is my first real flight, and I am filled with wonder. The strange, complicated workings of the coastline, its intricate indentations and shallows, sandbars and marshes, are beautiful and marvellous, the atlas made flesh. In a single instant, little Beaulieu lies far below, the village with its glistening river and lake, the silvery ribbon of the Solent and the low hills of the Isle of Wight ghostly pale. However, the stars remain as far away as ever, and after a while I feel instead that our sports car is not in the heavens but skimming the surface of the sea.

The land is black velvet. Now I know what German bombers see: almost nothing, except a flash of river or lake, and the occasional candlegleam of a car whose headlights are not fully darkened as it weaves slowly along country roads. The nightly blackout seems to be working. The waters widen as we pass from the English Channel into the North Sea, leaving behind the kindly shores of England.

Denmark lies ahead. For a time, we have the world to ourselves, Len and I. The propeller clatters; the engine keens with quiet insistence, occasionally murmuring and grumbling softly. We press forward without lights or wireless a few feet over the restless waters which as a girl I crossed with Father.

It's hard to believe we are in any danger. Len soberly assures me that we are. 'One problem could be,' he warns, 'if the Luftwaffe take it into their heads to launch a raid tonight, and happen to come this way. If they spotted us they'd knock us out just like that, without a thought. If we do go down, it'll be the cold that kills us. We won't have time to drown.'

'We're flying ducks,' I say. It's a joke – I'm thinking of sitting ducks, and those ceramic ducks people put on their walls. He doesn't hear, or doesn't think it's funny. Which I suppose it isn't. Strange that BP already know whether there's to be a raid tonight.

'I meant, we're easy prey. Anything expected tonight?'

'Nothing expected. Haven't seen hair nor hide of Jerry for a while. I reckon Old Adolf's got his hands full with the Eastern Front.'

Later, hazy shafts of white light pierce the sky from some point beyond the horizon. At first I foolishly imagine it's a town or city with no blackout. Len puts me right. 'That's Jerry looking for enemy aircraft. Atlantic Wall. When we get close you'll see they scan the sea too, for boats. You heard of the Atlantic Wall?'

'If I have, I don't recall what it is. Not a wall, presumably?'

'Oh yes!' Len exclaims, 'A real wall in places, a concrete barrier along the shore! That's mainly around the ports. Most of it is massive great bunkers, arranged so they can see from one to the next. Jerry wants the whole Continent fortified, from the Arctic to Spain. He wants it impregnable.'

If true, that would be a Herculean accomplishment. I'm not sure how Len has come by this information. Perhaps it is common knowledge. Perhaps it's something airmen have seen for themselves. Or perhaps it's mere rumour. I ask, 'How do we get past it?'

My brave pilot turns with a grin. 'We'll manage, Miss.' It was on just such a mission as this that Peg's equally brave and confident George was brought down and killed. Alarmingly, Len has a paper map folded open on his knees and taps it roughly with a gloved fingertip to show our route. With no wireless and only a compass to guide him, he is finding his way by eye and from memory to a landing field across the seas. 'This Atlantic Wall, see, Miss, there are loads of gaps. Like where we're going,' he says, 'between the Danish islands. They haven't put everything in place.'

Brave he may be, but I sense my pilot's nervousness. 'So far so good,' he says. 'We don't know who's there. Be very careful, Miss, when we're on the ground. Have you got a gun?' Perhaps stupidly, I haven't, because it would incriminate me if I were searched.

The shoreline is dark and uninhabited. We come down fast, poor Len following the directions of nothing but a flashing torch, dropping as steeply as a sea bird, the engine subdued to the whine and putter of a motorised bicycle. We skim watery mud and sand. It will not be possible to either walk or swim – should we happen to bail out right here. Two seconds later there's a grassy field beneath us, and on it we touch the earth again, bouncing awkwardly in three or four jerks. The torchlight is flashing, but we can't see who is holding it.

Stepping onto solid ground brings a horrible rush of awareness. Here is not mere waterlogged land and sleeping wildfowl, but a nation of men in the grip of madness, a monstrous Caliban of irrationality. It's hard to believe the same serene moon shines here that once shone – a few lost hours ago – on a similar shore in England. England! The very word rings out for liberty as I stand in this benighted Denmark.

The flashlight beams turn erratically. Some figures are at the plane, refuelling it. The moonlight doesn't show enough. The scene is like mere snatches of dream or nightmare, or staccato images from the blackest Film Noir. I must snap out of it and get a grip. Foolishly I can't keep Hamlet out of my mind! Deranged Denmark slain anew. "Whatsoever else shall hap to-night, Give it an understanding, but no tongue." Because no matter what is about to happen, it will never be spoken of, and will remain always mine alone, alive or dead.

As if on cue, two men approach, both tall and young. One is lean and wears a peaked hat on a head of snow-white hair. The other is dark and fleshy and, in the gloom, hardly Danish in appearance.

There are quick handshakes but no introductions, although they do announce, in a beautiful accent of curious squeezed vowels, 'Holger Danske. We take you to the other side. Come now.' No one has said the words Holger Danske to me before, so I don't know what it is. At first I assume they are saying their names.

But the password! They did not use the agreed words. In these circumstances, I am to say in German, *I don't remember when we last met*. They *must* reply in German, *At least two years ago*.

I say my piece, 'I don't remember when we last met.'

'Quick,' says the blond man. I see he has a pistol in his hand, but not pointing at me.

I am not inclined to turn back at this stage despite the password failure. I argue with myself. These men are part of their own organisation and not bound by our procedures.

My pilot is by now the only familiar, trustworthy presence anywhere. I take the opportunity to grip his hand. 'Thank you, Len. Have a safe flight back.' I know this is a ridiculously mundane remark and that his name isn't really Len. I can't think what else to say. Better might be an effusive kiss on both cheeks, but I refrain.

In a low voice he warns, 'Be careful. I hope it goes well for you, Miss. Good luck.' I can't tell if he has some specific danger in mind.

We drive without lights other than a torch held out of the window, sometimes fast, sometimes creeping slowly for reasons unexplained. From lanes and dirt tracks we switch to an ordinary two-lane country road laid straight across a flat landscape. The dark man drives and the blond sits beside him, literally with a pistol at the ready.

I'm in the back seat, unclear whether this is part of our plan. For all I know, I've been kidnapped. I don't know where I am, or where I'm going, or who these men are. They say little to one another, and nothing to me, but when they do speak, I understand not a word. They snap at each other irritably, and at one point the driver slams the brakes and stops in the dust, shines a flashlight briefly onto a map to settle some argument before racing ahead. Still I accept that all is as it should be. I've been told that these two will steer me across a channel of water, partly frozen, into Germany, and I must believe it.

We pass through a small town of unlit buildings and unlit streets. There's no one about, not a single person. Everything is shuttered and deserted. I guess it is under curfew. My companions, be they friend or foe, seem to know every narrow alley and back lane. We must be reaching our destination, for the blond man frequently turns to the driver and speaks in a low voice. Letting the car roll forward in neutral, he freewheels on rutted gravel towards the silhouette of a house. Through the trees I see moonlit water beyond.

We come to a stop beside the house. It's not a house after all, but some sort of derelict workshop on the water's edge. The men wind down their windows and look around as if they expect to see someone or something. Both check their wrist-watches and exchange a few words. The blond in his peaked hat – I recognise it now, just an innocent fisherman's cap – turns to me and gestures towards the water: 'Flensborg Fjord. We wait.' I was given only the German name, Flensburger Förde.

The men are anxious and uncertain. After a few seconds the blond opens his door, pistol in one hand, flashlight in the other, and moves swiftly to the ruined building, searching behind it for a moment and returns. He's shaking his head – not there.

The driver leaves the car and the pair stand together in whispered conversation. One taps his watch. My guess is they are agreeing how much longer to wait. The ground around them is gleaming with frost.

I open my window onto the night and inhale the chill. The moon has begun to fall in the sky. It's essential that our crossing is done well before dawn. Sunrise will be after eight o'clock, but there will be light in the sky a good hour before that. I look at my own wristwatch: nearly 2.40am. I am starting to feel anxious myself. I have a rail travel permit from Flensburg, created by SOE, that can only be used on this date. I'm to be driven to Flensburg by our contact waiting on the far side. What are they waiting for?

The allotted minutes of patience must have passed, because with sudden decision they come to me. 'We don't stay longer,' replies the blond. The gun is not on view. He's holding it inside his coat pocket.

'What's the problem?' I ask.

'The man to take you, only he can do it. He must be here.'

'I thought *you* were supposed to take me to the other side.'

A slight grin shows what he thinks of that idea. 'Impossible. There is sandbanks, mines, ice. There is surveillance at Brunsnæs and after Holnis Peninsula,' he gestures vaguely westward, 'Vorpostenboote – patrols. Unterseeboots made in Flensborg they are protecting carefully. Only he knows the safe way.'

'U-boats are still made in Flensburg?'

'Ja, of course, by FSG, biggest factory in Flensborg.'

I'm wondering if this is useful information to take home, or whether everyone knows already.

'Didn't the RAF bomb Flensburg?' It is embarrassing to ask. I should have been more fully briefed. All I know about Flensburg is where to catch my train.

'A raid on Flensborg was last summer. You missed the target and bombed us on this side of the fjord.' A pointed finger suggests the bombs fell near where we are standing. Idiotically, I am half inclined to apologise for the mistake, but he adds, 'In September and October, the RAF succeed to hit the shipyard. But the damage was so little, and repaired so quickly. Ach! Flensborg is lucky. We are not lucky.'

'Will I see the U-boat factory from the railway station?'

'No,' a shake of the head, 'from the fjord road by the harbour.'

'Except I'm trapped here because only one man knows the way across the fjord.'

'Ja, the boat is here, but not the man. Something is wrong. He is not Holger Danske.'

Only then do I understand that is the name of their group. I open my door and step out. The ground underfoot is hard with frost. 'This man, what is he?' I ask. 'Is he Danish or German?'

'Norwegian.'

I am floundering in incomprehension. The operation is unravelling for reasons no one anticipated. 'Show me the boat.' I'm trying to put two and two together and not coming up with anything. Suppose the Norwegian group has been infiltrated. For all I know , there could be rivalry between resistance groups, or the boatman has been arrested, or expects to be and fled in fear. Or he has simply gone for a stroll.

I step over rough ground to the other side of the building. On that side, I see, the brickwork has half-collapsed into the fjord. A slender, solid-looking wooden rowing dinghy is tied up. The water around it shifts and moves thickly as it struggles to freeze or remain unfrozen.

The little boat is perfectly sound, about twelve-foot long and recently used. Inside lies a ladies' bicycle, battered but sturdy. I stare at it for a while, trying to understand. The oars are in their rowlocks, still wet. There's also a loaf of bread, partly gnawed at one end, poking from a small cloth bag. In my judgment, the oarsman left the scene in haste and not long ago.

'Is the bicycle for me?'

The Dane considers, frowning. He doesn't know. Then, 'We must get away now,' he urges, as if he has had a most horrible realisation. 'This could be a trap. They know about you, are expecting you. We have a house for you, safe, until there is a plane for England.'

That too could be a trap. Return home without attempting to reach my objective? Something certainly has gone wrong. The operation can't be aborted just because of that. Whether they stay or leave, my two companions could be picked up soon, and me with them.

'The people meeting me on the other side, are they German?'

'Norwegian,' the blond replies.

'What's the name of the place?'

'Near Fjordhavn. In Deutsch, Fördehaven.' He points across the fjord to what could be a small harbour, then moves his finger a little to the right. 'A track through trees to the water.' I'd guess it's only about a couple of miles across the water from where we're standing.

The driver gives me a telescope, a clever device that packs away to something hardly bigger than a thimble. I gaze at the far shore, and make out low buildings beside a tiny fishing port with nothing moored. A darker patch could be woodland rising from the shore. A searchlight sweeps periodically across the harbour. Further to the east more powerful lights finger the night sky nervously.

I ask if I may see his map, the one from the car. 'It is not a marine map,' he warns. I study it by torchlight. True, it's not a marine map, but it shows the fjord in plenty of detail.

'There is no time. Please, we must leave,' he repeats.

'Let's go across.'

'Across the fjord?' The blond shakes his head emphatically. 'No, no, no. Not on our agenda. Too dangerous.'

'Then I'll see you here in three days as we planned.'

The men watch, doubtful and uneasy as I climb into the boat. I push away from the shore with an oar, a familiar, pleasant sensation.

'Say hello to Mrs Rosen,' Carol instructed the boy sharply. Aidan pursed his lips and gave Marjorie an evil stare. 'You remind me of my little brother Reuben,' said Marjorie. 'He was just like you at your age.' She had been put to bed, and sat up with the duvet pulled cosily around.

'How old is he now?'

'Don't be cheeky,' said Carol.

Marjorie smiled. 'I'll look after him. You carry on.'

This kid, she thought, is not like Reuben at all. At ten years old, Reuben was sweet and full of wonder, adorable and so bright. This lad is untutored, awkward and suspicious. He does have, though, the troubled innocence of boys. The cause of his troubles was plain.

When Carol left the bedroom, Aidan sat awkwardly at Marjorie's writing desk. She said, 'Fancy a toffee?' and miraculously produced from behind her pillow a bowl of Quality Street. He was impressed.

'Which do you like best?' she asked.

He picked one up and showed it to her.

'Can you like something without knowing what's inside?' Her tone was serious. She might have been discussing philosophy. Indeed, she was.

'Well,' he ventured, 'it's all toffee. And I do know what's in 'em.'

'Do you? How?'

'We had 'em last Christmas at me auntie's.'

'Here, let me test you.' She reached a colourfully wrapped sweet from the bowl. 'What's inside?'

Aidan gave his answer. Marjorie unwrapped the toffee and bit into it to check. 'Correct.' She pushed the bowl across to him. 'Help yourself. I have a good memory, too. Can you play chess?'

'*Chess?* Nah.'

'Well, never mind, it's only a game. Still, this game teaches you to work out what people are thinking, what they're going to do next, and how to make a smarter move than them.'

'Yeah?'

'I'll show you.' She asked him to put the chess board and the old box of chessmen on the bed. Together they flattened the duvet and set the pieces on the board, Marjorie explaining where each one stands and the move it can make. 'This was my husband's old chess set. I always keep it near me.'

'To play chess?'

'No. Because I miss him. You have white, I'll be black. White moves first. You must think ahead. Far ahead, not one move. Don't just plan what you will do, work out what your opponent will do. Work out what's best for you.' Each made a first move.

The boy tinkered with the pieces and brought out a second pawn. Marjorie said, 'Excellent start. What are you good at, at school?'

'Nuffink. Anyway, it's the holidays.'

'Tell me what you'd like to be good at, and I'll show you how. Everything at school is fantastically easy.'

When Carol returned to the bedroom, she found Aidan and Marjorie locked in intellectual combat over the chessboard. She did not fully understand what she could see. 'Come on mischief,' she said to the boy, 'leave Mrs Rosen in peace.' He ignored her. 'Aidan!'

'Could Aidan please come again tomorrow?' asked Marjorie. She turned to him, 'If you want to, that is. We need more time to finish this game.' It grieved her, this bright, troublesome, dissatisfied child about to start his final year in primary school so ill-prepared to become a big boy in big school. 'Would you put the board on the desk, Aidan, very carefully? Make sure the pieces don't move. When you come again we'll carry on.'

At once he did as she asked. Carol looked on astonished. 'Thanks for teaching me, Mrs Rosen,' he said, 'and thanks for the sweets.'

The usual knock and bright 'Halloo' and Carol stood in the bedroom with her truculent little boy. 'How are you today?'

'*Very* well!' cried Marjorie 'We've got a game of chess to finish, haven't we, Aidan? D'you want a glass of milk and a biscuit, first? Do you know any jokes?'

While Carol attended to the laundry and the kitchen, the pair played chess as he repeated playground jokes about the number of elephants, changing lightbulbs, knock-knock.

'A man walks into a bar… Ouch!'

She riposted with a few of her own. 'Why is six scared of seven? Because seven ate nine.'

When it was time for her trip to the bathroom, Marjorie sent him to the living room. 'On the table, there's a sheet of paper and a pen, and a book of puzzles. Do as many as you can. I'll give you twenty pence for every correct answer. Nothing for incorrect answers.'

'Why give me anything? Suppose I don't want to?'

'Don't waste time asking pointless questions. The sooner you get started, the better. Shut the door behind you.'

Carol protested, '20p a throw? Wayne would be furious.'

'Tell me about Wayne.'

'Once upon a time he had a heart of gold. Afghanistan changed that. He had problems out there. He's a hard man on a short fuse. He says it's better if I don't know about it.'

'Could be right. Sometimes it is better not to know. What's his idea of fun – women, booze?'

'Well, same as any bloke. But no, he's good like that. He's into fitness, running, cycling, weights and that.' Carol stopped what she was doing and began to explain. 'The trouble is, Wayne wanted his boy to be like that, too. He just isn't. He's a rebel. So Wayne thrashes him, and Aidan is against him all the more. It's a spiral.'

'Ah-ha. Well then, we'll break that spiral.'

* * *

The air is biting cold over the water, everything moist to the hand. Pearls of ice are starting to form on my coat and hat and in my hair. The coat, I take off and put back on inside-out, to keep it clean and dry. The hat goes into my handbag, to be replaced with a headscarf. From the cloth bag with bread inside, I cut pieces to muffle the oars. I row with care, making a good deal less noise than a bird that cries shrilly and splashes onto the water beside me. I hear a few other bird calls, distant. Nothing else.

A gentle south-west wind against me causes a slight choppiness – perhaps making it harder for anyone to spot the little boat. Broad, flat bands of tissue-thin cloud are being pasted across the sky. The muted moon struggles to trickle through, mere candlelight in the breeze. Despite its fleeting gleam, I feel enveloped all around by a growing blackness. Good. The darker the better.

I row, pulling hard, curiously unfatigued; alert, taut. There has been no sign of either sandbars or mines, nor patrols yet, nor ice. I rip mouthfuls from the oarsman's soggy loaf. Another piece of the bread I put in my handbag, wrapped in a handkerchief.

To the east, the sky lightens faintly. In shades of black and grey, the beach comes into view, peaceful, yet sinister. I see where the track emerges from trees at the water's edge, and another by a wooden jetty coated with frost. If anyone is there, I anticipate some sign of them now, perhaps a few flashes from a torch to guide me.

There is only calm and stillness. That's bad, and also good. Bad, because there can be no doubt now that someone has betrayed, or been betrayed, I cannot know which. And good, if it means that for the moment the Germans – police, SS or Gestapo – do not know about me. Or if they know about me, they do not know where I am.

The skiff touches gravel with a small grating sound. I wait to see if it has attracted any attention. It strikes me that I've hardly seen another human being since I left Beaulieu.

The bicycle I lift out straight away. Obviously I must drag the boat into cover. It's an almighty struggle to haul the thing even a few inches onto the foreshore, let alone all the way up the bank. This small craft is my only way back to Denmark. Without it I'm trapped here among the Jew-killers. One thing I mustn't do, is leave it where it might be noticed by a suspicious early walker, or the first coastal patrol of the morning. With all my might I can hardly shift it. A rising fear is that I am spending too long on the task, standing by the water's edge at first light, with a rowing-boat, red-handed. I could do with a Norwegian man to help with this.

A theory nags at me that the missing Norwegian boatman left a bike for me because he already knew the Norwegian on the German side of the water had been arrested. He himself took flight, on the

Danish side of the fjord, because any arrested man soon reveals everything he knows. And after he tells everything he knows, no one in this operation will be safe, myself least of all.

That's what they told me at Beaulieu. An ordinary healthy man lasts only a matter of minutes. The most resolute cannot endure torture for more than forty-eight hours, seventy-two hours in cases of those who can bear having body parts removed or being blinded without giving way. Then, in the hope of winning some measure of clemency or pity or compassion from God and the world, some respite from mutilations and agony, some grain of decency from one's captors, even the strongest victim begs to do any favour to please his tormentor. Even the best of human beings are frail, and breakable, and can be destroyed.

Instead of dragging the skiff over the gravel and out of view, there's another possibility, something easier, quicker and quieter. Of course, it means I shall be trapped here. I shove the boat back into the water until it is caught silently in the current and the breeze. It drifts slowly away. This confusing find for the morning patrol could suggest that someone has fallen in and drowned. At the very least, it means they won't know where I came ashore.

I am alone now with no escape route. Even supposing the two Danes are in place to meet me in three days as planned, there is no way to get back to them. Yet above all what I feel is relief.

The bicycle is a boon. What a stroke of genius by my absent ferryman! It's about ten miles to Flensburg. The bike is battered but sturdy, a solid machine with a wicker basket in front and a luggage rack at the back. Coat and hat are once again all correct. All this time, I've been wearing the German waterproof overshoes I was given at Beaulieu. I slip them off and sling them among the trees. With handbag in the basket and attaché case strapped behind, I push up to the paved road and start pedalling.

The little road rises and falls through quiet farm country, passing ploughed fields, wintry copses and meadows and streams to satisfy the heart of the most savage Teuton. From time to time corners lie whitened with snow from an earlier cold spell.

Just beyond sleeping Ulstrup two men stand in conversation at the roadside, my first Nazis, a pair of simple rural types. If anything goes wrong I have no protection except my charm and my punchblade. But they give a polite 'Morgen' with hardly a glance. I respond in kind. No mention of Hitler. As the sky lightens I cycle hard, sitting upright and making sure my coat and skirt stay modestly in place.

The road runs back towards the fjord – firth is a better word – and turns parallel with the water, giving views across a broad, handsome harbour. On the far side, shipyard warehouses and factories, covered and enclosed, project into the water. From the air, it probably looks like one huge jetty. These, then, are the U-boat works.

The ride refreshes me after the trials of the night, which already seem as if they took place not last evening, but last week. There is something uplifting and hopeful about the start of a new day. I could do with a cup of coffee, though, ersatz or not. At last the road becomes a street of houses, where in places tarmac gives way to cobbles. People are hurrying about their business: ordinary folk, young and old, no doubt Nazis all, Jew-haters to a man. Hardly anyone in military uniform. These, though, are the edges of town.

In the town centre, as at home, uniforms are everywhere. This is not like home, though. Amidst the winter coats march stridently colourful streams of militia outfits proud in brown, tan and green. And in every direction the awesome black symbol is raised over civic life, its mysterious geometry emblazoned on pure white and blood red, the vast shape like the broken wings of a raven.

There are no bomb sites that I can see, nor any war damage at all. It's very jolly. A Monday morning with a shining Germanic future ahead, Masters of the World. All cheerful on so sparkling a morning. Orderly lines have formed at a few of the shops, each neatly dressed woman ready with her ration book in hand.

Among the clamour of a town going to work no one takes the slightest notice of me. Parties of children – on their way to some sort of school or academy, I suppose – are smart in pale khaki that might be scouting kit, with neckerchief and cap. I pedal past a group of lads marching in step with voices raised in hearty song, *Die Fahne hoch! Die Reihen fest geschlossen!* (The flag high! The ranks closed tight!).

This is the famous Horst Wessel Lied, marching song of the National Socialists which has now become Germany's national anthem. It's brilliantly uplifting. A People goose-stepping to a glorious Future. Suddenly, in faultless unity, their right arms swing up into the fixed salute. Passers-by stop to listen or join in, rapt and delighted, and they too raise their right arms as the young men pass. God Almighty, what faces!

Hundreds of men and women are walking or cycling, or stand crowded in clattering primrose-yellow trams, converging on a railway station draped with three enormous swastika banners hanging from rooftop to pavement. Outside the busy station a group of respectable idlers, perhaps too early for their train and too old for military service, are gathered at a display case. Across the top of the cabinet are proclaimed the words *Deutscher! Dein Feind ist der Jude!* – "German! Your enemy is the Jew!"

I pause there too, curious. It's the latest issue of a newspaper called *Der Stürmer*, its pages clipped open for passers-by to read. The stories are delirious ravings about the pestilent Jews and the invincible greatness of Germany, with extraordinary cartoons depicting the British as caricature Jews. I glance sidelong at the other readers. They study the paper intently, endorsing the message with thoughtful nods of the head.

My first face-to-face encounter with the full leather-strapped regalia of state is approaching. Two youths are checking documents and permits at the station entrance. I struggle to relax the knot in my stomach. I slot my cycle into a bike rack beside scores of others. From a kiosk I buy the latest issue of the Nazi women's magazine *Frauen Warte* to hold in my hand and read on the train.

I do as others do, remove my hat, say Heil Hitler and hand over my papers with respectful, upright patience and an expression of modest admiration for our young protectors. I hope my neatly parted, dew-washed blonde hair and fresh complexion without a scrap of make-up, and almost-total absence of visible eyebrows, is all in keeping with Nazi ideals of feminine beauty.

'Heil Hitler, you go to, gnä' Frau?' He catches sight of the swastika pin on my coat.

'Home to Lübeck.'

'Uh.' He hands back the documents without a word and reaches for the next in line.

The station interior is like a monumental brick cathedral. Before the trip I was shown photographs of it to forestall any surprise and familiarise myself with the platforms. There's a snackbar of sorts but I'm wary of going inside. Besides, my train leaves too soon. I walk among passengers stepping up to the carriages. Not First, not Third, and definitely not Fourth (though I do see a carriage with 4 on the doors), it's Second class that passes most unnoticed, and for which I have a ticket. However, I have not passed unnoticed. Two men with no luggage pause in their conversation to turn their heads, their gaze following me, perhaps only in the usual male way. Another man, standing alone, further back, whose eyes turn my way, wears the grey-green of the Sicherheitsdienst security police. I decide to share with three ladies and two gentlemen – one of whom, though elderly and presumably retired, wears Wehrmacht uniform.

We greet one another with curt politeness and take our places on plush seats with pristine antimacassars. Entering the carriage, I give a quick Heil Hitler. My fellow passengers respond in kind. All of them discreetly observe my swastika brooch, and I discreetly observe that none of them except the old soldier wears a swastika anywhere on their person. I also observe in them a troubled moment of uncertainty and fear at the sight of it. I can guess why: no one knows who has what connections to the hierarchy.

I do admire their smart outfits and buttoned tidiness, as correct as shop-window dummies. Every one of them is scrubbed to a rosy spotlessness, and not a hair out of place. They are very decently clad and shod, and with nice baggage too, stowed on the luggage rack. Two of the ladies murmur in conversation, as does the man and the third woman. The uniformed man, solitary, is absorbed in a newspaper. I flick through my copy of *Frauen Warte,* lingering over certain articles and pictures.

The articles are well written, with stirring patriotic pictures, explaining in simple language (for ladies) how Britain's Jews started the war and how Germany's destruction of the Soviet Union will end the worldwide menace of Communism. No mention of slave labour or mass shootings. I read with interest. When Germany conquers Great Britain and liberates it from the hold of The Jew, there will be eternal brotherhood between the two nations. Turning the page, I find a feature on how to make a traditional Osterbaum – an Easter Egg tree – for the coming holiday. Then there are fashion pages, with stylish springtime ideas. These look much more ambitious than our own drab make-do-and-mend; here's a page of attractive things to buy or have made. Everything they suggest, I notice, smart blouses, shirt-waisters, costumes, dresses, has quite an emphatic collar. I look up at the ladies opposite: they all have emphatic collars.

It is jarringly incredible that so spruce and civilised-looking a crowd should be party not just to a madman's war to subjugate the world, but to torture, slavery and extermination. These neatly turned out creatures *look* human enough. No wonder they remind me of shop dummies.

All the while the wheels of the train rattle beneath us and my weary brain puzzles over the missing Norwegians. Fearful possibilities circle in my thoughts. I need to sleep, but must wait until tonight. A train carriage of Germans conjures a nightmare Utopia, an orderly population of effigies going about its tasks with relentless zeal. Red ants in a black nest. Black ants in a red nest. Crawling, crawling, devouring. Images of the restless night rise up like hallucinations. It would be nice to have some breakfast.

'Bitte, Frau! Entschuldigen Sie, gnädige Frau.' Wake up, madam. A commanding voice rouses me, and a firm tap on the arm. My eyes pop open. Standing inside the compartment and staring directly at me are two tall men in black-belted green jackets with black trim, jodhpurs, tight leather jackboots and high peaked hats.

I notice the SS symbol on their left breast pockets, and each man wears the death's head signet ring of the SS, yet it's not the SS, nor SD, at least, not if I remember what we were taught. This swaggering proliferation of forces and militias and squads and commandos and units, black and grey and green, with their holstered pistols and peaked hats, their own shiny ornaments, buckles, straps and symbols and insignia, is maddeningly confusing.

It strikes me with a quick, sick feeling, that it's possible they *do* know I'm on a train between Flensburg and Heideseebad, since one of the Norwegians may have been detained by now. It was the

Norwegian group who provided the travel permits. I struggle to compose myself and remain utterly calm lest I should start to sweat.

On the other hand, if the SS or the Gestapo *have* been informed of my movements, they will not immediately arrest me. If they have any sense, they will allow me to continue to my rendezvous. They will observe where I go and whom I meet. If they have any sense.

'Oh! Ich muss eingeschlafen sein! Entschuldigen Sie,' I say at once, with what I hope is a slight girlish embarrassment. 'Ist es meine Fahrkarte die Sie sehen moechten?' – Oh! I must have fallen asleep! Excuse me. Is it to see my train ticket?

Thank goodness even in sleep I was sitting bolt upright with legs pressed together.

'Nicht Ihre Fahrkarte, gnädige Frau. Ordnungspolizei,' explains one politely. 'Ihre Papiere, bitte.' Not your ticket, madam. Order Police. Your papers, please.

The other passengers are looking at me uneasily, from which I gather that they have not been asked for their papers. I hand them over, my identity card and Party card, holding back a surge of fear. Ah, yes, the good old Ordnungspolizei, whose intercepted messages, Percy Jarram told me, contain nothing except details of the number of people they have killed each day. The tiniest error in the documents may bring swift violence. Of course they have observed my brooch and my reading matter.

'You are coming from?' A silly question, because the train started from Flensburg and there haven't been any stops. Or might there have been an unscheduled stop while I dozed?

'Flensburg,' I reply calmly.

He examines the identity document thoroughly. He holds it up to look through the paper, and rubs it between thumb and fingertip as if checking the thickness or texture. I know, or think I know, that my papers were made by expert forgers working for SOE, copying documents taken from German prisoners, refugees, internees and others, using, as near as possible, precisely the same ink and paper.

'Going to?'

'Lübeck.' I have been worried for a while about having to say that out loud in front of other people, in case anyone speaks to me about Lübeck, or happens to have known Waltraud Weißmüller personally.

'Why did you visit Flensburg. Where did you stay?'

These questions, I know, cannot have been asked of every passenger. It would take too long, and would be impossible to check the answers. I give the reply I was instructed to give, and hope it works. 'At my aunt's house in Die Westliche Höhe.' I suppose Waltraud really had an aunt in Flensburg's Western Heights, but she too is now dead.

The officer nods thoughtfully. He hands back my papers with thanks and an apology.

When they have gone, I query my fellow passengers, 'Did they ask everybody, or just me? Maybe it's because I was asleep?'

One of the women says kindly, 'Don't worry, young lady. I think they are looking for someone who looks like you. They have to check, to be sure! One cannot be too careful.' Yet even her lips are pursed with doubt.

'Yes,' responds the gentleman in uniform, whose newspaper now rests on his lap, 'they are looking for a woman. A young woman on her own.' He gives a meaningful stare.

'Really! Ach, so...' The others exclaim with interest, grateful for this gem of inside knowledge which, in fact, is perfectly obvious.

'A foreigner, I suppose?' asks the other man.

'Oh yes, bound to be. A foreigner or a Jew or some such.'

I grimace slightly with distaste at the word *Jew*, as do some of them. 'Well,' I make my contribution to the discussion, 'if there is someone, they must catch her quickly. I'm sure they will. I have confidence that everything is in order.'

The other two women remain silent, and eye me with suspicion.

1

It was only four yards from the en-suite bathroom to the bed. Her world was becoming small. Marjorie sat heavily, her red, swollen toes just touching the floor. Carol raised each leg in turn, put the left foot through and then the right, stopped to fit a pad over the gusset. 'Up, Marjorie, lift up for me, darling. There! That's nice. Lift your arm for me.' For Marjorie had persuaded her favourite carer to ask the agency if she could do Mrs Rosen in the mornings as well.

'Can you stop saying *for me* all the time, Carol. Just *lift your arm* is fine.' She lifted it.

'OK. Now the other arm, Marjorie. Yes, lift it for me. Oh, sorry, I mean lift it! Higher, darling. Hand through. Can't you get your hand through?' Carol tugged the damaged fingers through the sleeve.

'How's Wayne this morning?'

'He's at work.'

'Still not sleeping with him?'

The carer pressed her lips together. 'I shouldn't've told you that.'

'No, you shouldn't. How many years have you been married?'

'I don't remember. I'd rather forget.'

'I was twenty-six when Harry and I got married. I remember it well, that day.'

As Marjorie recalled, a humourless clerk at Chelsea Register Office asked them to read the declaration, and showed them where to sign. It was over in minutes. Harry slipped the £3 Utility wedding ring on her finger and kissed her on the cheek. There was no wedding car. The new Mr and Mrs Harry Rosen walked away hand in hand along the Kings Road, and went to Lyons for tea and cake, the last occasion they were free to use their staff discount.

Just before the ceremony Harry mentioned that his name wasn't actually Rosen. 'Rosenzweig sounds like an enemy alien,' he said.

'Why didn't you tell me? You should change it officially, Harry.'

'Oh, and it isn't Harry,' he laughed, 'while we're on the subject.'

'Harry! Are you serious?'

'Yes, it's Chaim. I'm Chaim Rosenzweig. Pleased to meet you. Do you think Rose has a better sound to it than Rosen? More English. I should call myself Rose.'

'My poor un-English rose!' Marjorie mocked him. 'Rose, Rosen, Rosenzweig are *all* foreign, Harry. This should have been dealt with.'

Carol guided Marjorie to the living room (another eight yards), lowered her into her chair, plumped up the cushion behind. 'So, d'you marry during the war?' she asked.

'No, we had to wait till our war work came to an end.'

'Me and Wayne had a lovely wedding. White dress, bridesmaids, flowers, confetti, the lot. The reception was really glamorous.'

'We didn't think about flowers. Harry had a carnation, come to think of it. No reception.' She remembered that nothing could keep his hair in place on that lovely brainy dome of a head. She wore a decent jacket and skirt that was to remain her best costume for years. 'We had survived the war. Nothing else mattered.'

'I loved Wayne on our wedding day. Maybe I still do. Maybe he still loves me. It's hard to know.'

'Forget love. That's for the birds. The thing is to admire each other and enjoy being together.'

'It is *much* too late for that, Marjorie. We're way past that point. The point of no return.'

The carer became quiet for a few minutes as she wrote in her log book. At last she closed the book and put it in its folder.

'Carol, about not sleeping with your husband.'

'Come on, that's strictly *my* business! I wish I hadn't told you.'

'Wayne went off to work this morning. He's busy with his job. You're a grown-up woman, you know how a man's mind works. We won't go into details, but there's something he wants, and he thinks about it on and off all day long. Things catch his eye that make him think more. One way or another, he will have that thing he wants. If not with you then with anyone. Even against his will he'll do foolish things for it, risk everything for it, destroy his family for it. Whether he loves you or not. You do know that about men, don't you Carol?'

'Marjorie! You're not seriously suggesting I should sleep with him just because that's what *he* wants? *You* wouldn't have done that. Honestly Marje, what about *my* feelings?'

'Feelings!' Marjorie snorted. She gave Carol the advice she gave any friend. 'Don't think about feelings. Think about goals. My motto is, focus on your objective and do what you have to do. Tell Wayne straight, you want to make it up but he must be different with Aidan.'

'Blimey, I can't believe I'm hearing this. I'm shocked.'

'You want to stay married? A marriage is made in the bedroom.'

'So they say.'

'By the way, Wayne's a plumber, isn't he? D'you think he'd do a little job for me? Fix a leaking radiator and change a washer. I'd pay his normal overtime rate, cash in hand.'

'Be happy to, I should think.'

* * *

It's evening when I reach Heideseebad, the last few miles of the journey on the wooden seats of a dear little local Bummelzug rattling along a single track down to the Baltic shore. From the resort's small station I step out into utter darkness. It takes me a few minutes to find the walkway that leads to the beach. Even in the gloom one senses water ahead, can hear it faintly, sea touching land. I must establish first if anyone is following me. Stepping down a rough, grassy slope of sand dune, I stand stock still and gaze around. It's hard to get much impression of the place. I heard no footsteps. The glow of a cigarette might show anyone close by, but there is nothing.

Sand blows across the wooden promenade as I stride beside the beach. I turn abruptly to retrace my steps. Still no one is following. Reaching the guesthouse where I have a booking, I stand in obscurity, studying the place. It's a fine brick villa with a flagpole on which, presumably, the Nazi flag is raised in daytime. The original crest above the door – I suppose it was an eagle before, since the place is called Adler – has been replaced with the Nazi eagle. There are no motor cars parked, no one standing about.

Frau Schneider opens the door with wide-eyed, tongue-tied astonishment. Although I have a booking, she seems shocked to see me. Well-padded, middle-aged and tidy, she's wearing traditional costume, and could so easily be the relaxed and cheerful landlady. Instead, her welcome is flustered and nervous. She recovers herself quickly.

'Your train was late?'

'No, no. On time!' I reply pleasantly. 'Forgive me, I have kept you waiting. I took the night air beside the water for a few moments. The cold has never bothered me. It's so nice and so still tonight.'

Frau Schneider nods, clearly troubled. She first carefully points out the bomb shelter in the basement, then leads me upstairs to my room. It's charming and comfortable in country style, with carved, polished wood and an inviting bed covered with a heavy eiderdown.

Although the evening meal has been finished and cleared away, she kindly proposes a plate of food. I very willingly accept. I've had nothing since an early lunch in Lübeck. 'Please, before anything, complete the guest registration form.'

She watches as I write, scrutinising every stroke of the pen. I hand her my Party membership card for identification. She seems much reassured by the sight of it.

'You come from Lübeck?' she asks, reading my address with a curious expression.

'Ja.'

'Me too.'

My heart plummets. 'What those British murderers have done to our beautiful town! Have you seen? My family home, destroyed.' My heart is in my mouth lest she, of all people, be someone who knew Waltraud Weißmüller personally. There would be no talking my way out of that. 'Our home was destroyed too,' I add, to explain away any sign of stress on my part.

Thank goodness I took the trouble to visit the town! Apart from checking I had not been followed, and resting in a Gaststätte over a plate of meatloaf and turnips, the real purpose of my stop in Lübeck was indeed so that I could make sensible comments about the place. I had to look at the damage the RAF had done, assess how the population is taking it, and in particular see with my own eyes the address on my ID card.

'We lived in...' and she names a street. I think I'm supposed to know where it is.

'Let's not discuss it,' I suggest. 'We shall pay them back.'

'And my little sister in Essen...' she says quietly. 'I am not being unpatriotic, but one naturally worries. Even the Führer is concerned for his loved ones, if it is permitted to say so.'

With luck her sister is already dead or soon will be. Our intensive bombing of Essen and the Ruhr region, as far as I know, has been a great success and is still continuing. I hope it continues until the whole damn place is reduced to dust.

'Does she have children with her?' I ask tenderly.

'No, they have been sent away. Where they have gone, it is no longer safe there, either.'

Ah, I think, you thought you could sit safely in your new Germany and rub your hands in glee as you blow everyone else to pieces.

'And is she all right?' I ask.

'I haven't heard.'

I can only nod sympathetically.

At last my head rests on a soft pillow. Germans are good at bedding, I always found. Yet, tired as I am, my eyes stay open, staring around, at the ceiling, at the window, at the door. At night it's easier to imagine the unimaginable. Our instructors warned us: they don't beat you with fists or with batons, but with an iron bar. They don't prod or probe but swing it hard, striking at bones: cracking shins, knees, arms, crushing fingers. Women, there are some special injuries reserved especially for you. It can be helpful to have some phrase to repeat, or to count to twenty over and over again. I visualise being woken by shouts and kicks and dragged from my bed by the Gestapo.

What wakes me, though, is an extraordinary roar outside. As I peek from behind the blackout curtain, a huge number of planes approaches from the sea. Searchlights pick out the good old red, white and blue RAF roundel on their wings. They make a terrifying sight, a great moonlit armada filling the sky.

So this is what it's like when "our boys" reach their destination!

The thought of the pilots, fellows like Peggy's George in the cockpit of each plane, intent upon the job in hand while braced for death, almost brings a tear to my eyes, their young manliness, their fresh goodness and decency, their valour, their tremendous innocence.

Searchlights track several planes. The pilots take evasive action at once, turning and climbing steeply. Soon I hear the ringing crackle of flak, like fireworks. No doubt some of our young men have just been felled. I think of their mothers receiving the news, women in the narrow hallways and little sitting rooms of Britain. Then comes, from far away, the familiar thud of bombs ceaselessly exploding like the heavy tread of a monstrous creature, shaking the earth, crushing whatever lies beneath its feet. Ribnitz, perhaps, or Rostock.

Oddly, it brings Sodom and Gomorrah to mind, cities consumed by fire because of their inhumanity. Then, annoyingly, I find I am pondering a Biblical question… suppose there are ten good men in an evil city, should it be destroyed?

The bombs I made at Elstow were dropped long ago. I wonder where, on which cities, and if there really was anyone good in that city. Ten good people anywhere in this country, or ten thousand, or a million, would long for it to be consumed by fire. By now, everyone good has been executed, or fled. In any case, whether there are ten good men here or not, consumed by fire this land must most certainly be. I return to bed and sleep soundly.

Breakfast, as in any convivial Kneipe or Gaststätte, has everyone sitting around one big table in a gemütliche dining room warmed by a great log fire blazing in the hearth. Swastikas, together with a large framed portrait of Hitler and photographs of high-ranking Nazis who have stayed at the guesthouse, adorn the walls and mantelpiece.

I introduce myself, and the others give me their names very genially. We laugh about the night's air raid. Everyone is clean, tidy and smart. We are only five in total, four women and a man – two young wives in their twenties (myself included, of course), another married woman of maybe thirty or so, an attractive young Fräulein, and the avuncular Kapitän. This suits me well, as my plan is to be amiable to all, and pass some time with each of the women.

Frau Schneider, smiling with the bonhomie of her profession, lays out sliced ham, cold cuts, Würst and cheese, baskets of fragrant fresh Brötchen, bowls of quark and real butter and marmalade, as abundant as if there were no war. This morning she shows none of the fearful anxiety I saw last night, although she does glance in my direction too often and, unless I am imagining things, rather icily. Then, I'm not sure that she doesn't sometimes look at the others in the same way.

'I meant to ask you, Frau Schneider,' I say, 'what happened to the pier? It's only a few years since I was last in Heideseebad, and it was alright then. Was it the English?'

'No, not the bombs,' she answers. 'It was Nature. The pier and boardwalks were destroyed by sea and ice last winter.'

The Kapitän makes an amusing point: 'Bad as winter is, at least it is not as bad as those British Jews!'

That becomes our main topic of discussion as we tuck in, and the mood is of good-humoured outrage at the effrontery of the British who are out of their minds to take on the might of the Reich and have been duped by Jewish Financiers and International Jewry. I certainly don't argue with this, but am interested to see who among the women expresses doubt. Fortunately, none does. I would not want my contact to be in any way suspect.

A discourse on the fine distinction between Jewish Financiers and International Jewry leads onto the big news item, the Fabrikaktion or Großaktion Juden, which I gather is a final round-up of German Jews. I listen spellbound to the gentleman's account of how well it is being carried out, Jews being detained without warning at their place of work and taken straight to assembly points for deportation to the East. It's quick, efficient and humane, he declares. I must nod with approval. The ladies turn to discussing a peculiar protest in the heart of Berlin, about which I too am assumed to be aware, at which Aryan wives of Jews in detention have demanded that their husbands be freed. I gather, from what is said, that most of the men *have* been released – 'for the time being,' as our gentleman companion puts it.

The consensus at table is that such women should also be detained, and banished to Sachsenhausen or some similar camp. In whispered fascination the ladies murmur sotto voce how unthinkably disgusting it must be, to be *wed* to a Jew, and be, you know, by one! There are grimaces and horrified giggles as lurid details are contemplated without being uttered. The Kapitän smirks and pretends not to notice.

Venting against the Juden gives profound satisfaction, a pleasant sensation of being all of one mind. But these are no ordinary Jew-haters; truly they have a mania. I join in with the rest. For a moment I wonder why I do not feel afraid, but the only thing that alarms me is that my contact may dissent and so give herself away.

That's why I decide to use the password immediately, saying blandly, 'To change the subject to something more agreeable, I believe they make a kind of Pflaumenkuchen here, don't they?'

The slightly older married woman says, 'Yes, with Zwetschgen. Is it made here?'

The Kapitän growls with throaty amusement and shakes his head. He's been visiting the Ostsee coast since he was a child and has never heard of such a thing.

'But most places have something of their own, like the Spätzle in Schwabia, don't they?' says the pretty Fräulein.

The young wife confesses, 'I love Pflaumenkuchen mit Streusel!'

Frau Schneider laughs brightly at the confusion, 'You are thinking of Zwetschgenkuchen, Frau Jünger! We have Zwetschgen here only in summer! But no Pflaumenkuchen, Frau Weißmüller.'

I laugh. 'Ach, I must be mistaken.'

Later I mention that I shall walk into town, and perhaps look at the shops. Would any of the ladies care to accompany me?

One of them thinks that would be very nice. It's Frau Frick, the young woman who said she loves Pflaumenkuchen. She's not my contact. Which is good.

Yes, with Zwetschgen. Is it made here? is the correct reply, and *Ach, I must be mistaken* my response to that.

As the group disperses, Frau Schneider begins clearing the table. Seeing that I have not yet left the room, she enquires breezily, 'Frau Weißmüller, may I ask – what brings you here at this time of year?' I sense she is sounding me out for some reason.

'Just to be somewhere safe,' I reply, 'and to calm myself. Did I mention that my husband fell last year? In the East. I try to remain cheerful. I must get used to life without him.'

'Ach so. My sympathies. You must be proud.'

Frau Frick and I pass villas and guesthouses on our way into the centre of little Heideseebad. Frau Frick knows the resort, and leads us to a delightful confectioner's in the main street. I have no idea what is ersatz and what is genuine, but we buy some biscuits and a circular box of coffee-flavoured chocolates called Scho-Ka-Kola, which she says she adores. We pause at a shop selling postcards – yes, even in the midst of war – and I buy a few cards 'to send', as I tell her.

Hanging grandly across a civic building, a banner in large Gothic letters proclaims *Juden sind hier unerwünscht!* – Jews not wanted here! It seems weirdly redundant in a small resort where there are no Jews, either as residents or visitors, and probably never were many. The building is the local police station. I turn to Frau Frick, but she has not noticed the banner, which may be a common sight.

On the beachside promenade, I make a point of exchanging one of my biscuits for a piece of Frau Frick's chocolate. Later, we peer closely at my postcards, trying to work out how long ago the photos were taken, before making our way back to the Pension.

In friendly fashion, there we all sit down together for lunch. Afterwards, we move to a cosy lounge where a log fire crackles and burns in the grate. I take an armchair beside my contact, Frau Jünger. We talk amiably and politely. She's a handsome, guarded woman, must be in her mid-thirties, with good features, an elegant manner, dark blonde hair tightly pinned up, and lightly flecked hazel eyes that reveal nothing at all. She looks refined and comfortably off. She's wearing an expensive-looking fawn woollen suit in a boxy, slightly military style, and a pale blue blouse with a modest white bow at the neck and a lacework collar. She too wears a swastika lapel pin.

I ask her, as Frau Schneider asked me, 'How do you come to be here at this time of year?'

'My husband encourages me to go away for safety now that there are so many raids. I've stayed here several times. We used to come before the war, too, with the children. It was a lovely place.'

'Your children, they're not still in Berlin, I hope?'

'Both safe at Hitlerjugend KLV – Hitler Youth evacuation camp.'

I smile as if reassured. 'Ah, good.' I know it's risky to delve into personal matters. And inappropriate – after all, she can't question me, except as Frau Weißmüller. Nevertheless I do ask her, 'How old are they?' I am curious about this brave woman.

She catches my eye as if to warn me away from the minefield of our real lives. Yet she replies. 'My girl is ten years old, and the boy twelve. They enjoy the camps. They are perfectly happy.'

Am I to share in the happiness of these little members of Hitler Youth? Just because they are her children? I should not have asked about them. Such discussion is indeed pointless. It takes a moment to know how to respond. In the end there is nothing I can say. 'Fancy a walk before it gets dark?' I suggest. 'The weather is still nice.'

As soon as we are outside and walking, I explain how useful it would be to agree some sort of code, in case she should ever need to send a message, or refer to people or places, or arrange a meeting. She looks really alarmed, but I press on. 'It's very secure.' I explain how a book cipher works. 'We agree on a book to use. It could be anything, a novel, a dictionary, *Mein Kampf*, anything. Using page numbers, line numbers, the text of the book becomes your code. It works because no one knows what book you are using. You see?'

Frau Jünger brushes the idea away as foolish. 'In Germany every ordinary letter may be read. Everything is scrutinised. Everything is overheard. Everything is reported. Everything is known. Sending anything in code would lead at once to arrest, torture and execution. You may as well send messages without code – the consequence is the same.' She is emphatic.

We take a different route than the one I followed this morning, but again I make sure that Frau Jünger and I exchange one or two small items and look at magazines together. I see another *Der Stürmer* display, which we pass without a second glance. We continue down to the promenade and stop to gaze out to sea. I leave my handbag open and gesture towards it.

Gingerly, lest we damage our shoes, we step onto the sand and inspect one of the large, elaborate wicker beach chairs lined up at the top of the beach, away from the water. They are not something I am familiar with. 'Oh, yes,' explains Frau Jünger, 'these are common on the Ostsee beaches. Because of the wind. Each man his own suntrap!' As we lean forward, the two of us momentarily concealed by the wicker roof of a beach chair, Frau Jünger pushes a small package into my bag and clips it shut. The whole movement takes less than a second. We return onto the promenade, stopping to point at something on the shore and share an amused comment.

As we stroll, I ask if there is anything else she thinks we should know. She says something top secret is going on at a place along the coast, called Peenemünde, on the island of Usedom. 'My husband used to send me to Zinnowitz, near Peenemünde. It's a nice place, very popular, a Jew-free resort like Heideseebad. Now he says I must not go to Zinnowitz in case the enemy find out about Peenemünde, where a new long-range weapon is being tested.' She gives me the exact location of the Peenemünde works. Suddenly I realise that I like Erika Jünger very much. She strikes me, incredibly, as humane and intelligent as well as wonderfully cool and courageous. I wish I could speak to her 'out of character', but dare not.

However, I do say, 'Frau Schneider suspects something about me.'

'It's not that, exactly,' Frau Jünger reveals. 'Yesterday she told me in confidence that the Gestapo had visited her. They asked her to look out for a woman travelling alone, and inform the local Blockwart, block warden, if anyone arrives. Apparently she laughed it off, and told them most of her guests are women on their own.'

'Why on earth did she mention it to you?'

'Because of my husband's position. I've stayed with her several times. I'm above suspicion. She asked me to help her – to let her know if I have doubts about any of the other guests.'

'That's extremely lucky. How do you know she didn't mention it to anyone else?'

'She probably did.'

'Well, that does suggest she's not an informer. If she were, she wouldn't have said anything. All the same, take great care, Frau Jünger. They obviously have some information about me.'

'And you, Frau Weißmüller, be vigilant, even more so. I don't think Frau Schneider will go to the Gestapo. It would ruin her guesthouse to be involved with them.'

'Frau Jünger, may I ask…' Since we have already talked so frankly, I plunge in with another matter. 'I wonder if there is some way a train ticket… in view of your husband's position… to get across the border into Denmark.'

She shakes her head. 'Impossible.' We stop walking and I make a show of offering another biscuit. 'Especially now. The Führer has closed the border. The railways into Denmark are only for troop movements that will be announced tomorrow.'

'You actually know that, Frau Jünger?'

She nods. And after one second, 'If your travel arrangements have gone wrong, my dear, you are in very grave danger. So am I, because what I have given you could only have come from me, and we have been seen together. If you are captured... well, I'm sure you know, it will mean an unhappy end for both of us.' She smiles gaily and pauses to point out a large seabird. We follow it with our eyes.

The bird seems to stop in mid-air, hovering and watching. 'Nothing has gone wrong, Frau Jünger,' I reassure her untruthfully. 'I merely wondered if that would be a safer way out.'

'It is never safe to change your arrangements.'

We smile at one another and gasp with admiration as our bird drops into the water and emerges with a wriggling fish in its beak.

C arol's husband stood at the door with his toolkit in his hand. Carol's description told part of the tale. Big, well-built, with a no-nonsense manner and a ferociously insincere smile, a crewcut and a tattoo on each finger, he looked as Carol had described him, a hard man. Marjorie saw a man without focus, confidence or purpose. He lacked empathy. He was weak, aimless.

'Thanks for coming, Wayne! I'm Marjorie.' She pushed ahead with her rollator. Wasting no time, she straight away remarked, 'I met your son, by the way, Aidan. Clever boy.'

'You reckon? Always in trouble. The police have been round.' At her request he made two mugs of instant coffee. He clearly expected to get on with the job in hand, but she gestured him to pause awhile.

'Yes, Carol said he was a nuisance. Quick learner, though, isn't he? I taught him to play chess just like that.'

Wayne smirked. 'You what? Chess?'

'No really, he's brilliant. See that exercise book on the table? Says *Raven's Matrices* on the front. Carol said you were in the Army. In my day army recruits used to do this test. Do they still?'

'Nah, we do something on a screen. Army BARB, it's called.'

'Have a crack at these, tell me how it compares. Fancy a biscuit?'

He pondered the diagrams. She said, 'Now look at this.' She presented him with Aidan's answer sheet. She had ticked his correct answers, one after another, page after page. 'Aidan is super-bright. You should be proud of him.'

'Incredible.' Wayne threw out a laugh and drained his coffee. 'Must've been cheating.'

'There's no cheating with this. The answers aren't in the book. Look out for that boy of yours. Don't want to waste a brain like that.'

Wayne answered good-humouredly. 'I suppose you've gone and told the brat he's cleverer than his Mum and Dad.'

'I wouldn't do that! Trouble is, he probably already knows. He's smarter than other people. That's his problem. He wants to respect you, but he wants you to respect him, too. Tricky one for any parent, isn't it? I know what it's like, our three kids are *nothing* like me and my husband. Well, I'll show you the radiator. The valve is leaking. Couldn't change it to a thermostatic one, could you?'

She sat down on the spare bed to chat while he worked. He squatted to examine the radiator valve. She said, 'Carol mentioned you did two tours in Afghanistan, one in Iraq. She said it was tough going, and I can believe it.'

'Oh, Carol told you that, did she? Always blathering. It wasn't "tough". People can't imagine.'

'She did say you'd had some bad experiences.'

'No offence, but she shouldn't've said anything. She has no idea. You have no idea. No one does.'

'How d'you know what I've experienced? A lot of people my age have killed someone. A lot had a friend killed. A lot saw sickening sights, a lot did sickening things. Some of us women saw action, too. It's *you* that don't realise. We say nothing. No one wants to hear.'

He stopped what he was doing, put his tools on the floor. He was trying to work out if she had insulted him. 'To be honest, I did sort of forget you must've been in the Second World War. And, aren't you that lady that laid out three burglars? Carol told me.'

'Everyone in my generation knows what you're dealing with. Our house was destroyed by a bomb. My little brother got killed in the blast. Mother never got over it. Father died from a war injury, too.'

He looked up, thoroughly shocked. 'Sorry about your brother. What I meant was, *most* people have no idea. When your truck is blown up and your mate loses his eyes and his legs, and you're not allowed to go after anyone for it. We gave 'em sweets – literally handed out sweets. Hearts and bloody minds.'

'Is that what happened to you, Wayne?'

'Let's get on with this radiator.'

'Tell me about it, if you like. I'd like to hear every detail. There's nothing you can say to me that you shouldn't say.' She waited.

And in a few angry sentences he described the moment his truck was blown up, and the terrified, blood-soaked hour that followed. To which she listened in grim silence and then said only, 'Tell you what, you can go over that story again to me any time you like. Or anything else. Did you learn your plumbing in the army?'

'Yep. Royal Engineers.'

'It's not all bad, then. You've come home with both your eyes, all your arms and legs and a useful trade.'

'Yep.'

'You ought to build on that. Put your training to good use. It would all've been for nothing otherwise.'

'I've got a job.'

'No, I mean, sign up at Sandcliffe Institute for Level 3 plumbing. Go for the gas certificate. You'd earn much more, be a happier man.'

'You reckon?'

'I always say, the secret of happiness for a man is to make his family proud of him.'

Wayne laughed hard, turning back to the radiator. 'Oh, that's what you always say, is it? Got any more pearls of wisdom like that one?'

They chuckled like two men bantering. 'But it would be a good thing to do, wouldn't it, Wayne?'

'I don't know. OK, this valve is just loose, that's all. There's nothing wrong with it, literally nothing. Still want me to change it?'

'Hang on, Wayne, another thing about Aidan. I'd be happy to tutor him. No charge. In the holidays, on weekends, after school, anytime. I'll coach him to pass exams, or get the extra help for him.'

'What exams?'

'Entrance exam of a decent school. Somewhere like Yeobright's, in Dorset. He'd need a bursary to cover the fees. You know how to apply and all that?'

He shook his head in determined refusal. 'Jeez. Thanks, but no. We're fine as we are.'

'I thought of it because Carol's been so good to me. Above and beyond. And I admire what you did in Afghanistan and Iraq.'

'Aidan doesn't want to go to a place like Yeobright's. No way.'

'Yes he does. I talked it through with him, Wayne. Going to a top prep school with clever boys instead of –'

'Does my wife know? She's been keeping things from me lately.'

'No, I never discussed it with Carol. I thought I'd come to you first – you're his father. That's why I asked you to do a bit of work for me, so Carol wouldn't suspect anything. Seems to me your talents are being wasted and so are your son's. I hate waste. Especially, I hate to see talent go to waste. I discuss these things with Aidan while we're playing chess or doing a bit of studying.'

'Studying! Aidan?'

'It's up to you, Wayne. Talk it over with Carol.'

'Boarding school, isn't it – Yeobright's?'

'I thought you'd be *pleased*. Get him off your hands and be proud of him at the same time. And they get a lot of boys into Winchester.'

'What, Winchester, like Winchester school, y'mean, or–?' Perhaps he thought she meant Winchester Comprehensive.

'Winchester College, Wayne. They have fantastic bursaries. I do think Aidan has it in him to win a scholarship.'

'What, Aidan?' As blankly as if he had all along misunderstood what Marjorie was talking about.

'Yes, Aidan. I'll get the address of Sandcliffe Institute for you.'

'No, got it here.' He held up his phone to show her the web page.

'Good! And yes, change the valve for me. Help yourself to another coffee. I'm going to have a lie down in my room.'

* * *

In my room I unwrap Erika Jünger's package. It contains better material than I thought possible, scores of classified documents on microfilm, copies of one-time pads dated for future use, and code sheets printed on the finest silk.

I have only ever seen genuine one-time pads while in training, and those resembled a London bus conductor's book of tickets. These are far superior, absolutely miniscule, the pages thinner than anything I've ever seen, and print that it needs a magnifying glass even to detect that these are letters of the alphabet. On the squares of silk, a line of plain text details places and dates when the code must be used. The silk fits into the piping around the edge of my handbag. The pads I sew into the shoulders of my dress.

When it's done, there is little time left for an outing with the young Fräulein. I suggest a brisk walk to the beach and back, to sharpen the appetite. She happily agrees, laughing that her appetite needs no sharpening. A sea mist is building and dusk falls as we stand looking across the sands. I offer her a sweet. She shakes her head and declines. I propose that she have one for later. This she accepts with a mischievous grin. We stride back to the guesthouse in time for a convivial drink before the meal. All sit merrily around the dining table and logs blaze in the hearth. Frau Schneider brings roast pork, delicious potatoes fried with bacon, and heaps of tender, tasty kale. I haven't eaten so well in years. Ah, a good life in the brave new Germania. Not the place for anyone who keeps kosher, but there are to be no such people in the new Germania.

Frau Schneider willingly makes a packed lunch for my journey. 'So, back home to Lübeck, Frau Weißmüller?' she inquires.

'No, I am going to Greifswald. I have cousins there.'

'Ach so. That is a pretty town, if it hasn't been bombed.'

I settle the bill and bid farewell to Pension Adler. My first task is to visit the Heideseebad police. I gather from Erika Jünger that no one goes voluntarily to a police station anymore. Rather, they merely send anonymous notes denouncing one another for crimes real and imaginary. With its inevitable fulsome confession and plea for mercy, this is usually sufficient evidence for the Volksgerichtshof, the People's Court, to pass a summary sentence of beheading.

I climb steps to a double door between immense red swastika drapes. So few members of the public venture inside nowadays that they have done away with a reception desk. Instead, a gang of brutes pointing machine guns order me to state my business.

'Heil Hitler. I have information about a crime against the state. I must speak to an inspector very urgently.'

'Oh, ja? Write a letter, Frau,' replies one of the thugs indifferently.

Despite this poor beginning, I do end up speaking to an inspector. He is crisply turned out, tie perfectly knotted, cap on straight, leather straps and holster and jackboots all polished to a black shine. When our eyes meet briefly, it's clear that my upright respectability and dignity could be stripped away and reduced to whimpering and snivelling tears at the click of a finger. But then, as I hope he can see in my own eyes, so could his. In this mad hierarchy, only fools think they are safe.

We step into a small side room with a desk and two chairs, but remain standing as in confidential tone I give him my information. 'Herr Inspector, this is what happened in Pension Adler last night. The wirtin, Frau Schneider, told her guests that Gestapo officers had asked her in absolute confidence to look out for someone. Frau Schneider openly told us she would not report any of them. She even made fun of the Gestapo, and certain guests laughed. Some of us were very unhappy with her attitude.'

The inspector looks astonished. 'This happened at Pension Adler?'

'Shocking, isn't it? Not the sort of place… I don't know what has come over Frau Schneider lately. I came here as soon as possible. If officers did indeed ask Frau Schneider in confidence to look out for someone, she should not have told us, and her attitude… but please do not tell her I said so.'

'I will inform the Gestapo office. Some of our own men will also call on Pension Adler.'

I ask if he might also deal severely with the unpatriotic officer, standing outside his door, who insulted me and dismissed my concerns. Such people are a disgrace to the Reich. The inspector looks furious. He says he will see to it at once.

'By the way, Herr Inspector,' I add, 'Frau Schneider has the very best of food and drink in her Gasthof. I can recommend it.'

'Thank you for your diligence, gnädige Frau. Heil Hitler!'

'My duty as a German, Herr Inspector. Heil Hitler!'

A distraction at the Pension may delay things. They may even arrest Frau Schneider and some of her guests. They're all Party members, so I'm not concerned about their fate, except for Frau Jünger, who says she is above suspicion in any case. It would be nice to meet her again in another world, or another lifetime.

At Rövershagen junction I leave the train and change to another going to Ribnitz, the wrong direction. At a small station I get off again and cross the platform. No one else has left the train. No one is following me. I board another train, heading in the right direction. The copy of *Frauen Warte* stays on my lap though I've read it all the way through, and to pass the hours I sometimes even look at my dreadful novel, *Volk ohne Raum*. I show my papers as calmly as any other Nazi. They pass muster without hesitation. People come and go in the carriages, artisans, soldiers, old folk, young mothers, all eyeing one another warily. To everyone I say Heil Hitler. With so many detours and delays and screeching unscheduled halts to let troop trains pass, it's evening before I reach Flensburg.

When I step out of the station, there's an icy wind blowing and it looks like snow. A sheet of cloud is moving swiftly to cover the whole sky. People are hurrying across the square. Night is falling and there are no streetlights.

My bike is still on the rack outside. I strap my small case on the rack and ride one way and then another, making a circuit back to the station. No one has followed.

It's almost certain that there won't be a boatman waiting for me. Yet I feel Erika Jünger was right: don't change the arrangements. I shall go to the rendezvous point as agreed. If no boatman is there, I shall simply do whatever is necessary to solve the problem. That is the correct approach. Continue with the operation as planned even if it ends in failure, arrest and the L-pill.

I turn off the main road onto the quiet lanes I used before, cycling in the cold and dark as if all is fine. If challenged, well, my papers are in order. At last I spot the rough, potholed track that reaches down through the woods to the waterside pick-up point.

On an impulse I don't stop. I ride past without a pause in case someone is watching. Besides, I would like to know what lies along the shore. Approaching tiny Fördehaven harbour, I see steel fences, warning signs and searchlights. I turn back, looking for another way. A cart track leads past a farm in the direction of the forest. But a farm may have dogs, a farmer and a shotgun. Finally I make out a path skirting a field that leads into the woods.

The hiss of wind grasping at treetops drowns out any other sound. The fjord waters, visible beyond silhouettes of trees, shift and move as if preparing for a sleepless night. I place the bicycle on the ground, hide Waltraud's case among bracken and strap my handbag against my body. Unburdened I pass swiftly between trees towards the water.

The beach next to me is exactly where, just days ago, I tried to pull a little rowing boat across the unhelpful pebbles. I pause to take stock and only then do I notice: a small patrol boat, probably a coastguard vessel, engine silenced, hidden in shadows at the shoreline. It has plenty of military kit on deck, including fixed guns. There are no exterior lights and no light on board. Almost invisible, a swastika flag at the stern sways slowly back and forth as if alive.

This is a godsend indeed.

I sit down among the undergrowth and slip off my woollen stockings. From this point, I proceed more cautiously, sometimes lying flat in the frosty bed of fallen leaves. At the edge of the wood, where it meets the gravel beach, I'm hardly five paces from the patrol boat, which has backed up to the shore and let down a ramp. The glow of a cigarette, about twenty yards along the beach, catches my eye. Two uniformed men are sitting there on the ground, idly talking in hushed voices, waiting with their weapons.

It takes a while to realise that there is also someone on board the boat. An officer mans the bridge, standing or sitting by a narrow unlit window. It's impossible to see how he is armed.

With infinite care I assemble my ingredients like baking a cake. *Cool, calm preparation*, I almost hear the voice of my instructor. Knots tied in the stockings just as she showed me, hair in place under my headscarf, knitting needle to hand.

No sooner have I readied myself to board the vessel than something unexpected happens. One of the two men squatting on the beach stands up and walks towards me, a machine pistol swinging on a shoulder strap. I remain motionless. His boots stride unevenly in the dark, unsure of the stones underfoot. He pauses to open a hip flask and takes a swig. He puts the flask away and stares meditatively at the beach, at the trees, out to sea. He pushes his helmet back, sweeps a large hand over a skull rounded and muscular, shaved smooth. He walks again, passes the patrol boat and is now so near that I wonder if he'll bump right into me. I can smell the schnapps.

Seen so close, he's monstrous, powerfully built, a foot taller than me, with massive clenched jaw. Like a bull-terrier waddling about on its back legs, he takes a couple of weary steps into the trees. He is standing not a yard away and notices nothing.

He unbuttons his coat and reaches to his trousers. Under the coat he wears a belt with a holstered handgun and a sheathed knife. I'm surprised to see the silver pips; it is the uniform of an SS officer. In the dark, I had not recognised the men's outfits. The fingers of his right hand deftly unbutton the fly, feel inside and pull out his penis. Urine gushes out in a splashing stream. Some droplets fall on me. While he pisses, he raises the flask in his other hand, throws back his head and takes a deep draft. It's hard to imagine how a man could make himself more vulnerable.

There is little time to weigh up the alternatives. His coat and tunic could be a problem for the needle. As for a hand strike directly onto the neck, my position, his height, the darkness, and the possibility of his body making a noise as it falls are part of the calculation.

With no further thought in an instant I have pulled the stocking tightly around the unsuspecting neck. He puts up less of a struggle than the lifeless mannequins we used in training. The knots are well positioned, crushing the jugular and windpipe at once and, I think, killing him literally within a heartbeat. The creature falls against me like a heavy log, the naked penis suddenly weirdly erect like a final Nazi salute. I lower him onto the ground. He has no pulse.

As fast and quietly as possible, his jacket, knife and gunbelt are off. I put them over my own clothing. His companion, if he can see me at all in this darkness, may mistake me for him. There's a leather pouch of documents, too. I retrieve my stocking and, with his machine pistol over my chest, in a few strides I'm across the beach to board the vessel.

Practically at a run, I'm on the bridge and shutting the door behind me. Certainly this is a vessel of the Küstenwache, the coastguard. 'Obersturmführer, sind Sie das?' says a voice from the wheel – Is that you? Even as he turns to see who's there, he feels the knife edge on his throat. My training requires that he be killed at once and without a word, but I may need his help. 'Schweigen, oder du stirbst sofort.' – Silence, or you die at once.

I pull him away from the window. This one is a beast of a different shape, even more horrible to behold. Small and feeble, with large staring eyes, he looks like a deranged, hairless Chihuahua. 'Just a girl!' he exclaims. 'Are you the–?' At which I draw blood which runs down his shirt. He's in Kriegsmarine uniform, not Küstenwache, and, I guess, under SS command.

'Silence! Any further sound at all and I shall cut out your tongue. Take off your jacket and trousers.'

He shakes his head in disbelief and reluctance. Covered in filth and dead leaves from the woods, I must be an awful sight. Ferocious yet terrified, the little creature visibly trembles, hastily unbuttoning and unbuckling. With the uniform beside him on the floor, he begins to weep quietly, holding his hand over the wound on his neck as blood continues to trickle through his fingers.

This wretch is like a little boy with a burst balloon. He really has lost his bluster. It might be satisfying to let him know that I am not merely 'just a girl', but 'just a Jew'. There's no time for such nonsense, and no point in it. Instead I ask, 'Where's the wireless set?'

He shows me at once, frantically gesturing. The communications equipment has a simple on-off switch. 'Ach so. Now I need some rope. And,' I ask, 'where's the fire axe?'

No doubt he thinks I'm either going to hang him or cut off his head, as the tears begin to pour down a face contorted with anguish. He leans forward and suddenly wets himself, the liquid dripping out of his shabby underpants.

Everything must be done quickly. I fill his mouth with an oily rag from the floor, and tie my knotted stocking around his face, the knots pressing into his mouth. I may have tied it too tight; he may suffocate. Ah well, if he does, he does. I tie his hands and feet together firmly behind his back, strap the fingers together too, and rope the whole whimpering bundle to a metal spar close to the wheel.

One thing I don't recall, if I ever knew, is how to disable a marine radio, so I simply take up the axe and smash the equipment, reaching inside to rip out wires and crushing the glass valves under my shoe.

A torch shines up from the beach. At once the officer outside quits his post and is leaping up the ramp with Luger drawn. Oddly, this one too makes me think of a dog, with the bounding vigour and ferocity of a Doberman. I would have preferred to avoid gunfire, which could attract attention. Yet in the same instant I have already fired the machine pistol at his legs, aiming from the hip, and run towards him even as he falls to the deck. He makes a wild effort to pull his trigger, in the process shooting into his own injured foot. A metaphor for the whole German nation.

He cries out furiously until a length of rope is pushed into his mouth. He has to be disarmed, stripped and tied to the deck. I cut off his uniform with careful slashes of the knife, trying to avoid bloodstains as we'll be needing the uniforms. His injuries can be dealt with later, if at all.

Only the Chihuahua on the bridge is in a fit state to help me. I hurry him at gunpoint, shivering in his horrible damp underwear, across the beach to retrieve Waltraud's case from its covering of bracken. Seeing the bulky corpse lying there, despite the gag my Kriegsmarine officer groans in horror. I warn him to remain silent. The sight of the penis projecting causes him even more alarm. Full of fear, he finds the strength to drag the body as I walk alongside carrying the attaché case, a bizarre procession if anyone could see.

'Right, let's go. Come on. Schnell, schnell.' He drives the boat into the darkness. It seems he will do anything rather than be hurt. I wear the SS tunic in case anyone spies us from afar. Watching him at work, it's easy enough to get the hang of the controls. Detailed marine maps of Flensburg Fjord lie open at the wheel. They even show the location of all mines, marked on the chart by hand.

Through the boat's binoculars the brick ruin on the Danish side can be made out. There's no one at the site. I study the shore and the lanes and roads behind, and for a moment watch some distant coastal traffic intent on its tasks, swastikas on show. Our own livery and flag should ensure we don't attract any notice.

At last I see a car with no lights moving on the rocky headland.

'Also gut!' I announce. 'Schon gut! Ihr beiden! Zieh Leine. Abhauen.' All right, you two, hop it. 'Überbord. And take your friend.' The dead SS officer is pushed overboard, and his two colleagues must follow. They aren't keen. I give a choice of going over alive or dead. The Chihuahua is again overcome by trembling and tears as he helps me raise his injured partner onto the gunwale.

Cold will be their biggest problem, and will likely finish them off. I suppose they do have a chance. Each man sits on the side of the boat, as unsteady as a pigeon on a twig. Of course, I need my stockings back; I untie the SS man's gag before slicing his ropes and shoving him into the black waters. In the instant of falling, he manages to spit at me. A well-aimed ball of saliva hits me on the cheek. I feel a misplaced admiration for the accuracy of his aim, as well as for his steely defiance. In exchange, I toss the man a life vest, a heavy thing that he'll have to inflate if he has enough breath left. As soon as the Kriegsmarine officer's gag is off, he pleads for mercy, 'Have pity! We will die here!'

What perfect, fantastical buffoonery – a Nazi begging a Jew for pity! This poor fellow really is not up to the job of subjugating inferior races. 'Was ist los? Kannst nicht schwimmen?' I ask. What's up? Can't swim? 'Try to save one another, if that's allowed.'

He gets the push and splashes down, followed by a lifebuoy. The SS officer is swimming away strongly even with bullet wounds in his legs, determined to survive. To his credit, nugatory as it is, since he does not believe in pity he does not ask for any.

Their fate doesn't concern me. Strangely, I feel no sympathy for them. I feel nothing at all, other than satisfaction at a problem solved, and some amusement at the thought of the pair being picked up and questioned, perhaps tortured, by their Gestapo.

Inside a card Eleanor had written *Grandma Happy 87th Birthday, Love from Ellie and Adrian.* A long letter was folded inside. Some people love their grandparents. Others find everything about the elderly slightly distasteful. Nicola's daughter Eleanor was in the fond category.

Marjorie put on her reading glasses and unfolded the letter. Important news, good and bad. The good news was that Eleanor and her boyfriend Adrian were to make Aliyah – emigrate to Israel. The bad news was, 'Mum thinks you encouraged us to make Aliyah. She is very angry with you.'

Encouraged her? This was the first Marjorie had ever heard of Eleanor's wonderful plans! A deeper rift with her daughter would be bad news indeed. She depended on Nicola for countless small things. She reached for the angina medication, inserted the fine spray beneath her tongue.

Later, over tea and cake, Marjorie gleefully revealed to Joe and Eva Reznik that her grand-daughter Ellie was going to make Aliyah. The words were still coming out of her mouth as the eyelids closed and Marjorie slumped forward to the table. Her forehead struck her plate, breaking it into two. Her guests cried out in horror. 'Has she fainted? Marjorie, are you… is she all right?' Eva raised Marjorie's head from the table, pushed her back on the chair, repeating 'My God, my God, what's happened?' With tears in her eyes, she used a napkin to brush the crumbs from Marjorie's face. Eva and Joe stayed loyally beside their unconscious friend until an ambulance crew wheeled her away. Joe felt Marjorie's children ought to know. He called Philip, but Philip was not around. He tried Nicola's number.

Nicola was on a heart-pounding high of exhilaration and fury. Last night had been spent on a City pavement at the Climate Camp and today she joined the march to the Bank of England against the G20 London summit. Her placard read *No Borders No Prisons No Capitalism No Climate Change*. Without warning, the demo had burst apart and spun into nightmare. Young men with faces covered were running everywhere. Pinned into a side street, she had watched helpless as unprotected limbs and heads, many as old as hers, were struck with batons by police in full armour. Eventually able to escape, she fled back to her own home, and no sooner shut the door than the phone rang. It was Joe Reznik, about her mother.

Nicola would have preferred not to bother with Marjorie's health right then. Her mother would support the police, not to mention the G20 and the bankers, and scoffed at the coming climate disaster, and had even turned her daughter Ellie against her over Palestine.

Yet it was difficult to openly refuse to help. She said to Joe, 'I'll call the hospital. If they say it's serious, I'll go down.' When she phoned, a nurse described Marjorie as 'very poorly, barely conscious'. Nicola packed an overnight bag.

At 10pm, Nicola messaged her brothers: *At Sandcliffe Infirmary w Mum in Acute Admissions. She collapsed this afternoon, confused, can't speak, huge lump on forehead, horrible bruise across her face.*

Midnight: *Mum not yet seen. She doesn't make sense, doesn't know what's going on.*

At 2am: *Hi. Mum awake and recognises me. Nurse just asked if we would like a sandwich! At this hour!*

The dense mist began to clear from Marjorie's mind. She looked around and gradually understood where she was. Why Nicola, of all people, had come to her, she did not know. Eleanor's letter made its way back into her mind. She saw the opportunity to make closer ties with Nicola. She opened her arms and drew Nicola into an embrace. 'Thank you for coming, darling.'

In the curtained cubicle, they talked softly. Marjorie's thoughts wandered and her remarks were sometimes non-sequiturs. Nicola did not mention the G20 demonstration, which now felt impossibly far away.

4am: *Mum has no recollection of coming to hospital. Still not seen by a doctor.*

6.30am: *Mum still in Acute Admissions cubicle. Not seen yet.*

10am: *Doctor with Mum now. I've stepped out for some air.*

1pm: *Doc says it was another TIA (mini stroke), with mild concussion from hitting her head as she fell. Discharge later today, but could take a couple of weeks to recover.*

At 3pm, Nicola was free to take Marjorie home. She put her to bed and brought her a cup of soup. On the bedroom desk, she noticed, was written in huge, quaking letters the date of the next Social Services assessment. It was intolerably poignant to see how her mother was still struggling to cope on her own.

7pm: *Mum back home, but can't be left on her own.*

Philip replied: *What about if we get her some additional care for a few days, eg overnight?*

Max did not reply.

Nicola texted: *That's expensive. We must sort out who does what. I can't be solely responsible for her.*

Philip noticed that some of the posters had been changed in Nicola's windows. There was more now about climate change. The blood-stained BLIAR still held pride of place for the time being.

She offered him apple juice. He sat in the sitting room by himself, reading from her stack of *The Ecologist* magazines. Max arrived late. There was a short pretence of pleasantness with Nicola. 'How was the journey?' – 'Fine.' – 'Jelka and Ollie OK?' – 'Yup.'

Always before the three of them had put aside their differences and talked amiably. Last time, they agreed to have their mother's care needs assessed by Sandcliffe Council. It hadn't turned out as expected. The council had taken over Marjorie's care, yet she had to pay for it herself as her assets were above a £23,250 threshold.

This time Nicola began by saying angrily that she flatly refused to do 'everything' in future. Her brothers must share equally in dealing with Mum's needs and everyday affairs.

'Equally,' Philip said, 'except I must spend more than you?'

'I'm talking about *real* hassles, not writing cheques. You can afford it; we can't.'

Philip's tone hinted at his contempt for her. 'Don't want to argue, Nic – but as well as spending thousands of pounds, I've driven up and down that bloody A34 in all weathers ever since Dad died. Taking her out, checking she's OK.'

'That's normal. It's called being a grown-up son or daughter. But who sits with her in hospital all night? Who gives up three days to look after her? You don't realise, I'm doing the lion's share. Max, you do nothing. It can't go on like this. It really can't. I mean it.'

She would not put up with Max's protest that he lived too far away to help. Her resentment had taken on a sharper edge. 'Makes no difference where you live. Paris or Peru, she's *your* mother as well, you know.'

Max stood his ground. 'Mum wants to be left alone to struggle and get on with things in her own way.'

'Listen to yourself! You're *justifying* being selfish! Mummy has always accepted help when she needs it. It's sensible and practical.'

'*Selfish!*' Max's quick temper leapt up. 'Phil, *you* make so much of how much money you've spent. Which is actually totally painless for you. And Nic, a little stay by the sea, help yourself from her fridge, then make a big deal of how much *you* do.'

'Wow, *that's* not fair! I was up all night. I texted you at 4am.'

'You texted,' he jabbed a scornful finger, 'so we'd *know* you were there, and what a wonderful daughter you are. Mum didn't *ask* you to come. You thought it would *look* good, right?'

Nicola's temper too was on the rise. 'I didn't want to go. It's a long drive. I had just come in from the G20 demo. I was shattered.'

'Ah, now we have it! I have a theory that if no one had known, you *wouldn't* have gone,' exclaimed Max. '*And*, Nic,' he had not finished with his theory, 'I saw your Facebook pictures of Mum. Lots of Likes. What you don't mention is, actually you hate her! Dad too. You hated him.'

'That's not true!' Nicola grasped her mug, not empty, and hurled it at Max across the room. He ducked as cold tea sprayed out like a garden sprinkler, but laughed. He always found explosions of rage pleasing. The cheap, sturdy mug did not shatter. It hit the wall with a bang. Only the handle fell off. Nicola shouted, 'Why bring Daddy into this? I did *not* hate Daddy! I loved him! I miss him!'

'Just Mummy then?' he retorted.

Philip sat cowed, dabbing with a handkerchief at drops of tea on his jeans, wishing he had not come. He murmured, 'Max, that's incredibly hurtful. We all miss Dad.'

Max ignored him, intrigued by Nicola's fury. 'That was stupid, Nic. Tea fucking everywhere.''

Nicola moved swiftly to pick up a stack of folders from a kitchen dresser, holding them in her arms as she announced. 'My plan was, to go through these with the pair of you and divide it up. But why bother? Here's what *I* do for Mum. It's your job in future.'

She upturned a dozen files filled with Marjorie's online shopping orders, her bills paid and unpaid, bank statements, care assessments, letters from social services, email print-outs – flinging them into Max's lap. 'I'm not doing it any more. None of it. I'll be like you.'

'Thank God,' said Philip, 'Mum can't see you arguing like this.'

Max would not let it rest, 'She *can* see us, in her mind. She reads us like a book. She loves us anyway. But we don't love her. Not just you, Nic. None of us.'

This awful observation hung in the air. Nicola's rage was felled in an instant. She surveyed the confusion she had caused. Max picked up a few sheets of paper from the floor and read a few words. 'I see,' he said. 'Yes, you *have* done the lion's share.' There was no apology.

Philip said, 'I didn't realise there was so much stuff to deal with. We'll take it in turns, Nic, share it out, whatever, we'll all do some.'

Max went onto his knees and began to gather up scattered papers. 'No, you two carry on with the visits and sorting out crises, and I'll deal with this in future. You've done your bit, Nicky.'

That did sound like an apology of sorts. She joined him on the floor, collecting jumbled sheets that previously she had kept so neatly in order. Among the pages she found a bleak, echoing truth – that Max was right, the only love in Nicola's life was Marjorie's, for her.

Her brothers could hardly wait to leave, and Nicola was just as keen to see them go. Max wandered to Primrose Hill. He walked to the top of the grassy slope to look over central London. He had occasionally considered switching to a London agency. He had good contacts in London. Paris had the best reputation for photonews, though, and made a better base. And he did not want to interrupt Olivier's education or social life in Paris. But it could be done.

Olivier could take his Baccalauréat at the Lycée in Kensington; he'd qualify for a Bourse Scolaire. It was not obvious where they could afford to live within reach of the Lycée. He would ask Mum. He had a vague idea that she and Dad had lived in that part of London, before he was born.

* * *

I lay in a hot bath and SOE even treated me to a cold wave perm à l'Anglaise. In uniform and boots (and a fetching beret) I'm free to wander the estate. Beaulieu river curves through the woods in serpentine, marsh-edged bends. Something is afoot on the waterfront. Mysterious structures are being assembled under the trees. Requisitioned cottages beneath the canopy have become workshops. A shivering sentry says we are preparing for a major operation.

The codebooks and other material from Erika Jünger, along with the maps and documents from the patrol boat, were placed directly into the hands of a pair of BP dispatch riders, in the presence of two steely officers from SIS who arrived by car. All the rest, the German novel and magazine, travel papers and the rest, went back to SOE. I was stripped naked by two SOE nurses and examined as thoroughly as a girl can be.

My suspicion about who was betrayed, and by whom, is not dismissed out of hand, as I expected, but taken seriously. Anyone, in Britain or abroad, who knew my movements but not my cover name or objective is to be investigated. Our links with the Norwegian group are also under scrutiny.

The fact that my mission was compromised, and information leaked to the Germans, places a question mark over my value to SOE. I was sent to SOE for a joint operation, and that is complete. So it seems that I'm now the property of SIS again.

Wearing my own clothes at last, I board the early train. It's already jammed with soldiers smoking, standing, leaning out of the windows, sitting on their luggage. I open a compartment door and refrain from saying Heil Hitler. The passengers look up icily when I ask if the seat is free. Reluctantly they admit it is and I adore them. Their curtness, their phlegm, their reserve.

Through a window the New Forest slips away. Primroses and purple crocuses cluster on the embankment. Golden blossom shines among the gorse. Spring is coming, and I shan't be here to see it.

Across the road from St James Park station, I ring the doorbell of SIS, alias MI6. I'm taken up to a smart room with armchairs around a coal fire. Alec Hughes and a couple of other chaps are sitting by the hearth. All three rise sharply to their feet. Alec pumps my hand. 'Terrific job, Marjorie! Fantastic result. Marvellous, nabbing SS uniforms for the Danish resistance. Not to mention a patrol boat!'

It seems indiscreet to say these things aloud. 'Hello, Alec! Ernst couldn't be here, I suppose?'

'Not possible, I'm afraid. This meeting is between you and us. Rest assured Wardmann and Jarram know the mission was a success. We can't discuss that now.'

Percy Jarram! So he *was* involved.

'Marjorie,' says Alec, 'you've heard mention of "C". Head of SIS? Well, let me introduce you.' At this, one of the men takes a couple of steps towards me. I can barely hide my surprise. He's late middle-aged, balding, with a neat military moustache and the bearing to match, not to mention exceptionally well turned out in a beautifully tailored dark suit and gleaming black brogues. Even the tie looks as though it might have been specially made for him. As "C" holds out his hand, Alec intones, 'Sir Stewart, Miss Behrens. Marjorie, Major-General Sir Stewart Menzies.'

'How do you do? Honoured to meet you, sir.'

'How do you do? Most impressed with your achievement, Miss Behrens.'

One might suppose the nation's Head of Intelligence would come across as very intelligent. Instead he strikes me as merely very posh. Eton and the Guards would be my guess, inherited fortune, family seat in extensive grounds. Top-drawer connections.

'Thank you, sir. Shall I be going on another mission, sir?'

'No-oo! Nothing against SOE, of course,' he says, 'but it's good to have you back here with us. We must find something suitable for you. Be a shame to let your talents go to waste.'

'Thank you, sir. Shall I be returning to BP?'

'Not possible, I'm afraid. Don't worry, Miss Behrens, you have already performed great service there.'

'But sir…'

'First things first. The PM would like to express his gratitude in person. You'll be taken to him at three o'clock this afternoon.'

'The PM? You mean – the Prime Minister?'

'That's the chap. He's impressed by your work.'

Very likely I look flabbergasted. 'What's the form when meeting the Prime Minister?'

'Address him as "Prime Minister" when you're introduced. Shake his hand as normal. From then on, it's "sir", or "Mr Churchill". Don't discuss anything personal. Let him do the talking. Expect the meeting to be brief, under five minutes. Might be just a few seconds.'

Apparently Sir Stewart and his assistant were present only to give me that message. After they've left, Alec calls for sandwiches and tea, and we talk things over. '*Am* I going back to BP?' I ask. '"C" said it would be a shame to waste my talents.'

'Don't ask me, Marjorie! I'm in the dark too.'

After our little lunch, he picks up my suitcase and leads the way to my quarters. I expected to be taken there by car. Instead we go downstairs, along a basement corridor, upstairs again and through a door into as smart a place as I've ever seen. Soon we're standing in a huge paved hallway. It's opulent, grandly historic, with a carved staircase, immense crystal chandeliers, beautiful Oriental rugs, exquisite furnishings of polished wood.

'Where on earth are we, Alec? Is this still the same building?'

'We're now in Queen Anne's Gate,' he says. 'This house belongs to SIS, too.' A woman officer arrives to conduct me to my quarters.

Alec says, 'See you at three o'clock. No need to put on a coat.'

'What, is the PM coming to this house?'

'Yes, he's here now, having a talk with Sir Stewart.'

My 'quarters' are a magnificent flat of an elegance and quality I hardly knew existed, let alone ever experienced. Somehow I've slipped into the world of people who have their shoes hand-made and inherit priceless heirlooms.

A knock on the door and I am taken to meet him. The room is a small library, lined with books, extremely quiet. To one side stands an antique reading desk; on the other, four leather-covered armchairs and a low, circular table. The Prime Minister struggles to his feet from a chair as if inexpressibly weary.

For one dizzying second, I seem to be observing him from inside a photograph or a newsreel that has come to life. For a moment it even startles me that the Prime Minister is physically a real human being, a short, heavy, round-shouldered man swathed in a large expanse of pin-stripes. He shakes my hand with a real human hand, and with sparkling eyes and an astonishingly mischievous smile.

'Good afternoon, Prime Minister. It's an honour to meet you, sir.'

'Good afternoon, Miss Behrens. Congratulations,' he growls, 'on a successful expedition. Care to join me for coffee and brandy?'

I'm surprised to see we are alone. He doesn't have a secretary in the room, not an advisor, no assistant. I must remain calm and keep my head. One thing I hate is talking nonsense. Another is being overawed.

He is not wielding a cigar, and of course wears no hat, without which emblems he looks paler and fleshier than I expected. It strikes me that he is indeed elderly. The fine, clever head is almost bald but for a few lonely grey wisps. The voice, at least, is familiar, as is the bow tie. The eyes are alert and knowing.

'Let me say how impressed we are with your fortitude and your great accomplishment!' he replies. He speaks slowly, which seems to make this utterance unduly portentous.

'May I take the opportunity, sir, if it's not impertinent, to say the same of you? I am full of gratitude to you.'

He has an appealing, self-deprecating smile. 'Ah – well, that's much appreciated, Miss Behrens. Do I understand that you dispatched an SS officer with your bare hands?'

'With my stockings, sir.'

He chuckles. 'Better yet!' He lowers his voice to a jovial rumble, 'That's where a woman has an advantage over a man. Well done!'

'Thank you very much, sir. May I raise a concern, sir?'

His smile vanishes at once. He looks positively ferocious. 'This may not be the right moment, Miss Behrens, to raise any other matter, nor the right way. Sir Stewart is…'

'Sir Stewart mentioned that he didn't want my talents to go to waste. He wasn't referring to my hosiery. He meant an aptitude for memorising and decoding enemy messages. Yet I've been told I can't go back to Bletchley. And SOE say they don't want me either, for the time being. Do you have ideas for me, sir?'

He studies my face. 'Yes, I do. You have pre-empted me.' He gestures towards the armchairs. 'Let us sit.' At that convenient moment, our coffee and brandy arrives and is placed on the table. When the door has closed again, we sip coffee and he begins to explain. 'I chose to meet you in this room,' the grainy voice measured and subdued, 'to ensure complete privacy. There is no recording equipment in here. We cannot be overheard.'

In June 1941, Mr Churchill recounts, Germany betrayed its promise to the Soviets, opened an Eastern Front, and as a result the Soviet Union joined the Allies. This much everybody knows. 'You speak Russian, don't you?' This isn't said as a question. 'I've read up your background. SIS and SOE have done their homework.'

He puts the coffee aside and takes a big sip of brandy. I barely touch mine, merely raising it to my lips.

'Therefore in June 1941,' the Prime Minister returns to his topic, 'I was obliged to halt intelligence operations against Stalin. The FO's Russian section was shut down.'

Moments pass as he finds a cigar, cuts it, starts it burning, and blows billows of smoke around us like a heavily scented veil.

'Those fighting on the same side are not always friends,' he murmurs. 'It has been my wish, to set something up, in isolation from the intelligence bodies, to keep me apprised of what Stalin is getting up to contrary to our interests. A small group, obscure, of talented, discreet individuals such as yourself, each one carefully selected, engaged on the sort of work you've been doing for Sir Stewart at Bletchley. Reporting directly to me, not to him.'

'Does Sir Stewart know about your wish, sir?'

'Not he! Nor should he. Nor any of your colleagues at BP, SIS or SOE. Now or in the future. Nor your dearest family and friends. Nor, if ever a man is fortunate enough to win your heart, may you whisper it to him. Not even in the most intimate seclusion. This is a secret to which even the Secret Service are not to be privy.'

'Is that entirely proper?'

'Fascinating question! Yes, it is proper,' going on as if reading poetry, 'Under the powers of the Royal Prerogative. It is within the Prime Minister's authority. During a state of war. To take any action. He deems necessary. In defence of the kingdom.'

By the time I leave the room those outside are frantic with impatience. Sir Stewart chides me, 'You ought not have kept him so long!'

I reply that Mr Churchill did all the talking. 'I didn't feel it was my place to tell him to shut up.'

Alec Hughes asks, rather peevishly, 'What on earth did he talk about for so long?'

'Oh, you know, great military campaigns of the past, and so on. It was jolly interesting.'

'Come on. What really happened?' says Alec.

'Well, I found out what I have to do next to serve the war effort.'

'Oh, yes – what?'

'I'm to return to my job at Lyons' head office.'

'The *Prime Minister* himself told you that, in person?' Alec looks surprised and terribly disappointed for me.

L

She moved a knight. 'No, Grandma,' Olivier shook his head, 'think about your rook.' She took the knight back. 'This is hopeless. I can't do the crossword any more, and now I can't play chess.' She spoke as though half amused by some comical element in her disintegration. In truth she was not amused. She was afraid, as scared as she had ever been.

'You don't do your crossword any more?' asked Jelka.

'No. My mind goes blank. I can't see how to proceed.'

'That's what happens to most people,' commented Olivier, '*all* the time.'

Jelka wanted to be helpful. 'Try codeword instead.'

No one who knew the Marjorie of old would have suggested such a thing. Max had lived with his Serbian girlfriend for nearly twenty years, yet the two women had spent little time together. Even now they had moved to London, Marjorie saw hardly more of Max than before. He was often away, working in war zones, trouble spots, scenes of catastrophe on the other side of the world, drawn to disaster and conflict which he referred to as "great pictures". She did though, gladly, see much more of Jelka. They were getting to know one another.

She found Jelka interesting. One might blink to make it go away, but she saw in her a hint of something feral, a streak of toughness and savagery. Sometimes Jelka made her think of a scavenging cat, wary, quick-witted. A perfect partner for Max. Marjorie taught Jelka some of her recipes. She sensed the role she had started to play for her daughter-in-law – whose own parents had been killed in the Yugoslav conflict.

As Jelka explained how codeword works, Marjorie pointed at little numbers in the corners of the squares, struggling to focus her eyes. 'Numbers,' she said foolishly. 'Harry does numbers, I do words.'

'No, there's no arithmetic,' said Olivier, 'the numbers go from 1 to 26, and represent letters of the alphabet.'

'So 1 is A; 2, B; like that?'

'No, Grandma, that's the point. They're not in order. You have to work out which letter each number is, to make words. They give you a couple of clues,' – he showed her – 'see?'

'Of course I see, Ollie!' Her other difficulty was that she literally could not see: she first had to peer at the grid with her magnifying glass. As a trial run, she picked up her pen and began to complete the codeword. On the face of it, she wrote any word that came into her head, always the longer words, scattered all over, not bothering to enter the clue letters into the empty squares.

'What are you doing, Grandma?'

A slight panic flickered across her face. Had she misunderstood? 'I think the secret is to work out the longest words first.'

'No, but I mean,' he chose, as an example, the word *mysterious* which she had written in squares unconnected to the others, 'how do you know it's that, without using the clues?'

Marjorie frowned, unsure whether he was tricking her. 'M, space, S, six spaces and another S. There are only about five pronounceable combinations that would fit, only two ordinary English words, *misogynous* and *mysterious*. It couldn't be *misogynous* because look – the position of the Y. You can tell it's a Y from this word here.' Her pen touched an empty space of nine squares.

'What word? It's not filled in yet!'

'No, but it can only be *vasectomy*, surely? So from that we know which letter is M and which is Y.'

As horrified as if he had seen a magic spell cast, Olivier demanded, '*How* do you know? Can you see the words there before you have written them in? Do you know the whole English dictionary by heart? How did you know 21 must be M?'

'Nine-letter word with no repeated letters. And here's another nine-letter word with no repeated letters, with the same pair of letters at the beginning of one and at the end of another, so this one is *vasectomy*, and this, *mysterious*. So this other nine-letter word must be *manifesto*. Ollymentary my dear Ollie. No clues needed. That's why I prefer a crossword – that's all about the clues.'

Olivier gazed with fearful admiration. In effect, his grandmother had done the whole codeword in her head, in seconds, without writing the words. It was the nearest he or Jelka would ever come to seeing Marjorie's mind at work. Even in its poor, fractured state, it seemed, there were parts intact, parts unknown which had not been destroyed.

'Wow, you're fast!' said Jelka.

'Oh, I know. You should see me on the dance floor.'

'We'll have to find you a harder one to do.'

Marjorie opened another letter from the council. *Dear Mrs Rosen – Our Fairer Charging Policy.*

Next month charges for Home Care, Day Care and Transport services will change see new rates attached. Your contribution towards the cost of your care will increase as a result. According to records of the Financial Assessment and Benefits Team you have over £23,250 in capital. If this information is incorrect please complete the form below.

She did not complete the form. She had not quite got to grips with the 'contributions'. What was the difference between Home Care and Day Care, and what did Transport refer to? Her weekly payment increased from £26.05 to £258.30. It was an impossible, terrifying jump. It must be a mistake, surely? She phoned Max. He had no time to deal with it now. He adjusted her standing order and made sure the invoices were paid.

Marjorie checked the invoice herself. She explained to Max that in fact her savings now stood below the threshold. They *had* made a mistake. This came at a bad moment for him; he had a work opportunity in the Gulf of Mexico. He phoned Social Services to talk them through the totals.

Dear Mrs Rosen was informed that the amount she paid for care had been duly adjusted and backdated. This too was incorrect. Max phoned Social Services – he was now in Indonesia. It was agreed the demand had been sent in error, and could be ignored. The incorrect amount appeared again on the next invoice.

Dear Mrs Rosen, You have been awarded an annual Personal Budget of £13,701.30p I am writing to advice Your assesed

contribution towards Your care costs You curently recieve notified on
11 August continue to apply until Your next financial review takes
place next May. Yours sincerely.

Max could not understand this, the weird syntax, nor why it had
been sent, nor the concept of a Personal Budget that had been
'awarded'. It manifestly was not an award that one actually received.
Rather, it seemed she had to give it to them. He made no effort to
find out. Max was desperate not to be distracted from important
assignments. He had to choose either to deal with his mother's care
or pursue his own career.

At last came the Christmas holidays. Sandcliffe Council shut down
for ten days. In maddened relief, Max and Jelka escaped to old
friends in Paris, where he became immersed in convivial New Year
meals, free-flowing wine, and music too loud to think. There was
nothing Max wanted more than to get into a state of not giving a
damn about either his mother or his work.

* * *

I sit once more at a desk in Lyons' Labour Planning Office at
Cadby Hall. Otto welcomed me back with something like
sympathy. He must assume things did not go well for me in
Signals, or wherever he thinks I've been. That's not something we
can discuss. I continue to do the crossword every lunchtime as
though the crossword competition never happened. He doesn't refer
to my long absence. We chat only about work, raids and the latest
news.

Most of the work now is on the storage of army rations. I'm also
applying my mind to the future of Lyons' Corner Houses: controlling
portion size; speeding up menu choice; stopping customers stealing
cutlery. Some of the tea shops are damaged beyond repair. A lot of
Nippies have hung up their aprons and been given something more
important to do for the war effort. I'm setting up a team to look into
switching the whole tea-shop business to self-service. Otto is thrilled
by that. He says, 'After the war, Marjorie, you've a great future in
Lyons' management.'

Cadby Hall offers a greater puzzle than the crossword. The first clue came as a single sighting at lunchtime. Normally, I eat a sandwich at my desk. Occasionally I have lunch in one of the staff restaurants. There it was that I caught a glimpse of him. I stared and stared to be sure. Without any doubt it was Harry Rosen, from Bletchley Park, carrying a tray, looking for a table. He wore a dark grey Utility business suit, crumpled and untidy, and sat with people he knew. I ate my meal alone, trying to work out why a brilliant Hut 8 mathematician is in a Cadby Hall staff canteen.

From then on, I find I'm constantly scanning the population of Cadby Hall. Thousands, tens of thousands, work here every day and all night too. It's an immense site. There are food factories, research laboratories, a training college, bakeries with steaming, fragrant chimneys, a phalanx of office blocks around a busy transport park, five-storey buildings filled with clerks. Building X, the senior administration and management quarters rising up in one corner of the site, alone houses thousands. It's almost impossible that I'd see Harry Rosen by chance.

Yet there he is again, ahead of me in a corridor, carrying a ring binder. I walk faster to catch him. 'Harry Rosen? Hello. Remember me? Marjorie Behrens.'

'Hello, Miss Behrens!' – 'Oh, no, Harry, it's "Marjorie", please.'

'Of course I remember you, Miss Beh… Marjorie!' He grasps my hand and shakes it, or rather holds it, gazing directly into my eyes. I quiz him: 'How do you come to be in this place, Harry? What on earth brings you here?'

He grins boyishly. 'War work, of course. Like you. Can't discuss.' He must wonder what I'm doing at Cadby Hall as much as I wonder what he's doing here, yet he doesn't ask. 'Sorry, I can't stop now, late for a meeting.'

Away from my desk, going about the building, making my way across the site, I am always hoping to see him. I look at people going in and out of the crowded staff discount store, the medical centre, recreation club, staff library.

The third time he's sprinting up the stairs inside Building X as I walk down, glances at me, smiles, doesn't stop. 'Marjorie!' he says, 'All well?' and continues too fast to hear the reply. Late for another meeting, I suppose.

I wonder whom he meets, and what about. After all, he's a cryptanalyst. It's pretty hard to picture him in a meeting at all, especially at the head office of J. Lyons & Co.

What's the attraction? I ask myself, *I don't even know the man.* Something in me senses he will like me and find me attractive, if I can only make him notice me. On the fourth encounter, Harry Rosen and I meet face to face in a hallway. Lovely teeth, white and uneven, with a little gap between the two in the front. I adore the way his black eyebrows rise to an impish point. His dark hazel eyes sparkle with joie de vivre, intelligence and humour.

'Hello again!' he hails me, without the least astonishment at this continual coincidence. It's odd that he remembers me at all, or says he does. At BP he never even looked at me. 'Can't stop,' he says. 'Would it be nice to have a stroll later in Kensington Gardens? What about,' he suggests, 'opposite the Albert Hall, seven o'clock?'

Not just a stroll, but a mad jitterbug in the park, a Corner House dinner, and Harry has swept me into his West End world. He points out every low dive and every smart bar, every theatre and cinema, he's seen this play, that film, laughs and chatters, promises to take me to places into which I would never venture.

We don't come out of the dancehall until after the National Anthem, joining the crowd milling around in Piccadilly. It's a wonderfully balmy night, people surging mysterious and faceless along the blacked-out street, fleetingly visible in the feeble glow of painted sidelights on passing cars, lit up by occasional dimmed flashlights, or icy blue lamps outside restaurants. Nearly everyone is in uniform. Lit cigarettes dart about like fireflies. Harry lights one and hands it to me, and one for himself.

The noise and laughter, dancing and music still resound in my mind. In a single step we have left the crowd behind, turning into Green Park, where we drift across the grass, our hands never quite touching. We cross the Mall into St James' Park to see the great dark shape of the Palace. It has blackout, too, of course. Harry leads me towards the Embankment, and there, under trees beside the river, we sit on a bench in total darkness.

All evening we've hardly mentioned anything personal. Now, in a low voice, Harry tells me, unseen, 'You know, I'd just won a scholarship to continue my maths, when this ruddy war started and put the kybosh on it. What about you?'

'Father died at the beginning of the war. He had a business in Hull buying and curing fish. He had cold stores on the dockside, and warehouses and smokehouses, with his name painted across the roof in huge letters, the words *Fred^k. Behrens*. Written like this: Fred, small k, full stop, Behrens. We lived near the waterfront.'

'Hull, now that's, um – is it up north somewhere?'

'Harry, you great ignoramus! It's in Yorkshire. Hull is one of the country's largest ports. Bombed to bits now, though. Maybe you can forget about Hull, come to think of it. Hardly anything left.'

'How did he die – killed in action?'

'Not really. A war wound carried him off. Not this war; the last one. He was only forty-seven. Father didn't really live with us. He was away from home eight months every year, or he'd come and go for a few days at a time. His head office wasn't in Hull, it was in Lowestoft. He had warehouses there, too, and we had a second home there. Oh, I grew up in all these places beside the North Sea, ports and harbours, playing on quaysides.'

It's so intimate sitting beside one another like this, the sturdy bare branches over us like protective limbs. I sense that Harry is really *listening* to me. I wish I could see his face.

He says, 'My father's a cabinet maker in Shoreditch. I'd never even seen the sea before the war. You played on quaysides. I don't remember playing at all. I don't think we were allowed to play. There wasn't anywhere. Just the street, and there were goyish kids out there, rough kids. We were scared of them. Mad, violent people. My parents were scared of them, too.'

'When Hull was bombed, our house was destroyed. We slept in a warehouse for a while. Then Mother took us to Lowestoft. That wasn't safe either. She was in a bad way. Our home had been destroyed, Father had died. And her youngest –' I find it hard to say the words, 'my ten-year-old brother, he was killed in the raid.'

'Oh!' He does sound truly horrified. 'How terrible for you, dreadful for your mother.'

'Mother won't allow his name to be mentioned.'

'What was his name?'

'Dear little thing, killed by the shock wave. Not a mark on him. Reuben. Reuben Behrens. Mother couldn't cope after that. I helped her start a British Restaurant so she'd have enough food for us, my sisters and me, and the boys, three of 'em still at home.'

'Ah, good idea! Food without ration books!'

'Then the next boy was called up, and she was terrified he'd be killed as well. And then *she* was nearly killed in a raid. Her nerves were in shreds. She was in no fit state.'

'How is she now?'

'Nervous wreck. There are constant raids on Lowestoft. I got my papers and had to leave her in the lurch. They sent me to a munitions factory. Hardly seen her since. She's never liked me in any case.'

'Doesn't *like* you?' He falls silent.

The sound of traffic has almost stopped. We can hear the river lapping against the Embankment wall, the soft splashing. 'You know... I lost someone, too; not in the war. My sister Feiga,' Harry murmurs. 'It's only tiny, our house, where I grew up. A poky little back-to-back. Couldn't swing a cat. Someone ought to bomb it. There were twelve of us – I'm the youngest. They're all in the army now, my brothers. All alive, far as I know. We were skint; I mean really penniless. Hungry all the time, that was the worst of it. Feiga couldn't take it. She was never strong.'

'Oh, how awful, Harry!'

'My father blamed himself. What I hate about myself is that I blamed him, too. But really, everything we suffered was because we were Jews. It all goes back to that. Ach well, never mind.' He half laughs. 'It will end, one day, I suppose.'

'The war, or...?' I know he doesn't mean the war. He answers, 'Well, yes, I suppose the war will end one day, won't it?'

'Then it'll be – Men, back to your jobs! Women, back into your drawing rooms! Everyone, back to sleep.'

'Not a chance. People will never go back to sleep again after this.'

'No, I don't think so either.'

'What would you like to do if the war does end?'

I find myself answering, 'Sounds terribly earnest, but I'm only interested in doing the best for my country. That's all.'

'How extremely laudable!' He is mocking me slightly. 'Is it true? King and country?' I can't interpret his tone. Then I realise he's *not* mocking. His comment is not ironic; it's deadly serious.

'That's right. And you know what's funny, Harry. I didn't know that about myself until you asked. What do you think you'll do, after the war?'

In the gloom I see Harry sit up as if resolved to confess some secret. 'I'm going to tell you the truth now. I am interested in finding a mathematical interpretation of the workings of the mind, the way the mind uses algorithms to interpret the world and make use of it. And in the relation between our understanding of the physical *reality* of an object and our *idea* of each object as having actual or potential function. The point is, all perception can be given a numerical value. So I want to find a mathematical method of expressing mental processes. You see what I mean?'

Gosh! He's fantastically passionate about this incomprehensible topic! He assumes I have understood. In fact I am lost. For a start, I have never heard the word algorithm.

At this inopportune moment, sirens begin to howl in the distance. 'That's over in the east, isn't it?' I say. The local siren has not begun to sound. Bright flashes illumine the horizon. 'Flares,' I warn. 'Jerries choosing their targets.'

Nevertheless, neither of us moves. Echoing through the air from far away, the whiplash of guns. Beyond the City, orange lights float down from a burning sky.

Suddenly we hear the familiar rumble and a closer siren. Becoming quickly louder, the roar overtakes us faster than thought, and there's a din as if a gun battery has burst into action right next to us. A cluster of devices crash down a few yards upriver, becoming a multitude of dazzling balls bouncing around in all directions. 'Incendiaries,' Harry cries out. A cluster of them hit the further Embankment, flaring into life on impact. Two explode into flames apparently on the surface of the water. Something falls on our side of the river, shaking the ground, scattering white-hot pieces of fire like white confetti. The planes overhead, guns, sirens screaming, all together make an overwhelming noise.

Our tranquil midnight talk is well and truly over. 'Can we make it to the tube station?' Harry yells. I am lip-reading more than hearing the words. Most of all I can tell he's afraid.

We start running in that direction, but there is a flash ahead. He spins around to run the other way, but clearly it's too late to reach a shelter. I stop running and grab his arm, 'Stand quite still!' We need to see where exactly the incendiaries are falling, where fire has already broken out and in which direction it is moving. If possible we should try to put out any fire. Teams of brave, cool-headed Air Raid Wardens and Fire Parties are already tackling several blazes behind Westminster Abbey and back towards Parliament Square. I must help Harry remain calm. The poor man is in a panic. If we stay close to the Embankment wall we can jump in the water if we have to.

'Can you swim, Harry?' I shout into his ear.

'Good God, no, of course not!'

'Can't swim! Pity. It's much more useful than mathematics.'

'I don't see that.' Even now he's trying to be good-humoured. His voice shakes with anxiety.

The benches here are set on low stone plinths. Between the plinths and the Embankment wall is a small, relatively protected space.

'Lie down!' I order him. 'Close to the wall.' We drop to our hands and knees on the pavement as the ground shakes with a mighty thud, and scramble into the space behind a bench. Flashes of blue and orange flicker close by.

'So,' Harry says into my ear as we stretch out beside one another, squashed together on the ground, 'to go back to your question, I want to be involved in creating computing machines that can *decide* rather than *calculate*. Work has already started.' His voice is quavering, his body trembling, whether with excitement or fear I cannot tell.

It's thrilling and incredible to hear such things in this mad, blazing chaos, but surely he is touching upon his work at BP.

'Should you be telling me this, Harry?'

'I'm only telling you what interests me. In theory.'

'My dear Mr Rosen, you are too clever for your own good.'

'Yes, I feared as much.'

'Stick to dancing, is my advice.'

'Right you are! If we survive this night, we'll dance like madmen.'

At this moment my heart practically slams on the brakes, as without warning Harry slips his hand onto mine and rests it there, attempting to pass it off as a merely comforting gesture. I've been waiting nervously all evening for something like this. Dancing is one thing; this is another. And we lie like that, hand in hand, hoping for the best as hot, blinding fireballs roll past the stone plinth that protects us. Adding to the clamour, more aircraft roar over our heads. They are turning back, heading away from London. I picture them arriving soon at an airfield in Europe.

The Westminster all-clear hasn't sounded, but we hear one across the river, and in time all noise has subsided. We climb out and jump back to our feet, vigorously brushing the dirt from our clothes. The fire crews are hard at work, dousing small fires with stirrup pumps. Flames cast a bewitching light on us. With nervous relief, Harry giggles merrily and straightens his tie. Without a shred of modesty, I inspect my stockings from top to toe. Incredibly, they are unscathed. I look up at him and find myself laughing with the sheer joy of life.

'Well, I'd say we had a lucky escape,' I declare. 'Wouldn't you?'

He smiles beautifully. 'Except I don't know what "luck" means.'

'Luck is that marvellous, capricious déesse who governs our affairs.'

'Dear Marjorie,' says Harry, as if starting to dictate a letter, 'I've had a lovely evening. I think we could get on well.' In his eyes there's a reflection of distant searchlights, white traces scored into the night sky over south London.

'So do I, Harry.'

We follow the Embankment all the way back to Chelsea, sometimes arm in arm. He whistles a tune. It's not the quickest way home, but it's the nicest. The nicest ever.

M

'Little glass of sherry for auld lang syne, Carol?' The carer couldn't wait to get home, but she was always patient with Marjorie, and grateful to her. She poured the drinks. 'Happy new year, dear! Will you be all right on your own?'

'I'll listen to Big Ben at midnight. Ouf!' Marjorie gasped as a sharp pain struck her chest without warning. 'Angina, is it?' asked Carol. 'Use your GTN.' She meant, the angina spray.

'Not angina. Not in the right place.' Marjorie tapped the top of her belly, below her breasts. Nevertheless, she inserted the pink bottle under her tongue and pressed the button. She yelped with agony. 'Something I've eaten, do you think, or the sherry?'

Marjorie had eaten the same food as always. Her sherry stood almost untouched on the table. The pain worsened, yet Marjorie became less sure where it was located. 'Round the side,' she gasped. 'Damn this, I feel sick as well.' The glyceril trinitrate was still in her hand. She gave herself a second dose.

'Any improvement?' Carol began to feel anxious. It could, after all, be a heart attack. 'You shouldn't spray again so soon. If it's not angina, don't use the spray.'

Marjorie flinched at an agonising new twinge. 'Quick, I'm going to be sick.' Carol brought a bowl just in time. 'Look, this is no good. I'm going to phone 999,' the carer insisted, 'and get you to hospital.'

'Don't you do any such thing! You promised.'

'Never know, darling. Heart, lungs, stomach. Might be peritonitis. Maybe something's happened to your hiatus hernia. It could be pericarditis. Might need urgent treatment. It does no harm to check. They'll give you an ECG, at least.'

'I'm not going. If it's serious, so be it.' A new twinge made her groan and twist in agony.

'I must call an ambulance. If I don't, and it turns out to be serious,

I'll be at fault. I'd lose my job.'

'Go home now and no one will know. Please just go.'

Carol was dialling. 'No, I can't leave you like this, sorry.'

'Don't call an ambulance. That's all I ever asked of you.'

The carer grimaced uncomfortably. 'Not liking hospital is one thing. Saying you won't *ever* go is another. It isn't reasonable.'

A pair of paramedics strolled into Marjorie's bedroom, gentle giants, relaxed, purposeful and good-humoured. Marjorie, bending and turning with pain, refused to go with them. In consultation with the carer (whispering in the hall; Marjorie could hear them quite clearly), it was decided the patient was not rational. She was placed on a stretcher and carried out of her front door against her protests.

Carol had put Marjorie's toothbrush and toiletries, compression stockings and slippers into a holdall. Marjorie called out, 'My handbag, Carol, give me my handbag. The photo of Harry, by the bed, put it in my handbag. Give Philip a ring, let him know. Write a note for the cleaner and leave on the shelf outside the door, in case I'm not back before she comes. I'm afraid I'll *never* be back. Better blow out the Shabbat candles, Carol, on this occasion, just in case. Lock the flat when you leave. And by the way, I *am* rational.'

Siren wailing, blue light spinning, the ambulance cut through the New Year's Eve traffic. As it sped forward, one of the gentle giants filled in their report. *Emergency. Epigastric pain, sudden onset with vomiting.*

The rush was to no purpose. At Sandcliffe Infirmary distant merry-making echoed in the corridors. A&E was crowded, the bolted-down plastic chairs and most of the floor space occupied by a melée of patients not yet seen. Some were ill, some cradling a crying child. Some were drunks not in control of their bodily functions. Others, laughing at their wounds, were in festive mood, accompanied by friends or family. Marjorie was placed among a group of shouting, laughing women bleeding from tattooed arms and flushed faces.

In Paris the next afternoon, after a long, late Réveillon, Max turned on his phone and found Philip's enigmatic text: *Mum to A&E last night with chest pain not heart.* It was only for information. All the same, Max phoned Sandcliffe Infirmary. The receptionist said Mrs Rosen was now in Acute Admissions with severe back pain and had been given morphia.

'*Back* pain? That's new. And morphia, that's morphine, right?' – 'Yes. She'll be having tests.' – 'Today?' – 'Today? No, after the holiday.' – 'Could I speak to her?'

His mother sounded controlled and urgent. 'Get someone to come here, darling. I'm in real trouble.'

'Why, what's the problem, Mum?'

'Can't talk now. Let Joe and Eva know I need help urgently. And Philip and Nicola.'

'What kind of help?'

'Just phone them.'

'OK, I'll call them straight away. Happy New Year, Mum.'

'It's gone twelve, then, has it?'

'That was last night, Mum. It's New Year's Day.'

'Oh, I missed Big Ben. Max, this is important: find someone to come and help me, quick as you can.'

'I'll see what I can do.'

'Just phone someone. Thank you, darling. Happy New Year.'

* * *

Every day Harry asks if I fancy going out with him to the flicks after work. The cinemas are packed lately. Many in the audience don't care if they see a film. People come in during the second feature and leave half way through the main picture. Some come only to see Pathé News, others for a kiss and cuddle. Harry insists on seeing a film from beginning to end, and discussing it afterwards as we stroll in the unearthly sunlit evenings of Double Summer Time.

He has the most frivolous tastes. He'll splutter with amusement until his eyes water when we see a comedy. New pictures come out every few weeks. Last month we went twice to see *Double Indemnity* and *Passage to Marseille*, and we've seen *Casablanca* seven times. We have private jokes about them. Harry comes out absurdly with Bogart's "I stick my neck out for nobody." When we say goodnight, he pronounces melodramatically, "Kiss me, kiss me as if it were the last time."

Our favourite in-joke from *Casablanca* is not funny. Humphrey Bogart asks Ingrid Bergman to tell him something about herself. Her answer is a cool "We said no questions."

A letter is delivered to my flat and placed directly into my hand. 'From the Foreign Office,' says the messenger. It's not on FO notepaper, just ordinary bond paper with the word "Confidential" typed at top left. I'm required to attend for interview, on Sunday of all days, on the eighth floor of Aldford House, Park Lane. I've never heard of Aldford House and nor can I read the signature.

About half-way down Park Lane, the building appears to be a block of flats, a horribly ugly architectural masterpiece of stone and brick. I clatter the lift gates shut and ride slowly to the top floor.

A genial young academic type welcomes me. We join a dozen or more people, mainly of our own age. Only then do I realise that the young chap is in charge. It hadn't crossed my mind that someone as young as us could be the head of anything.

Considering the strict precautions taken so far, he is remarkably open and relaxed. 'Hello everyone! My name is Sinclair Bannerman,' he announces. Not his real name, I suppose. 'You all know why you're here – if you don't, speak up now.' I say nothing even though I have no idea what is going on, hoping it will soon become clear.

'You've all excelled at this kind of work. We're a select team.' He gives an appealing grin. 'We may look like a pretty mixed bunch, but we have a lot in common. We're all patriots, all first-rate problem-solvers, all fluent Russian speakers.' It's interesting that he knows all that about each one of us. I wonder just how much he has been told about me. 'You've just been carefully vetted, though you might not have noticed. So, what is our task here? We'll be provided with Soviet intercepts and follow established decryption procedure. The intercepts are coded using one-time pads, not really one-time because they are used by different services, together with a hand-cipher made on a grid using text from works of literature translated into Russian.'

He looks around. 'If you feel that one of your colleagues falls short, let me know at once. Don't put loyalty to one another before loyalty to the country. There is no hierarchy or rank in this team.' I wonder if everyone agrees with him about that.

I'm impressed by this chap Bannerman or whoever he is. He's nice and unstuffy, and has an air of competence. 'No one at the FO or BP or SIS or wherever you've been until now knows about this group. For security, your share of our work will take up only a short time each week. That's to make it possible to say nothing about it to friends or family. Continue your normal employment and leisure activities, and make no change to the way you lead your life.'

A dashing fellow with a Russian accent asks, 'Who are we? Does the group have a name?' I've been wondering the same thing. Bannerman replies, 'We'll refer to ourselves and this house and all that goes on here as Section B. Officially there is no Section B. This office belongs to the Commercial Section of the Diplomatic and Commercial Research Section under Commander Denniston, head of BP until last year. But we're separate from Denniston's office. We answer only to the Prime Minister.'

We end with cups of tea all round, a party atmosphere and a chance to say hello to one another. People talk quite freely, under orders to use only first names, not surnames. Some worked together at a place called Wavendon, apparently part of BP which decoded Russian intercepts until last June. Sinclair himself is a mathematician from Cambridge University. One of the women is a criminologist. And Sinclair's description of us as patriots is a little nuanced, as several are not British. It's an extraordinarily exotic bunch.

I notice one of the girls approach Sinclair and confer with him quietly, tête-à-tête. It looks as if she is either something more intimate than a mere colleague or else is part of the leadership of the group. I like the look of her. She's stylish and elegant with dark hair pinned neatly. I get chatting to her. She's from the Conseil National de la Résistance; her name is Yvette.

She points out some Polish intelligence analysts, and people from the Baltic States, and a pair of older men, real old-style Russians who were cryptanalysts to Tsar Nicholas. By comparison I am unutterably dull! Someone asks what field I come from. Slightly embarrassed, I admit I have no specialisms at all. 'I work for Lyons; you know, the tea shop people.' Perfectly true. 'But I am not here to make the tea.'

Section B is a friendly outfit. On fine days I walk out with Yvette for a quick spin in Hyde Park or up to Marble Arch for tea and a pastry. We've become quite matey, she and I, within the limits of what we feel free to discuss.

We do cautiously offer one another a few glimpses of our thoughts our interests, our backgrounds, just enough to look for common ground. As we choose a pastry, Yvette reveals, 'My family were pâtissiers. Pastrycooks. For generations! On both sides of the family.'

'You say "were"…'

'My parents are dead now, killed in the war. Eh oui!'

'I'm sorry to hear that.' A slight laugh dismisses my sympathy. There's no harm in telling her my father is dead too. 'He was a fish buyer. He was never at home, always away, following the herring, he called it, Lerwick, Peterhead, Yarmouth.'

'Maybe he had another family somewhere. Secretly. I bet he did.'

I laugh. 'I wouldn't have blamed him. A wife in every port. It's possible. Used to send us crates of fresh fish, though, the best of the catch. Boats would unload at the quayside, and a box was taken up to our house. We ate a lot of good fish.'

'You had the best fish – we had the best cake. Maman brought their family recipe book as her dowry. One of her ancestors had been a pupil of the great pâtissier Carême. Her gâteau de l'écureuil and gâteau de Savoie made Papa famous in our little region. And tarte au quemô, and her very own walnut gâteau with chocolate, sans pareil!'

'Sounds wonderful.'

'We sit here with a cup of tea and what passes for a pastry.' She shakes her head at us, poor fools that we are. 'Do you know what galette manougienne is? Non? Ah! A pastry like in a dream, with a spoonful of crème fraîche, and not with a cup of tea, but a glass of sparkling Valdon rosé.'

'Stop, stop, Yvette, I can't bear it!'

'Maybe we'll have one together one day. I'll give you the recipe!' We laugh at the absurdity of it, some future unimaginable, when sugar is not rationed, nor flour, with cream, and French wine.

Most of our conversation, like everyone's, is the war news, which is bad. The optimism ignited by D-Day has come to a disillusioned end. Our soldiers, even the Americans, are mired in French mud, being massacred; and the Germans have started a terrifying new bombing campaign against us with flying rockets, alias "doodlebugs". There's a mood now that the war could still be lost. Several of us would rather work against the Germans than the Russians, but it is not to be.

Yvette, chatting, explains that intelligence from each source always has its own code name. Intelligence from BP is called ULTRA. The Russian intelligence we provide, she tells me, is called ISCOT. Another group in our building gathers intelligence on "the Zionists", called ISPAL. 'Really, why them, especially?' I express fascination, and the detail is spelled out: whom they watch, and why. Of course, I don't know if it's true.

The sirens sound again as the doodlebugs crash down. Their sinister rattle comes into earshot and cuts out a few seconds before a huge explosion. In the tense silence, inevitably your thoughts turn to hoping this one will kill another person rather than yourself. Not just a bomb, then, but a fiendish moral test: Made in Germany.

'You have to laugh,' everyone counsels, 'or you'd cry.' The wireless offers a stream of uproarious farce. As important as the news report is the wild nonsense of *ITMA* – It's That Man Again (i.e. Hitler). At the same time there's the melancholy. Grief is not worthy of comment. Houses in any street have lost a fine son, or more than one; or father, or both, maybe a sister, daughter, grand-mother. 'You just have to get on with it,' they say. They mean, with life.

The doodlebugs provide an ideal pretext to tell Harry and Otto I must see how Mother is coping. In Lowestoft, I find the entire town given over to the war, uniforms everywhere, servicemen, wardens, Home Guard, volunteers, WVS. I walk up to the Denes, the bombed-out wharf where once I used to play. A wrecked smokehouse still has *Fred*[k.] *Behrens* painted across a half-collapsed roof. Our sheds are a waste-ground of broken masonry and jagged shards. The cold North Sea waves still toss against the quayside, and the memory of Father standing there is so vivid I might put my arm through his.

The British Restaurant is in a brick hut at Lowestoft Ness, most easterly point in Britain. Despite its hazardous location, the restaurant has somehow survived all the attacks on the town and the crash-landings of shot-down German bombers. Mother, her face now oddly gaunt for such a plump woman, sits on a chair inside. The place is an oasis of cleanliness and calm, done out in green and cream, linoleum on the floor and lithographs on the walls, tables in straight lines.

'Hello, Mother.'

'Oh, you, is it? Come for a free meal?' There's no other greeting. She's speaking French. Since Father died, she's forsworn the German tongue, and is almost as reluctant to speak Russian. Her French isn't bad. I suspect she barely talks to anyone in any language.

'No objection to paying my way,' I answer in English.

She gestures wearily to go ahead and eat. I tuck in to bean soup, and meat pie with boiled potatoes and cabbage, hearty and satisfying. Mother, across the table, raises a hand to her head in utter despair.

She mumbles unclearly about a raid one snowy evening in January. 'Alerts all the time, all the time. Awake for hours every night. On edge every day. Last year. This year. They even shoot guns at us from the planes as they fly over.' She returns always to the subject of the January raid. It obsesses her. 'A pilot came down low to shoot a little boy who was caught in the park! They don't just want to win the war. They want to break hearts. Germans, Germans, Germans. Germans.' She grimaces with such anguish that her face is hardly recognisable. 'All my life, they spoiled everything I had, God-forsaken swine, may they be blotted out.' I assure her I feel the same.

She chides me for leaving the British Restaurant entirely in her hands. The next brother has been called up, which means three of her sons are on the battlefield while I, she comments acidly, am 'hiding in an office.' Mother is so despondent that she no longer goes to the shelter, adopting a fatalistic attitude.

She joins me for a rib-lining pudding of plain and jam, with a pot of tea as strong as you like. The whole bill is only 1/3½d. 'Ach, it's on the house,' Mother says with grudging generosity.

'I don't mind paying.' In the end she asks me to pay for her meal as well as my own.

Dressed as for a funeral, complete with a black veil on my hat, early next morning I walk back to Lowestoft station for the train to

Norwich, and onward to Cambridge. The connecting service from there to Bedford is packed with soldiers and factory girls. After a long wait, I board a juddering old bus to Bletchley.

Ernst's billet is probably being watched. But Ernst and others at BP have a standing invitation to Friday night dinner with what is said to be the only Jewish family in Bletchley. He tries never to miss it. Their little terraced house is only five minutes' walk from the railway station, but comings-and-going at Bletchley station are constantly monitored. So I prefer to arrive by bus with time to spare, which I spend unwatched inside a church.

As the moment approaches, I make my way to the house. It too is under observation, and I don't intend to join them for the Sabbath meal. On the other side of the road, I pause to apply powder to my cheeks, looking in the looking-glass of my compact. I recognise most of the guests as they arrive. They walk straight in – clearly the door is not locked. At last I see Ernst in the glass, but he's with a friend.

Nothing for it. Before they have even noticed me, I cross the road and tap Ernst's arm. When he turns sharply to see the face beneath the veil, I have a finger on my lips. He understands at once and leaves his friend with an amiable 'You go in. Tell them I'm coming.'

'Sh, Ernst, walk with me. Cross the road. Something important.'

One half of me argues with the other, asserting that what I'm about to say to Ernst is not covered by the Act, because it's not to do with my own work. The more sober half says Yvette mentioned it in confidence, so it is covered. I go ahead and tell Ernst what I discovered, little as it is, about ISPAL. 'I thought you would want to know straight away.'

He listens; shakes his head. 'Marjorie, Marjorie! We already know about ISPAL. In fact… well, it's so complicated. There's much more going on than you may realise.' He pauses, and changes tack, explaining. 'It's not *us* they're after.'

His pause has awful implications. 'Ernst! You're not *helping* them spy on Zionist groups, are you?'

'Marjorie, the situation in Palestine, between us and the British,' there's another disconcerting pause, 'is delicate. There are differences of opinion, irreconcilable differences. We are all aware of their shortcomings concerning Palestine, but our own feeling is that the British – or rather, the English-speaking nations – are our best chance to defeat fascism and antisemitism, and our greatest hope for freedom. Our view is that it would be unwise to fall out with the Allies. And their view is that they don't want to fall out with the Jews. Because with the Arabs supporting Germany... one has to make the right choice in difficult circumstances.'

Ernst puts a hand on my arm, his expression frank and almost devoted. 'But I'm pleased and grateful you came to me. We won't forget.' He kisses my cheek. 'I must go now. Shabbat shalom.'

Pity the millions bombed out of their homes, on icy nights like these! And as if doodlebugs weren't enough, there's this latest thing to cope with, the new rockets called V2s (doodlebugs being V1s). Harry jokes that mathematicians are safe because they believe in the Theory of Improbability.

Well wrapped, we arrive at his new digs south of the river. He's going to show me the place before we go 'up West' for the evening. He unlocks the front door and in we go.

I'm in the hallway half turned away from the door – Harry has hung up his coat, I see him from the corner of my eye –

he's about to go up the stairs, his foot is on the bottom step – my own coat is off one shoulder, one arm out of its sleeve –

I notice Harry's coat on a hook, unaccountably trembling – the hook is quivering too –

there's only half a second to start feeling puzzled about it before –

Harry's front door is travelling down the hall faster than a bus, hitting the whole left side of my body, slamming me against the wall, banging my head hard on the wallpaper, missing the lethal coat hooks by a less than an inch. Blood is flowing over my face like... a dozen cracked eggs. In that instant I'm grappling with an almighty headache, a huge roaring bang of pain from nowhere, rolling round and round inside me like thunder,

and the clattering din of bricks and shattered masonry hurled at the other side of the door, followed at once by a bewildering emptiness as silent and dark as a whole universe being switched off. Then a bright light fills everything, shining like the sun through my eyelids.

At first I think it's the flash from a bomb, but everything has become perfectly still. The air is warm. Is it a fire? I hear voices far away. Through flickering lids I gather that I am no longer in Harry's hallway. My eyes close again and I retreat, trying to understand. I open my eyes again. With my fingertips I feel a cool iron bedframe. A nurse moves soundlessly beside the bed. This is a hospital ward.

'Is Harry all right?' I say. My words sound faint in my own ears, as if less than a whisper. Have I uttered them? I try to speak louder, 'Hello, nurse. Is Mr Rosen all right?'

She makes no reply but stares at me astonished, opens the door and calls out, 'Doctor? Doctor?'

I know now. Harry has been badly hurt. A V2 landed two streets away. Twenty houses down, dozens more wrecked, and several deaths – they won't say how many. Scores more in the hospital, mostly women, carried here by other women with their own injuries.

They tell us a V2 is silent because it arrives faster than sound, but as I recall there was something audible, a sort of gasp, as if the house has exhaled and at the same time taken the air out of your lungs.

Harry was blown right into the basement, together with the splintered staircase he was climbing. A piece of timber ripped his back open, twisting and tearing the flesh down to the ribcage on the left side. The right side, and his spine, are intact. 'We've given him morphine.' But they're busy with others, worse off than him.

'May I see him?'

'No, you must rest. Your injuries need time to heal. So do his.'

The doctor breaks it to me that I may never fully recover. 'Damaged tendons and joints, a lot of internal scarring. Oh, you'll be fine for normal purposes, just some weakness. It'll catch up with you in later life, that's when you'll feel it.'

More injured are hurried in from another V2 strike. Everyone's nervy, eyes darting at the sky, at the window. There's no siren. V2 explosions happen anywhere without warning any second, any day, any night, big enough to brush away whole streets in an instant, erase whole families, blind you, deafen you, flick your limbs off, and gouge a crater deep into the English earth before you know. Waiting, waiting for the next one. Behind you, or in front. I am constantly expecting another to land on this hospital and finish me off.

Yet this is the last roll of the dice for Germany's folie de grandeur. Yvette brings flowers and joyous news: even while rockets are being fired at us, the Red Army has raced through Poland and set up camp east of the ruined streets of Berlin. The Aryan supermen are running for their lives, helter-skelter, whipped and squealing across Europe, like dirty bathwater spinning down the plug. Fleeing packs of them give final vent to their bloodlust, shooting wildly, wiping out villages as they go. Very poor losers, the Master Race.

There comes a day when I slip on my shoes and coat, and make my way at visiting time to the Men's Ward. Harry's heavily bandaged around the chest, but cheerful and perky, his face as lovely a sight as anything I've seen.

He smiles sheepishly and we hold hands. 'Sorry about that,' says he with sparkling eyes. 'I promise it won't happen again.'

'How can you be sure?'

'Did I say I was sure? Just because I promise, it doesn't mean I'm sure. That's the difference between logic and linguistics.' He seems intoxicated and rambling. 'Or mathematics and language. Or words and numbers. Or something.'

I lean down to kiss his head. 'Shush, dear, be calm. Try to rest.'

He says, 'Oh, and Marjorie, as I was about to say, before we were so rudely blown up... will you marry me?'

I laugh, not sure if this is a joke, or the morphine. 'Yes, Harry, of course. One of these days, bound to.'

'You will?' His eyebrows rise in genuine surprise. 'Oh, good. I was afraid you might not.'

'Silly! Why wouldn't I?'

'Theory of Improbability.'

Luckily we're both out of hospital in time for VE Day. I'm called to a meeting. "C" is in the room – Sir Stewart Menzies – together with Sinclair Bannerman from Section B, and another man. It's a surprise to see Sinclair again as Section B is so secret, and anyway is to be wound up; or so we were informed straight after VE Day.

Sir Stewart introduces 'Sir Leonard Peters, from Vienna.' Holding out a hand without hesitation, the newcomer exclaims 'Delighted to meet you, Miss Behrens.' He has a crisp, top-drawer accent with a rather attractive slight lisp, and I find myself looking into intelligent, inquisitive eyes. The dark hair is neatly trimmed and brushed. He wears a beautifully cut suit. Whether he is head of station in Vienna or has some other position, I can't guess and probably don't need to know. His slight form and elegance makes me think of those strong, delicate steel cables that hold up bridges.

'Please do sit. Tea, whisky? I hear you were hurt. I hope you have recovered?' "C" wastes not another second in chit-chat. 'Someone who claims to know you has surfaced, and could be useful to us.'

I accept a cup of tea and a digestive biscuit. 'Who is this person?'

Sir Leonard Peters replies for him, 'As the Russians reached Berlin, a high-ranking Nazi turned up in Austria.'

'And do I know him?'

'No, not him – her. He and his wife managed to be re-classified as non-Nazis. They're currently stuck in the Russian zone. It's the wife who approached us. She asked me to find you. She didn't know your name and there's no record. I contacted Sir Stewart.'

"C" nods to confirm the story, adding, 'The lady wants me to check your identify by asking where Frau Schneider's pension is.'

'That's good, sir. She has a sense of humour. Frau Schneider's pension is in Heideseebad.' He is most contented with the reply.

Peters smiles, 'The lady simply walked into our embassy, asked to speak to the ambassador but was sent to me. Very useful meeting.'

Between them, the two men explain what was so useful about it. Peters does most of the talking. 'The lady and her husband have well-placed contacts in the Soviet Occupation Zone, most of them as anti-Communist as themselves. She says she has connections in the Socialist Unity Party; people who joined when they saw which way things were blowing. Your friend is extremely ingenious.'

"C" adds, 'The lady is able to travel frequently from the Soviet Zone in Vienna to the Soviet Zone in Berlin '

Sinclair says nothing; he has been completely quiet since I arrived. I have a feeling he thinks I am being told too much. Actually, I think *he* is being told too much. There's no reason for him to know about Erika. Or perhaps Sinclair has some other role, apart from Section B.

Peters says, 'Odd, I know, but the lady insists on dealing with you and only with you. She trusts no one. Refuses point-blank to work with the embassy, says it's too risky.'

Sir Stewart interjects, 'I feel quite relaxed about it. Two ladies, both civilians. I feel we should accede. Indeed, what alternative do I have? As she sees it, she's acting in the best interests of her own country, not ours. All the same, if a foreign national provides you with intelligence, and you share it with us, Miss Behrens, what objection could we make?'

There is a small smile, perhaps at the foibles of women. 'In any event I shall run it myself. A summary of what she sends, decrypted, together with your analysis, must come directly to me. *Directly* to me. *No one* else.' To protect Erika's source, no one is to know who she is or who I am. Except, of course, Peters himself.

Despite saying he'll run it himself, "C" now says Peters is to be my point of contact. 'Well, Miss Behrens,' "C" gets to his feet and holds out his hand, 'sorry, pressed for time. Mr Bannerman and I must take our leave. Delighted to meet you again.'

Sinclair too has leapt up and shakes my hand, 'Bye then, Marjorie. Nice to see you again.'

'We'll leave you and Sir Leonard to discuss details,' explains "C". He means codenames, passwords, mailboxes and cover story.

Peters waits until the door is closed. 'Right-o, Miss Behrens, here's what we know.' His tone is brisk and to the point. 'Herr Jünger was a senior official in the Deutsche Reichsbahn. Austrian railways was part of Deutsche Reichsbahn, so it was part of his remit. Since liberation, Austria has its own national railway system.'

'Ah – I see. So now he is…'

'Exactly: a senior official in Österreichische Bundesbahnen. The wife is a master of hiding in plain sight. She's a private secretary in the Bundeskammer, the Austrian Chamber of Trade, a specialist in negotiating trade deals between the new Austrian government and the Soviet Occupation Zone. In that capacity she regularly accompanies trade missions, on Austrian diplomatic papers, into the Russian Sector of Berlin. She has a contact there willing to provide her with highly sensitive information. This is confidential, Miss Behrens, under the Act. Never to be divulged. Could cost lives.'

'Of course, sir.'

'Now, Frau Jünger has excellent cover. What about yourself?'

'I'm in the head office of J. Lyons & Co., intending to pursue a career within the company.'

'I see.' He looks doubtful. 'You're not married. Any prospects?'

'Oh! Well, I do have a young man. We have an attachment.'

'Because you know, ordinary wife and mother, the comings and goings of normal family life, for a lady to pass unnoticed that's the very best thing.'

Tack, tack, on the window, pebbles tossed at the glass. I look out with a frisson of alarm. Harry is on the pavement, smiling up and singing. Traffic dashes past and pedestrians too, while he stands oblivious, serenading me with our French chanson. I open the window and call out, 'Not today, thank you!' but he is undaunted. *'J'attendrais, Le jour et la nuit, J'attendrais toujours....'* He sings well and with buckets of sentiment. Seeing me at the window, he holds up a red rose and redoubles his agonies.

Adorable, idiotic man! There's something truly touching in his buffoonery. *I'll wait, day and night, I'll wait always...* He's already won my heart, but he can't stop winning it.

Poor Harry Rosen is besotted. Mind sharp as a blade, immovably rational in argument, yet also ridiculously whimsical and emotional – and vulnerable, too quickly hurt, longing to be appreciated, and, I think, always expecting not to be. I rush down to let him in.

N

Sunday, January the second, a fine, cold morning at the start of the year which was to be Marjorie Rosen's last. Philip called Sandcliffe Infirmary to ask if she had been sent home yet, or was still in Acute Admissions.

'She's been moved up to Ward 26.' – 'What's Ward 26?' – 'Geriatric.' His call was put through to the ward. The nurse said Mrs Rosen was too confused to speak to him.

Was this true? Was there even the slightest particle of truth in it? His mother was the most unconfused person he had ever met.

'It's very common in ladies with UTI,' the nurse explained.

'UTI?' Philip could not understand how urinary tract infection had got into the picture. No one seemed to know if his mother had been admitted with back pain, stomach pain or chest pain. Now this! The nurse went on to tell Philip that Mrs Rosen was being a nuisance. 'She wanders around hassling other patients and taking their things. She has to be physically stopped from walking out of the ward.'

'We are talking about Mrs Marjorie Rosen? She can't take ten steps without help. She uses a zimmer frame. She can't wander around at the best of times.'

The nurse insisted it was so. 'If you *could* come in and have a word with her about her behaviour, that would be good.'

Speed limits and lane closures led the traffic slowly in single file between heaps of blackened snow. Inside Philip's car, warm air blew steadily from the vents. The wipers ceaselessly slapped away a fog of filthy spray. South of the M4 there had been no snow. Instead, under oblique sunlight a shining, skating lacquer of ice polished the road.

He arrived exhausted at Ward 26 in the middle of the afternoon. The nurses' station was unoccupied. Colourful streamers and *Merry Christmas* hung across an eerily deserted corridor. To the right was a room of decrepit men on hospital cots, many half uncovered. To the left, smaller rooms were lined with elderly women in unmade beds, dishevelled, fastidiousness utterly abandoned. Among them, his mother sat slumped in a bedside chair.

He went in. The hot air was acrid and choking with repulsive odours. 'Hello, Mummy.' She looked up with eyes glistening, their loose rims bright red, the flesh below tinted dark grey. Her gaze struck him as oddly unseeing.

'Philip?' in a faint, rasping voice. Her hand reached out.

'How are you feeling, Mum?' He could see she was wretched. For once, Marjorie did not declare that she was *very* well. 'Glass of water.' Her lips were crusted and white, scored with cracks.

He noticed *Nil by Mouth* posted above the bed, went to the sign and took it down. In cupboards beside a basin at the end of the ward he discovered plastic beakers and filled one from the tap. Marjorie sipped the water like a cat, dipping her tongue into the liquid. She held the cup close as if she would fight to keep it.

Philip had never seen his mother in such a mess. She wore her own nightdress, dressing gown and slippers, but everything awry, one slipper discarded, a shoulder uncovered. Thin strands of silvery hair tumbled loose from her bun. The pale face, with colourless eyes, hairless brows and high forehead, seemed strangely waxy. She was not wearing her compression stockings. The legs were swollen, stained purple beneath the skin.

'Gosh, there's a horrid smell in here!'

She seemed much recovered after a single cup of water. She said, 'This is the end of the line, isn't it? No wonder they call it Ward 26. Someone has a sense of humour. Ward Z might be better.' The smell, she explained, was because nurses did not bring bedpans and would not help patients go to the toilet. 'Some just do it and lie in it. I force myself to walk to the toilet. I haven't had a wash since I got here, and nothing to eat. Can you get me something, a sugar cube, anything?'

Two days with no food! At a volunteer stall on the ground floor, adorned with Christmas decorations, he bought yogurt, biscuits, take-away teas with sachets of sugar. He fed her the yogurt with a disposable spoon. She could not manage it on her own.

'Help me to the toilet, Philip, there's a good boy.'

'Course, Mum. And I'll help you wash and tidy up.' Marjorie screwed up her face with pain as he raised her. 'Where does it hurt?'

She pointed vaguely at her torso. 'Bad if I turn,' she said. 'Not bad if I keep still.'

He helped her along the ward, the flaccid thighs and breasts of pitiful elderly women to either side hardly concealed by their disarranged bedding. A crazed patient in a shabby gown, shuffling constantly from bed to bed, picking up other people's property, paused to utter words of her own invention. Another patient shrieked at her, another shouted, 'Help me, help me.' It was Bedlam neon-lit.

The washroom visit finished, Philip said, 'I'll find a nurse and see if they can get you a walking frame and put your stockings on.'

'Be careful. They punish anyone who complains. I mean, *really* punish them. Philip, you need to know, these are not ordinary nurses in here. Some of them are trying to kill me.'

He treated it lightly. She was in earnest. 'Don't believe me, do you? They watch us as we try to cope. Have you ever seen the faces of children pulling the wings off a fly? The fascination of cruelty. Turning a beetle onto its back. Stoning an injured bird to death. The nurses here have the same look. And,' she added, 'one of them stole my address book.'

'No, Mum, they wouldn't do that.' He searched for it in the bedside cabinet. 'Is my handbag still there?' she cried. Her handbag was still in the cabinet. 'My picture of Harry, did they take it?' The tiny silver-framed photo of his father was still in the handbag. 'My door keys?' The door keys were still there. He went to the bedside of the wandering, filching patient to see whether it had been taken there. At last he found the precious address book under Marjorie's bed, hidden among rolls of dust. 'Here, Mum. You must have dropped it.'

'I didn't drop it. They threw it there when they'd finished so it would *look* as if I'd dropped it. That's exactly what one would do. Or,' the idea struck her, 'did *you* have it?'

'Did I have it?' he smiled, alarmed. Being starved must have affected her mind. 'No, Mummy, I just got here after a long drive.' She might not believe him and he could not prove it. 'And Mum, the nurses here might be overworked or incompetent or lazy, I don't know which, but I really doubt that they are trying to kill you.'

'Why not? Don't you think,' Marjorie demanded, 'our enemies *would* take the chance while we lie helpless in hospital?'

'Enemies! What enemies? And what would be the point in trying to kill people who are on their last legs? The place to attack would be the maternity ward, not the geriatric.'

'How naïve you are! They're doing that as well!'

Sighting a male nurse, he dashed to ask if Mrs Rosen could have her compression stockings put on. The man, bearded and handsome, said, 'Of course. We will deal with Mrs Rosen later.'

'There,' said Philip, 'everything sorted!'

'Think so? Call Carol, tell her it's urgent.'

Philip put his bag in Marjorie's guest room. He looked around the flat, went into his mother's bedroom. Every item that ever she had used or touched was redolent with a sense of her. One side of the mattress was Mum's, with pillows indented, the other side occupied only by memories. Of Dad, of the two of them.

From this thought he drew back as if opening someone's diary. In any case he could not turn the pages. He knew nothing of his parents' relationship. He had reached the closed book of her.

He picked up a photograph of his father and studied the face. Philip was older now than his father had been in this picture. He knew he had disappointed his father. Well, Dad was dead now and his disappointment didn't matter any more. Of course, one day Mum would die too, and her feelings about him wouldn't matter either.

In the kitchen he heated some chicken soup, ate a bowlful and filled a flask with it to take to her. He made a list of her usual medication for the nurses. He was back at the ward by seven.

Marjorie had slipped a long way further downhill. They had not put her stockings on. She lay with eyes half open, stupefied. What had they done to her? Around the ward, call buttons were sounding and tremulous voices calling unanswered.

He roused her to try the soup. With a flick of the fingers she waved it away. 'Water, darling, pour me some water.' He put a plastic beaker to her lips. Grabbing it, she jerked half the water into her mouth, half onto her face. He wiped her with his handkerchief. Suddenly she uttered a horrible croaking cry. 'They're going to do me in, Philip. I heard them discussing it in Russian.'

Too blandly he said it was not so; that they were discussing some ordinary nursing routine. 'You think I couldn't understand them?' She struggled to emerge from the stupor, accusing him in hateful realisation, 'My God! You *are* on their side! You were *always* against us.' She fell back, eyes closed, expressionless.

Philip murmured 'Goodbye, Mum.' As he left, he saw a nurse. She assured him that Mrs Rosen was taking all the medication on his list, plus an antibiotic for the urinary infection. 'And morphine sulphate, to make her comfortable.'

'Does she really need morphine?'

'To make her comfortable.'

'When will she be seen by the doctor?'

'After the holiday. Probably have tests next Wednesday.'

'Can I mention, Mum's supposed to wear compression stockings every day. It's to do with blood pressure. They were prescribed by a cardiologist in this hospital, actually. Could someone put them on her? I left them on the bed. By the way, Mum doesn't sleep much, so she'll be awake most of the night, if anyone has time to do it then.'

'Oh, don't you worry, she'll sleep all right.'

There was little traffic in Sandcliffe that evening. A few reflected red and white lights skittered by on the frosted tarmac. Alone in the flat, Philip would have loved a drink. He found only an ancient bottle of cream sherry. He started a shopping list, with beer and wine at the top. He made two fried eggs, ate them with a piece of buttered bread and a glass of milk, watched television and wearily texted first Carol, then Max and Nicola. *Mum really bad. Weird and paranoid. Not eating. Still not seen by doctor. Not wearing her stockings. Tests scheduled for next Weds. Nothing till then.*

* * *

Hardly surprising that a young man who loves dancing and flirting is an enthusiast for the marital bed. Harry's romantic side continues at full strength. More surprising is the passion he evokes in a chilly, stick-in-the-mud girl. People speak of women 'consenting', 'giving themselves'; but Harry and I require no demands nor consent. We have passed through that door into a glorious private world, a conspiracy of delight in which all is permitted, all is good, all is us.

Afterwards, as we lie together, Harry holding me half-dreaming and satisfied, I find I am listening for sirens, explosions, gunfire. There is only peace and quiet and the warmth of his embrace. The sky is all clear. Gradually my mind returns to its concern. The arrangement with Erika must be re-thought. It doesn't work to use SIS mailboxes. The material is too sensitive, and it involves going to places hard to explain to Harry. We need something further from the service and nearer to home.

In the dull world outside the bedroom, with Harry (now smarter, under the guiding hand of a wife) in jacket and flannels, shirt and tie and polished brogues, and myself in cardigan, blouse and skirt, stockings and court shoes, and make-up neatly applied, I am sure the sight of Mr and Mrs Rosen does not bring sexual abandon to mind. That's our secret! Or are all young couples like us? No doubt.

In our rooms above the shop, we play chess, eat fish and chips, unravel crossword clues and make love. In the night Harry shakes me awake. 'Darling! 10 Across, I've got it!' A clue we failed to solve has been solved. Then I know for sure I have found the right man.

The more we make love, the sweeter is Harry. That's how he is when I ask, 'Harry, have you heard of the International Friendship Association? Or the Town Twinning Movement?'

I turn to gauge his reaction. 'I can imagine what they are.'

'Reaching out across borders,' I explain with a straight face, 'all over Europe.'

'Friendship, understanding,' he grins mockingly, 'an end to hatred. How silly people are, eh, dear? If only it were that easy.'

'I filled in an application form today. After all, it's an opportunity to get to know people abroad, write to them, even visit them.'

He's astounded, but doesn't want to be dismissive. There's a pause before he asks, 'Are you quite serious, darling?'

I answer that I am.

'Why, dear? I don't see the point.'

'I approve of the scheme.'

Harry accedes with a puzzled shrug and raised eyebrows. 'Well, why not, I suppose. To think world peace can be achieved simply by writing letters! Who knew? A friendly correspondence with Hitler and his gang would have spared everyone such a lot of trouble.'

On the application form, I ask to correspond with married ladies under forty who share my passion for Europe's historic ornamental gardens. Erika asks for the same. There is something absurd about the choice of topic. Most people have other things to think about. Here in Battersea High Street we don't have any garden at all, only a paved yard just large enough for a washing line. Soon I am contacted by the International Friendship Association with Erika's details, giving her name instead as Frau Jäger.

There's another name, too. A Frenchwoman, Mme Dubois, would like a lady pen-friend with an interest in turn-of-the-century botanic gardens. She wants to see how well Europe's historic gardens survived the war. Perhaps we could get together occasionally. She suggests Kew, the Riviera, Laeken, Munich. If Frau Jäger can join us once in a while, so much the better. This is fortuitous. We shall all write in the language of the recipient, and correct each other's mistakes. To keep my end up in our correspondence, I subscribe to a gardening magazine and borrow gardening books from Battersea Library. I read them when it's quiet in the shop. The subject is surprisingly interesting.

The door bursts open, jangling the brass bell, and there's a voice I remember. I look across the counter. She has a small hat pinned to her hair, which is now up in 'Victory Rolls'. She's very stylishly kitted-out, pale blue overcoat, kid gloves, sheer stockings, nice shoes, beautiful make-up.

It's three years since I last saw Yvette, three years since Section B was wound up, three years since my undercover work with Erika began, three years in which everything changed for me and for the entire world. I didn't expect to see any of the old team again, and certainly not in my shop. 'Hello, Marjorie!'

'Bonjour, Yvette! Come for some wallpaper?'

She laughs merrily and I like her for that. I always did like Yvette. 'Got anything in Russian style?' she asks.

'Hammers, sickles, that sort of thing?' I propose. 'Perhaps with a red border?'

She has a lovely, tinkling laugh. 'That would be perfect.'

I lift the counter flap and invite her onto my side. We hold on to one another briefly and exchange a peck on each cheek. 'This is a nice surprise.' She'll know I'm under no illusion that it's a social call.

She pulls off her gloves, tugging them finger by finger. She has a natural elegance. 'Oh, Marjorie,' she notices the bump, 'expecting?'

I hold up my knitting, soft white wool on the needles. 'A little jacket for him or her.'

'How gorgeous! Alors, since the war, we both became married women. Look!' She holds up her hand proudly to show the ring.

I assume she finally got hitched to Sinclair Bannerman. There was an intimacy between them at Section B. But I'm wrong. She tells me about Goff – Godfrey Oakeshott, an older man (she doesn't say by how much), a captain in Signals Intelligence, handsome and gentlemanly, so she assures me. They live in his grand house in Sunningdale, within easy reach of London.

'So, you are Madame Oakeshott now!'

'Owner of a real live man. Can we talk, Marjorie?' she asks lightly. 'It's about – you know.' The shop is empty, but it feels wrong and dangerous to say anything confidential in here. And they did tell us: *you'll never talk about this*. I have no wish to do so.

'No, frankly I'd rather not discuss it. Cup of tea, Yvette? And I made some pastries.'

'Tea would be nice. No pastry,' in a confidential, woman-to-woman tone, 'I really must watch my figure.' She looks around admiringly. 'This is so nice! We had a shop just like this one. This is how I grew up. It's boarded up now. I'd go back, if I only could, to how we were in those days, before the war,' she says wistfully.

'Ah, if only we could.'

'In spirit, maybe. Well, if ever we retire from this life…'

'If ever I retire and people wonder what became of old Marjorie, look for me on a quayside beside the English sea.'

'Except there is no retiring from fighting for what you believe in. That's why I'm here.'

The start and end of the day are the busy times. Customers queue for a bottle of turps, a roll of lining paper, a bag of cellulose flakes, a tin of distemper, or to borrow wallpaper catalogues. I stock odds and ends like nails, too, scooped and sold by weight. During the afternoon, hardly anyone comes in. I sit behind the wide wooden counter, taking the chance to read, to study and to knit. The touch of wool, a suit of baby clothes, tiny cardigans, adorable little bootees; the clack of needles is contemplative.

On the other side of the plate glass, a murmuring throng in old coats presses along Battersea High Street, easing past the market stalls. Costers' cries burst out, repetitive, London voices in the air. Quieter marketeers and racketeers offer meat or children's clothes, mixed wares second-hand or stolen. Housewives hand over tuppence or thruppence for a paper bag of whatever is rationed or not rationed nor price-controlled, with or without a ration book.

Mutilated men are everywhere, lean and dull-eyed. Bomb sites at both ends of the street are children's forbidden playgrounds. They build dens amid the debris. There is bitterness in the market that rationing continues so we can give food to the defeated Nazis. In every street there's pain for which there will be no healing in our lifetime. There is a seething, tight-lipped hatred of our enemy and his comrades, and of the nearby nation which pretended to be neutral in the war of Good against Evil. Everyone has seen the diabolical newsreels: skeletal bodies heaped like broken dolls on some hideous rubbish tip; British troops staring in wide-eyed horror as they rummage through stick limbs for anyone alive.

News reports shy away from mentioning who the dead are or why they were murdered, describing all corpses as 'political prisoners'. The 'J' word is not used. When it is revealed at last that those piles of cadavers and emaciated survivors are… Jews, audiences find their horror ebbing away. But this! It has affected Harry's state of mind and his digestion. I scan the hollow faces of the dead. Father's family are somewhere here, and Mother's; lying among these profaned people, their nakedness uncovered.

Three years later, though I think of it every day, that is like news from prehistory. For this is Year One of everything new, a new Britain, a new world. This year even miracles have come to pass...

'We should celebrate!' Harry bellowed like an animal in pain after hearing Ben-Gurion's momentous Proclamation. Instead he sat down on the sofa and cried. It was an odd, dry spectacle, a few drops pressed out between racking sobs, like squeezing bitter juice from a crab apple. He wept, or didn't weep. 'People can say what they like about us now,' he said angrily, 'it won't matter any more. We'll ignore them.'

My own emotion is a turmoil of regret that I am not among those fighting to defend the new state and rescue besieged Jerusalem. Rather wonderfully, our old Bletchley Park colleague Ernst Wardmann *is* among them. He has changed his name to Ephraim Vardi and works for the Jewish Agency in Tel Aviv. By the time we manage to contact him to ask how we can help, always bearing in mind that I am pregnant, the war against Israel is well under way.

'You're pregnant? Mazeltov! A good year in which to be born. You are useful where you are, Marjorie,' is his crackly answer.

'Where I am? I run a shop!'

'I don't know anything, Marjorie. I only know what I know. Stay on the British side of the line and keep me informed of anything that might affect us, as you did once before.'

'Ernst – Ephraim, I want to use my training.' He is one of few who know what I mean. It was Ernst himself who sent me to SOE, and no doubt also saw the debriefing report.

'That episode is closed. But you have other skills. Use your contacts.'

No sooner has Ernst remarked on my contacts than Yvette has turned up in the shop. 'Hello, Marjorie!' – 'Bonjour, Yvette! Come for some wallpaper?' – 'Can we talk?' I make two cups of tea.

'At the end of the war...' she begins.

I shake my head and say firmly, 'No, really, Yvette, I don't want to discuss it.'

'At the end of the war,' she persists, 'you remember, Section B was shut down. Some of us moved to GCHQ, others to SIS. Others, like you, Marjorie, went to normal jobs.'

On reflection, I suppose it's safe to talk when the shop is empty and the door shut.

'What's GCHQ?'

'New name for GC&CS. It's not at Bletchley any more, so we don't call it BP.'

'Ah, I see.' I resist the temptation to ask more. She returns to her subject: 'The trouble with anti-Soviet work is that GCHQ and MI6 both think the other is riddled with spies. MI5 even suspect there are Communists in MI6's anti-Soviet section. The Foreign Office believe there are Communists in both MI6 *and* MI5.'

'That's not my concern.'

'Something's come up, to do with Russian ciphers. Similar to the diplomatic intercepts we worked on. We'd like you to come back and help us.'

The hair rises on the back of my head. I don't want to hear such things in my wallpaper shop. 'I don't remember anything of that sort. I can't remember much about the war.'

'Well, if you do happen to remember, come over and talk to us. You're closed on Wednesdays, aren't you?'

'That's what it says on the door.'

'Your husband comes home late on Wednesdays.' They've been watching us. 'Are you free this Wednesday?' She gives an address.

'I don't know where that is, and don't need to know.'

'I'm sorry, it's quite a long way. Fourteen stops from South Kensington on the Piccadilly Line. When you get to Eastcote, it's a ten minute walk, far end of Lime Grove, Eastcote MOD, an old RAF place. And,' she pauses, 'while you're there don't mention Section B. Not even to people you think already know about it. They don't.'

'Well, we'll see. Sure I can't tempt you to a pastry?'

'For old times' sake, then! We often went out for our tea and pastry, didn't we?' Yvette smiles. It's clear how keen she is to be on friendly terms. 'This isn't proper pâtisserie, of course. Viennoiseries, we call them in France, I'm not sure why. No doubt your friend in Vienna would know! Still in touch with her?'

I practically jump with the shock. How does she know about Erika? Sinclair Bannerman must have mentioned it to her. He shouldn't have. Why would he?

Or does she know as part of her duties? In which case, why does she need to ask? No one was supposed to know about my contact in Vienna apart from Sir Leonard Peters and "C" himself. The *only* other person who had an inkling of it was Sinclair.

I have an unpleasant, sick sensation in my stomach. Could be the baby moving around. I try to control my breathing, breathe normally. 'Vienna? No,' as if trying to remember, 'no, I don't know anyone there.' If Sinclair did tell Yvette, she will know this is not true. If he just happened to mention it, that's not her fault. Very likely she asked her question in all innocence. I change my answer: 'Oh, I know who you mean. No, we're not in touch any more.'

'Ah! Anyway, famous for viennoiseries, Vienna!'

'Presumably.'

'Oh, and waltzes,' she laughs.

'I've never been there.' I still feel nauseous, like vertigo, like realising it's getting dark and I'm lost, like the ice I'm walking on is thinner than I thought, and the waters beneath colder and deeper.

With a jolly toot, the tube train rushes out of its tunnel into daylight. We rattle cheerfully past the fine new housing schemes of Middlesex. The carriages are almost empty, and remain so as the doors slide open and closed at stations I have never heard of in London's burgeoning suburbs. I suppose it's busier in the morning and evening. I sit in my seat for an hour, knitting and reading, and wondering what GCHQ want from me. Of course I must accept Yvette's invitation, and am also mindful of Ernst's remark about maintaining my contacts.

Extraordinary to see American soldiers manning a British defence establishment, but that's what I find at Eastcote MOD. The Stars and Stripes on a flagpole, rows of long white huts under watchtowers.

I expected to meet Yvette here, but I'm taken to the office of a man I've seen a couple of times before but never spoken to – military bearing but civilian dress, young middle-aged but with a head of silvery white hair. He introduces himself as a Bernard Wilworth, giving no title or rank. He's calm, affable and impenetrable.

We stroll to a garden beside a Wrens barracks and sit on a bench. I ask if I saw him at BP in Hut 4 and at Block B during the war. He says I'm correct on all points. He remembers me, too, or says he does. He asks how well I speak Russian. We swap a few words. 'I'm better in Spanish,' he laughs, 'but we're not spying on them.' Then for an added punchline, 'Well, we are, but that's another matter.'

The implication is obvious. GCHQ have formally switched their focus from Germany to the Soviet Union. 'At BP,' muses Wilworth, 'there used to be an ongoing debate about sharing intelligence with the Americans, didn't there?'

I remember it well. My beau of the time, Bob Shaffer was part of that early cooperation. 'Things have moved on,' says Wilworth. 'UK-USA intelligence sharing is in place for the long term. I'd like to talk to you confidentially about a highly secret joint project. This is all covered by the Act, Mrs Rosen. The object is to intercept Russian diplomatic and intelligence communications, and find supporting collateral, to discover the extent of Soviet penetration into Western administrations and into our own networks.' This is in line with the summary Yvette gave on her visit to the shop. Wilworth says, 'The Americans have a huge team working on it at Arlington. We only have half-a-dozen people so far.' I remember Ernst saying never to ask who put my name forward. It could only be Yvette.

'Based here?' Eastcote MOD stands at the end of a respectable street. I wonder what the neighbours would say if they knew.

'For the moment. We're setting up listening stations everywhere from here to Australia, and will need better premises than this.'

'May I ask, sir, what progress so far?'

He's as forthcoming as if I had already joined the team. 'What we've found is frankly shocking. An array of espionage permeating almost all our major institutions. The Soviets have a *huge* network in place. Some are embedded in our intelligence departments.'

'Inside GCHQ and MI6?'

He nods. 'That's right.'

'And who is aware of this operation?'

'On our side, only the directors and assistant directors of MI5, MI6 and GCHQ. No one else is privy to this material except the team itself. But we've hit a rock. The Russians tightened up their cipher procedure just when we were on the verge of a breakthrough. And that keeps happening.'

'Why, what have they done?'

'Thing is, they were very slapdash before. Some of their codes resembled each other. Trade codes resembled Diplomatic. One-time pads were compromised. Operators had private conversations mixing code and clear. Suddenly all that's stopped.'

'The Soviets must have found out about the project.'

Wilworth nods his head vigorously. 'Yes, our guess is it's one of Arlington's legion of Russian-speaking advisors. They wander about with the flimsiest of security screening.'

'Might it be at this end, even someone in your own group?'

Wilworth is amused by the suggestion that his own brand-new hand-picked team might so quickly have been infiltrated. He impresses on me that not even the Prime Minister has been informed about it yet. 'Above Top Secret', is how he describes the project. 'Politicians are not to know about it. For two reasons: they can't keep a secret and many may themselves be Soviet sympathisers.'

'What exactly would my role be, sir?'

'To decrypt, translate and analyse intercepted traffic and crack the cover names. We hope at least to identify their locations. You'd be one of a number of analysts at arm's length from GCHQ, people not known to our insiders or to each other.'

'Except Yvette,' I point out. 'She knows who I am.'

'She's not GCHQ. She's an MI6 officer who joined my team.'

So it is that I am inducted – "cleared and indoctrinated", in GCHQ parlance – into Bride, known as Venona in America. The name is irrelevant, for we are never to refer to the project by name.

Only at this point does Wilworth reveal, 'Right, Mrs Rosen, so actually you'll be working on intercepts from a new source – in Vienna.' For a moment I may have blanched, since he surely cannot mean Erika. But this is not about Erika. She is not mentioned. 'The source is the Russian Embassy itself. It's not a radio intercept. This comes directly from the telephone cables between the embassy and their military HQ in the Russian Zone.'

'Gosh, you mean a phone tap, sir? How exciting!'

'This is absolutely never to be spoken about, not even to colleagues on our own team. A separate unit of German and Russian speakers will study the material. You're now part of that unit.'

On the journey back into London, I step out of the carriage at a small station and wait for the next train. No one follows me. Why, why, have I agreed to do this? Now that the war's over, the baby due and things going so well for Harry and me!

Ernst asked me to stay on the British side, but it's more than that. True, this Russian phone tap could produce something for Ernst, and I hope it does. It seems though that I am in thrall to England, to something marvellous which I so admire – despite all the betrayals and failings, despite the wretched Foreign Office and their beloved Palestine, despite everything. Not England's destiny, if that implies the hand of God or the gods – but another kind of destiny, those accidents of history, geography, language and ancestry that direct a nation's steps.

Since I have been asked to take a part in its destiny, I shall do so. And the secrecy, is that really such a burden? Life is a solitary affair anyhow. None of us can be known, nor shared. In a way, being married is a constant reminder of solitude. I leave the tube at South Ken station, catch a number 49 and get home before Harry. The heart and mind are secret places. All the rest is play-acting.

The great game continued, but it was no game. Marjorie could see, anyone could see, that most ward staff were émigrés, émissaires or envoyés from enemy states. The old alliances were still ranged against us. She must stay alert. There's no one to turn to for help. Philip took their side over her address book. Did he think her a fool?

And she heard Philip mention morphine to a nurse. He was still mixed up in that business! Marjorie battled the narcotic as she had been trained to do. She was having some success, she believed, as far as its effect on the mind; in the body, it was harder to fight. As soon as the ward's overhead neon was dimmed, she saw more clearly. Since her macular degeneration became worse, bright light dazzled like driving into the setting sun. She detected fanciful, impossible visions and mirages, knowing all the while that there *is* a real world, out of arm's reach, crystal clear if she could but see it.

She woke again, unbearably thirsty, tongue like an immense wedge of cardboard, throat raw as sandpaper, as if trying to swallow a whole mouthful of dry, dead leaves. On the table at the far end of the bed stood a jug of water and a plastic beaker.

She managed to lower the bedrail and swing her legs off the bed. Holding the bedside, step by step she moved towards the water. But reaching it, the jug was as heavy as a cast-iron bollard. Nor would the disposable beaker fit inside. She plunged one hand into the water and wiped the exquisite liquid onto her lips and tongue. It would be easier to drink from the washbasin tap at the end of the ward. So began another mighty trek.

At the nurses' station, moon-faces turned from their chatter, amused at her ungainly progress. She cleaned her teeth with one finger and splashed her face as best she could, drying herself on her nightdress as the paper towel dispenser was empty. She stared in the mirror. She tried without success to find herself in the looking glass. Her thoughts were led as by some malevolent piper towards a dark Funfair and Ghost Train. It was, perhaps, the narcotic speaking.

She decided to go home to her own room and shut the door, and sleep until all this had passed. Until she remembered something odd: she *couldn't* go home, *could* not. It was not for her to decide. They could do with her here as they wished, kill or cure, feed or starve. Healing the sick transmuted from charity into cultish freemasonry, only the initiated understood its rites and magicks. Suppliants came and went like tide, flotsam in the corridors, lying prone, waiting to be examined, humiliated, cut open.

It was always so, Medicine next to Magic. For those never in hospital, as she used never to be, or those enduring the agonies and ecstasies of the maternity ward, or who rise healed after some quick procedure or are prescribed a simple course of tablets that banish ancient terrors, for them Medicine seems God's work, angels performing miracles. So what evil angels were those, mocking her at the nurses' station, using what foul spells?

Exhausted by the walk to and from the basin, she sat on the bed, pulled up each leg in turn and settled herself among the sheets. Philip had left a newspaper folded open at the codeword, with her magnifying glass and pen. The tiny numbers and letters swirled on the paper like gnats under a tree. Shape-changing words wavered in and out of focus. The precious grid of squares trembled and tumbled like a tower of children's alphabet bricks. Figures moved about on the page, real people, phrases uttered, lines crossed and criss-crossed, incalculable angles and code that cannot be broken.

It was not visiting time, but there was no one to stop Philip as he walked into Ward 26 the next morning with a carrier bag of food for his mother. Marjorie greeted him warily, with not a trace of warmth. To her alarm, he closed the curtain so they could not be seen. 'Let's get you into your chair.' He pulled back the bedsheet. Marjorie's legs had become repugnant, hugely swollen and rainbow coloured, suppurating from repulsive sores. He eased her down to the chair.

He poured a cup of water, and put balm on her sore lips. 'I brought you some breakfast.' From the bag Philip took paper towels and cleaning spray. The dirty bed table he sprayed and wiped, wheeled it into position and drew from his bag a flask of coffee, a carton of fresh milk, plates and cups, soft bread rolls, vitamin pills and a pot of ready-made oatmeal.

Soon they began a secret breakfast behind their screen, Marjorie slumped in the chair, Philip upright on the edge of her mattress. The stench made it difficult for him to eat, but there was no choice. Marjorie could hardly manage any of the things he had brought. Above all, she wanted only to sip at the water. They sat in silence. There seemed nothing more to say or do. He persuaded her to take a vitamin pill with a little coffee and some oatmeal that he tipped into her open lips with a teaspoon.

The plastic curtains clattered open. There stood a nurse amazed by the scene. 'Oh!' said she to Marjorie, 'Can I do your readings now?' She stepped forward to take her blood pressure and temperature.

And to Philip, 'We're busy. Come back later if you want.' At that moment Marjorie retched. The breakfast had not agreed with her and made an ignominious reappearance. Philip stepped away, leaving the nurse to deal with Marjorie's emesis.

Even as Philip drove disappointed out of the hospital car park, another small car drove in. The new visitor found her way along the corridors and in the lift to Ward 26. By then the nurse had finished with Marjorie, who sat dully in her chair.

There was no time even for greetings before Carol cried out, 'Oh Marjorie, my love, what's happened to you? Oh no, you've been sick. Oh, your legs!'

'Carol, thank God it's you – please do what you can to help me.

'I didn't know you were like this!'

'The nurses want to kill me. You don't believe me, of course.'

'Oh, I believe you all right. They probably want to kill all of you,' she rejoindered encouragingly, 'useless old biddies.'

Marjorie chuckled grimly, eyes glistening. She trusted Carol. She was an ally. Philip and Nicola were not allies, and as for Max, it was because of him that Harry died when he did.

'Could you help me wash and tidy myself? The shabbier you look in this place, the shabbier they treat you.'

Carol went back to her car and returned with her own washing kit and first aid box. She set to work with towels and wipes, washing Marjorie and her clothes, cleaning and bandaging the leaking sores, finishing the task neatly before a hasty departure. 'Keep coming to visit,' Marjorie urged her.

'It's difficult. There's new clients now in your old morning and evening slots. I'll pop in again soon, promise.'

'They daren't do anything while you're here.'

* * *

'**P**hilip's in bed. You're awfully late.' Harry arrives home, eyes glistening. I might suspect him of being drunk, except that such a thing is unimaginable. 'Did you really forget his birthday? You *promised* you'd be here. He so wanted to show the other children your balancing tricks.'

Harry is beaming. 'We switched Leo on this evening.'

'Go up to Philip, wake him gently and say Happy Birthday. Give him a big hug,' I command, 'and a damn good excuse for missing his party. He's terribly disappointed. I'll make you something to eat. What's Leo? Tell me after you've seen Philip.'

Instead of going upstairs he follows me into the kitchen, speaking excitedly. 'It will be revolutionary. They think of Leo as a business machine. Hahaha! They have no idea! Culmination of six years' work, darling. Shouldn't really say anything, confidential.'

'Then don't tell me. Go up and see Philip.'

'Confidential – not classified.'

Leo, it turns out, is an electric computation machine that ex-BP boffins and the Cambridge University Mathematical Laboratory have put together for Joe Lyons & Co. 'No one's going to torture you to find *this* out!' he laughs. 'Besides, it'll be in the newspapers soon.'

Harry guesses what has come to mind. 'Don't worry,' he forestalls my concerns, 'Cambridge will get the credit. Obviously BP can't be mentioned.' His tone becomes comically conspiratorial. I wonder if he really *is* drunk. '*You* know Joe Lyons' contribution to the war effort! Munitions factories, field rations, army laundry, Building X intelligence room. Well, here's the quid pro quo, a thank you.' He paces quickly around. 'But Leo is only the *beginning*, darling! It'll give Lyons the edge for a little while. The next step will transform other businesses, and then, the whole way business is done. Transform the world, eventually.' He laughs; or giggles, rather, and clasps my hands. 'Binary arithmetic! Boolean algebra!' I smile encouragingly, frankly mystified. 'It's the invention of the steam engine all over again,' he declares grandly, 'but this time for mental processes, not physical, do you see?' His eyes are moist with ecstasy.

'All the same,' I reply, 'go and see Philip.' Harry seems to know I was once at risk of torture. Perhaps it's only a figure of speech. The other surprise is his throwaway remark about an intelligence room at Cadby Hall. That's the first I've heard of it. It might explain what Harry was doing there.

The next day he is very kind to Philip, bouncing him crazily in his arms, singing 'We're going to the circus, the jolly, jolly circus, we're going to the circus, this afternoon.' Philip joins in, squealing with delight, and off we go to Battersea Funfair as another, unexpected birthday treat. Harry tells him he's a big boy now and it's time to start learning maths. Philip is proud and happy. Harry cradles our son in his arms, singing softly to him, like a lullaby, 'The area of a circle is πr^2, the circumference is $2\pi r$.'

Philip collects used cardboard from the market traders and sells it to the salvage merchant. He passes from stall to stall, sedulously gathering every discarded box. With businesslike concentration he ties up his little haul and wheels it on his tricycle to the salvage yard by the railway line. The adored bright red Triang Junior Boys Trike has a metal boot on the back, like a car. If the pack is small, Philip carefully places it inside and pedals there. It's not far; usually I let him go on his own. Sometimes I enjoy walking with him. Battersea High Street is full of foreign voices, refugees from all over Europe, living in maisonettes above the shops. The back streets are populated by working-class locals, most of them hard pressed and struggling.

We pass through iron gates into the oily yard where tattooed, muscular types in vests buy glass, paper and cardboard by the hundredweight. They're sweet to my cheeky little boy. If he turns up with only a pennyworth of cardboard, they toss it on the scales to show him the weight, and hand him his copper with a laugh.

Philip's delighted with that. He says 'Thank you,' politely, and so charming in his grey flannel shorts, pressed cotton shirt and owlish NHS glasses, adorably boyish with his ready smile, tousled fair hair and innocent face! He's too nice for a place like this. He's scared of the belligerent kids who roam in groups around the neighbourhood.

After delivering his cardboard, Philip and I carry on to the river. We make for the bleak, rubbish-filled waterside pathway next to St Mary's Church. Here the shore of the Thames lies beside us, a gravel beach strewn with wartime iron and an expanse of shiny grey mud, the quintessential awful sludge that might eat you up and swallow you whole. Philip likes to stand on the embankment wall and drop things into it. Every little item that brushes the surface of the mud instantly disappears. Philip, feeling what fears I know not, watches with horrified joy as his tiny pebbles and twigs vanish silently into the ooze. A few yards away, the dark, swirling river continues to surge past, a filthy lifeless stream of effluent. Laden barges toil up and down, travelling to docks and warehouses downstream, and beyond to the edge of the sea.

Until now my GCHQ work has been secreted among studies for the new Advanced Level General Certificate. It's mere cover – yet I'm as nervous as any schoolgirl when the envelope arrives, *Associated Examining Board* printed across the top. Harry stands close as I pull out the flimsy typed sheet and scrutinise it. I have passed three 'A levels', as they are called, in Russian, English and German.

'Three As at A-level! Very, very, *very* well done, darling.' Harry embraces me warmly and kisses me on both cheeks. I smile with unrestrained delight. He has a success to celebrate, too. His arrives as a grand certificate rolled into a cardboard tube. Harry has passed with distinction the new University of Cambridge Diploma in Numerical Analysis and Automatic Computing, in effect, he proudly explains, the first ever post-graduate qualification in Computer Science.

With Lyons' Leo project completed, and this remarkable diploma, it might seem an anti-climax for Harry to become a humble schoolmaster. Yet he wants nothing more now, he says, than to teach mathematics to clever young people. He's absorbed in theorems and postulations, hypotheses and logic. He stays late at extra-curricular classes, or attends lectures or indeed gives them at halls around London. I am learning, he explains, 'everything I need to know to be an Englishman.' There is something tragi-comic in his ambition. Devoted anglophile and loyal British subject, but Englishman he can never be.

Nor is this bright post-War world quite as we hoped or imagined at first. The dance of old empires continues to a different tune, in different costume. Did we suppose the Soviet Union would wither away, or somehow become our friend? The Soviet Occupation Zone has become a repressive state called the German Democratic Republic, the occupying powers are leaving Austria in charge of its own affairs, and GCHQ is making its move from the Eastcote huts to more serious-minded premises at Cheltenham, far from London and a very long way indeed from our shambolic, amiable, clever Bletchley.

As well as new alliances, new enmities are fixing themselves into place. It is forbidden to harbour animus towards West Germany, or recall any atrocities. Official policy is to patch it up and look upon them as allies and a buffer between us and the Soviets. The Kremlin is consolidating its grip on Europe's 'Eastern bloc' and has created a union of Soviet-controlled totalitarian states to confront NATO.

The Russians are far ahead of us in subterfuge, communications, microfilm and bugging. They run rings round us. We're making so little progress on Bride-Venona that work is grinding to a halt. Every development is stymied. Whatever step we take, the Kremlin seems to anticipate. Nor have we found out who amongst us informed them about our phone-tap tunnel in Vienna, Operation Silver. It had to be abandoned in haste, leaving behind precious technical equipment.

A new tunnel has been opened in Berlin, though, and this one – Operation Gold, alias Stopwatch – does seem to be producing a harvest. The analysts and interpreters have a new address: we've been moved to an office near Fleet Street, under the name London Processing Group, or LPG, part of Y-Section at SIS. Our cover is journalism; LPG translates and syndicates foreign stories for the British press. I'm supposedly a freelance translator. It really does sell pieces, for verisimilitude. Our Operation Gold reports go straight to a deputy head of Y-Section, Mr George Blake.

The bus from Battersea takes an hour. After work I take the bus back via Tooting Bec Lido to swim a few lengths and use the gym. Harry knows I've found part-time work for a Fleet Street syndication agency. He's happy for me and too busy to think any more about it.

Sweet rationing has ended. Philip demands ice cream. That's fine by me. I'll have one too, please. Nothing could be nicer than a cornet (with a 99 chocolate flake, of course!) from Notarianni's gleaming tiled ice-cream parlour nearly opposite our shop. Inside the house, Nicola lies in her pram in the hallway. I pull the white crochet away from her face and make sure she's still breathing. 'Any trouble, Joanne?' – 'Good as gold, Mrs Rosen. Haven't heard a peep.' Maybe Joanne slipped her a drop of gin to shut her up. Philip is sunny and cheerful, our baby girl always discontented.

Joanne helps me for a couple of hours every day, giving Philip his tea and minding Nicola. She looks after them in her own flat on Wednesdays when the shop is closed. She even does a bit of charring for me, tying on a pinny and getting down to some washing and scrubbing. She and her husband live in a housing scheme five minutes' walk away. Her flat's up five flights of cold stone and along an unlit outside walkway. She asks what I did in the war. People do ask each other. Between ourselves, Harry and I never talk about it. Everything we did was covered by the Official Secrets Act.

Even when Dr Turing's obituary was in the newspaper, we didn't discuss it. 'Found dead in his bed,' I read aloud. 'Suicide. Poor chap. Forty-one years old.' I held out the paper, but Harry didn't take it.

'What else does it say?' he asked.

'Reader in mathematics at Manchester University. Pioneer of the electronic calculating machine. One of the creators of the mechanical brain. Invented a way of giving memory to computing machines. Do you think it could have been suicide, really? A man like that? Of course, after what they'd done to him...'

Harry gazed for some seconds. 'What about his war work?'

I read it: '"Dr Turing served in the Foreign Office during the war." That's all.' Harry pressed his lips together and returned to his book.

My answer to Joanne is that I was sent to work in a bomb factory and was moved to the Labour Planning office at Lyons. Which is true. Harry always replies easily and at once, 'Nothing much. I was a corporal in an anti-aircraft division in Belfast. I was lucky.' Which is untrue. He calls it the power of the uttered word. 'Whatever you say, people accept. What else can they do – call you a liar?'

Certainly whatever I tell Harry, he believes. I tell him this area is not the right place to bring up Philip. I tell him we don't need the shop any more and should move across the river to Chelsea. There are a lot of controlled-rent flats available there. He simply agrees. Finding a new home is left to me.

There are many places to have mail delivered if you'd prefer it not to come to your own front door. The Institut Français at South Kensington is one that receives mail for its members. It's a short stroll from our new home in Dynsey Mews. Harry and I sometimes walk there in the evening to attend lectures or plays or concerts in the Art Deco theatre. The Institute's library carries the latest American and Russian journals, as well as French. I ask Lucienne and Erika to send their letters there, as Harry and I may be moving again soon. It's good cover. Easy to explain to Harry, too. I read and write letters in the calm of the library, occasionally needing to make use of the dictionaries, or over a coffee and croissant in the café-restaurant.

Lucienne and her bank manager husband Jean live in the rustic Charolais cattle country on the banks of the upper Loire, in eastern France. Every day, so Lucienne tells me, Jean drives through this pastoral scene to the quiet market town of Paray-le-Monial, there to adjudicate on loans to local farmers. Erika lives the sophisticated city life, in an opulent government apartment in Vienna with her husband Klaus, who remains a senior official with Austrian railways.

Three very different women, yet Lucienne, Erika and I have become quite close in our way, confiding all the innocent matter of family life to our sheets of Basildon Bond, ordinary handwritten letters between friends.

Erika keeps up her correspondence with Lucienne to maintain the cover. The three of us swap news of our children's triumphs and bitter disappointments, and of our own successes and setbacks, and the hopes and ambitions to which our husbands cling, and to which we too must devote our lives.

March 1956, London SW3

Chère Lucienne, J'espère que tout va bien. – Liebe Erika, ich hoffe, dass alles gut ist.

Harry is now the SE England chess champion. He has applied for a new job at a college in north London. We plan to take the children camping in France this year. Nicola is fine. Philip is worried about starting secondary school. And – we are going to have a third!

With love, amicalement, Alles Liebe – Marjorie.

Lucienne and I have made a little study of historic gardens, a couple of times visiting some fine examples together. I've learned how the composition of the soil affects what will grow. It's quite fascinating. On trips, I collect small soil samples to examine with my microscope.

This provides the reason to have a microscope on my desk. Most of Erika's letters contain at least one exclamation mark. I peel off the point of the exclamation mark and examine it under the microscope. These are microdot photographs of encoded documents provided by her source in East Berlin.

One day a packet arrives for me from Austria. Inside is a *Guides Bleus* touring guide to France. There's no note, just a colourful bookmark with the letters of the alphabet jumbled in the wrong order. A guidebook – what a perfectly inspired choice for a book cipher!

Erika and I always use the simplest techniques possible. On the flap of her envelope, a smear of correcting fluid acts as a seal. Nothing could be more innocent; everyone has correcting fluid on their desk. A broken seal means the envelope may have been opened. So far, it never has been. And each letter is numbered in sequence. The number appears in the date. So far, all have arrived safely.

While Sir Stewart Menzies was "C", he was extremely concerned that I should pass Erika's information directly to him and not to anyone else. Since he left, I don't report to the chief. Under the new man, such special arrangements, freelances, "illegals", irregulars, are not the thing. Everyone working for SIS must be part of the service, subject to staff procedures, with a section head, and play by the book.

The territory of the different agencies has become more clearly defined too, MI5, SIS and GCHQ with their distinct, separate remits. That's why LPG has been transferred from SIS back to GCHQ.

As a result, my position is more bewildering than Hampton Court maze: I am on loan to the service where I am permanently based. I'm like a figure in a drawing by Escher, going up, down and in circles at the same time. I report on Erika's material, under a cover name, to some young chaps who are part of a team of East Germany experts.

Yvette and I meet often for a chat over coffee, a shopping trip, or a good lunch, or even an outing to a theatre matinée. We talk with ease and confide in one another. The background to that is that we already do share secrets going back years – Section B, Venona, LPG. We still do not delve far into matters of home and family. It's enough to be two intelligent, capable women who like each other, who can help one another choose a dress or a handbag, discuss fine food, talk about a film or a play, without venturing across a certain line. Occasionally she throws out a titbit about former colleagues. SIS keep tabs on everyone still in possession of classified information. I ask, very casually, 'Still in touch with Sinclair Bannerman?'

'Ah, you don't know. Sinclair's dead. He left the service in 1946. He became a professor of mathematics. Died of cancer, years ago. Terrible waste. Still so young.'

'Died! Oh, shame! I didn't know. Awfully nice chap, wasn't he?'

'Yes.' She's upset.

From time to time she becomes curious about Harry. I say only that he is still a maths teacher. 'Do you have a picture of him?' Of course I don't; that could be risky. 'Here,' she says, 'this is Goff,' producing a small photo from her purse. He is even older than I imagined, lean, upright, dark blazer, striped tie, clipped moustache. I can't know if this really is her husband.

There's brief talk of getting together, the four of us, for dinner perhaps. We both know this is mere bluff and make the necessary excuses. 'Harry and Goff aren't at all the same type.' – 'Goodness, no!' – 'It's better just the two of us, isn't it?'

She teases me about my "Viennese friend". 'I'm wondering now, about this friend of yours,' she jokes, 'does she even exist? No one has ever seen her. No one knows her name!' Presumably Yvette means that no one has managed to intercept a message, letter or phone call from Erika. Which is reassuring.

'Why do you say "she"? Do people who don't exist have gender?'

Yvette grins. 'Well, *isn't* your friend a "she"? I say, Marjorie, you dark horse! Is it a man?'

I resist the temptation to say more. In fact, I'm not tempted. Something in me prefers to be tight-lipped. You can't be too careful. I stick to my guns and say nothing. In all these years, I've never even asked Yvette where she first heard about the arrangement with Erika. Because even to ask the question would reveal too much.

I laugh freely. 'I assure you, chérie, that my non-existent Viennese friend really doesn't exist, neither as a man nor as a woman!'

'So *you* say!' she says archly. I don't exactly trust her, but I like her and we understand one another. I feel she's my sort and, indeed, my closest friend. I should prefer all my dealings to be with her.

Then, even while it's happening, LPG learn that our Berlin tunnel has also been broken into. It's been working well for three years now, but this is a crushing setback. A terse statement is made to the team. 'The Russians have uncovered Stopwatch (Operation Gold). This operation is closed as of now.'

By what appears to be a bizarre coincidence, it happens while President Khrushchev is in the middle of his visit to London. In fact, he was about to walk into lunch with our unsuspecting young Queen when the Red Army announced they had found our tunnel. Straight away, the jubilant Russians invited the world's press to see the phone taps. They're so much more savvy than we are.

The Russians must have arranged for their 'discovery' of the tunnel to occur at just such a moment, expecting – or even knowing – that the CIA would take responsibility to avoid unpleasantness for the British during the Russian leader's visit. The purpose of Khrushchev's visit is to forge closer relations with the British. At the same time he has shown the British to be incompetent and powerless. It's masterful. The idea, I guess, is to drive a wedge between us and the Americans, and so weaken NATO. It's working.

Stopwatch's Russian and German Berlin staff are being hurriedly brought to London. The traitor could be among them. I contact Yvette at SIS to find out what she knows. We meet in a room at St

Ermin's Hotel, near the head office in Broadway. She says Red Army troops entered the tunnel from the eastern end. They couldn't have found it by chance.

I say, 'If it were up to me, I'd suspect everyone in Y-Section recently transferred *out* of Berlin. Surely the Soviets would make sure their man wasn't on the scene when they broke into the tunnel, wouldn't they? The list must be quite short.'

Yvette shakes her head and explains that the top brass at SIS and GCHQ are wedded to a belief that their fellows are all good, sound chaps. Their instinct is to suspect outsiders and bugging devices, not bad apples among the intelligence officers.

I stand at the window watching the goings-on outside. Young couples stride without formality, the young men without hats, young women pushing prams in which slumber the nation's babes, each one cared for by our Welfare State. In front of the house, Nicola skips with a rope, chanting in unison the words and rhythm, tap, tap, tapping, familiar from my own girlhood. And there's Philip, back from Cubs, running as in a madcap race. O fortunate, spoiled generation! O the goodness of what we have made! I call them in for tea. They must be in bed before our guests arrive.

Joanne and I prepare tonight's buffet, chatting like old pals, though of course I'm paying her wages and her bus fare. As a bonus, I pour her a glass of sherry, though I have only lemon barley myself.

Vol au vents and fish goujons, sandwich rounds and sausage rolls, breaded mushrooms, devilled eggs, salad-y bits and celery sticks; cream cheese, chopped herring, diced cheddar. Stacks of paper plates and paper napkins. A tureen of soup to be served in mugs. I pull off my apron and rush away to change. When I return to the kitchen, the plates of food look pretty and tempting.

The sitting room is soon rattling with laughter and talk. *Happy anniversary! Ten years! What's the secret?* Harry's in his element, jovial, flirting and killingly funny. He keeps up an eclectic choice of music on the gramophone, Duke Ellington and Louis Armstrong, Doris Day and Frank Sinatra, hits from *South Pacific* and *Oklahoma*. He drifts about clearing away empty siphons and topping up glasses. 'Babycham, sherry? Gin and tonic? Prefer coffee?'

Astonished gasps at his absurd party tricks – a book balanced on his nose, a bowl of olives on a fingertip, wineglasses stacked on his head (he can also dance with them in place). Suddenly Harry has ceased his foolery and calls for silence. I'm dragged up in front of everyone. There and then he surprises me with a gold wedding band. Amidst claps and cheers he slips it onto my finger above the three-quid Utility ring, gives me a kiss, and launches into a comfortable, relaxed speech. Harry has the knack of always striking the right balance of seriousness, humour and bonhomie.

Then, the gramophone is back on. Windows are pushed right up to let out the circling blue fog of cigarette smoke. Some take to dancing, Harry leading the way. Others hold glasses and loudly debate the topics du jour, Suez, Hungary, *Angry Young Men* and of course the dreaded Rent Act, which will turf them out of their Chelsea homes. 'Oh, but I can't possibly leave this area,' I hear a lament.

Others agree. 'I'd miss the art students too much, those willowy, barefoot girls.'

With the end of rent controls, the sensible thing to do now is buy, not rent. I reveal that we have already made our plans to move.

'We're looking at a place in Hampstead. Decent house, bomb-damaged but still sound, two thousand pounds. Space for a garden.'

'Oh my God, *miles* away from *anything*, darling!'

'And full of *earnest* types, Fabians and the like.'

'And penniless authors.'

'And Theosophists.'

'No, not Theosophists, I think.'

'Rather nice, though. Hampstead Heath and all that.'

P

In Ward 26, nursing assistants were removing the soiled bedsheets. Sandcliffe Infirmary was busy once more after the Christmas and New Year break, porters languidly pushing trolleys, assistants ambling with bundles of files, white-coated doctors strolling with stethoscopes around their necks, nurses cheerfully recounting their Bacchanalian holiday accomplishments.

At Marjorie's bedside Philip found Joe and Eva Reznik debating whether to stay or leave. Strangely, Marjorie – whose slumbers had always been as light as a sparrow on a twig – was soundly asleep, undisturbed by voices, lights or the late hour. 'We can't wake her,' said Joe. He meant it was literally impossible to rouse her.

They decided to leave. Eva promised Philip she would visit again soon. They warmly embraced him, and placed a Get Well card on Marjorie's bedside cabinet.

Left on his own, Philip used the opportunity to speak with an attractive senior nurse who had stepped into the ward. He read her name badge aloud: 'Anna. Hi Anna, I'm Phil Rosen – that's my mum there.' There was a pretty smile in return. She introduced herself as the Deputy Clinical Lead in charge of Marjorie's treatment. 'How can I help?'

Philip explained his concerns: no one helped Marjorie to the toilet, she didn't seem to be eating, and what would happen about the compression stockings now that her legs were in such a state?

Mrs Rosen, Anna explained, could not possibly wear her stockings because of the sores, and food is brought but she leaves it. Philip did not argue. He wanted to be on good terms with someone who could prove useful (and was very good-looking). 'And the toilet?'

'Does Mum finding toileting difficult? She would have been assessed on admission.' Anna took a blue folder from the end of Marjorie's bed, opening it to read. 'Marjorie Rosen can dress, wash, eat and toilet unaided, uses a walking aid, otherwise fully mobile.'

'What!' Now it was harder not to argue. 'That's completely wrong! Mum has daily carers to help her dress and wash.'

'Maybe she doesn't need them.' At the nurses' station, DCL Anna asked a nurse to confirm that Mrs Rosen could indeed walk to the toilet and back unaided.

'What, that lady? Yeah, she toddles along with her stick,' she chuckled. 'She gives us a thumb-up on the way back, so it can't be too bad.'

Philip was horrified. 'That's three times as far as she can normally walk. You realise the thumbs-up is ironic?'

The young nurse frowned with lidded eyes, suspecting she had been obscurely insulted. Even DCL Anna said, 'It's what?'

'The thumbs-up means *See, I managed in spite of you.*'

DCL Anna laughed it off. 'Any of the nurses would be very willing to help your mother. But you know, they are terribly busy. They can't come immediately. Some of the service users want nurses to come running immediately. Your mother must appreciate that's not possible We can fit her with a catheter, if that would help.'

'Do you have a commode she could use? And a walking frame.'

'No, not enough for everyone. Well, I'll see what I can find.'

'By the way,' Philip asked Anna, 'Mum is on morphine. Is that really necessary?'

'It eases the pain and makes her comfortable.'

'She's not in any great pain, is she? Mum hates anything that affects her mind. Hardly even touches alcohol.'

DCL Anna read from Marjorie's notes. 'Yes, she does have severe pain. Medical morphine doesn't affect the mind, if that's your worry. She'll be *Nil by Mouth* tonight to get her ready for tests tomorrow. But I'll ask the doctor for you, about the morphine.'

'Thank you, Anna. It's good of you to care. Mum's a remarkable woman. Very interesting, intelligent lady. Have a chat with her if you have time; she'd like that. Here, look,' he held up his phone to show her a picture, 'this is Mum when she was well.'

Anna glanced at the screen and at Philip's face. Good-looking guy, she thought. Quite old, but really nice. Terribly concerned about his mother. She liked that.

A crowd of voices burst into the ward. Finally Marjorie opened her eyes, frowning against the neon glare. It was a young doctor and her entourage passing from bed to bed, the doctor's voice occasionally pointing out some matter, sometimes not pausing. One at which the doctor did not stop was that of the wandering woman, no longer wandering but now unconscious on her cot. Another where she did not stop was that of Marjorie Rosen.

'Doctor,' exclaimed Philip, 'please would you take a look? My mother's legs are leaking fluid.'

'Your mother is not one of my patients.'

Philip retorted sternly, 'Doctor, you can't leave her like this!' Perhaps the doctor agreed, for she picked up a folder from the end of the bed. 'Nothing about legs. She will have X-Ray and ultrasound scan tomorrow.'

'Yes, but look at her legs.'

The doctor read on. 'They are investigating only epigastric pain.'

'What about the urinary tract infection?'

'No, there's no UTI. The notes say no infection.'

'No infection! And what about her legs?'

A substance was seeping from soaking bandages around the bloated calves. 'These dressings need changing,' the doctor said to a nurse, 'and I will prescribe furosemide. The patient's legs must be raised. When the swelling subsides, she must wear compression stockings.' Turning to Philip she said, 'Your mother's legs did not need to get like this. You really should have spoken sooner to the nurses. They would have dealt with it straight away.'

Marjorie remained silent during the exchanges. As the doctor and her party walked on, Philip said, 'That's good news, Mum, isn't it?' She looked sceptical. He fed her from a jar of baby food, which he thought might be more nourishing and easier to manage than a dish from the hospital kitchens. Afterwards she sat with eyes closed, the lids fluttering uneasily.

A frail patient in the next bed beckoned him. 'You might like to know,' she said, 'your mum doesn't eat anything at all unless you or her friends feed her. They do it on purpose, move the food and water out of reach. They think it's funny. It's a little gang of them. No one knows what's going on in this place.'

Later in the afternoon, Philip asked his mother if it were true. 'Are food and water *deliberately* put out of reach?' She murmured, 'Yes, yes. I am Tantalus trying to remember my sins.' He assumed this was yet more meaningless raving. She touched his hand in an unusual gesture. 'Philip, where does that tunnel go?' It took him a moment to understand. He explained that it wasn't a tunnel, just a window. 'Are you sure? I see trains coming and going. It's a railway terminus, isn't it? I think that passage goes down to the platform.'

At which, she half closed her eyes again. Philip sat with her until there seemed no reason to stay. He had to go back to his own home. He kissed her cool cheek and said goodbye.

It was raining outside. On his windscreen in the hospital car park was a penalty notice. He had overstayed the time limit. There was a fine to pay within fourteen days. Philip felt that he had tried to do good and been punished for it by the Fates. He was angry with the Fates and with the hospital and even more with ageing and sickness and mortality. It was a nightmare prospect for him and for everyone.

On Friday afternoon, Carol arrived at Ward 26. She had remembered Shabbat. She brought Shabbat candles, challah rolls and chicken soup. 'What about your candles, Marjorie, and your prayers?' By 'prayers' Carol meant blessings, but in any case it was not allowed to light candles anywhere in the hospital. 'You are a darling for thinking of that!' said Marjorie. Today, she was wide awake.

Carol then noticed, astonished and outraged, something on the bedside table: ignored and forgotten, a plastic cup of pills and tablets that no doubt were supposed to have been taken sometime today. Or perhaps they had been there since yesterday.

Marjorie admitted she had no idea when they were given to her. She was not concerned. 'O white forgotten pills,' she joked, 'if I never took you, what would happen?'

'A stroke, probably, or a heart attack.'

Carol took pictures of the unused medication with her phone. While she was about it, she took a few snaps of the disfigured legs, and wondered aloud if she should send them to Philip or Nicola to use in some sort of complaint. Marjorie implored her to send them to no one and say nothing. 'They'll punish me, Carol, if you do.'

When Carol returned on Saturday evening, Marjorie attempted a smile, but did not sit up and could not speak. She reached out to grasp Carol's hand with tremendous urgency. 'Can't you say something, dear?' asked Carol. The answer was clearly No. Not a word could she utter. Not a *hello*, nor a *thank you*, nor a *darling*.

Carol saw that since yesterday Marjorie had been attached to a fixed syringe pump, and could not be moved from the bedside. There was no need to walk to the lavatory, as a commode had been placed beside her. Carol changed Marjorie's dressings, fed her like a baby, and made the bed. There was, though, nowhere to wash. 'I'll help you with the toilet,' said Carol, pulling the plastic curtain around.

Behind the curtain, Carol studied the syringe pump. The device was giving Marjorie a powerful opiate, diamorphine, along with an anti-nausea drug, cyclizine. The opiate dose looked too high. Someone, she thought, should check this, but the nurses on this ward were definitely not to be trusted.

With kisses and strange, unanswered farewells, Carol left. Disturbed and anxious, outside the ward she wondered what to do, who to talk to. 'She really could die if we leave her like that,' she said to herself in the car. She resolved to take matters in hand somehow, make a note of the opiate dose and all Marjorie's other medication too and get some advice, and tell Marjorie's family, and above all come more often and look after Marjorie properly, and do something, but she did not know what.

Carol arrived at the hospital the next day. She put her coins in the parking meter, marched along the brightly lit corridors, took the lift, and in resolute mood reached the doors of Ward 26.

But the doors of Ward 26 were locked shut. On them was taped a note:

WARD CLOSED – NO ENTRY
No Visitors. Owing to an Outbreak of Infection this Ward is closed until Further Notice.
Signed: Ward 26 Clinical Lead.

* * *

Harry and I are nifty at putting up a tent. We rig up lamps, unfold the table and chairs and beds and set up the Campingaz. The neighbouring pitch remains unoccupied. I expected Erika and Klaus to be here by now. We'll be spending tomorrow with my Austrian pen-friend and her husband, who are passing close by on a camping tour of the Schwarzwald, across the German border.

'Have you got a photo?' Harry and the children crowd round to study the small snap she sent. A middle-aged lady in a jacket and skirt occupies the centre ground, looking too urbane for the setting of Alpine meadows. Beside her, even more incongruous, stands a man in a grey suit. Of course, Erika's picture is deliberately unclear. She never sent a photo of the family. She did not want to endanger her children. A family is good cover. That's the point of it. You do love them, though; the emotions, at least, are real.

Harry and I explore the campsite under a darkening sky as Philip runs ahead and Nicola skips beside us. The site lies on a slope of the Vosges hills, looking across the wide landscape of vineyards and villages below, where clusters of light are gradually coming on. We stroll from washing block to swimming pool to shop to snack bar. The pool is locked, the site shop closed, and the snack bar bleak. Back at the tent, I make a tasty soup.

It was a surprise to learn that Alsace, in eastern France, is half-way between London and Vienna. Harry is interested to explore the region. He insists we visit handsome, workaday Mulhouse before sauntering in Colmar's medieval maze of pretty streets and quaint squares and canalsides. As always he is indifferent to the picturesque. He wants only to see the abandoned and ruined synagogues, though he's the least religious man possible, and the degrading images of Jews in the stone carvings and stained glass windows of the churches. He refers to all such towns as judenrein.

Seen from the valley road below, villages lie on the hillside like precious stones on a chain. Their adorable cottages are the colours of confectionery, sugar icing and green marzipan. Flowers in abundance crowd tiny gardens, window boxes, hanging baskets. For Harry, picture-book charm doesn't make up for history. Everywhere are reminders of the Jews who recently walked in these lanes, or hid in them, whose families had been here longer than France itself, longer than Germany. Their ghosts brush unseen against our living flesh.

During the night I hear Erika and Klaus arrive: a car moving slowly, its doors closing quietly, low voices in German. It's too late to put up a tent. What will they do, sleep in the car? They become perfectly still. I hear only the bell-like note of a bird in the night, then in the distance the thin cry of another. Harry's slow breaths of sleep continue, and soon my eyes open again as a first hint of new morning seeps through the canvas.

There's no point in stirring from bed at this hour. In any case, this day needs careful preparation. Neither of our husbands may know anything about our previous encounter or our present arrangements. Fragments of memory like heaps of tesserae pour into my thoughts. I was much younger then, perhaps more easily impressed. Perhaps I won't recognise her at all. Which takes me back to breakfast at Pension Adler, when I did not know which of the prim Nazi ladies at the table might be Erika.

Eventually I untie the tent flap and peep out. The first light of day has a tantalising warmth. What's this on the neighbouring pitch? Erika and Klaus *have* arrived, but they're not in any sort of tent I have ever seen. It's a canvas room attached to the side of a camper-van. I slip on a presentable skirt and shirt, unfold a chair onto the worn grass and do nothing other than read and knit and take in the brightening sky and the cheering sight of swallows flying high. I hear one or two murmuring voices, a wireless set somewhere, a child. Early risers emerge in ones and two, clutching washbags and heading for the wash blocks.

I'm waiting to see who will appear from the Jüngers' strange van-tent. Perhaps it will be the unknown Klaus. But by seven o'clock, even Nicola and Philip are both up, yet there's no sign at all of the Jüngers. I hear Harry's usual morning cough. 'Marjorie?' he calls.

'Morning, Harry. I'm taking the kids to have a wash. I'll see if I can find some fresh bread,' I reply.

As we return – with a fresh baguette and a bag of croissants – I can see, even from a distance, that in those minutes everything has changed. A man and woman, who surely must be Klaus and Erika, together with a boy of about fourteen years old, are sitting at a large camping table loaded with brown bread, sliced cheese, sliced hard-boiled eggs and sliced ham. They must have brought these things with them yesterday. The most unbelievable aspect of the scene is that Harry is at the table with them, eating their food, drinking their coffee, smoking their cigarettes and chatting animatedly. Absolutely nothing could be more incongruous.

Nor did Erika's letter mention a boy. Her own children are in their twenties. 'Oh, Mummy,' Nicola exclaims, 'is that lady the one that's your friend?' Hearing Nicola's voice, the woman stands up, gaily calling out, 'Good morning!' in English.

The others spring to their feet. Every one of them is taller than Harry, even the boy. Harry, wiry, tanned and relaxed, is wearing his Viyella check shirt with a knitted tie and sleeveless pullover, flannel trousers and battered suede shoes. What's left of his hair needs a brush – there's something of Albert Einstein about his appearance.

Beside him, as stiff and upright as a sturdy wooden post, Herr Jünger is a huge blond man in his fifties, the shaved face and short-haired head scrubbed to a pink glow, which must mean that the weird van-tent even has its own washing facilities. He's so meaty and pink that it brings a rather unpleasant image of a butcher's block to mind. Yet he's dressed as a child, in a khaki outfit with badges, like a Scout, and embarrassingly brief leather shorts. The boy is no less blond, equally washed and spruce and similarly attired. Goodness knows what they make of my own gawky children, in their cotton shorts and sloppy joes. Or what my little darlings make of *them*.

But then, behold Erika. As Herr Jünger turns politely to greet us, I have a clearer view of her. She stares fascinated at me and I at her. Erika is not dressed as a Scout, nor as a Guide. Uncannily, her outfit is exactly as on that first morning in a Nazi guesthouse fifteen years ago: grey skirt and jacket, summer-weight this time, over a light blue blouse that appears to be… in fact it is, the very same one, with a white bow at the neck and ornate German lace on a white collar. It's too smart for a campsite. I wonder whether wearing the same shirt is a clandestine message to me, a sign, or just a private joke.

As usual, the male voices overwhelm our greetings. Herr Jünger pumps my hand and roars in fairly good, but terribly accented

English that Harry has been explaining how train timetables could be more easily created and changed using computers. Harry excitedly praises the Jüngers' ingenious camper van. I introduce Philip and Nicola to them, and we learn that the boy is Klaus's nephew, Hans, who shakes hands awkwardly and says in nervously uncertain English that he and Uncle Klaus go trekking in the hills today.

Klaus nods in vigorous confirmation. 'There are zo many many liddle liddle small small ways, ja, in the wineyards and hills,' he says. Despite his apparent love of Nature, I am informed, Klaus also adores hearty plates of food and plenty to drink, and expects to find both somewhere on their trek. I see now what Erika has in mind. If Harry can be persuaded to look after our children, she and I will be left alone for many hours.

Erika and I take a few paces away from the others. She takes my hand as if in formal greeting, but does not let go. She smiles slightly, looks into my eyes, says nothing. I study her face. Erika is no longer young. She must be in her mid-forties now, an attractive woman, mature and calculating and armoured. Lines all over her face are hidden by a sparing cover of foundation cream. The rich blonde hair is now dyed, I suspect, and her expression has become perfectly impenetrable and cynical. Or perhaps it was like that before. I don't remember. The hazel of her eyes, as if thinned by the years, is the mottled, indeterminate colour of shadows beneath foliage. I wonder if anyone ever tells Erika she has fascinating eyes, or if her husband has noticed them recently.

Face to face like this, I am almost shocked by her bravery, what she has done, is doing, in constant danger. Herr Jünger is ideal cover, though. I return her smile and speak softly to her in German. 'I believe they make a kind of Pflaumenkuchen here, don't they?'

The brows come together. She has forgotten that we used this as a recognition password. Then she remembers. 'Yes, with Zwetschgen. Is it made here?'

'Ach, I must be mistaken.'

She lets go of my hand. 'You know, I believe they actually do make Pflaumenkuchen here.'

'Well, then, let's go and have some. Nice blouse, by the way! Does it have any significance?'

'You forget nothing!' She shakes her head. 'I saw it while I was packing, and thought... na ja, let's see if it still fits.'

'It does, and still suits you.' We turn back to the others. Erika reminds her husband and nephew to get ready for their hike. Despite the Germanic feast he already enjoyed, Harry has no objection to joining me and the children at our table for buttered baguette, croissants and coffee. Erika joins us too, and chats in passable English. She says that although a camper van is good in some ways, the problem is you can't go for a drive without first packing up all your gear. She asks if I would mind very much giving Klaus and Hans a lift in our car to a place on the road above the village of Ribeauvillé, where they can pick up their hillside track. I gather from her expression that she most particularly wants me to say yes.

In the car, the four of us – Klaus and Hans, Erika and myself – speak in German. The husband and nephew explain in excessive detail which path they will take, what they expect to see on the way, their route back to the campsite, and what time they will arrive.

After dropping them off, we drive on aimlessly, Erika Jünger and myself together, alone and unwatched. The mood at once becomes very different, as if everything until now has been an act.

For Erika there is nothing sentimental or nostalgic about the occasion. She has some reason to meet me other than to eat Pflaumenkuchen and reminisce. Everything is part of the greater task. Erika believes she and I are on the same side, working to the same end, to restore democracy to a Germany made whole again. In truth, that's not how I feel. I enjoy seeing Germany punished by the Russians.

Simply having her beside me, this composed, groomed woman in the passenger seat and myself at the wheel, sets my mind chasing among these matters. West Germany has been embraced by the former Allies like the prodigal son. Erika is from eastern Germany. On the face of it Erika is helping the British, but of course it is all for the sake of a reunited Germany. That alone is what she is dedicated to, and what she works towards.

It raises questions as to what exactly *I* am working towards. Sir Stewart said about Erika, when he was head of SIS, 'She's serving the interests of her own country, not ours.' By inference, I must be serving the interests of the United Kingdom. What does that even mean, nowadays? Queen and country seem all but forgotten in this age of Cold War. The battle now is not between nations but ideas, ideologies, rival visions of a perfect world. Can there be any victory in such a war? The answer is yes. On our bookshelves at home is the Thomas Jefferson book Bob Shaffer gave me. I serve that philosophy, the one that saved and protected us, free elections, free expression and the freedom to take the authorities to court. Liberty, in other words. To that extent, Erika and I are on the same side.

Klaus was right, numerous lanes and unpaved tracks weave all over the hills. Unsure where to go, I drive further uphill through darkly shaded woods and shining sunlit meadows. Erika strikes a match, inhales deeply on a cigarette and gives it to me before lighting one for herself. Here, we can talk freely. At first we are silent, as if absorbing the significance of the situation.

Going up and down the gears, I take a winding lane that climbs and climbs, clinging at last to a high crest. On both sides of the road, slender, leafy trees conceal the vista below. Occasionally a break gives glimpses over the Alsace plain. At the next viewpoint, I stop the car. Turning off the engine reveals an ineffable tranquillity and silence. We get out and sit on a roadside parapet, a lovely, pearly view below us. Vineyards, countless grape bushes in parallel lines, lie across the land like swatches of yellow and green corduroy. A dark purple haze far away is Germany.

'So, together once again,' says Erika, in German. 'That was a good idea, to become pen-friends. I have something for you.' I am sure she does not mean some delicacy or souvenir. 'I'll give it to you in the car.'

She offers me another cigarette and changes the subject. 'You know, the Gestapo came to Pension Adler after you left. Someone had denounced Frau Schneider, of all people. You remember her?'

I decide not to tell Erika that it was I who denounced Frau Schneider. I suspect she has worked that out for herself. 'Yes,' she says, 'they came and helped themselves to food from her larder and wine and beer from the cellar. They took Frau Schneider away. And Frau Frick, too. I know you cannot tell me anything, Marjorie. Let me say, I admire your incredible courage. I admired it then, and I admire it now. It has inspired me ever since.'

'That's quite funny, Erika, because I found *you* an inspiration.'

In the car again, I wait for her to give me whatever it is she has brought. First, she smiles broadly. 'Oh, I must tell you what Klaus came out with this morning!' she says. 'He said, "Mein Schatz, I think your friend's husband is a Jew."'

'A Jew! Goodness!' I smile. 'And what did you say to him?'

She replies, 'Well, I pointed out that Harry enjoyed our ham!'

'Erika, anyone can see Harry is Jewish. You think a Jew is someone who can't eat ham? What makes you think that?'

'Oh, but that's a Jewish... no?' She is horribly embarrassed and astonished that Klaus' supposition is correct.

'When the Führer promised to cleanse the world of Jews, it wasn't because they don't eat ham. A Jew is a Jew whatever he eats. You may tell Klaus, yes, your friend's husband most definitely is a Jew, and so is your friend.'

It takes a second for Erika to comprehend what she has heard. 'My fr...? *You* are a *Jewess*? Can it be true?' She is all awkward smiles. 'It does not look so. Your appearance, and, and, your, ah...' – she is having some kind of struggle, finally resolved – 'Marjorie, in that case, I am even more impressed by your actions. I am terribly sorry for my foolish remarks.' She leans forward and kisses me on the cheek.

She opens her handbag and produces her gift. 'I brought you this.' It is a slender booklet. I flick through glossy pages. It's nothing but a catalogue of campsites in – where? In Switzerland. Not even Alsace. 'Fine, good. Thank you Erika, very interesting. Very useful.'

'No, Marjorie. Look,' she says, her voice low. She leans forward and opens the brochure at random and with her fingertip touches the spine – the gutter – where the pages are stitched together. Her hand brushes mine like an accidental caress, and we're so close together I can feel her breath on my cheek. 'On this side of the page, all the pages open up like envelopes. Unstitch the pages. Take the book apart.' Although we are completely alone she has lowered her voice further, almost to a whisper. 'Each page is two pieces of paper. Peel them apart. Inside each page you find another sheet of paper, something more interesting. Keep it out of sight until you are in private,' she counsels. 'Top secret. From the Presidium.'

I am sure I must have misunderstood. 'The Presidium of the Supreme Soviet?'

'Notes of a meeting. Extremely important.'

There's no point in asking how her source came by it. She cannot say and I would not want to know. I feel a page with my hand. It's thick, high-quality paper, about 170 or 180 grams. I can't feel anything inside it. She assures me there is something inside.

'This is absolutely brilliant. Wonderful, marvellous work. But,' something worries me so much that I can't ignore it, 'how did you do it, Erika? You couldn't have made this book by yourself.'

'No, of course!' she laughs. 'Someone at the embassy made it.'

'What?' I am dismayed. 'The British Embassy? In Vienna, you mean? Made it themselves, or *had* it made by someone else?'

'Naturally, the British Embassy in Vienna! I expect they made it themselves. They have people. Why, what's the matter?'

I think I must be open-mouthed in shock. 'Our arrangement was just the two of us – no one else involved.'

'Yes, but that was *my* choice, Marjorie. My choice alone. Because when I got out of Germany in 1945, I was not sure whom I could trust. I was on the wrong side – both wrong sides, you might say, or all three wrong sides – Nazi, Allied and Soviet. The situation has changed. Today we all know which side we are on.'

'Whom did you see at the embassy? Did you give your name?'

'Don't worry. I gave the name I used to see Sir Leonard Peters. Peters isn't there any more, but the name worked for the new man.'

My heart sinks. 'What name did you give? Jünger? Or Jäger?'

'No, a different name. Marjorie, the embassy in Vienna already knows about both of us. They have a file on us, obviously. They knew from the start,' she points out, 'and Sir Leonard knew who my husband is, and the work I am doing. I told him myself, years ago. That's how I made contact with you. Don't you remember?'

'I remember.' Together with the fact that Sir Stewart has retired and Sir Leonard has moved on, the memory is unsettling. 'It's still safer, Erika, being just us. Our friendly arrangement was good then, and it's still good. Be careful who you deal with in the embassy.'

Despite the polished, unruffled manner, Erika is perturbed by this comment. On reflection, she may have had her own doubts too. 'Don't worry,' she says, 'they don't know what I put inside the pages. They don't know I'm bringing it to you. They don't even know my real name.'

'All the same,' I say, 'be cautious.' The booklet is tucked into my handbag and we say nothing more about it.

Playing the tourist, we climb to the overblown charm of Haut-Kœnigsbourg on its rocky ledge, and down again to Ribeauvillé. As the road skirts pretty Bergheim, a sign points one way to the *Ancienne Synagogue*, former synagogue, and the other to the *Deutscher Soldatenfriedhof 1939-45*, German Military Cemetery. Our eyes meet oddly.

In Ribeauvillé we don't find any pflaumenkuchen. Instead we stop at a bakery with tables set out in a cobbled square, and order slices of rich kougelhopf, "kooglof", which Erika names Gugelhupf. With graceful generosity the baker pours golden gewürztraminer into two pretty, etched glasses, with his compliments. I take hardly three sips of my wine, persuading Erika to finish it for me. I order more cake. 'I'm eating for two,' I remind her. 'Four months gone now.'

'Family life agrees with you. How many do you plan to have?'

'We'll stop at three.'

She again takes my hand. 'You were just a girl before, a daring girl. Now look at you!'

'Erika, I've really so enjoyed spending this time together. But I must get back now to see how Harry and the children are getting on.'

'Klaus and Hans will be back at the campsite soon, too. I must be there to greet them.'

Harry and I and the kids travel a little way with them, as far as the main road. With smiles, brisk handshakes and jolly farewells we wave them off as they head back in their natty campervan across the Rhine into Germany.

Harry continues our drive between leafy vineyards and along cobbled streets of colourful Hansel-and-Gretel cottages. Steep roofs plunge to massive criss-cross wooden beams. Hanging baskets and window boxes overflow with bright geraniums. Philip exclaims, pointing out storks' nests on church spires, and Nicola claps her hands, saying the houses are so gorgeous she'd like to wrap one up and take it home.

'So,' says Harry, 'what was that all about, this Aryan lady and her Nazi husband?'

'Don't be horrible, Harry! Erika is my friend. I like them.'

'Really, you *like* them?' Harry's eyes twinkle with merriment. As we drive, he bursts into song. 'I love to go a-wandering, along the mountain track...'

The children join in with a chorus of singing and giggling. 'Fol-de-ree, fol-de-rah, with a knapsack on my back.'

Not Marjorie alone but all its patients seemed swallowed up by the locked Ward 26, made into its possession like prey consumed, digested entire, dissolved, disappeared from this world, their bony remnants to be disgorged in due course. Even though there was no entry, Carol continued to arrive at the door each day, hoping to talk her way in. She made it clear to Joe and Eva and to Marjorie's three children that no one can survive long with the amount of morphine being automatically pumped into Marjorie.

Nicola phoned the ward two or three times daily to find out more. She knew there was a mobile handset for calls to patients. The nurses' replies troubled her. Never did they give Marjorie the phone. 'She is asleep, is in the bathroom, is having lunch, is with the doctor. Yes, Mrs Rosen is wearing her compression stockings. Yes, she is eating and drinking normally. Don't worry. She is asleep. She is fine. She is asleep, asleep, asleep. And,' a nurse asked her, 'could you not phone so often?'

Family and friends of the other patients gathered unhappily outside the locked door. They did not believe in the infection. Hospital staff were allowed in and out of the ward wearing ordinary coats and hats, and shoes wet and dirty from the winter weather.

Nicola, Philip and Max spoke frantically to one another. Philip called Ward 26 and asked to speak to Deputy Clinical Lead Anna. She told him she could say nothing. The doctors and nurses, it seemed, had been sworn to the familiar omerta of their profession.

'Could you possibly,' Philip asked her quietly, 'as a favour, use your own mobile to let Mum speak to me when she wakes?' Anna whispered that she would try, 'if there's no one around. Keep your phone on.' Later, hastily given DCL Anna's mobile phone and told she could talk to her son, Marjorie struggled to articulate the words, 'Get me out, Max. Take me home. They'll finish me off in here.'

Abruptly, the call ended. She had thought she was talking to Max.

Philip felt obliged to pass on to his brother the words intended for him. 'But Max,' he warned, 'you can't take her home, whatever she thinks. Mum needs nursing. Her care package would have to be restarted, and that might take ages. It has to be arranged with Social Services and the GP and the care agency and everyone.'

Max did not like Philip's attitude. On Thursday afternoon, the fourteenth day of Marjorie's detention, Max and Jelka arrived at Sandcliffe. He made the same assumption as Carol, that somehow he could talk his way into the ward. They would not refuse him.

He was wrong. They did refuse. Max burned with the savage, flammable emotion that had dogged him all his life. It was intolerable: standing a few feet from his mother and not being allowed to go to her! That night Max couldn't sleep, lying in the guest bed with eyes wide open. At four o'clock in the morning, he phoned Nicola. 'OK, Nic, so who has their numbers, Social Services and all that? Or their emails? Do you have them, Nicky?'

While Jelka slept, he left brisk, urgent messages for the hospital's discharge team and social care team, its Patient Advice and Liaison Service, the Ward 26 clinical leaders, Sandcliffe Social Services and the council's community social work team, and the care agency. To Marjorie's GP he emailed *Fri 14 Jan: At her request I shall this morning remove my mother Mrs Marjorie Rosen from Sandcliffe Infirmary and take her home. She will need care arrangements in place urgently. Thank you for your help. – Max Rosen.*

At eight-thirty, with Jelka at his side, Max found the office of the Discharge Team at Sandcliffe Infirmary. 'Hiya, morning. I'm Max Rosen. D'you get my message? My mother hasn't been discharged, but I'm taking her home.' They strongly advised against such a plan. He had to explain, 'I'm not asking for advice and it's not a plan. I'm informing you so you can make the necessary arrangements.'

'No care package is in place,' they cautioned. 'You'll have to pay privately. It could cost thousands.' So be it, he declared. Jelka called for a wheelchair taxi.

Alerted by the Discharge Team, two nurses let Max and Jelka into the ward. With doomy warnings ('She'll die if you move her.' – 'It's against doctor's advice.' – 'She won't be treated next time if she self-discharges.'), the pair led them to the bedside.

Max did not recognise the wrecked, skeletal being in front of him. Was it the right patient? Marjorie, for a start, had never been thin; this person was deadly thin. Marjorie had an alert, perceptive, sceptical eye; this person turned to him with a barely conscious gaze. In the past, Marjorie had recovered from a dozen mini strokes, after each one 'losing a few pages' as she called it, but she'd never had a full-blown, disfiguring major stroke; yet this person's left cheek hung down and her lower lip drooped to the side.

She, unable to understand, wondered if Max and Jelka were a dream come true, or merely a dream, or were like the railway station tunnel on the other side of the ward which she now knew was merely a window. She made a curious sound like an animal, a yelp, a whinny, and they knew it was Marjorie. Max took the camera that he always carried in his pocket and within seconds had a score of pictures, of Marjorie, the other patients, the ward, the nurses.

Jelka discovered that Marjorie could not stand, her left leg limp and lifeless, the foot dragging on the floor. To Marjorie she said, 'Hold on tight.' To Max she commanded, 'Take her weight.' To the nurses she said, 'Remove the cannula.' And they, uncooperative though they had been, removed the cannula and lowered Marjorie into the wheelchair. At the nurses' station, a discharge form had been completed and Marjorie's medication placed in a bag.

Inside the flat, with his mother insensible on the bed, Max was beset with doubt – *does* this person need morphine, *how* to give it, *what* to feed someone who is starved, *how* to care for someone who has had a stroke, is too weak to stand, who cannot use the toilet, can barely speak – and who can't be taken to hospital.

The first visitor was the carer, Carol. With the bedroom door closed and tears in her eyes she tended Marjorie and washed her. She came out of the room as if offering condolences, 'The Marjorie I know is not there.'

Max grasped his head. 'This is a nightmare. She went to hospital an intelligent woman with a pain in her chest and came out utterly broken in mind and body. They destroyed her. Struck her down.'

'I'm so sorry,' said Carol. This was no mere sympathy. She meant, for her part in the catastrophe.

Yet Marjorie was not unconscious. She lay with eyes closed, listening, unable to do or say anything, debating a little whether it is better to live or die. *It is always better to live*, she said to herself. She became aware that she was no longer in the hospital, and that it was Jelka who sat with her. She opened her eyes and Jelka fed her, delicately, a dolls'-house lunch, a single spoonful of soup and one delicious ripe cherry with the stone removed.

A second visitor arrived: Marjorie's GP. The doctor bit her lip in shock at the sight of her patient. 'I'm not sure you've done the right thing,' she commented to Max, 'but I understand why you did it. Mum will need nursing round the clock, you know. It's clear she's had a stroke. She should be taken straight to hospital. We'll ask for an urgent brain scan to see the extent of the damage.'

'What, you mean, go *back* there? No. No way.'

The doctor frowned, uncertain how to proceed. 'Well, let's check if she can swallow normally.' She went into the bedroom and shut the door behind her.

'Oddly enough,' she concluded, returning to tell Max what she had found, 'there's no pain in her chest or tummy. Whatever *that* was, it seems to have cleared up for now. You know about vascular dementia? It's not the same as Alzheimer's; it's not a degenerative disease. Blood vessels in her brain have been harmed by the stroke, compounded by all her mini-strokes. I'm afraid it's knocked your Mum's mind for six. She needs to apply for NHS Continuing Healthcare.'

'Which is what?'

'Free nursing care on the NHS. Mrs Rosen would qualify. She has a physical disability, a terminal illness, mobility problems, long-term heart and lung disease and now mental impairment. I'll write the report for you.'

'Free? You mean she need never have spent her savings on care?'

'I don't know about *never*. You have to be assessed, but it's an assessment of need, not ability to pay. I must say, though, your mother is still remarkable for her age.' Nevertheless she gave Marjorie an injection and left them with a stack of prescriptions.

Only then did Max remember Philip and Nicola and the Rezniks. He tapped out his message to them. *We've taken Mum out of hospital and brought her home. She's in a very bad way. GP says she had a stroke while in hospital. At least she got out alive.*

* * *

Harry happened to be in the hall when the telephone rang. I hear his puzzled 'Mr *Ems*worth...'. Philip's headmaster has never phoned us before. I try to think of any reason he would personally call the parents of a sixth-former. Harry sounds bewildered by what Emsworth is saying. 'Off school? You mean, what – I don't quite…' I struggle to fill in the gaps.

'I'm awfully sorry, but I can't come in tomorrow,' says Harry. 'I've some arrangements that can't be changed. What about now? I could drive over straight away. No, of course. What about the day after tomorrow?'

A confounded shame that Harry took the call! Any kind of problem right now could hardly have come at worse moment for him. Whatever trouble Philip has got himself into, if only it had been me who answered the wretched phone, perhaps things could have been fudged until after Harry's interview.

In the end, Harry agrees that one of us will go in to the school tomorrow morning. He replaces the receiver and turns to face me, as stunned as a bird in shock. I wait as he musters the will to talk. 'Philip is suspended from school. Emsworth says Philip has committed a serious crime. It isn't a trivial matter. Emsworth wants to speak to us before calling the police. He says he has to see us tomorrow first thing. I said we'd go.'

'Well, *you* can't go,' I assert, adding '*What* crime?' I hear in my voice a sharp edge of indignation, for all the world as if I know Mr Emsworth's remark to be an outrageous lie. Which I don't.

'He wouldn't say on the phone. He suggests we try asking Philip. He almost implied that we know nothing about Philip.'

Tomorrow is the day Harry is due at West Midlands Polytechnic. For weeks he has been reading his old conference papers, rehearsing what to say at the interview, researching who his interviewers will be, considering how to dress on the day and how to explain that he, Mr Harry Rosen, would be the best choice for the college, ideally qualified to transform its first class Mathematics Department into a pioneer Department of Mathematics and Computing.

Philip hasn't come home for dinner. At the table we say nothing, for fear of alerting Nicola and Max. Only when Nicola asks 'Where's Philip? Doesn't he want any dinner?' do we let slip our 'Hope nothing has happened to him'. Sometime after eleven o'clock, the telephone rings. This time it's me who answers.

'Where are you, Philip?'

He sounds cheerful. 'Just to let you know me'n some friends, we're having a sleepover at Julie's. Did old Emma phone you?' That's the boys' nickname for their headmaster. I hear pop music in the background, and young voices shrieking and chattering.

'He didn't say what it was about. What's happened, Philip?'

With a slight, dismissive laugh, 'Nothing, really, just... well, don't worry about it. Anyway, letting you know I'm at Julie's.'

'At Julie's? All night? Are her parents there?'

'Yeah, they're here.'

'Can I speak to Julie's mother?'

'Well, they're not here *right now*. They'll be back later.'

'What time?'

'Well, I don't know, do I? *I* can't tell them to be back by a certain time, can I?' he retorts, reasonably.

'It sounds like a party.'

'It's just me and some friends. Depends what you call a party,' he laughs. The sound is muted as he covers the receiver. I hear him cry out 'For fuck's sake! Shut the fuck up! It's my fucking Mum.'

'Emsworth says as of today you're suspended from school.'

'Does that mean I can have a lie-in tomorrow?'

'Look, Philip, try to talk seriously for a moment. Mr Emsworth said he's calling the police. Come home and tell us what it's about.'

Philip says, no, he doesn't want to. I don't see how I can force him to come home. I don't even know where his girlfriend Julie lives.

Harry waits until I hang up the phone. 'Maybe it'll turn out to be nothing,' I say to him. 'Remember that storm in a teacup about

Philip's uniform?' On that occasion it really was nothing. This time, though, it's not nothing. It's something.

Harry's alarm is set for six-thirty, an hour earlier than usual. Neither of us has slept well. He puts on his pristine laundered shirt and tie, freshly cleaned suit and polished shoes, and takes up his briefcase. 'How do I look?' he asks. I tell him truthfully, 'Like a nice man, a good teacher and a brilliant mathematician. Just right for the job.'

First stop is the tube station. Harry kisses me and I wish him luck. He attempts a smile, 'I'll phone you from the college.' Next, with cheery waves I drop Max and Nicola at their little schools. I carry on alone to Hampstead Grammar. Fine red-brick Edwardian buildings and brand-new Science and Art blocks stand together in the grounds. Instead of leaving Philip at the gate, today I look for a parking space. Nothing could feel stranger than arriving at the school like this, with neither husband nor son.

Anthony Emsworth isn't stupid, and isn't a bad man. Indeed, he is a good, hard-working, decent headmaster.

And is Philip Rosen stupid, or so very bad? In fact, yes. He has been painfully stupid, and now we know how bad he is, our beloved. This is a disaster for him, just before his A-levels – and for Harry, coming at a moment when he must focus his attention on an important step in his career.

At last my phone rings. 'Have you seen the head?' asks Harry.

'I've seen him.' – 'Come on, dear, I'm pushed for time. What's it about? What did Philip do that was so awful?'

'I'm afraid it is awful, darling. He's been selling drugs at school.'

'Who says he has?'

'Not just at school,' I carry on resolutely. 'He sells it to other youngsters, too, at other schools. He was caught smoking hashish with some other boys, and then it all came out from the other boys that Philip is a sort of – well, a sort of pusher – around Hampstead. Not just hashish. Other stuff.'

'They're lying.' Followed by a horrible silence on the line as he realises they probably aren't, and that it would make no difference if they were. 'What does the head intend to do?'

'He asked what *I* would do in his situation. Difficult, isn't it? He's already decided to call in the police. Whether Philip's charged with anything is up to them. Either way he'll be expelled. For the sake of the other pupils, as Emsworth put it.'

'That's what *he* should do. What should *we* do? What can we change, and what can't we change?' he considers. 'We can't change the accusation or the evidence, but can we keep the police out of it?'

'Let's talk when you get back. Good luck with the interview.'

'I need Emsworth's phone number urgently. Have you got it, Marjorie?'

'Leave everything to me, Harry. How's it going, so far?'

'Get the number for me, Marjorie, straight away. Phil needs our help, that's what matters. Give me Emsworth's number.' I almost hear the words *That's an order.*

In the next call he says he's already back in London. He's brusque. 'Wait for me at the school gate. I'll get a cab,' says Harry. 'I've phoned Emsworth. He hasn't called the police yet.'

'But Harry – your job application, your interview?'

'It's no-go this time, Marjorie. Told them I had to leave at once, personal reasons. See you later, school gate.'

'Will you be able to apply for something there another time?'

'Forget it, Marjorie. See you in half an hour.'

My dismay about the job, the A-levels and my son's future are jumbled up with utter admiration for Harry, the emotions conjoined in precious agony. He is so completely on Philip's side, even when Philip is entirely in the wrong and will never thank him.

At the school gate Harry says he would prefer to talk to the headmaster on his own. I agree to leave it to him. He has an easy, human way of speaking, putting everyone in everyone else's shoes, cutting through complexity. I wait in the car for over an hour. When he returns, tired and grim, I assume nothing. He drops into the passenger seat and slams the door.

'Well?'

'Drive,' he says. 'Let's get out of here.'

I take him to the park. He says not another word until we're sitting on a bench. 'Emsworth *will* leave the police out of it, but Philip can't attend the school any more. He can come in to sit his A-level exams. The school won't stand in the way of his university application, but

Emsworth won't give him a reference. That's about it.'

'But that's *marvellous*. How did you do that?'

'I did nothing. I only begged him not to ruin a young man's life.'

'Really – and that worked?'

He snorts. 'Don't ask.'

Did he threaten Emsworth in some way? Does he have leverage over him? Are they both Freemasons or something? I reach out to squeeze his hand. 'Very well done, dear.' At which the poor man actually laughs. Ruefully, at fate, at the world, at himself.

Worrying about Philip's education and Harry's career, I sit for an hour in the French Institute library. At last I fold Erika's and Lucienne's latest letters into my handbag, button my coat and leave. From the top of the grand white staircase I look down into the foyer, which is crowded this afternoon with smartly-dressed people. They must be arriving for some private function. Instinctively I scan the mass of faces.

We pick one another out instantly, Yvette's eyes arresting mine as if all else had vanished. Both of us are more than surprised. Even from this distance I can practically see the wheels of her mind whirring. I continue my descent, until with amiable smiles I can shake hands and be introduced to her companions, an elderly French couple. The gentleman is well-padded, well-manicured, suave and worldly, the lady absurdly affected, smoking through an ebony cigarette holder.

'What a coincidence!' exclaims Yvette. 'Are you here for the Alliance Française meeting, Marjorie?' My blood runs cold. Of course, Yvette *would* be a member of Alliance Française and the Institut Français. I was a fool not to foresee the possibility. Yvette clearly thinks she's onto something.

I might say I popped in for some innocuous reason. At worst, Yvette may discover I receive letters here. That could be disastrous. At all costs I must protect Erika's anonymity. It's possible that with her promotion within the service, Yvette now knows for sure that I am providing intelligence from my own East German source. She may speculate that the shadowy Viennese friend is the conduit. Perhaps she wonders whether I am providing something in exchange.

Maybe *that* is why she has been so interested in finding out about Erika.

'Oh, is that what's going on this evening?' I glance at the lively crowd as if happy that their presence has been explained. 'No, neither I nor my husband are French, so not Alliance Française, but we are members of the Institute.' With uncanny timing this is confirmed by a member of staff, smiling as she passes, 'Bonsoir, Madame Rosen. À la prochaine.' – Goodnight, Mrs Rosen. Till next time.

I return her smile. 'Bonne soirée, Sophie.' – Have a good evening.

'Wasn't that the librarian?' puzzles Yvette. 'She knows you well.'

'Ah,' divines her gentleman companion, 'évidemment you are une habituée of the Institut, as are we.'

Yvette does not answer him, merely studying my face.

I nearly respond with *I've never seen you here before*, which would have been a mistake. I say instead, 'Oh yes, I love it here.'

Yvette raises an eyebrow. 'And is Mr Rosen with you? Or do you come by yourself, all the way from Hampstead?'

'Oh, Harry is far too busy. He does come sometimes, to see a film. What about Captain Oakeshott, I suppose he is here somewhere?'

Yvette evades my glance. It's the elderly couple who reply, 'No, sadly, but he is in good hands.'

I express my sympathy, though of course I don't know the man or what is wrong with him. Or even if he really exists. With handshakes and friendly smiles we wish one another a pleasant evening. I leave them quickly, relieved to get away, stepping through the Institute's big double doorway into the cool, moist, ominous air of South Kensington in the rush hour.

R

Everyone in the family knew by now that Max and Jelka had sprung Marjorie from the diabolical geriatric unit in Sandcliffe Infirmary. A gleeful exaggeration went around of how the pair had stormed the ward and with piratical verve swept her away from the hospital's evil clutches. It was assumed that, back in her own flat at last, properly cared-for, she would return to normal.

Philip and Nicola came straight away to join Max and Jelka at the flat. Putting aside their doubts, even they marvelled at Max's startling, seditious triumph. Seeing their mother once again in her own home brought a first hour of celebration. Then began the clamouring anxiety about the way forward as they saw how ill she was, or something much worse than ill.

By the end of the second hour, Nicola accused Max of putting Marjorie's life in danger by rushing her from her hospital bed. He nervously wondered whether his rashness had indeed led him, as often before, into a terrible mistake. Philip said, 'We should have made a complaint about Mum's neglect through the proper channels.' He proposed paying her GP privately to take charge of her. 'A GP can't deal with this,' Nicola protested, 'that's *precisely* why GPs refer patients to hospital. That's the best place for her,' she hissed, mindful that Marjorie should not hear such a thing. Max insisted she could not be taken back there. Philip angrily added that he supposed he alone was expected to bear any cost that arose from all this. And the GP was phoned.

The doctor arrived quickly, accompanied by a nurse pushing an array of equipment on a metal trolley. She brought as well the Discharge Summary from the hospital. 'It says here,' she read from the document, 'that Mrs Rosen was admitted owing to "severe cough and weight loss. MSU" – that's a urine test – "showed infection, and ultrasound revealed a markedly thin-walled gallbladder. Mrs Rosen is confused: MMSE 10 out of 30." That means a test for cognitive impairment when she was admitted to the hospital showed mental ability borderline *severely impaired*. That doesn't seem right, does it, for your Mum as she was *before* her stay in hospital? When I examined her yesterday, her MMSE score stood at 19, which is mild to moderate impairment. "Diagnosis: Urinary Tract Infection." That's all they found. "Co-morbidity: Parkinson's Disease." None of this is in our notes. She hasn't been diagnosed with Parkinson's, has she, your mother?'

Nicola said, 'Not that we know of. She was admitted with chest pain, not severe cough. Was she coughing?'

'Don't think so. No one mentioned it,' replied Philip. He revealed that when he first phoned the ward a couple of weeks ago, 'They didn't even know who she was. A nurse told me Mrs Rosen was wandering about nicking stuff from other patients. I told her it's been years since Mum could wander anywhere.'

The GP was unhappy. 'Even if your mother had been stealing things, such a comment is inappropriate.'

Philip said one of Marjorie's carers, Carol, had sent him some very damning pictures, including one showing medication his mother was supposed to take that had been put aside and not taken.'

'What! I'd like to see that one. Would you be willing to make statements? Have you got any other photos of your mother inside the ward? I'm minded to report Ward 26.'

Nicola said she would not make a statement. She did not want any nurses or hospital staff to be blamed: 'They are simply overworked.'

Max said he couldn't wait to make a statement, and had a stack of images.

The doctor said, 'You do understand that your mother will need full-time nursing care?'

'Oh! But you don't mean, put her in a home?'

'Well, yes. She can't stay here with no nurse on the premises. If you can afford to have nurses with her day and night here in the flat, that's fine… otherwise, the council website has a page on care homes with nursing.'

Max and Jelka were already installed in the guest room. Nicola slept on the sofa bed in the living room. Philip lay on the hall floor and spent the night like that. On Sunday morning Olivier, Eleanor and Adrian joined them. The new arrivals tapped on Marjorie's bedroom door and peeked around, half smiling in the hope of finding her reading or doing a crossword or codeword. She was deeply asleep. They took the opportunity to watch her for a moment, this woman whom few had ever seen sleeping. Her face was not merely old. Rather it was frozen and disfigured, the white skin crazed with red, one side dragged down, red eyelids hollowed beneath a troubled brow, forehead scored with anguish. Determined intelligence had been replaced by a look of fearful puzzlement.

Marjorie woke between clean sheets. Soft afternoon light filtered through curtains, sweetly illuminating a serene room. She turned her head and saw, on a bedside cabinet, the little silver-framed photograph of Harry. In the armchair beyond was a human form coming into focus as the good Jelka. 'Hello, Marjorie,' came Jelka's kind voice.

Marjorie was piecing details together, gradually understanding that this must be her own home, though where that was she could not recall, and nor did it matter. Marjorie had no idea whether it was morning or evening, and that too did not seem to matter. Jelka half opened the curtains, bent forward to kiss Marjorie's afflicted cheek. 'It's Sunday afternoon. You've had a nice long sleep.'

Marjorie wondered why it was hard to speak. She forced herself. 'Jelka dear, may I have a glass of water?'

As soon as Jelka left, Marjorie fingered her numb face. It was certainly not as it should be. She ran a hand over her body. She was wearing her cotton jersey nightdress and – what was this? How humiliating! A nappy! She felt cautiously; it did not need changing, thank God! She had lost a lot of weight, her hips, her stomach, her chest, her thighs, reduced to skin and bone. She fought off a stupid idea that it was not her own body at all, that she had metamorphosed Kafka-like into someone else, something else, a stick insect. She discovered, holding back panic, that her left side was enfeebled; the arm, the leg, and the left hand, already so weak with the damaged fingers. At least it wasn't her right hand. She tried vainly to muster her thoughts. She could not recall where she had been, what she had been doing. She struggled to think about yesterday, the day before, last night. Memories came in senseless scraps, bright and loud or darkly misted, or as empty as a country lane at night.

She made an effort to snap out of it. It struck her that there was to be no snapping out of this one. A sick fear grasped her entrails like the teeth of a savage little creature. Yet even as fear made itself at home, she became aware of paintings hanging, a pretty lampshade, and a pleasant murmur of voices somewhere. This, she remembered it properly now, was her own dear old bedroom, and this, her own dear old bed, and she, whatever may be amiss, her own dear old self.

Jelka returned with a little lunchtime-teatime breakfast on a tray. Marjorie said, 'What has happened to my face?' Jelka brought a mirror from the bathroom. Marjorie did not hesitate to look.

'Oh!' She studied the image. 'Have I had a stroke?'

'Yes, I'm sorry. It may get a bit better in time.'

She spent some seconds more staring at her reflection. 'Ach! I was never the prettiest girl in the class. And old age is not the prettiest part of life. To get older, or not to be, that is the question!' If she was distressed it did not show.

Jelka fed her the miniature portion of oatmeal. Both grinned gamely at how tricky it was. A piece of mashed banana followed, slightly easier, and a few sips of coffee, terribly difficult. She wiped Marjorie's mouth, arranged her bedclothes, made her comfortable and at ease.

Max came into the room with Olivier. Memory began returning like the tide. Awkwardly she attempted to hug the lad, eighteen years old and already more man than boy. Then came Nicola and Philip. The room was becoming crowded. Hardly any space remained for Eleanor and Adrian when they slipped in. Eleanor's quiet, unassuming 'Hello, Grandma' was answered by an equally quiet, 'Ah! *You're* here. Good.'

The bed-bound mistress of ceremonies gazed at her middle-aged-to-elderly children and grown-up grandchildren, recognising who had come to see her and why, and who was not there.

Speaking slowly and carefully she tried to master the weakened muscles of her face. 'I sometimes wonder,' she mused, 'when do you first realise you're getting old? Is it when you find a partner and settle down? Or when your child first cycles round the corner, out of view? When your children have all left home? When you retire and draw your pension? Well today,' she said, 'I know I am really *very* old because my dear firstborn baby, who cycled out of view long ago and in a way never came back, is about to draw *his* pension.'

She reached out to hold Philip's hand. 'You made the life you wanted. I hope both of us feel we used our time well, with not too many regrets at the end. Thank you, darling, for everything.'

Philip was speechless at the portentous remarks. Before he could consider his response, now her daughter received Marjorie's smiling benediction. 'Nicola, we haven't agreed about everything, have we? You opposed me and Daddy every way you could. You've stuck to your principles, though. You fought your corner. I liked that, though it was the corner opposite ours. You've been a great help in this last, awful period. Thank you.'

Nicola frowned, tears close. 'Disagreements don't mean anything, Mum!' Marjorie turned at once to her visibly pregnant grand-daughter, Nicola's daughter. 'Will you change your name, Ellie, do you think, in Israel?'

'I'm changing my name to Ilana, Grandma. You can call me Eleanor. Or Ellie. Adrian's name will be Ariel.'

'Ariel and Ilana,' she murmured the names, 'I'm immensely proud of you. I wish you happiness and peace and success together, and many healthy Israeli children. Bring the baby to visit, won't you?'

Even as they promised, Marjorie turned to her younger son and his wife. 'Max and Jelka! Thank you for rescuing me from That Place...' Suddenly too tired to go on, she continued indistinctly, to everyone's surprise mumbling in Russian. She was saying, 'Jelka, I can't thank you enough for the effect you've had on my son. I'm glad to have known you.' She reached out to shake Jelka's hand.' The others looked wide-eyed at the formal gesture.

Marjorie's eye fell on Olivier and rested there. 'Ah, you, Ollie...' He stood tense and motionless under her scrutiny. She struggled to form the words. Her eyelids fell half closed for a moment. '...are destined for great things.' The whole gathering was nonplussed by this majestic prediction. 'But first, off to Harvard to study law!'

'Government,' he corrected her, 'not law.'

She seemed to have more to say to him, but did not say it. She fell slightly to one side. Olivier quickly moved to help, but she refused him. 'Well then, goodbye my darlings, goodbye. Live! Live your lives, live well and make the world a better place.' A slight gesture with one hand abruptly dismissed everyone from the room.

Her guests departed and Marjorie leaned, breathless, dazed, face aching, arms limp upon the counterpane.

Her thoughts slipped around like mercury. She worked to grasp them. This little party in her room had decided her once and for all. The valuable gold and silver rings, necklaces and pearls must go to her three great helpers, Carol, Eva and Jelka. The cheaper jewellery to her beloved, undeserving Nicola. Joe and Eva to have first choice of the furniture and books. The Israel money would go in its entirety to Eleanor, and the Swiss fund to Olivier after he graduated. Her own three children would have to share in equal portion anything that was left. Just enough, perhaps for a glass of champagne to bid her 'Good riddance.' Eyes closed, awake yet dreaming, she felt herself moving away on the tide, breaking up in the open sea.

They took their seats in the living room, Olivier perched on the arm of the sofa beside his cousin Eleanor.

'Wow – that was weird!' Max shook his head. 'What *was* that?'

'She really pulled out all the stops, didn't she?' said Nicola, 'Did you notice how she said something to each one of us in turn?'

'Jelka, what did she say to you in Russian?' asked Max.

'Just a thank you.'

'Shut the door Ollie,' Philip said, mindful that Marjorie might overhear.

'Leave it open, in case she calls,' suggested Jelka. The door was left slightly ajar.

'It was like an audience with the Pope or something!' said Nicola.

'I almost felt she was, sort of, *blessing* us,' said Max.

'Blessing or… the other thing. Mum thinks we're all fools, doesn't she?' said Philip.

Nicola agreed. 'She'd swap all of us for Daddy.'

'Don't you think,' Philip asked, 'there was something *valedictory* about it? Goodbye, and thank you, and I loved you.'

'"I loved you despite your faults." That's Mum! I *loved* you, or I *love* you, do you think?'

'Or, I loved you not,' said Nicola.

At this Jelka interrupted their *conversation à trois*, 'No, she loves all of you. She would die for any of you.'

The three of them, even Max, stared at her with the impassivity of cats. 'No, Jelka,' Philip answered, 'you don't know Mum. It's not that simple. Mum would die for us *without* loving us.'

'And why "goodbye"?' said Nicola. 'Does she think she's dying?'

'She actually did say "goodbye", didn't she?'

Max shook his head. 'Not exactly dying. But part of her was lost yesterday and more will be gone tomorrow. Mum wanted to say farewell while there is still something left of herself to say it.'

'She said she wouldn't be herself any more if she couldn't do the crossword,' Nicola reminded them. 'Well, she can't do it.'

'All the same, she still *is* herself,' Philip said, 'at least, as far as I'm concerned.'

'When do you stop being yourself?'

'Tomorrow. Never today,' answered Max.

* * *

'Take my hand,' croons Harry. He has a rough baritone, and is in jaunty mood. 'I'm a stranger in paradise, la dah dah dah di dah dah.' The A12 leads beyond the vast new housing estates into the airy freshness of Essex. How green, rustic and old-fashioned everything quickly becomes! Our little Austin can do fifty miles an hour on the open road, even touching sixty. Harry disapproves, though, of people driving at such speeds. He stays below a modest forty. As others overtake, his serenade is interrupted by indignant exclamations. 'Lunatic! Look at the speed he's doing!'

His hands leave the steering wheel in operatic gestures. 'Some enchanted evening,' he sings, 'you will meet a stranger… dah-dee-dah-dah-dah-dah. Dah-dah-dee-dah! Dah-dah-dee-dah!' The man is happy; he has been shortlisted for another job, better than the one at

West Midlands, and managed to solve the Philip crisis.

I too am happy, and indeed experience something like an instant of joy, for this is very heaven, the good and simple life for which all humanity yearns. Nicola and Max slip about on the back seat playing I-Spy, and even Philip has promised to spend a few days with us, riding all the way here on his bike. I'm thrilled by the vision of him cycling so far, and that he still wants to come on holiday with us.

Harry has managed to get him a good university place despite the lack of a reference from the school. Philip will never know how much Harry put into it, sidestepping the admissions system by personally visiting university Vice-Chancellors in different parts of the country. Harry's own academic standing, his contacts in education and connections from the war made it possible to ask for an exceptional favour. He travelled hundreds of miles and was utterly spent by the effort, but vindicated; for Philip's A-level results arrived, closely followed by confirmation of his university place. Harry congratulated Philip, giving him all the credit! Harry is a saint.

Philip, in his youthful folly, doesn't realise what has been done for him. He accepts such gifts as his due and assumes things have been so ordered as to turn out well. He considers himself innately lucky. Which he is, to have Harry as a father.

Harry, for his part, considers only that one does what one has to do. We do not discuss how things might have been. He focuses his thoughts on the new mathematics for computing machines. His conversation is peppered with "COBOL", "FORTRAN", "ALGOL".

At the end of our journey a single-track lane runs ruler-straight across moorland dense with dazzling purple heather, aiming always to a distant white coastguard building. Poised on its clifftop, the coastguard's weather-battered watchtower faces a grey shifting sea, while the lower floor has been converted into a simple dwelling.

The dwelling, the coastguard and the whole heath are the property of the eccentric Mr Touter. In an unravelling red pullover and dreadful sagging trousers, Touter greets us with a theatrical wave and cries of welcome. Out of sight of the coastguard, Touter keeps a ramshackle old caravan, hidden amidst the heath. There we shall spend a week out of reach and far from view.

Inland, distant horizons and pale farmland lie flat as a tablecloth under the blue and white heavens. I walk alone to the cliff edge and look down. Cool air blows up lightly from the empty shore.

The nearly deserted coastline, long and unbending under a bright pearly haze, is a broad expanse of pebbles and stones on which it is difficult to walk and worse to lie down. Sometimes a distant fisherman can be seen towards Dunwich, sheltered by his canvas windbreak, or a solitary walker may look down from the clifftop.

Harry does not ask why this lonely place was chosen for our break. The caravan creaks in the night and moves in the breeze. Through the window I see starry darkness and hear waves and distant, fluting bird notes. It is to the birds I must go in the morning.

Harry agrees to look after Nicola and Max as with bird book and binoculars I set off to the nature reserve on the other side of the coastguard. Caring for his children is not easy for Harry. He's too absent-minded to be left in sole charge of anyone or anything. Besides, they can be difficult. Nicola has a demanding, discontented nature. Max is worse, an inquisitive, incautious seven-year-old who vanishes for hours on this heath where unexploded ordnance lies buried.

The pale sky is flecked with a blizzard of white clouds. It's warm. The reserve feels wonderfully cut off from the rest of the world, cloaked in reeds and grasses as dense as hanging tapestries. Only keen bird-watchers ever visit this place; I see no one. The silence is broken by low, conspiratorial chirruping and song, occasionally a panic-stricken screech, hooting and honking and whistling, sometimes a sudden brief cacophony, a marvellous din of cries and calls. In sensible skirt, jacket and walking shoes, I follow a raised path from the beach into the reedy heart of the bird sanctuary. Between tall grasses moving silkily there are glimpses of lagoons and waterways half-concealed. I scan the reserve with my binoculars. Leaning on the parapet of a slender wooden bridge stands Ernst exactly as arranged – my old Bletchley colleague Ernst Wardmann (now Ephraim Vardi).

He's much aged, but unmistakeable. You can see Ernst has become a man of importance. The tweedy sportsman's outfit, complete with plus-fours, is wonderfully dated and of the highest quality, and probably purchased in Jermyn Street especially for this trip. In his efforts to play the part he has rather over-egged the pudding. He has a pricey-looking pair of binoculars.

When I arrive, he speaks without any greeting. 'Sh, look there,' in a low voice, 'don't happen to know if that's an avocet, do you?' are his first words to me in years. Ernst still has the quiet demeanour of a thinker. He's lost a lot of hair, and instead of the neatly parted dark, wiry locks of youth, what remains is silver stubble around a tanned dome. I don't look any younger myself. What's left of my own hair must be worn in a bun to hide the unwomanly calvity.

'Is that what an avocet is like?' I peer at an elegant black and white bird striding eagerly in shallow waters on stilt-like legs. It has a rather ferocious-looking long curved beak.

'I think it's rare. Looks sort of rare, doesn't it?'

'I expect we're jolly lucky to catch sight of it, anyway. Ernst, are you completely alone?'

'Yes, of course. I have clearance to travel freely in the UK. Supposed to notify the embassy of any movements, but this is just a short outing.' His tone suggests he considers my question naïve.

I search the bird book and find an illustration. 'Yes, definitely an avocet. Who knows you're here?'

He shakes his head. 'No one. Officially I'm in London today. I came up by train to Saxmundham early this morning. Took a taxi to the bird reserve. I walked through from the other entrance.'

Harry and I don't follow every development in Israel. Naturally we notice when Ephraim Vardi is mentioned in the news, and I'm aware that he's a senior Israeli diplomat. I knew Ernst and his family had moved to Paris. I don't know what he does there, what protection he would have, or what sort of surveillance he might be under.

'What about your security detail?'

'No one with me. Marjorie, you once asked if you could help us. We are monitoring a huge surge in traffic between Moscow and Cairo and Damascus. Cyrillic text encrypted on old-style Soviet rotor machines. I think you may be familiar with them. How's your Arabic?'

'Scraped an A-level. Why?'

Suddenly he touches my arm. 'Look! To the left!' he whispers. At once I'm alert for someone observing us, but he murmurs, 'Huge bird of prey.' I see it dropping close, wings like sails. 'Is that a buzzard?' he murmurs. 'Some sort of hawk?'

'No, bigger.' I riffle frantically through my book. 'Could be a marsh harrier.' I hold out the page to Ernst. The bird flaps into the air and vanishes with unhurried ease.

'This year,' he returns to his topic, 'Russia rearmed Nasser. New submarines, armour, missiles, tanks, the lot. Soviet technicians arrived en masse. Now they're starting to build up Syria in the same way.'

He launches into a very dry account of how Israeli intelligence keeps track of these things. Aman, he says, is Military Intelligence. Inside Aman is the Intelligence Unit. Inside the Intelligence Unit is Yehida Shmoneh-Matayim, in other words Unit 8-200, specialists in signals interception and decryption.

'This is complicated.'

'That's just the start. All of that is the IDF. Soldiers in uniform. Then comes Shin Bet for internal security, and the Mossad, or Secret Intelligence Service, on foreign intelligence. See what I mean?'

'A tangled web indeed!'

'Now – we also recruit individuals in other countries. Top-quality, independent, under-the-radar sort of people with good cover. Our new man at the top has asked us to make better use of them. That's what I want to talk to you about, Marjorie. '

'And when you say "we, us" –' I take my binoculars and spend a few seconds looking round. There is no one in sight. 'Or is that another question that can't be –'

'Israel, obviously. Better to think of it as being for me personally. There must be no conflict of interest with your other work. We don't want that.'

'What other work?'

'Quite. What we're interested in isn't Egypt or Syria. It's the relations between the Soviets and the two opposing wings of the Ba'ath Party. And the role of the Ba'ath in the Kremlin strategy for the region. You know about the Ba'ath Party?'

'Pan-Arab nationalist movement.'

'Correct. You'll get a full briefing. The Russians use it very deftly. We're tracking arms deals between Russia and Iraq's Ba'athists. The CIA are mixed up with the Ba'ath Party too, and we don't want them getting in our hair. I say, look – that pretty little thing bobbing about. Look how long it can stay underwater!'

We stare in silence for a moment, waiting for the bird to reappear after a dive. 'Has it got a crest? That's a great crested grebe. Shouldn't there be security clearance before a conversation like this?'

'You've already been cleared. The work is risky and top secret. We'll open a bank account in Israel for your payment.'

'Ernst! What are you saying? I don't want to be paid.'

'Why not? We were paid at BP. In fact, we can't *not* pay you. And you'll get a Teudat Zehut – an Israeli identity card.'

'Gosh! How wonderful! How will I explain the ID card to Harry?'

'Harry has a card already. He's been vetted.'

'*Harry* has? I didn't know that.' I look at my watch. 'It's time I went back.'

'Me too.'

When I return to the caravan, Harry is in a rickety camping chair facing the sea, apparently daydreaming. He's clad in a sloppy green pullover over a check shirt with a favourite old tie, baggy flannels, battered brogues. A book lies on the grass beside him. He has no interest in my avocet, harrier or grebe, listening with a patient smile. We set up the chessboard on a folding table amidst the breezy heath.

Between moves, Harry tells me about the latest computing machines that can decrypt, analyse and interpret in seconds. He is sure that even more powerful problem-solving machines are just around the corner. Even in this remote place, I do wish he would not refer to our war work. Of course, Harry doesn't consider computing machines as to do with the war. I reply, 'They'll never come up with a machine which knows it's being deceived, or when not to answer the question.' Harry laughs, 'They will, dear, they will.'

Philip arrives at last, tanned and triumphant, golden hair cascading over each shoulder. He's been sleeping under the stars. The long cycle ride has done wonders. He's happy and well-disposed towards us for a change. What a joy that he is not being argumentative! It's thrilling to have him beside me as we tramp about among the heather.

'About university,' cheerfully he broaches the subject right there on the cliff edge. 'I've sort of realised, I don't want to go. Basically, I'm not going.'

'Oh, Philip, don't say that! Why on earth not?'

'I only want to do stuff I'm really into.'

'Stuff you're into?'

'And I'm not going to be forced to play everyone's game.'

'Yes, but what will you do for a living, then?'

Free of care, he laughs at my concern. 'OK, so –' he's bright with enthusiasm – 'me and Jez, that's a guy I know, we're going to buy this place. It's derelict at the moment. We're going to do it up. Live in it, and let rooms to students.'

'You mean, a derelict house? Where is it, in London?' – 'No, Oxford.' – 'Where will you get the money? Who's Jez?' Philip explains the madcap scheme, based on reckless borrowing and dubious funds he and his friend have amassed God knows how. No argument of ours would persuade him otherwise. I shut my eyes and, for a moment, feel that it might almost be better if he'd jump down into the waves dashing on the rocks below. '*Please* don't say anything to Daddy while he's on holiday. It will break his heart, after all his effort to get you a university place.'

Unconcerned, Philip makes his announcement to Harry that very afternoon. 'Oh, um, Dad – like, Mum said not to tell you – but I've decided not to bother with university after all? I'm not going. Waste of time. Me and a friend have got this plan to, like, do up a house? Live in it and let the rooms?'

Harry turns to me in disbelief. 'Did you know about this, dear? When did you find out?'

'Philip told me just now when we were walking. He's quite determined.'

The effect is devastating and immediate. Harry steps away oddly, twisting his body so his face may not be seen, biting back his fury and grief as he has taught himself to do. No doubt he is in the middle of realising that he cannot compel Philip to do anything, nor forbid him. Turning to us again, the face is red, a vein on his forehead crooked and enlarged. 'Whatever you decide to do, Phil, if you ever need help, you can always come to me.' The man's willingness to sacrifice himself for his children is heartrending.

'See,' Philip points out later, 'Dad didn't mind after all.'

Harry's old tetchiness comes closer to the surface, especially when we are alone. In his anguish, he reads and does not wish to be interrupted. He sits in a chair on the cliff edge. There is no more singing.

5

Max and Philip parked outside The Herons. Their eyes met without expression as they prepared to go in. For 24 hours the two brothers had been researching Sandcliffe care homes online and in person. There were many. All were rated 'Good'. Only three they had seen had vacancies, in neighbourhoods at the back of town, far from the sea.

The Herons was two Edwardian houses joined together. The entrance smelled of air freshener, the hallway of bleach, the corridor of boiled vegetables. Coloured paper chains draped from the ceiling, left over from Christmas. The manager, a middle-aged woman determinedly pleasant, showed them round. She pointed out that every resident had a room of their own. In cheaper homes, she explained, residents may have to share. They looked into bedrooms slightly scented with urine and sick. In a cosy lounge, residents were positioned in armchairs facing a television.

'On Sunday, they have a traditional roast. And a glass of sherry,' she smiled mischievously, 'with doctor's permission, of course.'

'What about if they need help eating?'

'We cut the food for them, or mash it if necessary. We take account of individual needs.'

A bell rang persistently from one of the rooms, but was not answered. Philip said, 'Get that if you want, don't mind us.' The manager said, 'Oh, that's nothing. It goes on all day. We have a quick look every hour or so.'

They asked about the fees, and she gave some figures in the tens of thousands of pounds per annum. 'If the resident qualifies, Sandcliffe Council will contribute.'

'Even that,' Max pointed out, 'leaves a huge shortfall.' He had not mentioned it at the other homes they visited, but this time confessed he was mystified. 'How do the residents afford it? I mean, they don't look especially wealthy. What if they run out of funds?' The proprietor smiled. 'If they own a property it could be sold, which usually raises enough to see them out. The family may help. Or there are less expensive homes. This, obviously, is one of the nicer ones.'

She gave them a leaflet. With smiles and thanks they returned to the car. Several minutes passed before the brothers spoke. 'That was the best of the three.' – 'It's not that bad.' – 'Mum's not going there.' – 'No way.' – 'What if there's no alternative?' – 'We'll find one.' – 'A different care home, you mean?' – 'No, I don't want her to go into a care home if that's what they're like.' – 'We'll look at the options.' – 'The problem is, she needs round-the-clock nursing care.' – 'Continuing Healthcare pays for the nursing.' – 'Only part of it. Anyway, whatever, Mum's not going into that place.'

Carol closed the bedroom door and carried out her tasks. In both mind and body Marjorie struck her as horribly, irrecoverably damaged. Marjorie knew it herself. She had a queasy, panicky sensation of not knowing where she had left her car, what she had done with her keys or her credit cards, where to find her passport. Come to think of it, where were those things? Did she have a car? The box of old family photos, where had it gone? Some precious possession – she tried to remember what it was – was not mislaid, but lost for good. She was unable to focus. She must fight to wake up. Something urgent had been left undone, she could not think what it was. She must grab at loose ends and tie them before she forgot.

'Carol,' Marjorie gestured that the carer should sit, 'your paintings, Aidan's ornaments – take them home today.' Her speech was slurred. 'Is there storage space in your place?'

'Just wardrobes in the bedrooms. We put stuff under the bed.'

'Put them at the back of your wardrobe. Keep the paintings dry. Careful with the china ornaments, extremely careful. Don't damage them. I have to explain something: don't tell anyone about these things. Put them up for auction at Christie's, in London. Remember, these things belong to you and Aidan, not me. I looked after them for you. Is that clear? You know what Christie's is?'

'Well, yeah, but I mean –'

'Carol, listen. Christie's can advise on a reserve price. The figurines I gave Aidan are rare eighteenth-century Meissen porcelain. Write it down. M-E-I-... that'll pay for his university education and more, fees, living expenses, the lot. Your lad will make a good start in life. The small painting is by Pierre Adolphe Valette. Heard of him? No. The bigger one is by David Bomberg. Never heard of him either? Well, they'll help you and Wayne retire. There's paperwork that goes with them. Open the wardrobe. See the green box file on the left? Everything's in there. If you need legal advice, my solicitor will help. He won't charge you. It's taken care of.'

Carol bit her lip. 'So they're really *valuable*, these things? Why d'you keep them here then? Bit risky.'

'I like Valette's painting of Hull docks. I played there as a girl. Bomberg's view of Jerusalem from the South means a great deal to me. The Meissen was something my grandfather left me that my husband liked. It was always on display at our old house.'

'I'd be scared to keep them. I'm not sure I can accept.'

'You already have. That's what a Deed of Gift is. I gave them to you years ago.'

'You're doing this even though I called an ambulance when you asked me not to?'

'Don't be silly, Carol. I gave you these things before that. They were already yours by then.'

'I'm so sorry about the ambulance! That bloody hospital ward, excuse my French.'

'Carol, it's spilt milk. Always know when to hold ground and when to move forward. Move forward now.' The unhappy carer pleaded that she would do things differently if she could only go back to that day. Marjorie watched with a calm eye. 'Just do things differently in future. Look after me nicely, whatever happens, *whatever* happens. I'm counting on you.'

The new care manager from the council had been due at one o'clock. She was coming to reassess Marjorie's needs in the wake of her 'unsafe self-discharge from hospital'. Max sat waiting with his mother in her bedroom. Still the care manager did not arrive. Marjorie murmured, 'Have you ever thought how care for the elderly ought to be funded?'

'Mum, don't worry about that.'

'People are spending their savings on something that's available free to those with no savings. That's a danger to society. Saving must never be discouraged. Here's an idea: Care Bonds, like War Bonds.'

Max tried to think of something sensible to say. He asked her to explain how War Bonds had worked. She said, 'No, this would be different. A decent, basic level of care should be free, like the NHS. This would be savings that social services can't take into account and can't take away, because it's a loan to the Government.'

'If care was free, though, they wouldn't need to take...' But at last the doorbell rang. The new care manager, in business-like skirt and jacket, plastic folders under her arm, introduced herself as Brianna, apologised that she was pushed for time and was briskly sympathetic. She saw at once that Mrs Rosen could not even get out of bed without help, let alone use the lavatory. A hoist would be needed to give her a bath, and two carers for complete safety. She noted that this service user could not even swallow her pills unaided.

When it came to ability to pay, it was to Max that Brianna had to turn, since Marjorie could not fetch her own bank statements. 'Offer Brenda a coffee, darling,' said Marjorie to Max. He caught Brianna's eye. She must be used to it, Brianne, Brenda, Belinda, Barbara.

With their coffees, the two of them sat in the living room and looked through Marjorie's savings certificates, building society passbook and bank statements. 'Your Mum needs high-dependency nursing care twenty-four-seven. In her own home, the level of nursing she requires would cost –' she set out some numbers frankly, 'over and above our contribution, that is.'

Aghast, Max wished some more canny person were here to advise him. He was baffled by the figures. Who could possibly afford it? At that rate, he thought, even Phil will end up turning to Social Services for help. Phil would have to sell his properties. Ah, of course, that's the idea! That's what they expect people to do: sell everything they own. Brianna said, 'It would be much more economical in residential accommodation.'

'What about NHS Continuing Care?' – 'That's nothing to do with us,' replied Brianna.

His mother's question, how care for the elderly should be funded, seemed suddenly being put to him again as if Brianna had yelled it in his face. Yet what *was* to be done? There was paying for a nursing home, or paying for live-in nurses. Both of which cost tens of thousands per annum. The only alternative was for someone to move in and devote themselves to caring for her as daughters used to do.

'There's a vacancy at The Herons,' said Brianna. 'Better than average. Rated *Good* by the Care Quality Commission.'

'As it happens, I went there yesterday. When was it inspected?'

Brianna said it had not actually been inspected. 'That's normal. Homes provide information to the CQC and are graded accordingly.'

'They're not even inspected? Anyway, Mum needs a Jewish home,' he declared. This had just occurred to him. His mother surely did not want to languish among Christmas decorations and gossiping antisemites or, in a couple of months, have 'Happy Easter' strung across her room in memory of various pogroms and massacres.

'All our registered homes care for people regardless of their faith. All faiths and none. I mean, if it's about kosher food whatever she requires can be obtained.'

No, Brianna, what Mum requires cannot be obtained. The faces, the voices, the words, tangled histories, Friday night dinner. To say 'Amen' without anyone thinking it's a faith.

'What about the Ruth Cohen? She has friends in there.'

'There are no vacancies. The Ruth Cohen care home has a very long waiting list.'

'Mum's been active in the community.'

'In the community?' Brianna repeated.

'Got their number?'

Brianna listened spellbound as he made the call. She was not used to Max's impulsiveness. 'Hi, Max here, Max Rosen. You know Mrs Rosen? Have you heard about Mum having to leave hospital in a hurry? They weren't caring for her properly. She needs a residential nursing place urgently. Social services want to put her in a non-Jewish place. It's very, very urgent. If you can fit her in anywhere at all. Thank you, thank you! That's brilliant – I'll hand you over to the lady from Social Services.'

At four-thirty the wheelchair taxi arrived. With not a farewell nor a goodbye wave, Marjorie left her flat in Durbeyfield Lodge.

'Hello Marjorie!' Two cheerful carers, one black, one white, both in their thirties, neither Jewish, wheeled her to the end of a corridor. The rattling sash window gave a view only of a brick wall. 'I like it,' Marjorie announced at once. 'Will you two be looking after me?'

'Yeah, most days,' said the black woman, 'I'm Raine.' – 'Rain?' – 'Well, it's Lorraine really, but only my Mum calls me that, and only when she's cross.'

'I am Róża,' said the white woman, 'call me Rosie, if you like. Or just whistle and I'll come.'

'Rosie and Raine. What are your uniforms – are you carers?'

'Yes, but we're registered nurses.'

Marjorie reckoned Raine, with a flirty manner and amused eyes, was a West Indian girl from the council estates. Róża was obviously Polish. 'Lovely names!' She sounded them slowly, held them in her mouth like sweetmeats, 'Róża ("Ru-ja") and Lorraine ("Loh-rrain"). Roses and rain. I'll call you R 'n' R for short. Rest and recuperation.'

They laughed, they liked her. A single bed with crisp white sheets stood at one corner. She longed to lie in it. In the other corner a wide doorway opened into a bathroom equipped for someone in a wheelchair, as she seemed destined to be.

'I say, Raine. Or Rosie,' she said, 'I need to see my solicitor. Can I meet her here?'

'Course you can,' said Róża. 'The home has a legal advisor. Let me know if she can help.'

'I don't need help. It's only to change my will.'

* * *

'Hello Marjorie!' Behind me on the jostling pavement, a voice deep, gentle, American. 'Marjorie Behrens, right?' Bob Shaffer is as handsome as ever. That rangy, powerful build has matured, now with tanned, craggy, smile-creased face. More than twenty-five years have passed since our days at BP. The shaved scalp disguises a bald crown. He's dressed in American style, buttoned collar and narrow tie. Beneath a check jacket, he's sturdy and upright. I'm pleased to see he still looks at me in *that* way, which is foolish of me at the age of forty-nine. 'I've a couple of days in London.' He does not need to explain himself, and he knows that no explanation would be believed.

'Marjorie Rosen now, Bob. Married woman and mother of three.'

'You'll always be Miss Marjorie Behrens to me.'

'I wrote to you after you left. You never answered.'

'Marjorie, I'm truly sorry. It was considered unwise for US intel liaison to get too involved with Brits. They told me to forget you. I've never managed to do that.'

I ask if he's married. He simply nods. How odd, though! No phone call, no letter, but a 'chance' meeting in the street that's as likely to happen by chance as winning the pools. It's clear that Bob has sought me out for some particular purpose.

He soon gets down to business. 'You have good contacts in Israel, including in the diplomatic service.'

'What makes you think that, Bob? Am I under surveillance?'

He laughs charmingly. 'That's what we do, Marjorie!'

As we walk, he sounds me out on helping a group of US intelligence officers anticipate Israel's response to traffic between Russia and the Arab League. 'We feel the Soviets are looking for a way to ease tensions,' he says. From this I know straight away there's something renegade about Bob's group.

'Surely the NSA are monitoring Israel closely already.'

'Yup, but there are differences of opinion in the service. And differences of opinion in the Israeli administration, factions inside the coalition parties. We are failing to tap into these factions. We need justification for supporting the right people.'

I'm not clear who he means by "we" or "right people". He's not talking about the United States government. I make it clear that I'd never do anything against Britain's interests, or Israel's.

'What about if their interests clash?'

'I don't waste time on unlikely hypotheticals, Bob.'

'Let's the two of us go out somewhere together and talk it over.'

'The only way that would work is to square it with Harry first.'

Despite being affronted, Harry voices no objection to my spending an afternoon with an old flame while he is visiting London.

I find myself choosing a dress with care, doing my make-up more carefully, and feeling a flutter of anticipation as I prepare my hair. Bob has booked tickets to an afternoon showing of the controversial modern *Macbeth* at the Royal Court. Even sitting beside one another in a taxi feels intimate. In the interval, we perch close together on stools in a corner of the noisy bar and talk about his group's objective, our faces nearly touching. His breath on my cheek carries me straight back to our young love.

I answer that I'm thinking it over. The truth is, I already know I'm not going to do it, but I like being with him. He guides me to our seats, places an affectionate hand on my back. Later we stroll along the King's Road and stop for a coffee. Streetlights are coming on. He is charming and admires me. It's flattering, the attention, the inappropriate, forgotten thrill of being taken out by a man.

Not that I want Bob to, God forbid, take me in his arms and kiss me, let alone the other stuff. I don't allow my thoughts to wander into the territory of Bob actually feeling desire for me, and I don't want to know whether he does or not.

When I get back home, Harry is in a silent rage. 'Had a good time?' he sneers. I answer calmly, 'Yes! Interesting performance, the way they've done it.' When he finds me at the dressing table, taking off a necklace I rarely wear, he explodes. 'Look at you, admiring yourself like a girl.' He slaps the table hard and sweeps my brush and hairpins and a bottle of perfume onto the floor.

This is Harry as he used to be, red-faced with fury. I plead with him to believe that the meeting with Bob was all innocence. 'No, no, go out with him,' he rages. 'Feel free. I don't want it thrown back at me that I *stopped* you. And I thought you were a sensible woman!'

I meet up with Bob only one more time to tell him straight that Harry won't wear it. 'It's better if I don't get involved with you or with the project.' I hold out my hand. 'Goodbye, Bob.'

'It's been fun, though, hasn't it?' He gives me a kiss on the cheek and holds my arm.

Nicola has taken to the new anything-goes look, long straight hair and knicker-revealing skirts. She becomes angry when I ask her boyfriend to stay out of her bedroom. 'Mum, I'm *sixteen*. And anyway, we already sleep together, so what's the difference?' Poor

Nicola! She has embraced every daft ideology in the book. She is even worse when Philip calls on us.

The word "fascist" is thrown around. Come the revolution they'd be happy enough to string us up from the nearest lamp-post. À la lanterne, the benighted bourgeois reactionaries who helped them with their homework. Philip repudiates everything we say and do; even repudiates the idea of 'parents'. Doesn't believe in it. He joins the demonstrations that take place all the time now in the West End, which are mere theatre designed to inconvenience decent working people, for whom Philip has nothing but contempt.

I forgive him the raging passion of youth. I was in the same mood myself at his age, with bright eagerness for the better world we could make after the war. Harry had another dream, though. He dreamed that his children would wear sound leather shoes and well-fitted school uniforms, have normal English haircuts, eat English food and speak correct English. They would be untouched by mockery and insults, and flourish as Englishmen and Englishwomen. The proudest prize, Harry imagined, would be honour and respect from the world, not having to shy away from its taunts. His own worthless past could then be obliterated from his mind.

Now Harry's vision has evaporated like a mirage. The future, it turns out, was only air. The children won't be as he dreamed. Nor will the world. Fate continues to mock him. It pours contumely into his soul, that secret place of torment.

Yet at last some good news. Today he opened a letter and read it aloud to all of us: he's got the job as head of the Mathematics Department at Sandcliffe College, on the south coast. It becomes a university this year, and he's to start in post in the autumn.

Nicola flatly refuses to come with us to Sandcliffe. She insists she will stay in London with her boyfriend.

My own career news cannot be read aloud, and is not so good. The LPG team is to be moved from London to Cheltenham and integrated into J-Division, the GCHQ Soviet section. I'm no longer in the team.. On the eve of my fiftieth birthday, I'm out.

The wartime generation is being pushed aside. Young graduates sit at our desks and regard us as obsolete. Without warning Yvette has retired. She never replies to my letters, never answers the phone. I drive past her house in Sunningdale. The windows are boarded up. A sign warns it is 'under surveillance'. Maybe she's on a world cruise. Heaven knows she deserves it. Her husband must have left her a tidy sum.

Male and female created he them. Despite Harry's disappointment at the unsuitable match, there's a perverse mood of triumph. That a daughter of Chaim Rosenzweig be wed in this lovely English church by an Anglican priest, and to such a pasty, lacklustre, willowy Anglo-Saxon lad with not a spark of intellect and no prospects, gives its own peculiar satisfaction to a man like Harry.

Ach, such a house of worship! Such a nishtikeit of English youth! Here's a Yiddishe refugee has set his child's feet firmly among the native people of his new home. In these days, there are no taunting neighbours. No one minds that a man is a Jew, so long as he doesn't look, talk or act as a Jew, nor do, think or believe anything Jewish. Keep all that under wraps, and none but the most deranged will point to your Hebrew origins.

After the ceremony, we welcome everyone to the reception. Bursting with merriment, Harry raises himself nimbly onto a chair and beams around the chattering room. Every face turns his way. In this unconventional, lofty vantage point he presents a jovial picture, playful, and even on this wedding day cannot command his wild wisps of hair to stay in place. Goodness knows what the husband's family make of him.

Harry twinkles with intelligence and wit, glitters with bonhomie and good-humour. I hope he doesn't fall off the chair. For the moment, he keeps his balance and, as Father of the Bride, launches into a speech with the amazing courage of those who can address a crowd without preparation. He's a fish in water, a bird in flight. The jokes come, and the anecdotes, poignant memories of his darling little girl, and wishes for years of happiness as a wife and mother. There is the clink of glasses, the roar of laughter, clapping hands.

Harry at his best. It's one of those moments when I love him most. Because only I know what he is hiding and how well he is hiding it.

Max paced the wet promenade, following Sandcliffe's wintry sands from end to end, passing the locked-up beach huts, cafés closed for the season, a forlorn windswept pier with shuttered attractions. Occasionally a walker, buttoned against the weather, passed without a word, or a headphone-wearing runner in lycra dashed by with grim determination.

Yet the scene was majestic to his eye, the exhilarating sky a panoply of racing cloud, and the wide shore empty but for a whirling flock of gulls, their shrieks lost in the wind.

And he felt that the wearisome problem of what to do with his mother had at last been solved. She was in good hands. He made his way back to his car and drove to the Ruth Cohen care home.

He pulled into the driveway of the Edwardian mansion, inevitable end for most of Sandcliffe's small Jewish community. There was nothing remotely welcoming about the place, its lowering brick obfuscated by the shade of looming conifers. In a large day room women advanced into dotage were slumped in armchairs facing a booming television, a few studying the picture attentively, a few glassy-eyed and mumbling, a few catatonic.

Beyond was a large conservatory or sun room where, near a window, his mother sat unaided in a wheelchair. She looked out, blankly or meditatively, to a well-kept lawn, green as a gem, enclosed by pruned bushes and wooden benches.

Something astonishing had been done to her hair. The neat bun, essential part of his mother's profile for the whole of Max's life, was gone, cut clean away. Instead, short, grey strands grew from the edges of a white scalp entirely bald from crown to frontal. All these years, he had not known! Mum was bald! The trimmed locks reached only to her ears and the collar of her shirt. In part she appeared to have been transformed from respectable matron into suave gentleman, and in part (with her thick reading glasses, lofty brow, and the elvish frailty brought on by being starved nearly to death in hospital) into a rather gamine superannuated bluestocking. He wished she had not done it. She had passed from elegance to eccentricity in a single haircut.

Also bewildering was that in the chair beside her sat his brother Philip. Only this morning Max had texted his brother and sister *Mum now at Ruth Cohen*. That Phil would drive all the way here at once was frankly amazing.

Their mother had an air of stunned detachment, despite the noise. For the conservatory was not quiet. Mingling cacophonously with the television, a radio played pop requests and phone-ins. At one end of the room, a group of chatting women laughed loud and often.

To be heard at all, Max had to call out in greeting. 'Hi Mum! Hello! How *are* you?'

'Max?' She stared and stared, trying to find him in the fog of macular degeneration. '*Very* well,' she replied, delighted. She clearly did feel much better than yesterday.

Max turned to his brother. 'Hi Phil, you decided to come down?'
'Yah.'

'And I see you've gone for, ah, a different hair-do, Mum. Shorter.'

'Final chapter of this strange eventful history,' was her reply, 'sans teeth, sans eyes, sans taste – sans hair. I won't ask if it suits me. Nothing suits me. I'm free of all that now. A hairdresser came and did it this morning,' she explained. 'My hair won't be done the old way any more. I can't do it myself and can't expect anyone else to do it. I live here now. Voilà.'

'You said once you'd rather be dead than in the Ruth Cohen.'

'Yes, well,' a rueful chuckle, 'very foolish of me. I said that before I *needed* to be in the Ruth Cohen.'

Max smiled. She did seem to have made an astonishing recovery.

'Yes,' said Philip, 'you'll be comfortable here. Home from home.'

The three of them went to the office of the Ruth Cohen's manager, Agnieszka. Letters of Agreement had to be signed concerning the care home's fees. Under Social Services rules, as the fees exceeded Mrs Rosen's "personal budget", a "third-party top-up" could be used to cover the shortfall. It could only be paid by a third party, not by Mrs Rosen.

'How much is the shortfall?' Max asked.

'About £100 a week,' said Agnieszka.

Max was shocked, and drew back from signing. Instantly Philip said quietly, 'Max, it's fine.'

Max felt sick of the tedious figures, unable to follow them on their tangled route to the bottom line. He had to remind himself that the important thing was for his mother to be cared for. The finances were like a storm raging outdoors that he hoped would soon clear up.

Marjorie was shown the agreement but could not read it clearly. She felt it would be more prudent to let her children deal with these matters. She would give them power of attorney soon anyway. She signed in an uneven hand that she approved the arrangements.

Afterwards she was wheeled to the dining room, where dinner was served at 5pm, with teaspoons if necessary and bibs tied. The two brothers kissed her goodbye.

Relieved to get out of the building, both men took deep breaths as if they had been suffocating. The passing traffic was a reassuring reminder of normal life. Max said, 'It's generous of you, covering the shortfall.'

'Totally spaced out, isn't she? And sick all the time, apparently.'

'It must be a terrible shock, suddenly changing so much.'

'Frightening. Want to go for a drink or something?'

Max demurred. He wanted to be alone. 'Hey, Phil, why *did* you come down? It's a long drive.'

'I needed to make completely sure Mum would be happy here.'

Max couldn't fault the sentiment, yet still it mystified him.

Marjorie's GP visited the next Monday, as arranged. Marjorie said, 'I didn't know it was Monday! I need my wall calendar, to keep track of the days.' The calendar from her flat was brought. Nothing had been written on it since last December. She had even missed Olivier's nineteenth birthday. How awful, she thought, how selfish of me. 'The most difficult thing about being here,' she said to the doctor, 'is that nothing is required of you.'

* * *

Blustery night falls on Saltington's yacht harbour. A strong breeze draws ragged cloud across the curve of a pure white moon. On foot I follow the water's edge from quay to boatyards to pontoons. Great sudden gusts blow against my face. As the wind grows stronger, the rigging of moored boats strikes up, becomes a frenzied percussion, hundreds of vessels loud with clattering, drumming, rattling, ringing, the ropes a chorus of screaming and yowling, whistling in mad celebration, the masts swaying in wild rhythm.

A storm is rising tonight. Black surging tide beats the harbour walls. This first evening in Saltington is unspeakably exhilarating. If I want to sail again, where better than here? I long to find a small craft of my very own once more and put out onto this unruly sea.

We move into our new home in the first days of autumn, now just Harry, Max and me. A short drive along the coast from Sandcliffe, the little town of Saltington rises from a wide estuary between shining mud flats, salt marshes and water meadows. Its bustling Georgian main street, angled down to the water's edge, is a model of English provincial charm. On the inland side of town lies the edge of the New Forest, to which for years I have longed to return, yet find so very different from what I remember.

The house is all we ever wished for, in a petit-bourgeois paradise of trimmed privet, clipped front lawns and flowering trees. People are pleasant and polite, and birdsong – not traffic – continues from morning to night. Max rides his bike to school and Harry makes his short journey to Sandcliffe. In the afternoon they return to a clean house and a cup of tea. After supper, Harry and I ponder the crossword and play chess.

Yet Harry is not content. Disappointment smoulders inside him. The atmosphere at work is strained, too. His colleagues wanted the job to go to a senior member of the existing staff. Deeper inside lies some other bitterness. The angina grips him more firmly. The doctor orders him to walk more, worry less. In the Forest he strides quickly along paths not just through dying bracken and fallen leaves but in the labyrinth of his thoughts. My beloved husband, once so buoyant, is struggling now, battling with his depression and his health.

Absurdly he even reminisces about the childhood he was so keen to escape. 'You know what, maybe it would be nice to go to synagogue occasionally.' Is this *Harry*, hard-boiled rationalist, sceptic and dyed-in-the-wool atheist? The twists of fate have forced his mind back towards its starting point. 'We have to join Sandcliffe shul anyway, for Max's barmitzvah.'

It's yet more grounds for Philip and Nicola to mock us. Nicola arrives on a Friday evening to find the twin candles of Shabbat burning. 'You're not becoming *religious*, are you?'

'Being part of a community is not religious. It's sound common sense,' I answer 'It's useful.'

She presses her point. 'Dad, you don't believe in God.'

'So what? Still Jewish, aren't we?'

'And Mum, wouldn't you say you are an atheist?'

'I wouldn't say anything of the sort, darling. I never bother with such things.'

But Nicola wants to argue. 'What *do* you believe? You believe the world was created in six days?'

'I believe in the IDF,' I reply tartly – the Israeli army.

Nicola tuts her disapproval, as if to say we are beyond reason.

Harry is suddenly enraged. 'I don't go to synagogue because of what I believe. I go to stand in the place of a man who is not there any more, someone murdered for being Jewish.'

Nicola stares at her father. 'OK.' She is reluctantly mollified; impressed, even. 'Good reason, Dad.'

While Harry is at work, I drive or cycle searching for the Forest of my memories. Ponies and cattle still wander across the roads, marvellously ignorant of traffic. Everything else has changed. No rolls of barbed wire, no searchlights, no armed men on manoeuvres, no Land Girls toiling. At Beaulieu, I cannot work out where my training mansion was, the German house, das Haus as we called it. Nor can I place the field from which I took off one clear night. Today, no doubt, it's just a paddock or a meadow beside the sea.

From Saltington's quayside, a waterside path separates the Solent from the salterns. There I rest my eyes on the long horizontal lines of the coast, the narrow waters, bands of cloud, the low island on the far side. Thousands of birds are at work, solitary or in pairs, or great gatherings, myriad varieties, nippy waders and elegant, long-legged fishers, gulls screeching, bobbing divers and master flyers skimming the surface at speed. Vanishingly high, a single skylark trills in fluting upper octaves its 'hymns at heaven's gate.' The bird world is terrifying in its complexity, its ceaseless conflict, struggle for territory and dominance, subtleties of disguise and display, each individual bound to the diktats of instinct. A flock takes flight, in seconds covering a distance that would take a running man an hour, then returns to its starting place. Maybe we are the same, flying in circles, migrating to and fro, going nowhere.

Scores of sails pass in the middle distance on small boats as pretty as a child's drawing. They are a local type of scow, gaff-rigged, appealing and manageable. At the Yacht Club, so a neighbour tells me, someone's put up a scow for sale. Its owner invites me to meet her at the Club. She's a few years older than me, in sensible sailing kit, an old deck jacket over a polo shirt and trousers.

She thrusts out her hand, introducing herself, 'Audrey de Baar', with unmistakeably upper-crust brio. I like her immediately. We walk down to her little scow on its launching trolley outside. There's not much to see; a tiny flat-bottomed dinghy with a centreboard, a tight squeeze for two. There's no motor. On touching the water, it becomes quick and deft, weightless, eager with nervous energy.

'It's easy to rig,' Audrey enthuses, and so it proves. 'Want to helm it up and down the river for a bit?'

'The two of us? All right.'

'Once we're in open water, pull down the centreplate, like a keel.' Instantly we're away, dashing close-hauled into the flow of the estuary. I am overwhelmed with joy.

Audrey and her friends are all excellent, intelligent women and jolly companions. They know the area well, say sensible things about tides and currents, ponies and pigs, talk lyrically of Crown Lands, moors and meres, enclosures of old beech, holly and English oak.

A letter from Erika. I receive Lucienne's and Erika's letters at home now. It's risky, but I can't find a sensible explanation to receive them anywhere else. This latest contains an exclamation mark.

With a pin and a pair of tweezers, I peel the point of the exclamation mark off the paper and place it delicately on a microscope slide. The image is clear and in focus. Erika has sent photographs of top-copy documents in plain Cyrillic text. These are internal minutes and memoranda concerning the future of East Germany and the great opportunity presented to the Kremlin. The West is creating a strategy to abandon the Hallstein Doctrine (which considers East and West Germany as one country) and recognise East Germany as an independent state. Things are not going the way Erika would like. For Erika, it's a catastrophe. It seems she has lost her long battle to see Germany united and democratic.

Straight away, another letter from her. Always until now they have come at intervals of a few weeks. I hold it in my hand. For the first time, her seal of correcting fluid on the back is cracked. Impossible to know, but we must assume it has been opened and read. The envelope has been stuck down again meticulously, another bad sign. Who might have done this? I've always thought the people most likely to intercept Erika's letters would be on our own side.

I open it and unfold the paper. Erika's news is that Klaus retires this year. Step by step I decipher her message using my Guide Bleu codebook. She wants us to meet face to face as soon as possible. Most puzzling, she insists our pen-friend Lucienne and her husband be there as well, if possible – and, she says, it is I who must invite them. 'Ask Lucienne to reserve a restaurant table for dinner. Say they will be your guests.' The code from the guidebook shows a village in eastern France, called Brisault, beside the autoroute south of Beaune, not far from the Swiss border and an easy drive for Lucienne and Jean. The date, July 13th, is peculiar; the noisy, festive eve of a national holiday. Presumably that is deliberate.

Unless there's something I don't understand, I can only suppose Erika needs Lucienne and Jean as cover. That she wants Lucienne to make the restaurant booking means she knows our own communications have been compromised. Which means we are both in danger. From whom, I don't know.

Editors soon forget you ever existed. Commissions were drying up. Max spent too much time on his mother's affairs and too often had to say 'no' to them. It pained him to see other photographers' work in slots he could have filled. Brilliant images were coming out of the Arab Spring story. Max felt he could have done just as well. It was maddening! Even though she was now in a care home, he still had to drop out of press trips to deal with her urgent appointments, important emails, unstoppable correspondence.

The Department of Work and Pensions demanded immediate repayment of Attendance Allowance to which Mrs Rosen had not been entitled while in residential care. They threatened prosecution. However, they noted, there were other benefits she could claim. He applied for them online. As a result her assets had to be recalculated. Wasn't this covered by NHS Continuing Healthcare? Apparently not. What exactly was Attendance Allowance? He had forgotten.

Marjorie's income he could not grasp, shown on bank statements by incomprehensible abbreviations. FOX, CSX, TP. Only DWP did he know. The others, she herself claimed not to know, saying they were long-forgotten occupational pensions. Her capricious outgoings confounded him more; bills and statements, invoices and demands, direct debits and standing orders. Were the amounts correct? How would he know?

He opened an urgent council tax demand. In her flat his mother had been entitled to a twenty-five percent reduction for living alone; now that she was in a care home the discount fell to ten percent as the council regarded her flat as a second home. She had underpaid. What is a second home if you are in residential care? He phoned: she has to pay *more* for council services now that she is not using them? Yes.

Max sat at his desk filling in application forms for the two kinds of power of attorney – health and welfare, and property and financial affairs – agonising over each stroke of the pen (*This lasting power of attorney could be rejected at registration if it contains any errors*). Her GP refused to confirm Marjorie was sufficiently compos mentis to appoint an attorney. Joe Reznik agreed to sign instead, which was permitted as he had known her so long.

'Dzień dobry!' Marjorie greeted Róża – Good morning! Delighted at being addressed in Polish, Róża responded in kind. 'Dzień dobry! How are you today, Mrs Rosen?'

'*Bardzo* dobrze! A u ciebie?' – *Very* well. How are you?

'Goodness! Do you really speak Polish?' Róża was amazed. She helped Marjorie from the bed and walked with her to the bathroom.

'One picks up a few words. So, Róża, tell me your troubles.'

'Troubles?' The carer laughed merrily. 'I found a job, a boyfriend and a place to live. What do I want with troubles?'

'You like the job?'

'All you need to know about my job, Mrs Rosen, is that many residents are double incontinent, a lot completely immobile, some don't know who or what or where they are. My job means getting saliva, piss, even semen on me.' At this last revelation, Marjorie wanted to ask – why, how? But she did not ask. 'Yesterday, worse,' said Róża, 'one lady shit into my hand as I am removing her pad.'

'Oh, ghastly!'

'She can't help it. She would be sorry if she knew. Hardest part of the job is to remember that they are human. Everybody is human, everybody wants a good life and to be happy. Even these. I ask God why they live. Why, God, do you want them to live?'

'Does he answer you?'

'I think we know God's answer: if we do not have compassion for one another, he will destroy us. My other question for him is, why do *they* want to live? For this, I don't know his answer.'

'Can't you find a better job, Róża? You are a clever girl. You speak good English.''

'This job is the best.' Róża briskly continued with her work. 'Sometimes they look at you, and give you such a beautiful smile. Like the smile of a baby. That, for me, is the reward.'

Róża lowered Marjorie onto the lavatory seat. In the bedroom, she was joined by Lorraine, the two young women chatting as they made the bed and prepared to give her a shower.

After breakfast, for those still able, came morning activities, keep-fit, music and entertainment, arts and crafts. 'Playschool for a second childhood,' scoffed Marjorie. – 'Oh, come on,' urged cheerful Róża, 'it's *fun*!'

Lunch, then more activities. Afternoon tea and cake was a welcome landmark in the passage of the hours. Television, sunlight through windows or rain upon the lawn, the hairdresser's visit. Supper time came early. Carers served and fed the residents in the dining room, or assisted those who were bed bound.

At seven o'clock night falls on the care home. Everyone is taken to their room, undressed, put on the toilet and lifted off again, washed and brushed, medication washed down. Moving the immovable, helping the helpless, remembering that everyone is human.

Before clocking off at eight, Róża and Lorraine write their reports. 'Mrs Rosen is improving well and settling in. She enjoys solitude. She asks if she can have more time alone in her room.'

'That would not be beneficial,' decides manager Agnieszka. 'Encourage Mrs Rosen to socialise more.'

Marjorie sat in her chair, and switched off the radio. To Harry's photo on the shelf she murmured, 'To be or not to be, that is their question. Why they live? asks Róża. They live because something is better than nothing. She knew that on this topic, Harry certainly agreed: Something cannot be compared with Nothing.

Carol stepped into the Ruth Cohen always a little afraid of making an embarrassing faux pas or reacting inappropriately to some unfamiliar Jewish custom. She came to see how she could help Marjorie, for whom she was filled with love and gratitude, and regret.

She sat with Marjorie in the conservatory after helping her with the evening meal. 'I wish I were back in my flat,' said Marjorie. 'I don't get enough time sitting quietly on my own. The girls here are very nice, but they won't let us stay alone in our rooms.'

'How could you manage in your flat when you can't even walk?'

'I want to be in my flat whether I can manage or not. Anyway, I *can* walk.'

'Let's see you walk, then.'

Confined to a wheelchair almost all the time, Marjorie's walking had become worse. Raised to her feet, she leaned backwards for fear of falling forward, and could hardly move without losing her balance. She had a vertiginous, irrational sensation, caused by her ruined eyes and her wrecked mind, that the floor was dangerously far away.

'Sit down, Marjorie, before you come a cropper. Did I ever tell you I was in rehabilitation nursing? I can get you back on your feet, using a zimmer or rollator like before. You have to put in the effort, though. Want to try it?'

'You bet.'

'When you can get about on your own, and do a few other little things, you'll have a good case for nursing care in your own home.'

By the end of the day, there had been a change in Marjorie's outlook. She *would* get away from the routine and racket of the Ruth Cohen care home and return to her lovely, tranquil flat and sit on the balcony with a cup of tea all by herself and look at the sea, and think.

* * *

L ittle roads are lapped by tender green vine leaves, clusters of unripe grapes hanging as viticulteurs tend the tiny fields, labouring in every 'climat' and 'clos' as we pass on the D974. Well-kept, prosperous villages come quickly one after another, their names like a roadside carte des vins of fine burgundies. In mansions and village squares growers sell the bottled product of their terroir and vignoble. Everywhere strings of tricolore flags are being hung in preparation for the Jour National revels that begin tonight.

It's hardly ten minutes' walk through vineyards from the campsite into Brisault. Parked cars have been banished from Place de la République where now a long, long dining table is being set up and spread with white paper covers. Tee-shirted young men are positioning loudspeakers around the square.

Lucienne has booked a brasserie table within sight of the Place, from which drifts a racket of brass band and speeches. There we meet Lucienne and Jean for an aperitif. Their son and daughter-in-law, Alain and Sandrine, have joined them, together with their twelve-

year-old son Thierry, 'to keep Max company.' The arrival of Klaus
and Erika brings further friendly introductions amidst laughing, air-
kissing and handshaking. Our jolly party is a model of international
harmony. Erika catches my eye. Her glances dart around the
restaurant.

How weary she looks. Erika must be about sixty now. Klaus has
put on weight. They are the very image of Germanic respectability.
While Lucienne and Sandrine are gorgeous in fitted summer dresses,
and I am casual in slacks and blouse, Erika has a buttoned-up
formality in her woollen summer suit. The men are in open-neck
shirts and casual chinos, except Klaus, who wears a tie, pressed green
trousers and a collarless, military-looking tracht jacket, which seems
thoughtless on the eve of la Fête Nationale. One can imagine
everyone asking what these two did in the war.

Cigarettes are offered and drinks sipped. A bottle of Brisault is
ordered, and the four-course menu. We move from summery crudités
to fillet of bream. 'Can Thierry stay with us tonight?' pleads Max.
Thierry makes the same eager request. Alain and Sandrine agree
cheerfully. 'We'll bring him back to you tomorrow!' I promise.

The only interest Brisault has for Klaus is its renowned white
wine, of which he has ordered a second, pricier bottle. He says it's
his treat, and pours liberally. He drinks much of it himself, too
quickly, and is getting rather tight, and too raucous, with a savage
jollity. 'Also, here is one great *white* wine,' he booms, 'while around
all great roten burgunderwein find, ja?'

He swirls the golden liquid around his glass, and around his
mouth, with determined appreciation. Each swallow elicits Teutonic
shouts of delight. Harry hardly touches his glass. He considers all
such bibulous behaviour 'very goyish.'

I take a sip. Rich and flowery, not at all sweet, it's among the
finest wine I have ever drunk; but this will be the limit of my tasting
experiment. I want my wits about me.

Soon after dessert is served, the sounds from the village square
begin to rise. 'Come on,' yells Max, 'they're starting the fireworks!'

The street is overflowing with clamour and excitement. The evening
air becomes sensuously pleasant. In this sumptuous warmth, the press

of women and men in summer clothes conjures a heady intimacy. The crowd eases past locals still assembled at their long table en plein air, spooning crème into their mouths, smoking post-prandial cigarettes or grasping cups of coffee. The brass band plays.

'Stick together,' Harry warns. Erika calls to Max and Thierry, 'If we lose you, stand by the Hôtel de Ville, so we can find you.' The Sapeurs-Pompiers, the firemen, arrange huge fireworks in the midst of the crowd. Max and Thierry push through the crush to watch. 'They aren't going to light those here?' I grab Harry by the arm. 'Don't let the boys get too close. It could be dangerous.'

'Klaus,' Erika instructs her husband in crisp, imperative German, 'help Harry to look after them.' At that moment the music stops abruptly. The hubbub of voices falls quiet, expectant, and at once the bandsmen strike up again, now playing *La Marseillaise*.

Diners push back the chairs and rise to their feet. The entire crowd bursts into song with defiant pride. Klaus and Erika and Harry stand respectfully listening. For some reason I am moved by the sight and sound, and though not French I join in, singing the anthem with feeling, though what the feeling is, I could not say; pathos, perhaps.

This is such a fantastic firework display – and in a small village, of all places. The brass band has been replaced by raucous electric guitar and French pop songs on crackling loudspeakers. Dozens of rockets scream up from the heart of the crowd, exploding into a ceaseless kaleidoscope above our heads, sparkling droplets tumbling. Necks are craned to see everything. No precautions are taken. Giant catherine wheels and roman candles are lit within a few feet of us, shooting great flames bright enough to illuminate the walls of the church and town hall and the shifting faces with vivid, shimmering colour. Insouciant firemen light and light one after another.

'Did you know it would be like this here tonight?' I ask Erika. She knew, of course.

'Keep walking, keep moving. I don't want to be watched or followed.' Unusually, she speaks in English, her face close to mine. Hidden within the excited crush of people, certainly it would not be possible to keep track of us. Klaus, Lucienne, Harry, the boys, are lost from view. As they go one way, we go the other.

Erika says, 'There has been a development, and I am very afraid.'

'Yes, I thought there was something.'

The din of the festivities drowns out her words. She repeats, speaking directly into my ear, 'I am being watched, Marjorie, or followed.'

I shake my head to reassure her. 'No, no one knows about you. Your name is not in any reports. Followed by whom?'

'Now I must tell you. All this time you didn't know.' A rocket explodes directly overhead, releasing a snowstorm of silvery flakes of light which tumble harmless among us, a wonderful sight. 'My source in Germany, in the DDR—.'

'No,' I put a hand up to stop her, 'don't tell me. It's too risky. Honestly, I don't want to know.'

'He is a foreign intelligence analyst in the Hauptverwaltung Aufklärung – you know HVA? Part of Staatssicherheitsdienst – the Stasi. A colonel. He works in the KGB liaison office in Berlin. Surveillance of foreign trade missions is his responsibility. I knew him in the old days, the good old days, when we were young.'

'The Stasi! My God, Erika, don't speak of it. I wish you hadn't told me. He's in enough danger! Who else have you told?'

'No one. It's so you will understand the situation, yours and mine. Listen.'

Even though I don't want to hear what Erika is telling me, it's fascinating, the curious circular elision of Gestapo and Stasi and KGB, each a mere stone's throw from the other, made of the same steely alloy of omniscience, surveillance, cruelty and ideology. I'm suddenly reminded of the SOE interviewers asking me about my politics. Somewhere in the polarity of Left and Right, Fascist and Socialist, is a greater divide, Human and Inhuman. All ideology is Utopian. All Utopias are inhuman.

Erika slips her arm through mine and, with a turn of the head to look back into the square, leads me aimlessly forward. Every face is filled with smiles and carefree wonder. 'His section,' she says, 'has been alerted by a KGB agent inside British intelligence that high-quality Soviet intelligence is being sent from the DDR via an unknown female British agent based in Vienna.'

'How can anyone know that?'

'The point is, Marjorie, they do know. You yourself told me, it was you who warned me when we met in Alsace, you said the KGB may have penetrated the British Embassy in Vienna.'

'That was to advise you to stay away from the embassy. We don't work through the embassy. They don't know you, Erika.'

'Except, of course, they *do* know – both of us. Do you suppose the MI6 station in Vienna haven't identified me after all this time? And if they have, then the KGB have too. Your last letter to me had been unsealed and re-sealed. Very professionally.'

'And yours to me.'

'It means everything I send you is read by a KGB agent in London and sent back to Moscow. I have something for you...'

Huge, dazzling flashes of colour and light slice through the darkness in a great climax. Everyone around us cries out, entranced and thrilled. We too stop and gaze up amazed. Just minutes later, the celebrations start coming to a close. People are streaming away from the square and along the village street.

Erika hands me a piece of tissue paper folded into four. 'These are the Soviet agents in London that my Stasi officer found out about. He says the information may be out of date. Not their real names. Their code names and call signs. Quickly, Marjorie, take it.'

As my palm closes around it, I merely glance at the paper. Just three people are listed. I don't recognise any of the code names, but then, I wouldn't. One is female, at SIS. Another is male, at GCHQ's J-Division, the Soviet section in Cheltenham. The third, male, is or was at LPG. Any of them could have seen my Erika analysis reports and become curious about my source. The two males use an almost identical call sign, from which I gather that the agent at LPG may be the same one as at J-Division. I screw the paper deep into my handbag. My mind is churning with anxiety and uncertainty; how much credence should I give this? To whom do I report it, without knowing who the individuals are, and without revealing the source?

'And Marjorie, there is something else important I must tell you.' Erika squeezes my arm urgently. Yet she stops at once, and calls out 'Ah, hello!' Lucienne and Jean, together with both the boys, are right in front of us. Harry and Klaus, close behind, must have found some common ground after all, for they are chatting animatedly.

'I need to tell you something important,' repeats Erika into my ear, 'about you.' She smiles broadly as Lucienne approaches.

'Meet me in the campsite washrooms at twelve-fifteen,' I reply.

There is general delight at the haphazard way we have found ourselves together again. Everyone speaking at once, we tell each other how much we loved the fireworks. Max and Thierry excitedly recall every detail. Lucienne's eyes sparkle. She says she has had a wonderful evening. It's time, she says, to make their way home with Alain and Sandrine. It's getting late for the boys, too, don't we agree? We do agree. With kisses and effusive goodnights, we wish them a safe drive, and promise to see them tomorrow evening.

Erika and Klaus have booked one of the fixed mobile homes. Harry and I are in another part of the site in a pre-erected family tent. At midnight, Harry is ready for bed in his pyjamas and dressing gown. I'm still dressed. Thierry and Max are quietly giggling in the second sleeping area. 'Go to sleep now,' I instruct them.

'That chap Klaus,' Harry says, 'what a bore!' I apologise that my friend has such a dull husband. He laughs, 'I hope that's not what Erika says to *him!*'

'Just popping out for a walk around the site before bed.' That's not unusual and he's not surprised. I put on a headscarf and light jacket. It has become quiet. In the distance, occasional fireworks still fly up from the horizon, festivities in other villages. Their specks of light make not a sound that I can hear.

I've already studied the well-lit route Erika will take to the toilet block. For myself I follow a more round-about course, and pause in dark shadows, so that I can listen and watch. I want to see if it's true that Erika is being followed. I fear an alternative possibility.

I do have a strange unease, a sort of sixth-sense awareness. Slight movements, something concealed, could be a bird, some small creature, a man. I double back abruptly, but there is nothing. Behind high gauzy cloud a gibbous moon moves serenely forward. Erika comes into view.

She walks quickly under lamps along the pathway. She's encased in a long, shapeless garment, something between a nightdress, a nun's habit and a housecoat, secured by modest buttons from chin to ankle. Some plausible reason must have been given to Klaus for using the communal washing facilities instead of the bathroom in their mobile home.

No one follows her. She arrives at the deserted toilet block and steps inside. I remain still. After a few minutes, I walk across to join her. The ladies' washing area is cool and dank, the air sharp with the tang of some cleaning product. Erika stands waiting between shower cubicles and a row of washbasins.

'Hello, Marjorie.' As always when it's just the two of us, she is brisk and businesslike. 'Go ahead, Erika,' I say at once, 'tell me.'

She has not even drawn breath before the door swings open with a bang. At a run, two men and a woman rush inside the room. As I feared, it was me, not Erika, who was being followed. Stupidly, I have led them to her. The woman addresses me, 'Frau Rosen?' She's a native German-speaker. There is no need for a response. In any case she gathers her answer from Erika's astonished expression. 'Leave now, please,' the woman urges me, 'so you will not be hurt.'

All three are casually dressed in grey shirt and trousers, dark blouson and running shoes. They are fit and purposeful and appear to have pistols in holsters beneath their jackets. Not just their hair, but their whole visage seems wonderfully blond and fresh. The men move fast and take no notice of me at all. Clearly they believe that a couple of old ladies will be a pushover. They may be right. I've passed fifty; Erika is ten years older. These people are half our age.

They reach Erika in less than a second. She is still wondering who has come into the room by the time her arms have been grabbed by the men. These creatures are rippling with muscle, in the full energy of a chase. I must not let them touch me, as they are far stronger.

The woman is quickly unzipping her jacket. What I thought was a gun holster is a leather pouch. With a deft, practised movement she pulls out a strip of tape and slaps it across Erika's mouth.

Erika's toilet bag and folded towel rest neatly beside a washbasin. I dart forward, upturn the bag and grab two items that fall out with the rest, swinging them straight into action. As if in slow motion, Erika's head turns to me in wide-eyed terror. The woman reaches again into her open jacket and withdraws a syringe.

The can of hair lacquer, in my left hand, I spray directly into the eyes and nose of the woman. She has just time to strike the side of my head while I am still in reach. It's quite a smack. The nail scissors, I slam deep into the biceps of one of the men. He is impressively stoical, staring amazed at the injury yet making almost no sound as the arm falls limp. His other arm releases Erika and makes a fierce, well-aimed lunge for my scissors, now heading towards the underside of his jaw. If he manages to grasp my hand, I won't be able to match his strength. He could break my bones as easily as eggshells, take the scissors away from me and slice me to shreds with them, although no doubt he has a knife of his own. I lower my aim, directing the points into the patella tendon, across his knee. Again I quickly step out of reach.

This time there is a pained sound as he falls, jaw clenched, turning like a corkscrew. The woman spins towards me, the side of her hand striking my neck with the force of a thrown brick. The first man, unscathed and intent upon his work securing Erika's arms and legs, looks up at the woman and snaps: 'Nein – nicht mach!' – *No, don't.*

From that I realise they are under orders not to harm me. The spray can clatters to the floor as I fall against a washbasin and grasp at it for support. The impact causes some agonising little injury to my hip. The effort to remain upright wrenches my shoulder in its socket. I manage to keep hold of the scissors.

While she is within reach, I poke my fingertips into the woman's eyes. Blinded and in agony, she still has the presence of mind instantly to pass the syringe to the man.

I reach the woman's head and bring it down sharply onto the edge of a washbasin. Either it's the skull or the basin, but the impact creates a nauseating echo around the washroom. She falls onto the tile floor as heavily as a sack of potatoes.

I squat beside her tearing at the pouch, anxious to lay my hands on some sort of weapon. There is nothing but a pack of filled syringes like the one she handed her companion. I take them all, unsure what is inside. I'd guess it's for Erika. It could be morphine or ketamine.

Without finesse the man has plunged the needle straight through Erika's strange garment into the flesh beneath. The effect is dramatic. As her legs buckle, he takes the weight with ease, lifting her like a roll of carpet and carrying her fast towards the door.

I doubt that they want to kill her, at least not straight away. Presumably they want answers to questions. I feel that I must save her. We were warned against such emotion. *Cool, calm preparation* is the right approach. It might, in fact, be too late to help Erika.

The injured man is raising himself from the floor with unearthly determination. I take a hypodermic and insert it into his shoulder muscle as his colleague has done to Erika. With all his strength he unclips his holster to pull out a small black pistol. Like Erika, he fades fast, the hand falling from the gun, eyes closing like a patient succumbing to anaesthesia. I pull the gun from his sleeping hand, and help myself to the two spare magazines attached to the holster. The little marking, K100, by the trigger, shows it is a Makarov belonging to East Germany's security services.

Outside the toilet block, it's a surprise to find hessian matting unrolled on the ground. It leads to a car parked in the shadows. The man who carried Erika away is placing her into the car. There is no question of firing the pistol – not here, not now. I try to remain clear, and to understand the situation.

The car is a Wartburg, a large saloon, colourless in this light. The number plate, black on white, is impossible to make out. Erika is lost. My best bet is to get away from here.

Bruised, grazed, with a painful hip and throbbing shoulder I step into our tent. If the boys are asleep I don't want to disturb them yet. Harry hardly looks up from the pillow, 'Nice walk?'

'Harry, a fellow set upon me at the washrooms. Grabbed me.'

'What?' He's out of bed and holding me. 'What happened? Did he do anything? My God, your face!' He grimaces at what he can see. My fingertips caress a tender swelling above the cheekbone.

The tale I tell is that I fought the man and he ran off.

'Go to the police at once. We could dial, is it 12 in France?'

'No, no, I'm not bothering with the police. It would take hours, making a statement, being questioned. I don't want that.'

'The police do need to know,' he insists.

'It was so dark. I'd never identify the chap. Can we just leave? I don't feel safe here.'

He makes no move. Reaching out to hold both my hands, his eyes are aching with concern. 'Now? That would not be sensible, darling.'

I answer. 'Truly, I want to leave this place. We'll take Thierry to Lucienne's and find somewhere else to stay.'

'Everywhere will be fully booked for the holiday.'

In reply I start to pack. Harry, in pyjamas, watches bemused as I quickly put clothes and kitchen equipment into bags. I give him a box to carry to the car. With whispering excitement Thierry and Max awaken and rush about helping to pack. A ghastly thought strikes me. If we leave now, on the evening that Klaus reports his wife missing, the police will assume we know something about her disappearance.

That's why as we set off, I say to Harry that I need to leave them a note, writing in great haste.

Liebe Erika und Klaus, Etwas ist hier letzte Nacht passiert und wir haben beschlossen, den Campingplatz sofort zu verlassen... Dear Erika and Klaus, Something happened last night and we decided to leave the campsite immediately... A strange man assaulted me near the washrooms. It was very upsetting. Erika you should beware. Please would you tell the office in the morning and explain why we have left. Thank you. I'll call you soon. *Liebe Grüße* – Yours, Marjorie (and Harry).

Harry pulls up outside the Jüngers' mobile home. 'Look,' he exclaims, 'their car isn't there!' He's right: strangely, the lights are out and the car has gone. The mobile home has no letter box, so I leave my note on the step with a large stone to hold it in place. At the public telephone in the village square, I jump out to call Lucienne. I apologise profusely for disturbing her so late, and explain why we must bring Thierry back to them at once.

Harry has driven hours already today and is too slow. Despite the painful hip and shoulder, I insist on taking the wheel. Beyond Puligny, Chassagne, Santenay, vines come to an end, and the ground rises into woods and pasture beside a canal glinting in the moonlight. The boys are soon asleep. I pick up speed past dark, featureless landscapes and unknown towns. Harry too is deep in sleep as I find a way through a final tangle of Charolais byways. They wake as I slow down near the house, between meadows where herds of white cattle stand ghostly in a half-light, waiting for summer's early dawn. Lucienne dashes down to embrace me.

She is all kindness and sympathy, offers ointment for the bruises, plasters and ibuprofène. Extraordinarily generous, she cries out, 'Stay with us for a couple of days. It would be our pleasure.'

As soon as we are settled, I tell her, 'I'd really like to go out for a quiet drive on my own.'

She laughs slightly. '*Now*, mon amie, in the middle of the night? After you have just driven from Brisault? Leave it till morning.'

'No, I'd like to be alone for a while. I need to calm my mind.'

Lucienne touches my arm, concerned at my mood or even my sanity. Yet she says she understands, and makes another generous offer. Since our own car is small, and packed with our gear, why don't I take hers? She doesn't need it until tomorrow afternoon. She suggests 'Follow the Loire and the canal. Cross the river at Digoin. It's so peaceful. There are many pretty places to stop by the water.'

I set off in the opposite direction, east towards a faint brightness over the Saône valley. Her car is better than ours, faster and more comfortable, and the left-hand drive easier on my arm and hip.

Who in the world knows about Erika and me? My mind races over what I can remember, arranging and rearranging things said and done over the years. Constant questions about my 'friend in Vienna'. Three names on Erika's list: two GCHQ men who may be the same person, a woman at SIS. Not Bannerman after all: he left the service, and is dead.

Ringing in my thoughts are *galette manougienne* and *a glass of sparkling Valdon*, which Yvette mentioned once, years ago when we were young. 'If ever we retire from this life…,' she said, 'except that there is no retiring.' What is "manougienne"? On the main road, the N6, there will be all-night petrol stations. I'll fill the tank and buy maps. There are many things to sort out, and not much time if I'm to be back at Lucienne's by this afternoon. No one is following me, no one knows where I am, and even I don't know where I am going.

V

Jelka noticed at once the improvement in Marjorie's walking. She had learned to compensate for the drag in her left foot. Even the drooping face and mouth did not seem so marked. 'It's Carol's exercises. They're working!' Marjorie declared. 'She's teaching me to get back on my feet, and feed myself. We do speech exercises, too. She says I'll be able to go back home when I can walk.'

'Really? I didn't know that.'

'Yes, Carol says I could be back in my flat for my birthday.'

'What?' Her birthday was just two months away.

'Yes, at home again for my ninetieth birthday. You're all invited.'

'Well,' Jelka said doubtfully, 'that's marvellous. Fancy a drive?'

This was the routine, she knew, when Max came. He had told her all about it. Take Mum for a drive by the sea or in the Forest or to a garden centre. Stop somewhere, get her out of the car for a few minutes. She quickly becomes exhausted, so go straight back to the care home. Mum will then recount in detail, step by step, every single thing done on the outing, concluding, 'We've had a lovely day, haven't we?' Jelka did not mind doing that for Marjorie. Giving the old woman a little treat, humouring her, it was all fine.

But this time, Marjorie did not want to go to the sea, or the Forest, or a garden centre. She said, 'Take me home for a quick look.'

'To your flat?' Jelka had been told not to take her to the flat. It was considered unwise. Everyone agreed it might cause depression and homesickness.

'Take me to my very own kitchen and help me bake a Rosen's cake. Then we'll sit down and eat it.'

'What a great idea! It would be fun.'

The chill and emptiness of the apartment seemed perverse. Both of them were conscious that Marjorie might so easily still sit in that armchair, still sleep in that bed. Breathing deeply, clutching her angina spray, Marjorie stared around. The large framed picture of Harry looked out encouragingly from the mahogany cabinet.

In the kitchen they started work, Marjorie directing, giving tips. They chatted as Jelka beat eggs, folded in sugar, buttered the dish and mixed ingredients. She explained to Marjorie what Max was doing today, picture research for a news magazine.

'Yes, he's moving more into that. Less travelling. Ah, this is lovely, isn't it? Baking reminds me of home. Not London. I mean, home before you know what.'

You know what was the Yugoslav war, a subject never discussed. Now Marjorie said, 'No, dear, I don't know. What happened, Jelka?'

'Hasn't Max told you?'

'He said you are a Serb from Croatia. He saved you from, what?'

'He rescued me from the local militia. Our neighbours. We were trying to leave town, us and the other Serbs, to go to the Serb border. They ambushed us. They beat my Mum and Dad with pieces of wood right there in the main road, and shot them. Shot them dead.' She spoke calmly. Marjorie too remained quiet. The oven had reached the correct temperature. 'Wait a minute, Marjorie, while I put this in.'

Marjorie struggled from her chair to inspect the cake mixture. She rested a hand on Jelka's arm. 'You saw it?'

She nodded. 'Then they dragged me to a barn. Tore my dress. This guy just appeared. He had a bullet-proof vest with *Press*, you know,' she gestured, 'across his chest. Mad-looking guy. This guy was Max. He went to them without hesitation. They could easily have killed him, but they didn't. Max understands people, sees hidden things inside, their weakness. He has no fear of them.'

'That was always his problem. Fear is a good thing. It enables you to be careful.'

'He pulled me from their hands, shoved me in the back of his car and drove all the way to Athens. Like that. He took me to a colleague's flat, a very kind woman, and I stayed there with her. She cared for me, until I decided I wanted to be with him instead.'

Marjorie sat amazed. A turmoil beset her that prompted a hug for her daughter-in-law. 'So, I nearly lost him that day. The militiamen, I suppose, were Croat nationalists?'

'Ah, so you know about this.'

'And your parents must have been Serb communists?

'Yes, they had been partisans.'

'I see, yes. A terrible story, dear. I'm sorry.'

Together they peered through the oven's glass door. Marjorie said, 'Help me to my bedroom. While it's in the oven, I'll have a lie-down on my very own bed. I need to rest.' She meant, to think.

Jelka arrived back home that evening and confessed that she had taken Marjorie to her flat. She told Max about Carol's scheme for Marjorie to move back there. 'Maybe Carol doesn't realise we can't afford live-in nursing care,' he said.

Just a day later Max was given the opposite information when Nicola phoned with some news. He took the call as he walked from the tube station to his car. 'Hi,' she said, 'has Phil spoken to you?'

'What about?'

'He's taking Mum's flat back. He's evicting her. He told me himself: according to the tenancy agreement if the flat is unoccupied for twenty-eight days, he can repossess it. I told him what I thought about it.'

'He's doing that to *Mum*? Enforcing a contract against his own mother? I didn't even know they had any formal agreement. Mum's expecting to move back there. She told Jelka.'

'Really? Well, Phil says the truth is she's never going back. He's made bloody sure of that because he's going to rent it out to paying tenants.'

On an impulse, parked in a car park, Max called Philip and spent two tetchy hours urging him not to go ahead with the plan.

'Why?' retorted Philip. 'It's just normal. Old people who go into care don't get to keep their home.'

'But what keeps Mum going is the idea that one day she'll go back there.'

'Mum *knows* she won't ever go back. That first day, when we visited her at the Ruth Cohen, she said, "I live here now." Remember? She's the ultimate realist.'

'At least wait until after her birthday. She wants to celebrate it in her flat.'

* * *

To the right, night lingers, together with all that has occurred during its sleepless hours. To the left, across wide flat farmland, daybreak tints the sky a delicate eau-de-nil. Soon a streak of blazing red sprawls along the length of the horizon, as though just beyond morning's edge the whole world is in flames.

On the long bridge over the Saône, a sign announces the town of Trévoux. The road becomes a street of old stone houses, climbing to a ridge overlooking a huge bend in the river. The lofty towers of a little fortress peer down from green slopes above the rooftops. I park beneath handsome plane trees and consider the view.

I am in needle-in-a-haystack country. My task is slightly mad. No different, then, from the other puzzles and riddles we solved, the knots we unknotted over the years.

I expected everything to remain closed for the Fête Nationale, or at least to open late, but before six a bar is raising its blinds. I step inside, first customer of the new day. There's no time to waste. As soon as she places my café crème on the table I ask the patronne if something called galette manougienne can be bought in Trévoux.

She chortles at such naïveté. 'Wherever there are tourists in La Dombes, there you will find galettes, madame,' she replies wryly. 'Is it le vrai galette manougienne?' She shrugs. 'Oh, bien sûr, if you are in Manouges, it must be authentic galette manougienne. But elsewhere?' She shrugs. 'Voilà!'

'What do you mean by La Dombes?' For I have never heard of it.

'La Dombes, madame, is where you are now!' She smiles indulgently. 'In times gone by, Trévoux was its capital. You see that grand building there? That is the Parlement de Dombes. That's history, that is. That's from the Ancien Régime. Voilà.'

Having started chatting, the poor woman can't stop. She gives her view that galettes, no matter how many eggs are added, or how briochée the pâte, it's nothing compared to a proper pastry. In fact, I learn, she has never been keen on galettes, not even with sugar and cream, no, not even with red fruits. Voilà!

'The reason I ask,' I explain, 'is that a friend once told me about a pâtissier in a village near here who made the most delicious galettes au sucre, and marvellous gâteau de Savoie, and tarte au quemô, and gâteau de l'écureuil, and the best gâteau aux noix nappage chocolat ever. It was before the war. I wonder if that shop still exists?'

She has never heard of such a place. 'And, vin de Valdon is made in Trévoux, n'est-ce pas, madame?'

She suppresses a smirk at this idiotic ignorance. 'Vin de Valdon is made,' she points out, 'in Valdon. Evidemment.' Obviously. 'On the other side beyond La Dombes, madame, up in the hills. Voilà!'

'So is Valdon a village?'

'Non, non, non. It is a combe, a little vallon.'

It's twenty to seven. Between margins of overgrown greenery, the direct route to Manouges is arrow-straight and narrow across an undulating terrain of rough pasture and strangely shaped fields, copses, stud farms and glinting waters, occasionally curving to miss a marsh or a lake.

It climbs at last to the portals of a walled medieval cité. A few early risers are sauntering along the cobbled lanes of Manouges on this gorgeous jour de fête. The town is picturesque to a fault, a model of historic charm where once stench and squalor ruled. It brings to mind something fossilised, embedded in its ancient stone. Today everything is decorated with ribbons of tricolores.

The centuries-old inn in the main square is full of atmosphere and style, with quarry tile floors and wooden beams, stone fireplaces and stone walls hung with tapestries. There I sit, hopefully to discover for myself the pleasures of the local galette.

I quiz the waiter. Wasn't there once a pâtissier in La Dombes famed for his galettes, and his walnut cake with chocolate, and his gâteau de l'écureuil and tarte au quemô? 'Ask,' he advises, 'someone who knows everything,' a vieille fille he calls her, an old maid; that is, a spinster, or at any rate a woman, by the name of Claire, a true Dombiste, who will be sitting in the square with her cronies.

The galette is a succulently rich, tender pastry with a hint of something fruity and alcoholic and a lemony, sugary, butter topping. It arrives with an earthenware jar full of tangy, tasty cream served with a ladle. It is beyond delicious. With a smile I decline the accompanying glass of vin de Valdon. 'It's too early in the morning,' I explain, 'but I'd like to buy a couple of bottles for later.'

Claire and her friends, reserved, polite, suspicious, want to know whether I am a foreign tourist, or a French one. They sit in the shade of a tree, two on a bench, the others facing on straight-backed chairs. All are indeed very elderly, heavy-jowled, round-shouldered, with lips tightly creased in seeming permanent disapproval. All wear dark dresses with thin cardigans. They look at me and wait for my answer. It is quiet but for the squeal of swallows swooping above the square.

I tell them truthfully that I am a touriste anglaise, adding untruthfully that my sister came to La Dombes in connection with the war. I say my sister wonders if the pâtisserie she found in a village nearby is still open. Unfortunately, she cannot recall where it was. I tell them the cakes for which it was renowned.

Claire studies my face closely, calculating and perceptive. She makes no comment on my bruises. 'Your French is very good,' she remarks quietly, 'for an Englishwoman. You could pass for French. Yes, you could really pass for French, if you had to. Perhaps your sister is the same.' The others agree. They scrutinise me as if an unfamiliar bird has landed in front of them.

Claire has heard of a master pâtissier and his family brutally killed in the war. There were many such killings, she says, betrayals, reprisals. France is full of such things. Families with secrets. Her companions remain silent, casting a wary eye in her direction.

She mutters that it is more complicated than I shall ever know, with a terse, strange, oblique, 'Eh oui. Les anglais.' This, I suppose, may refer to the Resistance, or to the Normandy Landings, or to the Hundred Years War for all I know, or to something else. 'The young,' she reflects, 'they will never realise.'

'The whole family killed?' I ask.

Claire urges me to go to the hamlet of Notre-Dame-des-Etangs. 'Ask for Suzanne's house. She will be there. She's housebound, the poor one, and welcomes visitors. She sees very few. She is a little…' There is a slight hand movement beside the head, to indicate one whose mind is not all it should be. 'But she can answer your questions.' Her friends shuffle uneasily, their lips as tight as ever.

It is half past ten. The narrow road pushes through a world nearly flat, more and more empty, sometimes shaded by lines of tall poplars, sometimes shimmering and watery, always under a big sky. Low, blue hills lie to the east, where I suppose vines climb terraced slopes.

Through the open windows of the car a warm breeze blows, with a choir of whistling, trilling, chirruping, quacking, squawking from ponds and water channels and hedges. Occasional simple dwellings appear to the side, built of nothing more than gravel bound with mud.

My concern has been that Claire will telephone ahead to warn Suzanne of my arrival. Now I'm here, it seems unlikely that Suzanne even has a phone. Yet somehow she does appear to expect me.

She too is a very old woman, but of another kind. Wiry as a reed, slender as the rushes whispering behind her house, Suzanne uses two sticks to come to the door but is otherwise fit and energetic. After a few moments, it's clear Suzanne has nothing wrong with her mind at all. She is slovenly, in a shabby housecoat with food stains on the bust, but quick-witted and sharp-eyed.

I tell Suzanne what 'my sister' would like to know. Without asking why, she replies, 'Pâtissier Delacroix' and invites me inside.

I'm not sure I ever knew for certain that Yvette's maiden name was Delacroix. We were under orders to use first names only in Section B. The next time I met her she had become Mrs Oakeshott.

The room is dark and cool, and quite astonishingly simple, like a display in a folk museum. The decorated floor tiles are unglazed, and the walls blackened by years of candles, cooking and the hearth. A tiny white ceramic sink in the room has no tap. I would not know where to buy such a small sink.

Suzanne is troubled by my injuries. I say I was attacked by a man, but she is frankly sceptical. She offers a glass of water from an earthenware jug. It is cold and refreshing. As I sip, she leaves me, returning with a glass jar of a pale waxy paste. 'Balsamum,' she says oddly, and insists that I apply it to my grazes and sore places. Soon she is rubbing the ointment onto me with her own fingertips. It is astonishingly soothing. I say the worst pain is in my hip, and loosen my trousers so she can spread the balm over it. After this peculiar intimacy, we sit next to one another on upright chairs by a French window opened wide. Dozens of swallows scoot past at speed.

Suzanne leans slightly towards me and mutters, 'The pâtissier and his wife were résistants, but Communist, loyal to Russia, not France. I must say though, his cakes, they were really delicious.'

'What happened?'

'The story goes that they were tied up and made to watch as their daughter Yvette was raped and tortured to death by a group of local lads – collaborateurs, Milice. She suffered terribly. Then Madame Delacroix endured the same: raped, tortured, mutilated, murdered, while her husband had to watch. Enfin, Monsieur Delacroix was himself tortured and shot. They thought he was Maquis. Deep down, the poor man was nothing but a kindly maître-pâtissier. Everyone knew the lads, and we know them to this day. They are vieux gars now, evidemment, old-timers, those that are still alive.'

Yvette dead? I spend a while mulling over what has just been said, struggling to understand. I'm wondering where Suzanne's account came from. Don't they know, round here, that Yvette is still alive? At last I ask, 'How did anyone find out what happened?'

'The older girl, Monique, it was she who related the story. I don't know where she was hiding. Under the floorboards, I believe. She managed to escape somehow. After the war, she never returned to live among such neighbours, until this year. Now she is back. She is aimable, she is friendly. They say she married an English milord, and did not have children. Not many know the history any more.

'And the shop, does it still exist?'

Suzanne shrugs. 'The building, yes. Monique lives there now, above the shop. But it is not a shop any more.'

She invites me for lunch and asks that I help her cook. It would be impossible to refuse after the help she has given me. At a kitchen table of bare wood we prepare a fish. The dish is complicated and takes precious time, and seems too elaborate for a hot summer's day. As we work, Suzanne talks, gradually putting together a sinister jigsaw of wartime rivalries and lingering hatreds. We cook on an little stove fired by bottled gas.

She lays two places at the table. 'Stuffed carp à l'ancienne,' she explains matter-of-factly. It's meltingly delicious, in a lovely sauce, and served with creamy, tender pommes dauphinoise. I drink no wine, but Suzanne fills her glass three times.

By the time our chat is over, I am ready to continue my search, probably to its completion. My watch shows twenty to three. I ought to have returned Lucienne's car. I must call her when I see a phone.

The village forms little more than a crossroads. A few cottages stand along the two streets. Most have shutters closed, as if everyone has gone away for the day or forever. There's one modern block, a maison de retraite, retirement home, with a phone box outside.

My plan is to admit to Lucienne that I've come all the way to La Dombes, and apologise for staying away later than agreed. Her number rings and rings without an answer.

Yvette's place is shockingly run-down. Patches of rendering have fallen from the walls, showing layers of round stones and dried mud beneath. One ground floor window is covered with wooden shutters, the other has glass opaque with grime. A pair of garage-size double doors are rotting at the base, with holes large enough for a rat or a cat to pass through. Upstairs is a single shuttered window. Paint long ago flaked off the shutters and doors, right down to the bare wood.

Why would Yvette spend any time here? *Pâtisserie Delacroix*, faded almost to nothing, can still be made out on the wall. My knock echoes emptily inside. I peer through the dirty window glass, but see only abandoned counters and shelving and unused spaces. Not very ladylike, I press my face to the slender gap between the double doors. It is too dark inside to see anything.

A path leads round to the back of the building, where a rusty metal gate creaks open into a nicely tended vegetable plot. The back of the building is quite different. It's tidy. There's a newer front door, clean windows with modern shutters clipped open. There's a garden shed and, attached to the back wall of the house, what may once have been an outdoor privy.

I understand now: her parents' bakery faced the street, while the family home was at the rear. I ring the bell. My handbag is unclipped, the Makarov in easy reach. There is no answer.

I try the door. It's locked. The windows, too. I turn to the shed. There are tools, hefty old things in there, big wrenches, hammers, cold chisels, a sturdy adze and a long-handled French shovel. On hooks around the wall, lengths of steel wire hang, and rope and rubber hosepipe, and all the jumbled kit for which a practical man expects one day to find a use. Boxes ranged on shelves contain rusty nails and screws, bolts and unrecognisable scraps of metalwork.

The little outhouse that I took to be a privy is not a privy after all. It's a wood store. There's a stack of mouldering cut logs, together with an axe and a saw, rusting and abandoned. I leave the door ajar for a little light. Enormous spiders and dozens of large wriggling millipedes as long as my hand scurry around wildly as I poke about. The wood store is attached to the unrendered back wall of the house. Where I touch the surface, it crumbles and breaks easily, leaving a tawny dust on my fingers.

I take a cold chisel and a large hammer and try them on the wall. The narrow blade digs deep into the clay around a loose stone. It falls to the ground almost at once. Half a dozen hard strikes release a dusty cascade of crumbling masonry. Stones can be knocked out, one after another, each with a single blow. I'll have to get cleaned up afterwards. The far side gives way easily, making a hole into the house. Quickly I see it's not the house after all. It's the old bakery.

In a few more minutes I squeeze through. The bakery is connected to the house by a locked door. Steps lead to a room above the bakery, a kind of grenier, an attic of junk scattered on bare floorboards. Here the outside world is concealed not only by bolted shutters on the window, but also by wartime blackout blinds still in place after all these years. The room is cool, and the daylight subdued, but not dark, for from a skylight a sunbeam streams through air alive with floating dust motes. In one corner of the room, an ancient wireless receiver and transmitter have been smashed and tossed aside.

In the other corner, a modern radio transmitter and receiver stand on a desk, together with a telephone and tidily arranged papers and notebooks. I step forward for a good look. Clearly Yvette has complete confidence that her hiding place would never be discovered. She has even left, on the desk, a notepad in her own familiar handwriting which appears to be a schedule of wireless frequencies and call signs, and a tiny Russian one-time pad made of cellophane.

In the desk drawer is a sealed polythene bag of one-time pads, new and unused, which one can see at a glance are Russian. In the drawer below is a microscope and a pile of correspondence in Cyrillic, and an ordinary school exercise book. I flick through the pages. It details times and dates, names, phone calls, addresses and all the movements and contacts, right up to yesterday night, of a single target individual. The individual is *Mrs Marjorie Rosen née Behrens*.

I pull aside the blackout blinds and unlatch the window. With arms stretched, I unbolt the wooden shutters and push them wide open. Swallows, swifts or martins dart to and fro, keening in the blue sky. All the warmth and light of summer pours into Yvette's little den.

I really must get cleaned up and, too, urgently need the toilet. There's no alternative but to break through the door from the grenier into the house. It swings into an upstairs landing. I look into each room in turn: Yvette's bedroom, an unused guest room, cupboards, a bathroom. I wash my hands and face, give my headscarf a good shake, brush and tidy my hair, re-do my lipstick, dust off my clothes and shoes, all the while listening for her arrival, with the pistol ready on the washstand.

It's gone five o'clock. I have to phone Lucienne, but can't use Yvette's phone, unless I want to risk alerting whoever is tuned in to her line. When at last I do hear a sound downstairs, I return to the grenier and take up my position.

There's a steady tread up the stairs. I listen attentively as she reaches the landing. She has gone straight into the bedroom. I hear a few quiet movements in there. No doubt she is looking at herself in the mirror, I imagine she arranges her hair, checks where grey is showing. I hear something placed on the dressing table, the slide of a drawer, a wardrobe door. Maybe she is thinking of changing her clothes. I have to catch her when she is most vulnerable.

I step out of the grenier onto the landing, hair tied back, handbag across my chest, the cocked Makarov in my hand. It takes not two seconds to reach Yvette's bedroom door. She is standing in the middle of the room, ready and waiting for me, pointing a good old-fashioned double-barrelled shotgun straight at my chest.

Without a pause I continue fast into the room, moving swiftly to one side and towards her, grab the barrel with one hand and twist it from her grasp with no effort. The other hand strikes her face, not very hard. She is brave, but too slow, too weak, and taken aback by my response. I knock out the shotgun cartridges and kick them aside.

Yvette instantly and charmingly recovers her cool. Of all her traits – elegance, wit, cleverness– it's Yvette's composure that I admire most. Anyone else would be terrified.

'Ah, it's you, chérie!' she smiles as if amused by the situation. 'Useless to threaten you with a gun. You have been trained to deal with that. Or so it says in your file.'

'Hello, Yvette – or Monique.' At this she does look unnerved. 'Good to see you again.' In truth, I am delighted by the sight of her. I've always liked Yvette. Can it be called friendship when one party is merely dissembling, intent on betraying the other? Maybe it can.

'What's happened, have you been in an accident?'

'Actually, it was your people did this, yesterday.'

'Oh, I told them not to hurt you,' she says. 'That looks sore! I knew someone had been here. Obviously I noticed the shutters, then I saw the bathroom door had moved.'

'Oh yes, I'm sorry, I did use the bathroom.'

'I didn't think it would be you, though. How on earth did you find this place? Would you mind awfully, Marjorie, putting that gun down? You don't want to shoot me.'

'I hope it won't come to that, Yvette!' It's true, I don't want to shoot her. I keep it trained upon her nonetheless.

'We are not going to fight, like men, are we? We are not men. We are women. Civilised, intelligent women. We won't hurt each other, or damage one another's bodies as men would, or anything foolish of that sort. We are going to talk sensibly, Marjorie, just talk, like reasonable human beings. Talk things over and understand one another. Come to an understanding. That's right, isn't it?'

I lower the pistol. 'Yes, let's talk.'

The thing I most want to talk about is Erika – what has happened to her. If I were to say so, Yvette would merely protest that she knows nothing about it. My hand leaves the gun at the top of my bag. In its place, it pulls out Yvette's exercise book, the one filled with the movements and meetings of Marjorie Rosen née Behrens.

'Let's talk,' I propose, 'about something I found in your desk.'

Yvette and I sit at her kitchen table and she tells me what everyone has heard before. The brotherhood of man. Class, patriarchy, exploitation. Nations are a confidence trick played on the workers. The better world Socialism will construct. The familiar credo is rehearsed. I peek at my watch.

There is no point in replying, except to ask, 'What I don't quite see is why you worked on Venona exposing Russian agents.'

'No, dear Marjorie! To *prevent* our people being exposed. To keep Moscow informed, protect our undeciphered agents and block its progress. Why were Moscow always one step ahead? Why was Venona so ineffective? There were several of us on the team, and in the Soviet Section at Arlington Hall.'

'So why recruit me?'

Yvette shakes her head as if this too is obvious. 'To keep close to you, Marjorie, and share confidences. If I had not recruited you, you might have gone to J-Section, outside my control. Most important of all, I had to learn about your elusive contact in Vienna.'

'What exactly have your chaps done with her?'

There is still every possibility that Yvette will say she knows nothing about it. But she replies, 'How did you find out it was me?'

'You never asked about any of my other friends.'

'Hm, yes,' Yvette nods, 'that *was* an oversight. It's taken me twenty-five years to track her down.'

'I've always wondered if it came from Sinclair Bannerman.'

'He didn't know what he'd said. We were lovers, you know. When Section B was wound up, one evening Sinclair and I chatted about what we would all do with ourselves now the war was over. I said I would stay with the service. He mentioned he thought you would stay with the service too because you had a source in Vienna. I passed that on, and was asked to find out more.'

'You befriended me only to find out the identity of my contact in Vienna?'

'Yes, that was my main task after the war. But I did consider you a real friend. You never relax, never gossip, are constantly alert, always cautious. It's impossible to draw you out. I love you for that,' she laughs. 'After all, it wasn't *you* we wanted. It wasn't even your contact in Vienna. The person we wanted was her source.'

'But you retired from the service. Had you completed your task?'

'Not quite. We still had to decide when, where and how to pick up your contact. It was better if I wasn't on the scene any more.'

'Why move back here, though? You always came across as rather a sophisticated, urban creature. Why not Paris?'

'Sophisticated creature! No,' she laughs again, shakes her head, 'That's cover. I feel closer here to my parents and sister. You don't know what was done to them by the fascists, right here in this room.'

'Yes, I do know.' I reach out a hand to hers. I feel sorry for her.

'I remain alive to avenge them, and carry on my parents' work. Your Viennese contact and her husband were Nazis. Why should we care about them? Anyway, they're dead by now. We'll read it in *Le Progrès* tomorrow; Austrian tourists in a tragic autoroute accident. She will certainly have told the Stasi officers everything about her source. They're good at getting what they want. And soon the men who murdered my family will also have a surprise. That's why you will leave me in peace, and move on. We can even remain friends. '

For one instant it's as though we really do understand each other. 'Yes, all right. And by the way, Yvette, while I'm here – if we are friends – you once promised to show me your mother's recipe book.'

'Really, did I?' From a selection of cookery books on an old dresser, she reaches a black ring-binder and rests it on the table. It's smaller than I expected. Together we leaf through it, side by side, her head close enough for our hair to touch. 'What do we do now?' she asks. 'Call it quits?'

'Maybe. I'm not sure.'

As she turns the pages, my hand brings a disposable syringe from my bag. Without hesitation I plunge the needle through her linen skirt into the back of her thigh and press the syringe. She exclaims, gazes down with rising panic, stares horrified, tries to move away.

'No, Marjorie – they'll come after you!' Already she is too weak to pull her leg away. 'Think, darling, please think. They always have to settle the score, you know,' she warns, 'always. They will find you. You know that.' The plunger has almost reached the end of the tube. 'Wherever you are, dear, however long it takes, that's –.' Her eyelids drop and knees buckle. The last of the liquid has drained away and is circulating inside Yvette's body.

A surreal phone call from the village kiosk, a codename not said aloud for thirty years, and I am given my instructions. I race Lucienne's car towards Lyon. La Dombes lies on the marshy plateau between the Rhône and Saône, narrowing as the rivers converge. Long, straight country roads head towards their confluence in the centre of the city. Cutting across from the Saône to the Rhône, I take a main road on the right bank, mercifully empty of traffic for the national holiday. Beside Pont Wilson, a gateway swings open for me. From the boot of Lucienne's car two men take out the unconscious body. I hand them the key of her front door, together with two bags filled with every scrap of paper from her desk, evidence beyond doubt that Yvette is a double agent.

Dinner is long past when I draw up outside the house. They're on the terrace, at a long wooden table set out in the balmy evening air, under the light of electric bulbs strung onto a tree. All of them rise to meet me, Harry afraid, Lucienne angry, Max frowning.

Lucienne says, 'Bonsoir, Madame. Where *have* you been all day – and all night? I needed my car. Did something happen?'

I hand her a gift bag from the inn at Manouges. Inside are two bottles of Valdon wine and a galette manougienne prettily packaged in a box. 'I went to La Dombes,' I explain, 'I really don't know why. I tried calling you but there was no answer. And, you see, I met this very old woman who told me what happened to her family in the war. It was a terrible, tragic story. I helped her make lunch and sat with her. She had no phone. It would have been impossible to leave before she had finished. Then I got lost, and went an hour in the wrong direction. And I still couldn't find a phone. I'm so sorry.'

It's clear that these excuses don't cut the mustard. My unexplained absence has been too long and caused too much inconvenience. Dinner was put aside for me hours ago. I eat it too hungrily while the others watch. The gift of wine and galette is left indoors, untouched.

Even Harry hardly knows what to say to me. We retire to the bedroom where he slept alone last night. As we undress he is horrified by the bruises. I assure him I feel fine.

'You do know we'll have to leave first thing in the morning? We can't possibly stay here now. I don't think anyone believes your tale of the old woman who lives in a shoe, or whatever it was,' he says.

'Oh! The elderly woman who had no phone? That happens to be true. She was telling me her wartime memories. Dreadful things were done around there. Not the kind of thing I could walk out on.'

'Ah, so it *was* true. Where were you? Or shouldn't I ask?'

'No, don't ask.'

Harry knows the ropes; we agreed never to probe. He doesn't look well. It's his blood pressure, his heart, his digestion.

I take his hand. 'It's over.'

'Good.' He puts his arms around me, kisses me and holds me. The poor man really shouldn't have to take any more strain.

The Venona work has ended, and now so too has Erika. There will be a final debriefing about Yvette when we get back. That's it.

'There's nothing more,' I tell him. 'It's finished.'

On this fine spring day Marjorie would leave the care home and return to her own dear flat. There could not be a better ninetieth birthday present. Carol's efforts had been a success. Pushing a rollator, Marjorie could now travel on her own two feet all the way from her bedroom to the Ruth Cohen conservatory, even to the dining room.

'My brain's coming apart at the seams;' she chuckled, 'my body is breaking up like a ship in a storm. But I can walk again!'

Marjorie's carers Róża and Lorraine kissed her cheek and gave her a badge to wear, *90 Today*. With laughter and hugs, Philip, Max and Nicola met her in the day room, her three darling children.

Mum would tire easily, they realised; she would need a rest before and after the party. The party should last no more than an hour or so, and must be at lunchtime, because later the Ruth Cohen would also lay on their usual birthday tea in her honour. The food must be no trouble to eat and easy to digest. She – or rather, they, her children – had invited just a handful of her friends. In any case, most of the people Marjorie called friends were lost to this world in one way or another. No one from Saltington or London was close any more; her swimming partner Lara was in a home with advanced Alzheimer's, her dear friend Peggy died long ago, her yachting companion Audrey had recently died. They booked a carer to come along and look after the party girl.

In tremendous good humour, giggling with pleasure, Marjorie said a grateful goodbye to Róża and Raine. She was driven to her flat in time for the first lie-down. Believing she was home again for good, she eased her way joyfully from room to room in wonder and delight. There were flowers everywhere. Faded eyesight caused her to stand in contemplation of quite ordinary items, a shelf of videos, her hardly-used computer, books, television; oh, the neglected balcony garden, she must deal with that! She would set to work on it tomorrow. She gazed at her bed; and for a long time at the framed photograph of Harry on the corner cabinet, coming slowly into focus.

In the kitchen Jelka busily set out the buffet. It was, after all, only for a dozen people. A chocolate walnut cake (made by Jelka to Marjorie's recipe) stood at the centre of the table, adorned with a single candle in the shape of the number '90'.

'Can I do anything?' offered Marjorie keenly. 'No, no, no!' cried Jelka. 'This is your treat. Though you could give me the cream from the fridge while you're standing there.'

Fridge, cream. Marjorie felt struck by an inner, mental blindness. Fridge, fridge… she tried to remember what was meant. She could not place the word, the idea or the object. The room was full of light but she could not recognise a single thing. She looked around bewildered, unable to find the refrigerator.

Noticing her confusion, Jelka said kindly, 'On second thoughts, have a rest before your guests arrive,' Marjorie remained in the kitchen. 'Guests? Do I have guests?' Nicola guided her to her chair in the living room, where in an instant she had fallen into a light sleep. She was awoken by the doorbell. Max was put on duty to answer the door and bring new arrivals to her armchair.

The gathering made to Marjorie's faded eye a whirlwind of sound and movement. For all she knew, she might be sitting in the midst of Piccadilly Circus. Joe and Eva and her friends from the synagogue were there. Carol, too, chatting to today's carer. It made a jolly scene as with plates and glasses they found places around the living room, chatting and reminiscing. Marjorie herself ate and drank almost nothing. Nicola and Jelka helped open her cards, read the messages aloud, unwrapped gifts and explained to her what they were.

Standing beside Max as he took pictures, Phil muttered, 'You can see she's never coming back here. Look at the state of her. As soon as this little do is finished I'll move her stuff out.'

'Really, Phil? I'm sorry to hear that.' Max went into the kitchen to help. There Nicola and Jelka were arranging tea cups on a tray. He told them what Philip had said. Philip too stepped into the kitchen to lend a hand. Nicola hissed, 'Phil, is it true? You're going through with it, evicting Mum from her home?' She approached him angrily.

'Nic!' Max pushed the door shut. 'Keep your voice down.'

'I've let Mum have this place rent-free all these years, I've looked after her and been as nice as pie to her the whole time.'

'You absolute fucking bastard. You're thinking how much money you can make out of Mum's home.' She looked on the brink of slapping him.

'Don't argue here,' said Max. 'Not today.'

'Actually, Nic,' Philip jabbed a finger at his sister, 'anyone who lets Mum think she can come back here is the bastard, setting her up for disappointment. You should've helped her to be *happy* at Ruth Cohen, which is the right place for her.'

Max urged, 'Look Phil, why not give Mum just a few more months. It means such a lot to her.'

'She *will* get three months more under the rental agreement – that's the notice I have to give.'

'Tea is ready,' said Jelka. 'Take the cake in first.'

Nicola led them into the living room carrying the handsome cake, its candle flickering, her brothers all smiles. Surrounded by warm cheers and a chorus of *Happy Birthday*, with a little help Marjorie blew out the candle. Joe led 'For she's a jolly good fellow' and 'Hip hip hooray!' Jelka cut the cake into slices handed around the room by Philip and Max as Nicola poured tea.

Marjorie looked around slightly uncomprehending, fingering the incongruous *90 Today* badge pinned to her cardigan. Thin distorted lips, slightly parted, barely smiled, and there was occasionally something of fear. The fragile dawn-blue of her eyes seemed to have become – a trick of the light, perhaps – as bright as stained glass.

She was already drifting into catnaps as her guests left with kisses and kind congratulations. After a short sleep in her bed, Marjorie was helped into Philip's car and driven back to the Ruth Cohen care home. She protested mildly, hurt and surprised as she was led to the car. 'I was hoping to move back home today. Back into my flat. Because I can walk now. I thought…'

Hearing no reply, she asked, 'When am I moving back, then?' Philip's answer was, 'The Ruth Cohen have laid on a birthday tea for you! You don't want to miss that!'

She struggled to understand, knowing that there was a lot she didn't get these days, wondering if she would be brought back to the flat later. Max and Nicola remained silent.

She was placed among the old folk assembled in the Ruth Cohen day room. A large cream cake was smilingly brought in, inscribed with pink sugar icing, *Happy Birthday Marjorie 90.* Her children again sang 'Happy Birthday dear Mummy', joined by people she didn't know or didn't remember knowing. She did not want any more tea or cake. She felt entirely at the mercy of others. Max took photos. Róża and Lorraine said 'Have you had a lovely day, then?' and told her it was bedtime. 'Am I going home?' she asked them. They laughed sweetly at her error.

* * *

The children have been asked many time not to phone me at the shop. 'Darling?' I want Max to understand that I'm busy.

'Mum, are you free to talk right now?' It takes me a couple of seconds to realise he is in deadly earnest. 'Dad mustn't hear about this.' I step into my little office and close the door.

When he's finished I can think only of the damage it's going to do Harry. This is bad news indeed, and at a very, very bad time.

'You there, Mum?'

'Of *course* Daddy will have to know, Max. Not yet, he's just had an operation. He mustn't have any anxiety at all. No stress.'

'God! The operation! I forgot. Is it his heart again?'

Max has already been told about this. 'No, his oesophagus and stomach. They're removing some tissue. But the operation is a strain on the heart, which can cause complications.'

I hurry across the High Street to the car park. Passers-by nod in greeting or say hello. Some have heard that my husband is terribly ill. Some know it is the "C" word. Between ourselves we speak only of malignancy, of tumour. The "C" word, we prefer to avoid. People are kind and friendly in Saltington. They call me "Mrs Rosens" (in the plural or the possessive I cannot tell) or, "the cake shop lady". Everyone in town knows Rosen's Continental Pâtisserie, the coffee house opposite Boots' Lending Library. In season it attracts the better class of tourists, and all year there's a loyal following among the sailing crowd, the riding set, the local gentry and the comfortably-off retirees, as well as the town's foreign residents. I haven't gone for English quaintness but for a Mittel-European style. Rosen's is renowned for unusual, wonderfully delicious cakes.

Gâteaux rest on the counter under glass covers. I'm using their English names, or have given them one. Gâteau de Savoie sounds grand as Savoy Cake. Then there's Squirrel Cake, Cream Cheese Tart and best of all, Walnut Cake with Shining Chocolate. Satisfied customers sometimes ask if they could have the recipe. I tell them it's an old family secret. You can buy a whole cake, or I'll bring you a slice with a jug of cream, but the recipe you may not have.

In the meantime, the recipe book stays under lock and key in our bedroom, unless I need to check a recipe. Because on closer study there was much in Yvette's (or Monique's) recipe book that was difficult to understand. Some words are underlined, some contain highlighted letters. I can make no sense of them. There are curious abbreviations, in Yvette's own hand, that are not to do with ingredients, nor with cooking. I'll have to sit down with this book one day and figure it out.

A few of our family favourites, too, are on Rosen's bill of fare, the kugel Harry loves, his lokshen pudding, his babka and kokosh. A few croissants and viennoiseries I buy in, delivered every morning. The only savoury dish is soup. Galette manougienne has become Rosen's Galette, light, rich and tender, soft and buttery with the faintest hint of bilberry liqueur. I don't have Valdon, but can do a similar sparkling vin doux rosé, at a price. Not many ask for that. What they want in Saltington is a nice pot of tea or a jug of good coffee. Every night I bake cakes. Every day I join the girls serving in the shop.

Everything that preys on Harry's mind also gnaws at his guts, sets fire to his stomach, stokes his heartburn. He's always been like that. As he sleeps through the long, quiet hours of these frightening days, I sit downstairs in case he needs me. It seems a good moment finally to start work on Yvette's recipe book. At the bottom of some pages are enigmatic strings of letters. In the margin of a few pages, a meaningless doodle that I now see represents a Cyrillic character.

Transposing highlighted letters from the recipes, slowly unravelled strings turn into words and phrases, then into pairs of questions and answers, passwords, names. Yvette's own code name, I discover, was Hirondelle. Swallow. In a remembered sky, I see again the swallows over her childhood home, dozens of them zig-zagging fast, and hear their whistling note in the warm afternoon air.

I already had an inkling of it at the debriefing. I was asked if I had come across a codebook among Yvette's papers. SIS had studied the contents of the two carrier bags and been over her house and garden with forensic thoroughness but found none. She must have had one. They wonder where it is and what it reveals. It's possible that others also want possession of the book. And if I were Yvette's controller I would certainly want to stop anyone getting their hands on it.

On the third day Harry feels strong enough to come downstairs for an hour and tap out tunes on the piano. On the fourth day, he stays longer and picks up his clarinet. He still can't eat properly. I give him soup, juice, cottage cheese. He works through chess problems, helps me with the crossword, returns wearily to bed.

He'll be furious when he finds he has been kept in the dark about Max. When I tackle the subject, he is downstairs, propped in an armchair. It pains me to bear the tidings that will spoil everything.

'Harry?'

He looks up, quizzical, almost smiling. 'What?'

'I've got some bad news.'

The half-smile lingers as he wonders whether I am joking. 'Why, what's happened? Can things be even worse?'

'It's Max.'

He grasps at once that it's serious. The smile fades away completely. There is quite a different expression, that familiar hard face, the lips tight, eye steely. 'Police?' It's not a question, hardly even a guess. For some reason he has leapt to the right conclusion. He is reliving the agonies he went through over Philip.

''Fraid so. He's done something exceptionally stupid.'

Harry says he expected it, sooner or later.

I tell him what Max has told me. He and a crowd of friends came home late from some sort of discotheque. Most of them were fellow art students at the Slade. Everybody was high on drink and drugs. 'The usual scenario. In the morning Max found this figure in his kitchen, someone he didn't know, helping himself to food, making a mess. Max asked him what he was up to. When the fellow took no notice, there was some sort of row. Max whacked him round the head. You know what a temper he has. The chap fell unconscious to the floor and Max called an ambulance.'

Apparently unmoved by the tale, Harry asks, 'Any witnesses?'

I nod unhappily. 'A neighbour saw everything from her balcony. She even saw the other man fall to the floor.'

'Damn her. And it was she who called the police?'

'Yes. There might be other witnesses. The others in the house, maybe people in the street.'

I expect anger, blame, raised voices. Instead Harry's thoughts immediately turn to damage limitation. 'Has he got a solicitor?' For such an emotional, mercurial man, Harry remains strangely phlegmatic now. He is too worn out for anything more.

'Yes, Max called our chap Stevens. He went to the police station.'

'Good man.'

'He told Max to give what's called a no-comment interview.'

'What's he charged with?'

'Well, first of all, GBH – grievous bodily harm.'

Harry spends a long moment taking this in. He is considering the implications. 'What a start in life.' He shakes his head in weary misery. 'Maybe we can get the charge reduced?'

I take a deep breath and tell him the worst. 'I'm sorry, Harry, there's more. Possession of cocaine, LSD and cannabis. Stevens says Max must expect to go to prison. Could be for a couple of years.'

Harry's face becomes a horrified grimace, and he begins to rap his knuckles in strange, shocking punishment against his own forehead. He grapples with his despair, determined to stay afloat, finally mastering himself. Then, with odd calm, 'Well, we must do whatever has to be done. In custody, is he?'

'No. On bail. This happened last Sunday. He was released on bail on Monday and went to college as normal. It's Friday now, dear.'

'It's *Friday* is it? This happened on Sunday,' he repeats, puzzled. 'So, that means – Marjorie, when did *you* find out?'

'Max phoned me on Monday.' – 'Why didn't you let me know?'

'You were in the operating theatre.' – 'On Tuesday, then?'

'The doctors said it was very important that you have no strain. Any strain impedes recovery.'

'You dealt with this by yourself! It's been on your mind all week!'

'Yes, well. Max has had it on his mind, too. You know what he's *most* worried about? What *you* will think of him.'

'*Think* of him? I don't have any opinion about him.'

'Yes, you do. You think he is a fool.'

'All three of them are fools. They've brought us nothing but sorrow. We'll still do what we can for him.' Harry struggles to sit up, breaking into a sweat. 'I'll drive to London tomorrow to see Stevens.'

'Harry! Don't be ridiculous. You're not to drive for six weeks, the doctor said! It could be dangerous.'

In the end, he browbeats me into agreeing. I promise to do the driving. 'A criminal record! For violence! How shameful. Where does he get it?' He thrusts a hand across his eyes. 'This is even worse than Philip.'

When we see Max to discuss things over lunch, it gives the lie to what I've said about him being worried, or caring what Harry thinks of him. He tucks in to his food. 'Not hungry, Dad?'

'Daddy had a stomach operation on Monday,' I remind him. 'He can't eat.'

'Oh yah, right. Was it awful?'

'Max,' Harry replies, 'When making your statement, describe what happened more like this –'

'I've already told Mum what happened.'

'No, hear me out. It's very, very close to what you told Mum.'

As Max eats, Harry speaks. 'The man tricked his way into the house. Maybe with a view to obtaining drink and drugs, maybe stealing something. He said he was a friend of a friend, but you didn't believe him. He became violently abusive and threatened you with a kitchen knife. You were really scared and struck out as hard as you could to protect yourself.'

'That's crazy, Dad. That's not what happened at all. Nothing like.'

'No, it's a question of creating doubt.' Harry ought to bear in mind that Max can't abide being told what to do or say. He carries on, 'The witness didn't see the knife, but we'll take a look at the angle of her balcony, work something out. It could help undermine the rest of her testimony. Now, there's also the matter of the drugs.'

'What knife?' Max is shaking his head in protest as Harry presses on. 'You hit him in self-defence. The man collapsed. You tried to help him, and called an ambulance. By then the witness had called the police, who misunderstood the situation and arrested you.'

'This needs extra work, Harry,' I point out.

'We must find out who the other witnesses are, and what they will say. We'll look into this man. Has he got a history of violence?'

'Harry, that's the solicitor's job.'

'Dad, this is mad. I'm just going to tell the truth.'

'Truth!' Harry gives a contemptuous flick of the hand. 'Don't make any statement, verbal or written, to the solicitor or the police, until we've perfected it.'

'Dad, I'm not a *liar*! I'm not ashamed of anything I've done. I want to be up-front about it, and honest, and I'm sure that's the best way. And, you know, tell it like it was.'

'Why?' Harry is exasperated. He's over-tired. The stress he is supposed to avoid is already at work. 'What's the point? Is it such a virtue to tell the truth when it will be used against you?'

Max affects sardonic amusement. 'Great, isn't it? Most parents tell their kids to be honest, but you tell me to be a liar. *Truth* is what I'm totally into. I want to look truth in the face! Stare at it. It's what my art is all about, my photography, my life.'

Harry scoffs. 'Truth! Art! Life! What nonsense! What platitudes!' Then suddenly tender, plaintive, 'Max, I'm trying to help you. Let me help you. Please.'

'Well, look, Dad – don't bother. I don't want your help.'

'Please, Max,' Harry urges, 'tell a truth that serves your own ends. What *you* are talking about, not telling fibs, that's for kids. This is the grown-up stuff. We don't care about fibs here in the real world. This is about pain and hardship, being locked in a cell, the end of your hopes, your career, your health, your relationships, your mind. The only way to avoid prison is if you struck this man in self-defence. So start believing it.'

Max wipes his plate with a piece of bread. 'No, I just want to tell the *actual* truth, if someone like you can imagine such a thing.' He pops the moist bread into his mouth.

Harry hardly ever loses his temper nowadays, not in the way he used to, not the explosive rages. Instead we see the curious expression that comes across him, lips together, face reddened, the vein on his forehead larger. He does not shout as he used to. The voice is only slightly raised. 'My dear chap, it's all subjective. There's no truth, only viewpoints and self-interest.'

'Dad, is it true that two plus two equals four, or is that subjective?'

'Numbers are the only damn thing that is true. The rest is all cant and self-deception.'

'Anyway, the drugs will be enough to get me sent down.'

Both of them simultaneously look to me for support. I ask my boy, very gently, 'Max, have you spoken to anyone else about this?'

'Yah, yah, all the others in the house. I told them I whacked the guy because he was so gross, and rude to me. They said they were cool with that.' Under Harry's contemptuous gaze, he bites his lip and looks away.

'Well, Max,' I say, 'from now on, never tell anyone what you've done. Not a single word to a friend. Nor to Philip and Nicola. Nor to your solicitor. Only to us. Only we are on your side. No one else.'

'Yes, some of them do want to go home,' remarked Agnieszka. It was only natural to have such feelings, she said kindly. 'A few actually do leave us. That's their choice. They don't last long afterwards.'

They thanked her for Marjorie's ninetieth birthday tea and left the care home. Outside, the fine spring day had become a fine spring evening. Nicola and Philip parted coolly and left in their cars. Max and Jelka had come on foot, and now set off towards the town's public gardens and the seafront.

In the public gardens, fistfuls of pink blossom weighed the slender cherry branches. Dazzling yellow and red covered the azaleas. 'When this is all over,' said Max as they walked, 'I'm going to wash my hands of Nic and Phil. I don't need them.'

'All over – you mean when your Mum dies?' asked Jelka. She was doubtful. 'Even if you wash your hands of them, hate them or love them, your family are still there.' They paused to admire bushes in bloom, scarlet and purple, white and cerise and fiery orange. 'Even after they're dead.' That had been her experience. 'Isn't this lovely! Like walking through a rainbow!'

Brianna from Sandcliffe Social Services arrived with her folder and clipboard in response to Marjorie's formal request to go back home. She sat in Marjorie's room and asked her what she 'honestly' thought of the Ruth Cohen care home. Agnieszka from the office was present, as was Max.

Marjorie did not appreciate that the question was about the care she herself was receiving. 'Well, it's hard to say without more information. How many residents are there, and how many carers? Who is responsible for providing the care, what are the constraints on what they can provide? And they have to work within their budget.'

Eventually she understood the question. 'Oh, fine, I suppose.'

'Will they help you have a bath?'

'I don't need a bath.'

'Haven't you had a bath recently?'

'Yes, yes, of course. The staff are extremely helpful.'

'And the food, do you like the food here?'

It seemed unfair to ask while Agnieszka sat beside her. Marjorie had often mentioned to Max how dull and tasteless the food was. He replied for her: 'The thing is, Mum has always been a first-rate cook. She even had her own restaurant. So it's hard for her to say.'

Marjorie finally gave her own judicious answer. 'The food is fine. At least it's kosher. Naturally, I'd prefer to be at home cooking in my own kitchen.'

Everyone present knew that Marjorie could not possibly cook a meal any more.

Brianna completed her report: *Marjorie Rosen (Mrs). Widow. Ethnic origin: White British. Age: 90. Requested move from residential to domiciliary care.*

In the care of the Ruth Cohen rest and nursing home, her mobility, strength and health have greatly improved. She now requires only one carer for transfers. Speech is near normal. She can eat and drink unsupervised, except for hot drinks, and is provided with a kosher diet. She self-mobilises with a rollator. She has capacity to make decisions though confused at times. She needs assistance with toileting. She requires supervision of medication at different times of the day. She requires support stockings daily but cannot put them on or take them off unaided. She requires assistance with all personal care. She finds Ruth Cohen's Day Room and Sun Room too noisy, she proposed that Ruth Cohen create a Quiet Room alternative.

Comments: If returned to domiciliary care, Mrs Rosen would need a substantial package of personal and nursing care, initially five nursing calls per day and emergency support all day and all night, and all meals delivered prepared and kosher. She needs support for laundry, housework and shopping. Adaptation of her home would be required for safe mobility. Sheltered housing may be an option, but the same issues would arise as in her own home.

> *Ruth Cohen are willing to continue residential care. I asked that*
> *Marjorie be permitted a routine of managed quiet time in her room,*
> *this has been agreed. Marjorie is an independent lady who needs*
> *time to accept the change in her life. Marjorie would be vulnerable at*
> *home, at high risk of falls and accidents. Despite her request, I am of*
> *the view that Marjorie Rosen is not capable of living at home safely.*
> <u>Decision</u>: *Placement at the Ruth Cohen to continue.*

Marjorie was bitterly disappointed by the decision. Max and Jelka drove down to Sandcliffe to console her. The french windows of the conservatory stood open to the garden. They were offered coffee. Sunbeams revealed dancing, ephemeral figures in the steam rising from their cups. Jelka told Marjorie she was looking well. The carers had dressed her neatly today in dark slacks, cream blouse and a fawn-coloured cardigan. The short vestiges of hair were clean and brushed, and reading glasses hung around her neck on a chain. She asked, 'Am I a prisoner or something? Just put me in your car, Max, and take me home like you did once before. We'll sort out the red tape later.' They did put her in the car, but drove only as far as the clifftop so she could look at the sea.

* * *

The trial has finished Harry off. He's been ill every day since, too ill to get out of bed. The months of fretful obsession, working on Max's case, took all his strength. Then came the fortnight in court, those journeys up and down the motorway, that wretched hotel, the quick canteen lunch. The courtroom was hot and stuffy, yet in the public gallery ventilation blew cold onto our backs.

Between racking coughs Harry talks constantly about the trial – 'when the judge', 'that witness who suddenly', 'they didn't look', 'unfair', 'didn't let him answer', 'should have said', 'jury didn't understand'. It caught him by surprise that the drugs were regarded as more serious than the assault. He hadn't prepared for that. The announcement of the verdict he relives without cease, describing it several times every day. The foreman intoned 'Guilty' as the charges were read out in turn. The judge was not minded to impose a custodial sentence on this bright young man; instead, a crippling fine and costs. The barrister declared it a good result.

We, of course, have to pay. Max has graduated, but has no income to speak of. Harry insisted he must pay us back. Max cheerfully agreed to that, settling on a monthly rate that will take more than ten years. Max wasn't aggrieved at the verdict. 'After all, it's the truth, isn't it? I *was* guilty.'

Sunrise on a fine morning in April is the loveliest moment of the year. Summer raises its veil to give a seductive glimpse of the balmy pleasures to come. The dawn chorus is wildly eager.

Our struggle is nearly over. The freezing fog of diagnosis, therapy and hope has dispersed. In its place is a strange, other-worldly dream. Alone together on our desert island with no chance of rescue, our beautiful marriage is detached from everything and everyone, and from the future and the past, even from the present.

Harry and I spend our last days immersed in companionship, each moment suffused with intimacy. Death, impatient, tries to force a wedge between us, but we look away. It matters not whether we stay at home or go out, sit silently or talk, agree or disagree, are busy or have nothing to do. We smile ruefully and are stoical.

Back in the bedroom, I help Harry get up, take his pills, wash, go to the toilet, shave and dress. I run the razor over the top of his ears, and trim the hair that grows inside them. He says, 'I bet they never do that in an old people's home. The good thing about dying is not needing to be cared for.'

'I think I'd rather be alive with hairy ears, than dead.'

'So would I, but I'm looking on the bright side.' Even now joking.

Harry's not in much pain, he tells me. The nurse says he probably is. She urges me to put him in a hospice. I promise him I won't.

On my birthday, he leads me to his study. He has bought a present for me, a book, *A History of the American Republic*, which I shall read and re-read until my own dying day. Someone must have got it for him; he can hardly lift it on his own. He holds me in his arms and gives me a kiss, a gentle touch of the lips.

'Biz hundert un tsvantsik.' To a hundred and twenty.

'Haha! Same to you, darling.' I don't want to live to a hundred and twenty without him. I did expect, though, that we would make it to sixty-five together. It is not to be.

He wants so much that 'the kids' will join us on this day. Philip is first to arrive, the gravel crunching beneath his wheels as he draws up on the driveway. At once he exclaims, 'Dad, you look terrific! Is that a new suit?'

Almost skeletal, Harry has taken to wearing suits he kept from younger, slimmer days. They hang on him with deceptive elegance. With easy frankness, he assures Philip it's one of the oldest things in his wardrobe. Nicola arrives just minutes later.

We start tea without Max, who has been delayed on his way from the airport. This birthday is the smallest, quietest affair imaginable. At last Max does come through the door, slipping in quietly, shyly smiling, curly hair unkempt.

Harry beams. 'Ah! The whole family!'

All is well for a few minutes. Then Max says quite casually, 'You know, I've often wondered – why haven't we met, why don't we know, the *rest* of our family? We've got uncles and aunts and cousins, like everyone else, haven't we?' The other two look up with interest.

I tell him that I drifted away from my brothers and sisters. I watch Harry's face to see how he will deflect the question. Instead, in one unaccustomed movement, he thrusts his head down onto his hand and utters a sob. It is a strangely high-pitched sound. 'Feiga! Feiga!' he moans. 'I'm sorry!'

We stare fascinated, unsure how to react. We are so unused to the idea of Harry crying that none of us recognise what he is doing. The children are confused: they don't even know Feiga is a name, let alone that she was their aunt. Max rushes to embrace his father's emaciated form. 'Dad, I'm so sorry! I didn't know it was the wrong thing to ask! I didn't know it would upset you! I didn't mean to!' The rest of us continue to gaze in horror.

Harry allows Max to comfort him for barely two seconds. At first I thought it was addressed to Feiga, or perhaps to his father, but the 'sorry', I see, is an apology to us. With the same abruptness Harry brings himself under control. The weeping ceases, no trace of it remains and he is as upright as before. Max moves away as if the incident never happened. 'Yes,' says Harry calmly, 'my sister Feiga, she was my favourite. But very sadly she… she died.'

If any of them want to ask more about the past, they draw back now, dissuaded by the sense that there is some untellable story concealed there. One day, too late for an answer, they will realise how many things should have been said, how many questions were not asked. No one says, 'Daddy, I want you to know I love you.'

For Harry, anyway love is an irrelevance. In his view, a man does not expect to love his children nor be loved by them. He expects to support them, and be willing to sacrifice himself for them. He is not compelled, nor is he under any obligation – duty is more than that. Doing what you must do, and doing what has to be done, are two different things.

To lighten the mood, Philip asks, too brightly, about our latest 'holiday' in Israel. He says, 'You got a fantastic tan, Dad.'

'Oh,' I say, 'Harry always goes as brown as a nut in no time! I look more like a strawberry.' We all laugh. There's nothing more I can tell him than was in our postcards.

I hoped they would give Harry an easy time of it in his last days, especially after those shocking tears, but out of the blue Nicola pipes up. 'If,' she quizzes him, 'Israel played England at cricket, Daddy, which side would you cheer?'

'Firstly,' Harry responds at once, 'it's inconceivable that Israel would have a cricket team good enough to play England; and secondly, it's inconceivable that I would ever watch a cricket match or cheer either side.' Nicola alone does not smile.

Harry and the children sing *Happy Birthday*. I don't know if they have taken on board that this is the last time we shall be together as a family. We tuck in to sandwiches and slices of birthday cake, with cups of tea. A happy birthday for me and a last goodbye for him.

Harry is shaking me. 'Marjorie!' I turn on my bedside light. The alarm clock shows 2.46am. He whispers, 'I must talk to you about something, right now.' I rouse myself and sit up. He adds, 'Not supposed to, still classified.'

'If you're not supposed to, then don't,' I caution.

'No, listen. About Bob Shaffer.'

'Oh, darling! *That?* It was *nothing*. I'm so sorry about that! Have you been thinking about Shaffer, after all this time? I chose you. No one else has ever been of the slightest interest to me. You know that.'

I do wonder why he says the subject of Bob Shaffer taking me to the opera is 'classified' – in other words, an official secret.

'No, no, listen, I want to apologise, Marjorie, please let me. The thing is – I *knew* you weren't interested in Shaffer. But I had to *pretend* to be jealous, because—,' his expression is of the most awful, agonising regret, 'you see, darling, otherwise, you might've *realised* that I knew. And if you realised that, then you might guess that I also knew what he had asked you to do for NSA. And if you guessed that, you would wonder how I knew.'

What a revelation at such a time. 'But how *could* you have known what Bob said to me in the street? That's impossible.' For whom, then, was Harry working without my ever becoming aware of it? MI6? Ernst, perhaps? (Ephraim, rather.) 'Harry, *what* did you know about Shaffer?'

With only a slight movement of the head he brushes the topic away. 'You see,' he gives my hand a squeeze, 'after the war, after Section B was rolled up into J-Section, obviously I couldn't say anything. But believe me, dear, when Shaffer reappeared, I never, ever, suspected you of anything.'

I can't take it in. Section B was Above Top Secret. Harry couldn't have known about it, nor about J-Section at GCHQ.

'And your work after the war, I didn't mean to make life harder for you. I was always at your side.' His mind seems to be wandering again. 'It was the right thing for you. It was what you were good at. I only wanted to help you.' Actually, no, his mind isn't wandering.

Does he mean Erika? He might have guessed about Erika, but not what she was giving us. That must be what he means by my 'work after the war'. He can't possibly have known about Venona. Literally no one was aware of that unless they had been inducted into it.

My head is spinning. I'm flabbergasted. 'Harry, you mustn't talk about this. You might let something slip. To the nurse, the children. We might be overheard. The house might be bugged, I don't know.'

'It isn't, darling. Had it checked.'

'*You* had it checked?' I feel the floor is tilting, the room turning. 'How did you have it checked – who by – when?'

He waves that away. That's not what he wants to talk about. 'You remember when we met?'

'At BP?'

'No, Cadby Hall. When we started walking out, the first time.'

'We went dancing, and walked to the river. There was a raid. We lay under a bench on the Embankment and had a lovely talk.'

A real little smile of happiness, but he is gathering his thoughts. 'I only asked you out that night because I had to write a vetting report on you. I had to draw you out, see if you would say indiscreet things. There was some anxiety about you.'

'*You* were vetting *me*? Report to whom?'

'High-ups.' There's a slight, dismissive flick of the fingers. 'Wrote the report, recommended you. And fell for you.' His eyelids creep down to the pupil. A half-moon of the hazel iris remains visible. 'Fell for you hook, line and sinker. Cleverest woman I ever met.'

I don't know what he is talking about. Is any of this true, is it Harry's febrile imaginings, his deluded memory, an overactive mind in its death throes? Is it the morphine talking? Or *is* it true? Clearly yes, for he seems to know more about me than I know myself.

In dizzying realisation, as if stepping backwards off the tilting floor into emptiness, it dawns on me that I don't know this man beside me, Harry Rosen, Chaim Rosenzweig.

'You were writing a report on me?' I repeat idiotically.

Then I notice Harry's eyes are closed. He has fallen into sleep. I hold his hand and struggle to order my thoughts. The point is, I suppose, that whoever he is, whoever we were, or are, we are still *us*.

That first evening out feels vanishingly far away, a lost world. Cadby Hall was demolished years ago. The great J. Lyons & Co. disappeared without trace. The people we knew are dead and buried. Hitlerism was defeated and Erika's longed-for united, democratic Germany finally created, though she did not see it. The Soviet Union itself is falling apart. Even Jerusalem has been won. Our living, breathing days are turning into stone monuments and memorials, museum pieces and pages of history.

He springs into wakefulness and resists, but I have strapped him into the back seat of the car. At the hospice, he becomes quite calm as nurses wheel him to a room with a few other men. At times he is nearly lucid. He says. 'Marjorie, I'm scared.'

I would be too. I try to comfort him in a common-sense tone. 'What of, dear?' I lean forward and kiss his forehead as if all is well.

'I don't know. The great black wall that I am rushing towards.'

I promise to stay with him.

'Marjorie, let's say goodbye properly, goodbye and thank you.' He speaks without a trace of drama.

'Oh darling, not yet.' My voice is much too calm.

'Please, just let me say it. I've always admired you. Always been proud that you chose me. I loved you, darling, with all my might, all my strength and heart, ever since we met. And never shown it.'

'Oh, Harry! You show it all the time, every day! And I love you, darling.' My words sound trite in my ear because *I love you* isn't the sort of thing we say to one another. I am trying to remember what we do say, how to say, in my own true words, that I love him. At the same time I'm wondering what the point is of such declarations; and what exactly I would mean by it, and what Harry means by it. Other than in a birthday card or signing off a letter or a note, Harry has hardly ever used the word *love*.

'And the children. Tell them I said so. I couldn't tell them myself. They will always feel that I provided for them but didn't love them.'

That is an awful thing to say, and probably true. 'Darling, you showed it by everything you did for them.' Except, he's right, they don't know what he did for them.

'I wanted to be able to admire them, you know, but...' He shakes his head. He urges me to listen. 'About Max. The fine he's repaying. Write it off. Let him move on.'

He drops back against the pillow, his breathing shallow and laboured. While he sleeps, I slip away for a quick cup of tea and some air.

When I return, the man in the bed opposite relates what has happened in the meantime. 'A rabbi popped in to see your husband.' I instantly assume Harry was either fast asleep or gave the rabbi short shrift. However, the man explains further, 'Your husband was wide awake. The rabbi, he says to your husband, "Would you like to say the Shema, Harry?" and your husband, he's like, "No, and anyway I don't know the words." So the rabbi, he goes, "Let's say it together," and your husband, well, turns out he did know the words. So him and this rabbi, they said the whole thing together, in unison like, and then your husband, he went, "Thank you, rabbi," and fell asleep.'

He is unconscious, not asleep. The difference is small. I sit beside him, his hand always in mine, imagining that he may yet open his eyes and say something clever or funny. By evening, Harry is still not conscious. His breathing has become a horrible gurgling. 'Prepare yourself,' the nurse advises me, 'call your children now if they want to be with him at the end.'

Max is in Iraq. I ask the agency to send a telegram. Harry is wheeled into a room where we can be alone. Philip and Nicola arrive, and the three of us sit around his bed, listening to the awful sound, watching as Harry struggles to take his gurgling breaths.

With startling abruptness the sound has stopped. The chest is perfectly quiet and motionless. I touch the head, the face, but he is not there. Harry has left us, bequeathing books, papers and a clarinet, and a cadaver that used to be a strong, virile body.

Max arrives too late; too late even for the funeral. He collapses kneeling onto the dining room carpet, where he lies banging his head on the floor and sobbing uncontrollably. I have never seen a man weep with so little restraint. Into the fabric of the carpet he whimpers, 'Dad, Daddy, Dad,' sometimes twisting in agony.

Nicola, too, is crying on her bed, with the door closed. Through the window I see Philip sitting in his car, unable to face the rest of us, his head in his hands. He too is weeping.

Only I have no tears. With a flask of coffee and a packet of biscuits I take to my usual place in the sitting room, directly facing Harry's empty seat. There I remain. During the morning they return, one at a time, red-eyed, shocked to find me still in the same chair.

They offer a breakfast that I refuse. They say a few words that I wave away. I remain fixed to my spot, deaf and blind to everything. At last the children say their goodbyes and leave me.

It was Nicola, not Philip, who broke the news to Marjorie that she had to quit her flat. She was disbelieving, then outraged when Philip confirmed on the phone that it was true.

'I'm sure you understand, Mum.' – 'When by?'

'By the end of September.' – 'You said I could stay until the end of my days. I'm not dead yet.'

'Yes, and you could if you were still living there.' – 'No, but I'm going back to the flat. That's my plan.'

'You live at the Ruth Cohen now, Mummy. It's been decided. You can't manage in the flat.'

He was annoyed with Nicola. 'If you hadn't mentioned it, Mum wouldn't even have realised. Now she'll just get upset.'

Marjorie did get upset. She said nothing to anyone about her feelings. She considered Philip was ungrateful, treacherous and disloyal and had broken his promise. It was splitting hairs to argue that she didn't live there any more. It was still her home! She did not want to abandon all hope of sitting again in her own living room, or lying in her own bed, or baking a cake in her own kitchen.

But abandon all hope she must. She asked Jelka to take her to the flat for the last time. 'There's one more cake I want to teach you. A special cake. And I want to choose a few things to have by me in my room.'

If she were doomed to stay in the Ruth Cohen, she may as well have a few of her own books and a couple of her own pictures on the walls. She must be practical and sensible.

'Which books would you like?' Jelka asked.

'False choice, false question. Ask instead which I would be glad to cast away.' It wasn't easy to decide. 'I must have all Harry's books, of course,' – she meant, books Harry had written – 'oh, and some

Pushkin, John Betjeman, Sassoon, Rilke, Yeats,' she pointed out the volumes she wanted, 'Burns, Dryden, Wilfred Owen, and John Donne – ask not for whom the bell tolls!' She gave a short laugh. 'Cavafy, Wilde, Natan Alterman, and Bialik, and Tagore, Dylan Thomas' *Under Milk Wood*, and plenty of Tennyson, Keats, Wordsworth, yes and I think Allen Ginsburg too – *Kaddish* would be highly appropriate! – and of course Shakespeare's sonnets, Pope, A.E.Housman, and… no, there won't be space.'

'All these writers I never heard of!'

'Poets. Great poets.'

'You can't read them any more, can you?'

'This is for people to read *to* me. Oh, and could you bring Harry's old chessboard and box of chessmen? I like to have those by me.'

With care Jelka packed bags and boxes to take to the care home. 'What about your photo albums?'

'Yes. Can you and Nicola take everything else and look after it? I don't want Philip to have my things.'

At the kitchen table she said, 'You know, Jelka, this old recipe book of mine–' she tapped the black ring binder, '–it's one of my most important possessions.'

'It reminds you of your shop in Saltington?'

'No, something else. It belonged to a couple in France, partisans, like your parents. During the war they too were tortured and killed by local militiamen. This book is all that survives of them.'

'My God! How did it come to you?' It crossed Jelka's mind that Marjorie was making this up, that it was demented fantasy and imagination, like in the hospital.

'It was given to me. I want you to have it, to keep. You are the right person. Take it home with you. Look after it.'

'No, it should go to someone in their family.'

'There's no one left. These are what I call my secret recipes. In fact it's their secret, not mine. This book contains other secrets too, and is always to be kept secret. It's like a memory that can never be talked about. It's in French, but you can read French, can't you? And the cakes are all fabulous.'

Jelka had no idea what Marjorie was talking about. But then, that often happened. This time, Marjorie said a calm adieu to her flat as she shut the door. They took her special occasion cake to the care home and put slices aside for Max, for Carol, for Róża and Lorraine.

First thing next morning, Jelka phoned Nicola. 'Before Philip takes possession of the flat, your Mum wants us to take out everything of hers. She doesn't want him to have her things.'

'That's right! Why should he profit from her things?' Nicola willingly complied, ransacking the flat in her effort to take as much as possible before Philip could lay his hands on it. Lampshades, bathroom fittings, ceiling roses, even lightbulbs and door handles she boxed up and put in the boot of her car, fitted carpet she ripped off the floors and rolled up for house-clearance men. Book dealers came to clear the shelves. It took removal men barely two hours to pack up some furniture, the new television and kitchen appliances to take to her own place. Charity volunteers collected everything she did not want.

When Max next came down, he opened the door into an echoing, empty space as shocking as a carcass picked clean. Not even the ghost of Marjorie remained within its naked walls. He stayed at the Premier Inn and called Nicola to find out what had happened. She explained: 'Jelka said Mum wanted us to.'

'I don't think this is what she meant, Nic. Where is everything? Is it in storage?' – 'I gave it to charity.' – 'Not the books?' – 'Jelka said Mum has chosen the books she wants.' – 'And her furniture?' – 'Gave it to charity. I took some. I'm keeping it safe.' – 'What about her clothes? Her jewellery?' – 'I've got her jewellery.' – 'You took Mum's jewellery?' – 'Looking after it.' – 'Even the light fittings have gone. The door handles.'

Nicola cackled gleefully. 'That'll show him. Bastard.'

At the Ruth Cohen Memorial Rest and Nursing Home for the Jewish Aged, the milestone in every week is Sabbath, ancient drumbeat of time. Yet each Shabbat and each week seemed to Marjorie merely a return of the last, as if she lived the same week again and again and again. Nor did she notice, and nor did it matter. For whether she was caged on a treadmill or running forward in an endless race, that week of life was hers, its bright minutes trickling anew through her fingers. Friends dropped in and left again, Carol walked her round the garden,

Eva stopped by; a cup of coffee, a biscuit, a conversation, yesterday or today, a chat by the window.

Marjorie moved slowly, pushing her rollator. A rollator is a walking frame with wheels, brakes and a seat. Marjorie gripped the handles, moving between bedroom and day room, sun room and dining room, the rooms of her small world. Always the same book lay casually on its seat, *A History of the American Republic*, Harry's parting gift. With an impossible pretence that she was re-reading the huge volume, it rested there as if to say – *this* is what I am, not the lame, senseless, half-blind, crooked-as-a-stick crone you think you see before you! *This* is my reading matter. Indeed, there were evenings alone in her room when she gingerly turned some pages, and through her reading glasses tried to focus on a line of text, and recall what she once was, and what her husband had been like.

The phrase *absent-minded* had never felt so literally true. There were long periods of absence, when none of her conscious mind felt in gear at all. Hours came and went like smog moving in the streets. Only the trams, on their rails, carefully moving forward, were fully functioning. The footpath ahead was lost, this way and that, disappeared frighteningly from view. When suddenly she did not understand even her hand in front of her face, where she was, where her room was, how to sit, to stand, open a door, what to do with a cup, recognise herself in a mirror, was always a sickening, fearful moment. She kept calm and waited and found the way.

Urged out of her room to sit with the others, she joined the women who spent most of every day in a circle of armchairs at one end of the conservatory. After a while Marjorie realised that she was getting to know them, Sylvia, Rose, Gertie, Gloria, Hilda, harmless people, some half remembered from somewhere, friends of a sort. It had become accepted that Marjorie sometimes preferred to sit quietly on her own. That was no crime. Senility excuses any eccentricity.

One of them said, 'I wish I could go home.'

'I thought I was going home, once,' said Marjorie.

Another cackled dismissively. 'You haven't got a home, either of you. None of us have. Home was where you lived with your husband and brought up your kids.'

'Oh, I have a home,' Marjorie insisted, 'I have a home, but I can't go back to it. They won't let me go back, because – because it's in the past.' Whether she meant Durbeyfield Lodge, Saltington, Hampstead or Chelsea, she did not know. They were all one in her mind.

'No, Marje, that's what I mean,' explained the other full of regret, 'a home in the past ain't no home at all.'

'Look on the bright side,' mused another, 'at least you're cosy and well fed, and got a chance of dying peacefully in your bed.'

'Yes, but…,' Marjorie looked away, 'I never wanted to die peacefully in my bed.'

Philip came rarely; he assumed he was unwelcome. In truth Marjorie was thrilled to see him, or any of her children, daydreamed of seeing them. Nicola's visits were even more infrequent. She said, 'What's the point? Mum doesn't know if I've been.' Max said, 'If she doesn't remember, you should spend more time with her, not less.' As a result, he felt he had to call on his mother more frequently. Rising early to beat the rush hour, he drove from London every few days. He knew it wouldn't last forever. Though, of course, she might live another ten years like this. He'd be getting old himself by then.

'Max? Is it you?'

'Yes, Mum.' He offered to fetch tea or coffee.

'Ah, good, good. Come closer. Is it tea time, did you say?'

He kissed her. 'No, Mum, it's not tea time. It's the morning. You've just had breakfast.'

She laughed at her mistake. 'You know how a clock runs? A spring keeps everything in balance. My spring is broken. My clock still ticks, but its hands are broken. Like being adrift in the seven seas of time and no land in sight. I sail on without bearings.'

In any case she did not want any tea or coffee. She asked to be taken out either on foot or in the car. After every outing there was a price to pay, more pain, a bad day, but it was worth it. It pleased her to be on the move. They strolled round the block, Max pushing the wheelchair along quiet streets near the Ruth Cohen care home.

'I don't recognise anything,' she declared. 'Whereabouts are we? Which way is Hampstead Heath from here?'

'This isn't Hampstead, Mum! Look around! It's Sandcliffe!' Max was ashamed that his immediate reaction was to mock her absurd mistake. 'Hampstead is over a hundred miles away.'

Marjorie hid her shock and incredulity. How skilled she was at covering these gaffes and weaknesses. 'Darling, I do *know* that! I'm saying what a difference there is between this and our old home near Hampstead Heath, eh? That's what I'm saying.'

'Well, that's true,' he humoured her.

Arriving back at the Ruth Cohen, now she did want some tea. For safety, these days Marjorie had to have her hot drinks out of a heat-proof plastic beaker with a lid and spout. The Ruth Cohen had taught her to abandon all embarrassment. Like that they sat and talked. Max took a photograph of her trying to manage the beaker.

'What's marvellous is,' Max said with sincere admiration, 'that you never complain.'

'About what?'

'Anything. Hassles. Aches and pains.'

'Oh, I would love to complain – if only I knew to whom I should address my complaints.'

Max smiled broadly. 'And I suppose you do know, don't you, that your mind isn't what it was?'

'Oh, I know I'm losing it.'

'Actually, Mum, when your mind is gone, where does that leave emotions – have they gone too?'

'Emotions are in the driving seat.'

'Emotions in the driving seat! Wow. Is that good?'

'Awful! Emotions can't drive.' She laughed.

'For you, that's almost a change of personality, isn't it? Or d'you feel ninety-year-old Marjorie is the same as nine-year-old Marjorie?'

'Are you the same Max as the lovely little boy I remember?' She pondered his question. *We know about mourning someone who has died. Many know what it is to mourn someone while they are still alive. And for oneself, too, there can be a kind of grieving. She lives, I lived.* 'I haven't felt truly myself these last twenty years. I don't know who I think I am instead!'

He said, 'I suppose somewhere in the mind you're forever you, ageless, like in dreams.'

'I do ask myself these things. Pointless questions with no answer.

My life now is spent in strange rooms that are nothing to do with me. I feel I'm someone that *used* to exist. Does that make Marjorie Rosen nothing but memories? I don't know what memories are, or where they reside. If the memories are part of me, and I am remembering them *now*... you see the conundrum? I was, therefore I am.'

'It's not pointless to ask, even if there's no answer.'

'"*The unknown passing through the strange.*" You know Masefield's poem?' He didn't know it. '"*Sad in the fruit, bright in the flower*"... I see now how life is really lived twice or three times over. Like a dog walking with its mistress, we run to and fro, to and fro on our path, ahead and behind, living and reliving, anticipating and remembering. "*Those who follow feel behind their backs, when all before is blind – Our joy, a rampart to the mind.*"'

'So, Mum, do you ever think about – about that, about death? Does it feel closer than it used to?'

'Darling, I plan to live forever.' Her own mortality did seem just beyond the visible horizon of the imagination. 'The problem with that is being *unemployed* forever. Everyone needs a part to play, a job to do and something to look forward to.' She knew how absurd it was. There was nothing useful she could do any more.

After tea, the peasouper began to descend once more, dense and confusing, its bewildering tendrils entangling her, paths branching, disappearing, lost. She fought to see the way, tried to remain calm, excused herself at last by saying she was tired.

Max kissed her goodbye, vanished into the great world outside, left her alone in her room. In the mirror Marjorie studied her face. *Was* she still the same person? Gently, with fingertips she touched the glass. There was something in the eyes she recognised, or that recognised her.

Max, she considered, had redeemed himself in the last few years. She wished Harry could know. To the photo on her bedside table, she said, *Look, Max turned out a good boy after all. A good husband, a good father and a good son.* Harry appeared unconvinced.

Her eyes opened. She was uncomfortable and thirsty. She listened to the silence, remembered where she was, gazed at the faint glow of the nightlight and the luminous bedside clock. She felt nauseous. Her stomach was swirling with some putrid foulness which she could taste in her mouth and nose, while lower down, her guts felt full and heavy like wet concrete pressing to emerge. With horror she realised that her incontinence pants were leaking. With one hand she fingered the elastic edge; sure enough there was sticky moisture. She pulled up her hand and sniffed. Her worst fears were realised. Now the stuff was on her hand. The colour she could not see, but it was something dark. She turned to the clock face: 3:34am. Oh! She had to sit on the toilet, had to be sick, had to get this nappy off, had to wash her hand.

The call button was on the same side as her good hand, the one with something on it. If she could turn enough she might be able to press it with the clean hand. Blast, this was getting difficult. The urges of nausea and diarrhoea were growing out of control. The carer on duty might not come immediately. Even for them it took several minutes to walk down that corridor. She could not wait.

The rollator stood by the bed, but with this mess on her good hand... damn it all, the bathroom was not five yards away, surely she could manage that! With her bad hand she pushed herself into a sitting position and rose to her feet. She had been sick so often there was supposed to be a bowl under the bed for just that possibility. She could neither see it, nor feel it with her foot. There was another bowl in the bathroom, she knew. Flailing with her hand for balance, she hurriedly tottered forward, fighting to take each step. '*See*,' she said, 'I *can* walk, without anything or anyone to help me.'

Determined to manage, she did reach the bathroom door. It occurred to her that she should have pressed the call button *as well* as coming to the bathroom – it wasn't an 'either-or' thing. The alarm wristband that she hated, she ought really to wear for occasions like this. She would sit herself on the toilet just as soon as, with fumbling hands, she had undone this overloaded...

From the loosened nappy wet faeces ran in a fast-flowing rivulet down the length of her thigh beneath her white nightdress and dropped onto the bathroom floor. A great splash landed on her bare foot. She stepped backwards to avoid the stinking substance, a manoeuvre far beyond her ability. Sliding on the dark puddle, losing her precarious balance, she reaching out with both arms, the good and the bad, for something to hold. In panic, desperate not to fall into her own faeces, with furious effort she twisted her entire body, turning to the wall which might save her. Like a ninepin tumbling, her feet slipped quickly away. She heard the crack of her poor hairless cranium on the shiny bathroom wall and understood that she would, after all, lie in her own faeces.

* * *

There is a springtime after every death, and a summer. Bushes and shrubs, hedgerows and verges have become prettily speckled with new green. Full, golden bloom covers the gorse. Flowering trees are at their breathtaking best, the cascading branches heavy with delicate white and pink, bringing bouquets and young brides to mind; and the blowing petals, handfuls of confetti.

Inside my wardrobes and chests of drawers, Harry's vests and underpants are still neatly arranged just where I put them last, his socks and pullovers and cardigans, long-sleeved casual shirts, short-sleeved shirts, his smart white shirts, jackets and carefully folded trousers on their hangers. I don't know what it is I feel about them. I bought most of these clothes, knitted the jumpers, darned the socks, ironed the shirts. They have taken on an alien quality, a slightly unpleasant quality, peculiar to maleness. They are Harry's, redolent of him, yet no longer his. They are mine. Everything is tidy. There are his roomy summer shorts, his capacious bathing trunks. I stare at ties I helped straighten. Men's leather lace-up shoes in a row. They need to go. All of it.

And not just Harry's things. Satin half-slips and nylon stockings, garter belts with metal clips, brassières for a younger woman. I feel an impulse to empty them into a bin liner. My high-heeled shoes and half-veil hats and a smart grey suit not worn in years. At the back, at the end of the rail, dresses and skirts, some twenty years old, some older, back to the fifties and sixties, calf-length, knee-length, above the knee. With shocking clarity I see myself in them, moving and alive and smiling, as if looking not at clothes, or even at memories, but at someone in front of my eyes, someone I hardly know. I can hear voices and laughter coming from our Chelsea flat. And music. Standing beside her, this other me, there's a bright, gap-toothed fellow with a mischievous grin; Harry when he was young and happy and ambitious. There's a smell of mothballs. I would never be able even to get into these things any more. What possessed me to keep them all this time? I suppose I had spent a lot of money on them, and didn't realise I would never wear them again.

Charity shops in Saltington High Street are veritable emporia of retro style, overflowing with obsolete good taste and high quality. Racks and shelves are loaded with fine faded jackets and frocks, pearls and brooches, pristine crystal, leather-bound volumes, jazz LPs, interlined curtains, and veneer furniture from the fifties, relics of a bygone modernity.

The charity shop to which I take our things is at the top of the High Street near the church. It raises money for the hospice where Harry spent his last hours. I owe them something.

In a strange reversion to youth, since Harry's death I seem to move backwards through the years. Autumns pass walking alone in drifts of copper leaves, springtimes among blossom scattered on the breeze. New foals are born and taken away. I move gradually further and further back into maidenly unmarriage and childlessness. At night I wish Harry goodnight like a lovesick girl, and in the morning get up alone. Harry is a photograph, and a grave to tend. Nor do I see anything of the children and grandchildren I once had. Everyone is busy, far away, has their own life.

My day is full, though. From dawn to midnight, I have chores, duties, tasks. I cook, I bake, serve in the shop. I knit, I read. Like a young woman (but with a bad hip), I go out for a swim, to concerts and plays and exhibitions.

Working late in the pâtisserie kitchen, I hear a sound, too loud for mice, too quiet for honest folk. I turn off the lighting isolator switch and listen. Footsteps on bare boards, unmistakable, not one, not two, but three people have come through the back door of the shop.

By their flashlights I glimpse three strapping young men. One carries a crowbar, another a screwdriver. They're looking around, staring about, searching. They ignore the till on the counter. They open drawers, look in cupboards, along shelves, taking nothing. I fear someone has come at last for Yvette's codebook, her old recipe book.

Why now, is hard to say. After all, the Kremlin has a policy of openness, perestroika. HVA and the rest of Stasi no longer exist. Just months ago, the KGB itself was dissolved and replaced by the FSK.

The whispering is not German, nor Russian. These lads are English. The darkness gives me an edge. I can find my way around the shop without light, while they can't. I pick up the first tool within reach, which happens to be only a hand-held blender I use for grinding nuts. I know I can expect no mercy. Nor shall I give any.

They reach the kitchen. A swinging door is a useful weapon in itself, as is surprise, and it's amazing what frightful damage can be done with a cordless blender. You must be quick and use every ounce of strength, strike without hesitation, never have doubts or hold back. He drops his torch. Using his own crowbar against him, a man's joints can be easily disengaged from one another if you know how. Speed and clarity of mind are the essence, and willingness to do the unthinkable. Their screams of horror and unbearable pain as flesh is sliced make an unseemly racket for this time of night. One of the three, unharmed, leaves in panic, but I follow.

I'm slow nowadays, and never break into a run. As I try it now there's a sharp pain, like the twanging of a huge elastic band inside my chest. A moment of agony pulls the breath right out of my lungs. Even so, I reach the car in time to see him face to face, a scared man in the driving seat of a new Range Rover. He slams the door onto my left hand, crushing the fingers. I hear them crack. For some reason, I do not cry out – habit, I suppose. With my good hand I open the car door and make a grab. He is too strong for me, has slammed the accelerator down, and speeds up Saltington's empty High Street, towards the moonlit church and the silent main road.

The broken fingers hang loose, misshapen and unusable. Thank goodness it's not my right hand. I pick up the telephone and dial 999, speaking loudly over the caterwauling of the wretches on the floor.

When the police and ambulance arrive, I am assured that they were petty thieves, chancers looking for the till and the safe. 'Got more than they bargained for, didn't they? Oh, my God!' The officer grimaces horrified at the disfigured faces. 'Oh, my God! Look at the state of his nose! And – oh, my God! – what's happened to his knee? Oh, my God! Did you do this?'

'They were swinging at me, so I hit back.' I give the officer the car number and a description.

'Stupid of them to think a coffee shop would keep enough cash on the premises to be worth stealing.' He sizes me up with impudent admiration.

Even so, it's odd that there were three of them, that they had a brand new Range Rover, that they looked on the bookshelves and in drawers, and were professional enough to disable the burglar alarm.

In my corner by the counter I sit filling in the crossword awkwardly. I can't bake with these damaged fingers, or serve customers, or knit, and won't be able to for quite a while. This blasted hip is so bad I can hardly walk without a stick. What I am thinking, as I sit in my corner, is that the intruders did not find what they wanted and may be back.

Philip urges me to give up the shop. He says I ought to sell it as a going concern before my health problems affect the value of the business. He's right, of course. It's not the shop alone. The house is too big for me. The garden, more than I can manage. The drive to synagogue and back, too far. Philip says if I found a nice little flat by the sea in Sandcliffe, he would buy it for me. There to retire into quiet obscurity.

'If you did give me a flat–,' I answer Philip.

'Oh, I wouldn't *give* it to you, Mum! That would not be proper. You'd buy it, and I'd buy it from you. It would be mine, but you could live there as long as you like. A nice comfortable place by the sea. Rent free. Until the end of your days.'

'The end of my days! Goodness.' That awesome phrase.

It's amazing how time closes over. The past is ever alive, life nine-tenths hidden from view, sinking further into the deep. Only the shimmering surface is clear.

Sometimes, though, I catch sight of myself, my whole self and all the years that are mine, in a single glance; as though a hind glimpsed running among trees, or a seabird soaring across a beam of sunlight. For an instant all is illuminated. That brief moment, I tell myself, that brief moment was me and my life.

Z

It was blood, rather than faeces, that Róża saw when she looked in on Marjorie at first light. The sight caused her to recoil, gasping, uncomprehending. She struggled to master a quaking weakness in her knees. On the floor Marjorie lay as if sleeping in a sticky rust-coloured lagoon. A huge gurgling crust of blood ran across her bare scalp. Her white cotton nightdress was wet with dripping vermilion. Strange, shocking streaks of carmine red were fingered down the wall like some insane murder scene, and for a dizzying instant Róża wondered if that was what she beheld. The air was dense with a suffocating, gagging chemistry of blood, shit, piss and sick. A footprint smeared across brown slime showed where she had slipped.

Róża steeled herself to kneel in the ghastly mire and feel Marjorie's pulse. It continued to beat, weak and slow. Blood seeped horribly onto Róża's tunic and apron as she leaned closer. There was breath there, too, infinitesimally shallow. Róża slammed her hand onto the alarm. Across town, an emergency ambulance turned on its siren and picked up speed. As it drove through Sandcliffe's morning traffic, Róża wiped Marjorie's face and hands and feet with a wet cloth and handfuls of paper. Working quickly and tenderly she raised the nightdress and cleared the faeces, vomit and blood from her body.

At the touch of Róża's hand on hers, Marjorie's eyelids flickered and, to Róża's astonishment, opened wide and alert. The eyes looked into hers, the grip tightened and there was a faint smile of satisfaction before they closed once more.

* * *

It is not allowed to talk, to ask, to smile, to look insolent. We sit silent, expressionless, afraid, attentive, lest we be punished. Every girl sits upright at her little desk, in straight rows up and down the classroom.

Miss tells us to begin our work. Each girl takes her slate in its wooden frame. I finish my work at once, within a minute, and sit at my desk waiting, not writing, arms folded across my chest as we have been instructed, hands out of sight.

Miss is dressed like a nurse, with a high collar, a stiff white apron and a pleated cap. I am in my gymslip. The two of us sit and sit as the labouring slate pencils squeak like mice, moving, pausing, moving, pausing, the sound low yet piercing, continuous, yet rising and falling in waves.

I look at Miss, and Miss looks at me, both of us erect, silent and motionless, waiting together for the rhythmic squeaking to die away as each girl completes her task, puts down her slate, folds her arms, and sits in silence.

* * *

Carefully I wipe my shoes on the mat. If there is a speck of dirt on the hall floor, Nanny will give me such a smack. Mother told the new nanny that she may chastise me if I am a bad girl, so she does. Before going upstairs to give the passbook back to Mother, I turn to see if I have made a mark.

Our house has five bedrooms (not counting maids' quarters), two sitting rooms, a kitchen and scullery, and a bathroom. The mortgage is three pounds ten shillings a week. Mother trusts me with the money. She gives me three pound notes and a ten-shilling note, and the book, and I walk on my own to the Building Society. 'Mind you go straight there, madam, and straight back.'

When Father is at home, he likes to come with me. He says to Mother, 'I'll keep her company.' Father and I set out to the Building Society, but before we arrive, he says, 'I have to see someone, pet. Go on and pay the money, all right?' He taps my shoulder kindly. 'Not a word to Mother, mind! Eh, lass? Or to anyone. You can keep a secret, can't you? Good girl! See you back here in a few minutes.'

I ask him who he's going to see. He puts his finger over his lips and smiles. 'Sh! Not a word!'

I push open the door of the Building Society and reach up to give the money to a lady at the counter. She writes in the book, and I run back to meet Father. When he arrives, he gives me the sweetest smile, and we walk back home, happy as pie.

* * *

There in the distance, on the jetty, my dear ones! I swim towards them against a cold, cold tide. Icy waves roll down the estuary, ice on my skin, so cold I'm seizing up.

Fight it, Marjorie! Come on, girl! Pull, breathe in, pull, breathe out, pull, breath like waves, like swell, like oars, like wings, like sails. Pull hard, push hard, hard against the current, against the wind, against the cold, against the heavy, shifting sea. My nostrils and mouth are splattered with oil and froth and stinking brown scum. Dog-tired, I swim hard towards them, grab for air, lunge for air.

At last they come clearly into view, every one of them. And the tide turns to help, lifting me forward. And the eager new tide rushes high and fresh and clean, washing my face and body. Its swell breaks on the shore, on pebbles, pulls back, sh-sh, sh-sh, like breath, like breath.

Oh, marvellous, their welcoming faces! I stretch out my fingers to the jetty. Father reaches down, grasps my hand and draws me up, out of the water. 'My clever girl! I knew you could do it.' How wonderful to hear his voice, to feel his strong hand in mine.

Three smiling children stand in greeting, little Philip, Nicola and Max, good and lovely as can be, my darlings. Dear Peggy holds up a big white towel to wrap around me. Behind them, Harry watches with a mischievous gap-toothed grin, eyes twinkling with humour and intelligence, his face beaming with joy and grace and life.

Printed in Great Britain
by Amazon